M. S. West

Vampire's Bane

Volume One of the

Bonded in Blood Saga

This is a work of fiction. All of the characters, organizations and events portrayed in this novel are either products of the author's imagination or are used factiously.

VAMPIRE'S BANE

ISBN: 978-1-927526-77-4
Ebook ISBN: 978-1-9275-2672-9

Other books available by the author

Bonded in Blood Saga
Bane of the vampires
Call of the Werewolf
Siren Obligation (coming soon)

Others
The Sound of Silence

Dedication

To my co-writer and spouse who listened to my crazy ideas and understood where I wanted to go with them and of course who then helped me make this book a reality.

Prologue

The accumulation of almost two thousand years of a breeding program lays in a wailing mess on the table largely ignored for no specific reason other than the fact that the attention of the breeder has turned back to the mother. As it is, if the mother had not required further attention the breeder would have been very disappointed at what he would have seen on the birthing table for that squalling baby is vanilla in every way, not at all what he had been hoping for.

The idea for his breeding program had come upon him on a whim. He had already been on this earth, neither alive nor dead, for over a thousand years and had become bored with existence. He was seriously considering doing something rash so that others would assist him in leaving his poor existence when he heard the scream of a woman. It was a scream of terror and the sound of it made every dead nerve in his body come to life. Shortly thereafter, the shifting wind brought to him the coppery smell of blood, which awakened his hunting instinct. Lusting for that blood, he ran over building rooftops toward that sweet smell of blood and the sweeter smell of pending death.

Arriving at the scene, he pounced upon the man and tore the artery of his neck with teeth formed for that very purpose. The man barely had time to scream before his lifeblood bathed his attacker in its succulence and so into his feasting was the creature that the whimpering sound of the woman was almost lost to him… almost.

A quick turn of the head revealed to him a woman lying against the darkened wall of the building. She had one hand clutching to her swollen and badly bleeding belly the other was buried in her mouth trying to stifle the whimpers that continued to escape past a throat clogged with horror.

She smelled wrong to this entity. No, not wrong, just different.

He managed to pull himself from his meal and make his way to the woman. What he discovered would make most people heave their stomach contents, but to him it only generated interest. The woman was obviously near death for her stomach had been ripped asunder most likely by the man whose blood was now pooling and cooling in the gutters. She was trying in vain to keep the contents of her belly inside. Even as he watched, her hand fell limply aside and the contents spilled out.

The sack hit the dirt lane, something inside pushed against it feebly. It was trying to escape as if it knew it was in danger from the watching entity. The very creature it feared reached forward and ripped open the sack to get at the contents. Out spilled an almost fully formed human baby, a girl by the looks of it, the creature finally concluded.

He watched memorized as the object of his attention commenced its feeble life. It had been a long time since he had the blood of a newborn and he could not even remember taking from one so newly born.

There was no reason in particular for him not having hunted newborns before, even ones this new. In fact, if it was readily available, as in this case he was more than willing to take the substance. The amount of nourishment a newborn can supply is a trifling, but so sweet, sweet enough to make him feel alive again. This time the baby had some luck so to speak, for the creature watching it had just fed. Therefore, it did not pounce on it just yet.

The creature, never before being interested in watching its food in its first few moments of life became fascinated as the human baby's lifeblood commenced to pump through the tiny body and then as it became aware of its new life. It watched as it started to squeal for food or at the cold. The creature did not know which nor did he care.

The newly born human did not live long after that, however the seed its short life implanted into that creature's dead brain stayed firmly rooted for a hundred years before it flourished in all its glory.

It started as a hobby, which soon grew into an obsession. The breeder started with crossbreeding the smallest of the fairly folks, the pixies and fairies. Luckily for him, these matured quickly or he would have been another thousand years, if ever, trying to get where he was today.

He made plenty of errors at first, but errors did not bother him. As it was, it took him thirty years to determine the proper time to crossbreed the fairy and the pixie to achieve an offspring. Years that to a creature like this was meaningless.

Once he accomplished his first successful crossbreed, he crossbred the offspring to another creature and then another and another and another.

As often as not, he bred brothers to sisters, fathers to daughters, and mothers to sons in order to enhance a quality he desired or that had caught his interest. This resulted in him accumulating many twisted and mad creatures. Their state of mind mattered little to him, for all that mattered to him was if the product was capable of breeding, not to mention the blood.

After a time the blood became everything, so sweet, so nourishing and so energizing. Fairy blood had always been the best. Fairy newborn blood was as succulent as the finest wines. However, even that blood could not compare to the blood that his bred creatures started to provide. Thus, just as wine masters experiment with grapes to meet their needs, this creature experimented with his creations.

His entire breeding program almost came to naught two hundred years ago when he tried to breed his creatures to a werewolf. It would have been easy to have the werewolf turn his creature, if that was what he would have been after that is. It was not though, for the whole purpose of breeding this particular line was to see if he could have one birthed.

It took going back to the basics learned from his first crossbreeding with a fairy and a pixie to discover it was all in the timing. Still, it was a tricky process for a number of reasons. His discovered that the sperm had to be ejaculated from the male into the female in the midst of change for only at the point where the werewolf was neither human nor animal did conception occur in this specie.

After he figured that out there was the trouble of keeping the mating pair alive after the change for the werewolf's first instinct after a change is to rip whatever is closest to it to shreds. It took a feat of engineering involving straps and restraints to accomplish it, not to mention the death of a few of his specimens. He persisted and tried time and again until success was finally his.

For this line, it was not the blood that he was interested in. The sole reason for this line was in seeing what he could ultimately create. Therefore, it was shortly after he succeeded in his first werewolf cross that he started to wonder if he could insert his own genetic coding into his specimens.

How to bring the vampire into the mix stymied him for a number of years for vampires are completely incapable of natural breeding, or at least have been for as long as anyone can remember. Still, he did not give up and the experiments began on how to insert his genetic coding into a baby before its birth. His goal he finally concluded could only be achieved if he was able to bind and intermingle his genetics with the baby's before birth and then to see if the resulting creature could pass it on to future generations.

Only if he could accomplish the seemingly impossible could he ever hope to say that he succeeded in doing what had not happened in thousands of years and what such a creature would be was what inspired him to try and then try again.

Once again, it came down to ingenuity and timing. After many failures he discovered that only when he flooded his saliva infused with blood that he recently devoured into the umbilical cord and just as the baby sparked to life inside its mother would his genetics bind with the baby's.

When he finally succeeded at binding his genetics and getting a live birth came another wait. A wait until the creature grew and the to see if his creation could pass on the trait to its offsprings and if it did, if it would result in a creature born and not bound to a forefather.

So now, after almost two thousand years he has come to the accumulation of all his failures and successes in this line. So many deformities, so many failures, and so many discoveries all started for the sole reason of giving him a purpose in life; what is he to do for the next thousand years.

He barely manages to pull the second baby out of its mother before the mother expires. This one, like the latter he lays on the table and orders a thrall to clean before turning back to the expired body.

He losses himself in time. He ponders the new possibilities of what he had just pulled out of the female. Twins. It has been thousands of years since he had a set of twins. The last set he had bred together had accomplished a leap in his breeding program that would have otherwise taken a hundred years to accomplish.

Eager to see what he has in the babies he begins to wonder where the thrall is with his new creations. All she had to do is wash them so she should be back by now.

Two hours later they find a bawling male baby, however the female and the thrall is nowhere to be found. He fumed at the lost of the twin and sent out orders to find the one that dared take one of his possessions. The thrall had been wise in one aspect; she had escaped during the light of the day, thus assuring herself some time to evade his brood.

Chapter One
Twenty-Five Years Later

As of today I am a month away from my twenty-fifth birthday. That is exciting enough. What is even more exciting is the fact that today I am going to be officially recognized for six years of hard work. For the last six years I have been working my butt off studying chemical engineering and today I am going to obtain my doctrine for all that hard work.

This is something that I never imagined I would obtain, especially not when I use to live with my aunt Gretchen. Back then I was lucky to have rags on my back and food in my stomach. Not that Aunt Gretchen didn't try her best to keep us fed and clothed it's just that her best fell far short of what was needed to keep us comfortable.

As I have grown older and maybe wiser I've come to pity and have some appreciation for her. The truth is we were always hungry, however she tried and she never brought any of the Johns that paid her for an hour of her time home so at least she protected me from that.

The day she was killed was the day that turned my life around. Oh not right away, I went through some hellish years, moving from foster home to foster home and getting in more trouble than I care to ponder on these days. They were trying years that eventually lead me to Jackie and Martin, the two people I love more than anything in the world and the two people who I am proud to call my parents.

Even after fourteen years I have nightmares of the day that Aunt Gretchen died. Our latest move had put us in a small city in the mid-west United States and it was the dead of winter. That winter had been a cold one, making me pray that our next move would put us somewhere warmer. A move that was due to come anytime now. I knew this for we had already been living there for half a year, which is the longest length of time we had ever spent in one place from what I can remember.

My aunt's death is not the only thing I remember all too well about that year for that was the year that my insanity started. The first time the voice visited me I was able to ignore it. My insanity persisted however and I finally gave in to it.

I already had enough trouble fitting in a school and when I started listening to the voice things got worse. On the day my aunt was killed my insanity had caused me to do something stupid, which had resulted in me having to spend an hour in detention after school. I wonder now, as I have often wondered in the past if I too would have ended up dead that day if it were not for that detention.

It was already dark by the time I was making my way home that day. I was freezing and looking forward to the feeble heat that our run down apartment would offer me. At the very least it would get me out of the wind.

When I got to the apartment building I made a quick check for the man that had been… well the best way to describe it, as silly as it sounds is sniffing around me. He had moved in a couple of months before and every day thereafter he was waiting for me when I got home. Everyday he would stop me to talk. The first few times I managed to push my way past him without incident. I'm sure he wanted from me the same thing that Auntie gave her customers and that was a road that I swore I would never go down. He persisted though and just like my insanity he finally wore me down. The first few times I it was nothing more than a hello. That eventually stretched to a minute or two of conversation, but never any more than that and even then I made sure I kept enough distance between us that if he made a move I could run away.

As far back as I can remember Auntie had warned me about monsters that came out at night. She never elaborated on the monsters, just kept telling me not to get caught out at night and not to talk to strangers. Therefore, me being out late that day was certainly going to bring on another lecture from her. When I entered the apartment building I was ready for that lecture and at least on this night I did not see that strange man hanging around the stairwell so I didn't have to deal with him.

I had no idea that this strange man was one of the monsters Auntie had been warning me about. He must have been for when I opened the door to our apartment that night I found him standing over my aunt's dead body. I know she was dead, she had to be for there was blood all over the place and hers was not the only body in our apartment that night. There was another body tucked away in the corner, which I barely took note of at the time for the glowing yellow eyes of that man that had been sniffing around me had me frozen in place.

I had never been so frightened in my life. Not since and not thereafter. I am not even certain if the man ever told me his name. He must of at some point, however if he did I have long since forgotten it. The one thing I have and will never forget is how scary the man looked with his eyes glowing yellow and my aunt's blood all over him. I was certain I was going to be the next to die. I was certain that the man was going to tear my throat out like he had done to my aunt's. I knew I had to get away, but my feet refused to move. That is until the man growled at me to run away, to get the hell out of there. Well I was scared, but not stupid. His growl like voice un-rooted me and I didn't even look back. The police found me six miles from home the next day. All I remember of that day was thinking that six miles was not nearly far enough.

As far as I know they never did find my aunt's killer and as I did not have any other family I ended up in the U.S. social system. The next three years that followed were… trying to say the least.

The men in the foster homes that they put me into were always trying to bed me and the women hated me. The first time it happened I tried to tell the social worker. That did not go over well for the man and woman made me out to be a nutcase, so of course the social worker didn't' believe me.

What could I do? I remember asking myself over and over. Maybe they were even right for the voice was coming more often and getting me into even more trouble. My insanity was making me do some really stupid things. However, letting a man touch me was not one of those stupid things I was going to let it talk me into. That was the last time I ratted on the men and women in the foster homes. I started protecting myself. I started barracking myself in my room at night and I learned to scream loud enough that when the men finally broke down the door my screams would wake up the neighbourhood.

I went through more foster homes than I can remember. It was even worse than all the moving around that Auntie and I use to do. Each new foster home was worse than the last. Once more, I was in rags, once more I found myself hungry more often than not. Eventually I started stealing to get money to feed myself.

I suppose from there it was only natural that I got into drugs and booze. I couldn't get enough. Being drunk out of my mind or high allowed me to escape my miserable life and best of all it made my insanity go away.

I have to admit I was not much of a thief and I spent a lot of time in juvie after that. The need for escape became the sole reason for my existence and it was that need combined with my piss poor stealing ability that finally found me in a back alley on my knees in front of a man getting ready to do something that I promised myself I would never do. I probably would have done it too, if the police hadn't showed up and once again I found myself in jail waiting to be brought up in front of yet another judge.

I was fourteen by this time and I knew it was not going to go well for me. I had been caught screwing up too much so I was pretty certain that I was going to be put away for a long time. I'm not sure I really cared. The treatment in juvie was actually better than what I received in the foster homes. At least in juvie you get fed, however the drugs and booze I would miss.

It was the thoughts of how I was going to miss the drugs and the booze that was foremost in my mind when I was hauled in front of the judge the next day. Little did I know that on this day my entire life was going to be turned upside down.

Jackie was not sure why she stopped. The girl being hauled into the courthouse in shackles didn't look anything like the daughter she had lost, a loss that she was still reeling from even after two years.

Therefore, she had no explanation as to why the girl tore at her still tender heart. She tried to keep driving past the courthouse, she even pressed on the gas and yet she found herself in the parking lot. Throwing the car into park she sat in that parking lot for fifteen minutes trying to talk her way out of what she knew she was going to do. She told herself that she was being stupid and that she had no right doing this without talking to her husband first. She even tried convincing herself that the girl deserved whatever she got for whatever she had done.

However, after fifteen minutes of self-incriminations she walked into the courthouse knowing full well the stupidity of what she was about to do and the fallout that was sure to come.

When the girl was dragged in front of the judge she was a pitiful looking thing. It was obvious she had not washed for some time and her clothing were worn to threads and the sight of her rail thin trembling body pierced her heart.

Once again, she asked herself what she thought she was doing and yet when the judge inquired as to why nobody was there to represent the girl, she found herself standing and talking.

Yuma Arizona was not so big that she was not known. After all it was impossible to keep in the background when she was a past supermodel of astounding beauty and currently involved in many charities. Her husband Martin was also well known for even though he spent almost as much time working overseas with the military as he did at home, he was just as active as she was in the community. Therefore, the judge recognized her when she stood up to ask if he could see himself giving the girl over in her care.

The judge was surprised at her request for he knew about her losing her daughter to a hit and run driver. How could he not, for he had been the one to hear the case and he was the one that sent the man to jail for a three-year stint. As such, he would never have expected her to make such a request for any child, especially one as troubled as this one seemed to be. Therefore, he asked her if Martin knew about this.

For the first time since marrying Martin she lied about something that would significantly impact their lives. She told the judge that they had heard about the girl and that after a long discussion they had decided that it would be best for the girl if she went to a stable home and that was what they were offering her.

On the outside Jackie looked confident as she told the judge her lie. On the inside she was shaking like a leaf for even as she was telling her lie she knew that she would be lucky if Martin did not kick her to the curb before the day is done.

The judge asked her many more questions. None of which she remembers answering and yet she must have answered them to his satisfaction for in the end he granted her request.

I was standing in front of the judge and he was trying to stare me down. Well good luck there, for much scarier men have tried that. The judge finally asked me if I had anyone to speak for me. I was shaking my head no when Jackie had stood up and said that she was. The judge looked just as surprised as I was.

Jackie was… is the most beautiful woman I have even seen. I have since found out that she was a super model before she married and on that day she looked more radiant than I could ever have imagined a woman could look. Much more beautiful than I could ever hope to look that is for sure, for I have long since admitted to myself that the best anybody could say about me, even to this day is that I am plain.

The judge obviously knew Jackie. Looking back now I realize that most of the folks in the city knew Jackie, not only for how beautiful she looked and her past modelling career, but also for all the charity work she was doing. If that was not enough to make her well known the fact that she had recently lost her baby daughter to a drunken driver made her even better known and not only locally at that.

I stood there rooted like an idiot as she walked up to the front of the courtroom and told the judge that she would like to take me home and care for me. The judge questioned her reasoning. Even asked her if Martin, her husband knew what she was doing. I think she lied about that when she said yes for Martin was not happy at all when he came home that night and found out what she did. The judge finally agreed to give her a chance with me. Knowing that she had just kept me from going to juvie, which in turn would give me a chance to escape so that I could go back to my drugs and booze I allowed her to drag me out of the courthouse.

Martin was beyond furious when he got home that night. His look said it all. He hated even the sight of me. I locked myself in the room that Jackie had given me and listened to them argue long into the night. Mom, Jackie that is has since told me that was the first argument they ever had and the first time that Martin refused to come to her bed. I am sorry for being the cause of that now. Back then I didn't care for the longer they argued the less I had to worry about the man breaking down my door to try to molest me.

I hated Martin and he hated me. He was and still is in the military and I couldn't stand him and his all too upright military bearing and rules. Luckily he ignored me for the most part or that first year would have been even worse than it was.

I hated Martin, but I loathed Jackie. My insanity loathed her even more for she took away my freedom. She refused to leave me alone. She all but locked me away in that house, she even had Martin put bars on my window and an alarm on my door the first time they caught me trying to sneak out of the house. I fought with her every day, I screamed and rally against her and yet nothing I could say made her back down or throw me away as many had done in the past.

At first, I am sure it was my withdrawal from the drugs and the booze that caused a lot of the arguments. Later it was her forcing me into home schooling. All along the voice screamed at me to escape and I would have done it to if she had left me alone for a minute or two. I had never felt so much hate towards anybody in my life and I told her this more times than I care to remember. I know it hurt her and back then I didn't give a dam. I just wanted to get away.

That hatred had finally peaked the day I hit her. It came as a surprise even to me for I had never hit someone before. On that day the voice had been especially loud and Jackie had been pounding away at me with my studies. I was frustrated, mad and going insane so when everything came to a head I finally broke. The next thing I knew my fist was landing against her cheekbone.

The look on Martin's face when he came home that night and saw the bruising on her face scared the wits out of me. It was almost as frightening as the night I caught the man hovering over the body of my dead aunt. So scared was I that I ran to my room, locked myself in and curled up on the bed.

I was not surprised when a few minutes later he was pounding on my door demanding that I open it, as if...! Three times he pounded on the door and told me to open up and I ignored him every time. He didn't ask a fourth time and I sat on my bed wide-eyed as the door to my room came crashing in, after which he literally proceeded to tear it off the hinges.

He had a crazy look to his eyes and I was sure I was dead. I was getting ready to use my old screaming defence and would have, if he would have attacked me just then instead of standing in the broken doorway breathing hard. For a long time we stared at each other, me in defiance, him I'm sure trying to keep from tearing my head off.

When he finally did speak it was to tell me to get up and go outside. The only reason I even listened to him was because I was sure they were finally going to wash their hands of me and let me get the hell out of there. I was almost jubilant at the thought of getting my freedom back.

Jackie was standing wide-eyed at the bottom of the stairs as Martin led me towards the backyard of the house. I think I even called her a bitch on the way by. As usual she ignored it, which made me hate her even more.

Martin heard me however and stopped me in my tracks. He commanded, I couldn't believe it, he actually commanded me to apologize to Jackie for not only calling her a bitch, but also for hitting her. The only reason I did so was because I knew he would not let me get out of there until I did.

When we finally got to the back yard he threw me to the ground. At this point I really didn't care. It was no big deal. I would allow him his temper tantrum as long as in the end I got my freedom.

However, he surprised me yet again, for after a couple of minutes of looking down at me, wishing he could kill me I'm sure, he told me to get up. I willed death upon him for a few seconds before I did.

"Why did you hit her?"

I was still shaky with fear for he still looked like he was ready to rid the world of me, but I was also pissed. It didn't help my attitude that he had so easily manhandled me so I guess my response was flippant at best. "Because her face got in the way."

I didn't even see the hit coming. I did hear Jackie scream before my ears filled with ringing and the next thing I knew I was laying on the ground.

Never had a man hit me so quick and hard as he had just done and yet I've been in this situation before. I knew that the next thing he was going to do was try to molest me and that Jackie was going to stand there and let him do it so I opened my mouth to use my old screaming defence. He didn't come after me. Instead he did something no other man has done after hitting me; he talked.

"Get up."

Glaring bullet as him I decided it best to obey.

"Why did you hit her?"

"Because she's a fucking bitch!"

Once more I didn't see the blow coming. How a man could move so fast I could not even begin to fathom and yet there I was, back lying on the ground with my nose spewing blood. I remember thinking that surely now he would try to molest me.

"Get up."

"Fuck you!"

I was just as surprised by the kick to my ribs as I was to the blow to my head earlier. I even tried to release that scream that had so often saved me. Yet I couldn't for my lungs refused to fill with air. Through tear hazed eyes I saw Jackie standing in the back doorway with her hand to her mouth and fear in her eyes. I remember thinking of how much I hated her. I remember thinking that it was that bitch's fault that I was gasping for breath.

"Get up."

What was wrong with the man? Why didn't he just try to rape me and get it over and done with! It made no sense, yet not looking forward to another boot to the ribs this time I decided to listen to the man and stood.

"Why did you hit her?"

I was about to give him another flippant comment. I would have too except I didn't want to end up on the ground again so instead I stopped to think about it. This is something I had not done in a long time, if ever. So instead of answering right away I thought about what had happened that day that had finally caused me to hit Jackie in the first place.

"She made me mad." I finally admit to him and then waited for the blow that I was sure was coming.

Once more the man surprised me for instead of hitting me again he designed to speak. "So when you get mad you want to hit?"

"Yes! No, I don't fucking know. It's just..." I hissed at a lost of how to explain my insanity. How can I explain the voice's screams of pain? How can I explain how the voice tells me to never allow myself to be locked up? How it screams for escape, even death.

"Are you mad now?"

"Yes!"

"Hit me then."

I looked at him mouth agape. This was not the way things were supposed to happen. This man should be trying to molest me and that woman standing over there should be hitting me. That has always been the way it was, this was not making any sense to me.

"Hit me you pussy." He said in a most insolent voice.

That did it, the voice inside my head screamed and I attacked. God how I tried to hit him. I ran at him screaming, I tried scratching his eyes out, I tried to kick him, tried to punch and slap him.

It was no good for the man wouldn't co-operate and stay still. He was never where he is supposed to be and had me stumbling around like an idiot. On the other hand he had no problems hitting me and by the time I had finally worn down my anger I was a bruised and bloody mess.

"Have you had enough yet?"

I looked up at him totally drained of all emotions and energy. He had beaten me with more than his fists so I nodded my head in submission.

"Get up then."

I climbed to my feet and this time I was praying that he was not going to knock me down again for I was tired of the crap. Thankfully he designed to talk instead of hit. "Follow me."

It was a pretty meek me that followed him back into the house as he led me to the bathroom. I had no idea what he was up to and as such by the time I was standing in the bathroom alone with the man old fears were churning my stomach into knots. In defence I crossed my arms across my non-existent breasts and waited for his next move.

Instead of coming after me he reached into the medicine cabinet and pulled out a toothbrush, which he handed to me. "Clean the bathroom."

That's all! No yelling, no more hitting, no attempts to molest me, just clean the freaking bathroom. Fuck that!

I glared at him and sized up my chances of escaping from the nightmare of a man. Up to today, he had been more than happy to let Jackie deal with me. Never before had he interfered. That he had done so today had surprised me and yet surely I could still get away. Maybe not right this minute, because he was blocking the doorway, but I was certain that I could outwait him and when he got tired, well then I was out of that hellhole.

We stared at each other throughout the night, neither of us willing to be the first to give ground. When Jackie got up the next morning that is where she found us. Martin was still standing in the bathroom doorway and I was sitting on the toilet still glaring daggers at him.

Later, when she returned to him with a cup of coffee he took it without comment. When Jackie went to hand me a glass of orange juice he shook his head and would not allow her to do so, which just made me hate him all the more.

The morning dragged on into afternoon; neither of us saying a word to each other. By then I was dog-tired. Still I refused to give up and as my body had long since learned not to go to sleep when a man was standing over me I stayed awake. Surely I could outwait the man, I kept telling myself.

I am the one that broke first and late that afternoon I found myself scrubbing the bathroom with a toothbrush. Every stroke of that brush was making me madder and long before I finished the voice was screaming to high heavens at me, making me see nothing but red.

I am going to kill you. You have to sleep sometimes and when you do you will never wake up, both my voice and me screamed throughout the ordeal.

"Good enough."

Martin speaking after the hours of silence startled me from my deadly thoughts. I looked around the bathroom, not really noticing any difference in cleanliness. What I did notice although was my cramped and sore fingers. I glared at the man responsible for my misery.

"You need to go outside again?"

My first reaction to this was to tell him to screw himself. However, I surprise myself by nodding my head instead.

It was seven in the evening by then and I was attacking Martin with a vengeance. He still wouldn't play fair and I couldn't get a hit in anywhere. Just one hit, that was all I wanted by this time, just one lousy fucking hit! Martin on the other hand was casually smacking me around and throwing me to the ground.

That evening I went back to my bedroom bone tired only to discover that I still didn't have a door. Well, I was going to be dam if I was going to ask "that man" for one, so even though my body protested I sat on the bed all night waiting for what I was certain was to come.

Somehow I managed to stay up all night, waiting… waiting. Once more "that man" surprised me for not once did his shadow darken my doorway.

For the next three days I caught snatches of sleep during the day and stayed up nights waiting for him. By the third night my body was so tired it was screaming for sleep. However, I refused my body the sleep it craved for I knew, I just knew that tonight would be the night the man showed up.

That evening, like the nights before turned out to be another long night without the man's shadow darkening my doorway.

Come morning it had come to the point where I thought I could not take another sleepless night. Therefore, that morning I did something I had never done before. I asked something of someone. "Jackie, I can't sleep without a door. Do you think you could get Martin to replace it?"

It took her a few seconds to answer me. She looked at me with some kind of emotion I didn't understand in her eyes. When she did answer it was not the answer I was hoping for. "That, you are going to have to ask him yourself."

"No never!"

Never say never I have since learned for after another two more sleepless nights and longer days I found myself in front of Martin. "Can I have a door?"

"Are you going to barricade it?"

"It's the only way I can sleep."

He looked at me for a long time after that. I am sure he just wished I would disappear. He made it no secret that he was not happy when Jackie brought me home with her and his attitude towards me had not changed. So I was shuffling from foot to foot when he finally designed to answer. "I'll put it up if and only if you agree to open it when we ask you to."

I nodded gratefully for I really did need that door if I was ever going to get some sleep again.

"This is your only chance Michele." I remember him warning me.

Funny enough this whole thing became our first bonding. Oh I was not ready to admit that and I'm sure they weren't either or at least Martin wasn't. Jackie on the other hand, she never gave up on me.

Jackie refused to give up on the girl. She knew there had to be something special about her, for she firmly believed that there was something special about every child. The problem was finding that special before it was too late. So far Michele was more trouble than she had ever imagined that she would be. She was not at all like the daughter she lost and yet she would never give up on the girl she promised herself at least a hundred times a day.

She had thought the charity work she had done would have prepared her for Michele. Not to be, for even the work she had done at shelters and abuse centres did not prepare her for the girl's anger and stubbornness. However, she had gotten herself into this and if nothing else when she set her mind to something she was even more stubborn than Michele, so she endured day after day and month after month.

The day of the blow up Jackie kept herself busy throughout the day, avoiding the standoff going on in the bathroom. Poor Michele, she thought more than once for the girl has no idea what she is up against.

In a way, she was glad that Martin had finally become involved with Michele. However, even as she gave thanks for that she feared the manner of his involvement.

The next year turned out to be a much better year for us. It was far from perfect. Jackie, not knowing of my madness had come to the conclusion that I was a genius. She told me that it was boredom as well as lack of sleep that had kept getting me in trouble at school, so she started challenging me in my schoolwork. Being home schooled, she was able to push me hard, much harder than I had ever been. I can't remember how many nights I crawled into bed grateful for the respite. It was gruelling, however it kept the voice at bay so I let her keep pushing me. I was surprised when on my sixteenth birthday she told me that I had more or less caught up on that schooling.

It was near fall of that year that Martin turned both of our worlds upside down. On that particular evening, he and I had just finished what had become a nightly ritual for us; that ritual being me trying to beat on him and him not letting me for the most part. Those nightly sparring matches were always brutal. I had gotten to the point where I actually hit him once in a while. My hits were feeble at best. Him on the other hand, well he was responsible for more bruises than I ever had in all the years before meeting Jackie. The up side was that I had not lost my temper since we started so I kept going back for more. We had even started to communicate during the bouts and I was starting to believe that maybe, just maybe this man would not turn on me some day to molest me.

It was after the bout when we came back into the house that Martin dropped the bomb on us. "She has no social skills. She needs to go to a regular school this year."

We both panicked. I know we did for I saw my panic reflected in Jackie's eyes. It had been two and a half years and not once did she let me out of her sight. I was scared of what would happen if she did. It was my fear of what I would do that was being reflected on her face. How could this man tell us that it was time for me to go unattended to a public school?

"No, I can't." Jackie responded much to my relief.

"You have to. She's bright and mature when it comes to street smarts, but a child when it comes to socializing. It's time Jackie."

"But..."

The argument went on long into the night. Half the time they talked as if I wasn't in the room. I didn't mind for I knew that Jackie was the best chance I had of getting out of the madness that Martin was suggesting.

It didn't go as either of us wanted it to go and in the fall of my sixteenth year I found myself back in a pubic school. Jackie drove me to school in the mornings and I'm certain worried about me all day before coming to pick me back up after school. I'm just as certain that everyday, she lived in fear that I would get into some major trouble at school or worst yet, that I would not be walking out that door when she came to pick me up.

She had a right to fear for I was fighting my insanity. It wanted me to escape now that she had finally taken the chains off us.

I probably would have given into my insanity if something strange had not happened to me over that last year. My nightly bouts with Martin and Jackie's hard work at getting me caught up in school had made me come to have a grudging respect for them. I don't really know when it had started or even why. I certainly didn't understand the feeling and yet... Maybe it had something to do with the fact that I did everything I could to drive them away and every step of the way they refused to give up on me.

Therefore, when the voice started in again I fought my madness with every ounce of willpower I possessed. It was not without its bumps, but for the most part the trouble I got into was no more than what any other student in the school did.

Three quarters of the way through the school year it was my turn to drop a bomb on Jackie. My madness had left me alone for some time and that morning when I woke up it was a bright and beautiful morning, a sure sign that spring was well on its way. When I made my way down to the kitchen I found Jackie waiting for me. That was not unusual for her as she was always waiting for me, what was unusual was that in my light mood I choose to say something to her this morning. It was something so unlike me that when I did it I saw the wonder flash across her face.

"Good Morning Jackie."

She was so surprised that it took her a few seconds to say good morning back to me. After she did. I dropped a second bomb on her.

"It's going to be a gorgeous day. Can I walk?"

I saw the panic flood her face again. I can't blame her for I was asking a lot. I was pushing the envelope. Not only hers but mine also. I was pretty sure I could do it without breaking down and yet…

Jackie had a death grip on the edge of the kitchen island to keep from falling. She was trying to take in air. I know that she was on the verge of refusing me. I couldn't blame her for I would have refused myself in her place. Maybe I was even wishing she would.

"I think that is a good idea." Martin said as he came into the kitchen.

That was a long day for the both of us. I know Jackie feared that I would disappear from their lives forever that morning. Heck I even feared it as I made my way to school. It didn't happen however and that night when I got home we were both drained from the stress of the day.

Our fear of me disappearing from their lives forever that first morning never did materialize nor did it for the rest of the year. I finished off that school year and spent most of the summer much like any other normal, just turn seventeen-year-old girl. All was going well until about mid-summer whereas Martin put Jackie and I through a real test.

I had been with the Appletons for three years and never once in those three years had they left me alone at night. Never once in those three years had Jackie and Martin gone out for so much as a soda or dinner together. They had put their lives on hold for me so when Martin came home that evening and told Jackie that they were to attend a military party that coming weekend it put both Jackie and me on the verge of panic.

The appointed weekend came much too quickly for either of them and Martin had to literally drag Jackie from the house when it came time to leave.

"I can't leave her!" Jackie stated when they were in the car.

"Yes you can."

"NO! Something will happen I just know it. She is not ready."

"She's ready Jackie. She a different girl than the one you first brought home."

"Martin, please!"

Martin knew that she was ready to go into a full-blown panic attack and the military party really was of no consequence. The only reason he had agreed to go in the first place was because he felt that Jackie had to get use to being away from Michele for it had occurred to him that his wife had an unhealthy attachment to the girl. Well he had accomplished getting her out of the house so he was willing to compromise.

"Tell you what let's pick up some food from a drive-through and then we can come back and park down the street and watch the house."

She was quick to take hold of the slim lifeline that Martin was throwing her.

After getting their food they drove back and settled in to watch the house. For almost two hours they watch. It was not a quiet wait either for every fifteen minutes or so they had the same conversation.

"Are you sure she is still in there?"
"She's still there."
"It's been long enough, let's go back."
"Not yet."
"But what if something has happened."
"Nothing has."
"She could be dying."
"She's not."

The television was on when Martin and Jackie left to go to the party and even though whatever was on was blaring throughout the house I didn't have a clue what was on. Instead I sat on my trembling hands, legs jiggling, toes tingling, and filled with fear.

The voice was telling me that now was the time to escape these crazy people. This was the chance I had been waiting for. They had finally left me alone and I could be well on my way before they came back. It told me that now that I was older it would be unlikely that anybody would even come looking for me. Now… Now… Get away it kept screaming at me.

The voice was wearing me down. I wished they would get back home for I was not sure how much longer I could hang on. The voice was telling me to go out and enjoy the world, to go and…

The sound of the front door opening was a balm to my maddened brain. Wide-eye with the sudden relief of tension and barely daring to breathe I stood to face the door. Jackie entered the house first. I am sure I was pale as a ghost. I couldn't even more. All I could do is stand there and tremble like a frightened mouse.

When we saw each other we both lost what little composure we had. Jackie ran to me and took me in her arms, causing us both to break down and start sobbing tears. Strangely enough this was the first time the two of us embraced and the first time either of us shared an emotion that had nothing to do with anger. We held onto each other in desperation. I didn't ever want to let her go. I felt weak without her by my side and by the hold she had on me I think she felt the same way about me.

It was in the middle of this sobbing that I heard her whisper. "I love you my daughter."

It was too much for me. I had no way to respond to such an outpouring of emotions so I couldn't even reply. I just stood there and clung to her and continued to cry.

We finally did manage to release each other. We had only just done so when Martin surprised me and brought back my old fears.

"I'm proud of you." He told me as he gave me a hug. My body tensed, fully expecting his next move to be to grope me. Instead, when he felt my body tense he released and backed away from me. This was not the way a man was supposed to behave and him backing away from me confused me as much as him telling me he was proud of me.

It is amazing how little gestures and words can change people and lives. The hugs that night became the crack in the door, the one that slowly opened throughout the next few years. I never forgot those whispered words. "I'm proud of you." What did he have to be proud of me for? I was nobody. I have never accomplished anything, and I had as good as ruined his and Jackie's life. Why would he be proud of me for doing that?

It was those words that I hung onto whenever I had to fight my battles. It was those words that forced me into trying to make myself a better person. That comment that drove me to prove to them that I was worthy of those small puzzling words.

I am not certain when we changed from calling each other Jackie, Martin, and Michele to Mom, Dad, and Daughter. It just happened. I never asked and I never questioned it, I assume it was a natural progression.

The next couple of years passed much as they would for any family I suppose, except for one difference that is. Unlike many families that learn how to love and the meaning of being family from the start we had a large gulf to close and a lot of time to make up. I think that maybe this is why I have grown to love them so much. Mom and Dad became to mean more to me than anything else in my life. I learn to love them a thousand times more than I had hated them when Mom had brought me home.

Mom and I became each other's reason for living. Mom told me that it was me that allowed her to get up every morning to greet the day. That it was me that allowed her to slowly accept the death of her real daughter. She even told me about the first time she saw me. How on that day she was considering how to end her lost and how the sight of me being hauled into the courthouse had awakened something in her. I'm glad I saved her from that, for she is truly the most wonderful lady I know. I am sorry for the long road that it took for us to get to where we are today, but now that we are here, there is nothing that the two of us together can't overcome.

Mom also became my emotional anchor. I had never truly felt love before. The first time it hit me I was so confused over the emotion that I didn't even recognize it for what it was. That resulted in many days of emotional instability and Mom was there every step of the way helping me cope with it.

The night Dad asked me if it would be all right if they adopted me was the best day in my life. By then, they were already my mom and dad in everyway but name. I don't know why a piece of paper makes such a difference, but it does, and I have been proud ever since to be known as Michele Appleton.

I am happy to say that Mom and Dad started getting their lives back in order. Not having to worry about me every minute of the day Mom slowly re-established the friendships that she had put on hold for me.

We often talked about my anti-social behaviour so when Mom and Dad started to introduce me to their friends I was worried. Mom would bring home her lady friends and Dad slowly started inviting his army buddies to the house.

The first few times I found a corner to crawl into. I would try to make myself as inconspicuous as possible and yet the people keep coming and slowly but surely they began to pull me out of my shell.

It surprised me to discover that there was nothing special about me that made men want to molest me and women want to beat the crap out of me. None of the people that Mom and Dad introduced me to even made so much as a despairing remark to me. This became another confusing emotion that I spent a lot of time discussing with Mom. This was not the way things were supposed to be and I spent a lot of time grappling with those emotions.

It took time, but eventually I started to trust people again. I even learned to like a few of them. Mom and Dad did such a good job at it that it eventually came to the point where I asked Mom to get back into her charity work so I could help others that may be in the same situation that I had been in. I know my asking surprised her and you know what, I discovered that I like surprising her.

An even bigger step towards me accepting other people was the army buddies that Dad brought home. A woman wanting to beat me was bad enough for me to deal with although I had gotten use to that. It was the deep-seated fear of men trying to molest me that I feared the most. Dad understood this in ways Daddies do so he was careful with whom he invited over. They never cornered me, they were always polite to me, and they never so much as talked to me unless I talked to them first.

Ever so slowly I learned that there was no reason to fear all men… ever, ever so slowly.

The big breakthrough with men came the day I agreed to let one of Dad's army buddies join in our sparring match. Dad had been asking me if that would be okay for some time and I kept telling him no. One day I broke down and finally agreed. I think the only reason I had even agreed to it on that day was because the man Dad had brought home was a fellow that I had grown to have a crush on; another feeling I was having trouble with. That sparring match was not much of one. We had to follow strict rules that Dad put down and enforced. By the end of it I was actually laughing instead of trembling every time the young man got a hit in on me. That was the start of it and Dad was always careful whom he brought home to spar with us. In time, I got to the point where we could go at it full force without the old fear cropping up. Even them pinning me to the ground got to be just another mistake on my part instead of mental rape.

Having been behind in school from the start, I was nineteen when I finally graduated high school. I graduated at the top of my class and my latest IQ test put me in the genius level so it was not my smarts that made me graduate so late in life, it was the fact that I was so far behind in the first place. It was shortly after I graduated that Dad asked me where I wanted to go for college or university.

I am now ashamed to say that when he asked me that, my old fears and insecurities came back to haunt me. My hackles came up for I was certain that this was his way of getting rid of me, his way of pushing me out into the world so that he and Jackie could have their life back.

I didn't answer right away. Instead I asked him to come out and spar. That night's sparring session turned out to be a fierce one as I beat out on my dad the feeling of being betrayed.

I think Dad knew that something was bothering me from the start. He didn't say anything about it and allowed me my frustrations. He even taunted me more than usual during the match. He kept getting me to come after him and every time I ended up on my ass wondering what had just happened. It was not until I finally wore myself out both physically and mentally that he finally spoke to me.

"Are you ready to tell me what is wrong Sweetie?" He asked when he thought he had me in the right frame of mind.

"I thought you liked me a little." I finally replied after a long silence.

"A little." Dad replied and I could see that he was trying to keep from smiling. "You know I love you more than just a little, so do tell." He finished off while cupping my face in his hands.

It is a measure of the trust that I had learned to have in him that allowed me not to flinch when Dad took me in his arms and held me tightly. It is an even bigger measure when I held him back. I rested my head on his shoulder with my nose to his neck. For a long time I let it rest there, to take in the sweet scent of his sweat.

"You want to send me away." I finally mumbled into his shoulder.

"I'm not sending you away. Most parents get eighteen to twenty years with their children before their children leave to make a life of their own and your mom and I are not even close to getting those years from you Sweetie."

"Then why?"

"Because you need to keep going with your education. Your mom and I will not live forever and we need to know that you will be able to take care of yourself after we are gone. You are a genius Sweetie and you have to do something with it."

A long silence followed after that. I didn't know what to say. I didn't know who or what to trust.

"Have I ever lied to you pet? Trust me. You pick where you want to go and I'll get a posting there."

By this time, Dad was a general in the army. His advancement mostly due to his performance in the field so I didn't doubt that he could get a posting anywhere he wanted, what I was still having trouble with was his promise that he was not trying to send me away.

I knew that he had never lied to me, not even when he hated me did he lie to me. Deep down inside I knew this, I knew I should trust the truth in what he was saying, but I couldn't let go of those old haunts. Therefore, after some consideration and childish on my part I know, I told him I wanted to finish my education in Europe for no other reason than to test his resolve.

Much to my surprise, although hindsight being twenty-twenty I should never have doubted, we all ended up making the move and for the next six years, Mom and Dad continued to provide me a stable environment as I worked my way through university.

I didn't think my love for them could get any deeper than it was. I was wrong. Over the years I got to loving them so much that even now I get choked up every time I think of it. I continued to feel some insecurity, my insanity even comes back to visit once in a while. I know I will be wrestling with that for the rest of my life, however the one thing I will never wrestle with again is the love that I have for Mom and Dad and the love they have for me.

Today, thanks to Mom and Dad I am not the same person I was back then. I have come a long way thanks to them and today I am actually getting recognized for achieving something.

I have never forgotten those small words Dad said to me so long ago and on this day I feel like I have finally accomplish something to make my dad proud of me.

Chapter Two

Vladimir and the portion of his brood that serve him personally reside under a house that backs up against a Colorado mountainside. The building is impressive and large enough to house the thralls that serve him personally and yet for him it is what is under the house and what it backs up against that had caught his attention in the first place and that matters most to him.

As it is, the house is built on top of a massive underground warren. The thralls get the use of the building and make it look lived in while he and the brood use the underground warren, which is in fact much more impressive than the building above it. The house is located a few miles from Denver and locals commonly believe that an eccentric old man with more money than brains owns it. As such, nobody ever makes the trek up there to bother him and that is the way he likes it for it gives him the solitude to play with his experiments. He is analyzing the results of one such experiment when Edward's voice interrupts him.

"We got a hit on her!"

The figure that straightens up has a narrow face, a pinch nose, thin lips and short black hair. He is neither ugly nor beautiful and looks no more than fifty years old. That is unless you look into his eyes. It is always the eyes that give away an age and his eyes speak of eons. The only really spectacular part of him, if you don't look too closely is his nails… no, these days nails like his can go unnoticed so the six-inch black nails hardly raise an eyebrow anymore, therefore only the teeth and pointed ears make him disguisable in this day and age.

Vladimir Narishkin is one of the few remaining forefathers left in the world and Sire of the North America brood. Looking up with interest, he asks one such brood member where 'she" has been seen.

"Europe."

"Europe? What the hell is she doing in Europe? Are you sure it's her?"

"As certain as we can be without capturing her and of course…"

"Yes, yes I understand."

Vladimir loses himself in his memories for a time and Edward hears him mumbling something about the loss of time and resources spent looking for the girl in every state in the U.S., every province and territory in Canada, even in Mexico where his people are not too welcomed only to discover now that she has been in Europe.

"What part of Europe and how long has she been there?"

"Zurich, Switzerland. It seems she was going to University."

"University. How the hell does she get from an orphan and misfit to a university in Switzerland?"

It is obvious by the quietening of Vladimir's voice that he is becoming even less happy and if Edward had been paying more attention, he would never have given the off-handed answer he did. "I guess that is something we are going to have to ask her when we get her back."

For almost twenty-five years, Vladimir has been waiting for this day. Ever since his thrall had walked out with her, he had been waiting. How the thrall had managed to break from his influence and spirit away the girl is still a mystery to him. He would have been more worried about that if he had not made sure that the thrall had met a very painful end. Even that had gone wrong. Of the two he had sent to play with her, only one had returned telling stupid tales about a pack of werewolves and as expected of those who displease him, that one is no longer among his brood. Even then he had not been overly concerned for it had given him her location. In fact, after destroying the one that displeased him he became curious of how the child would survive without the thrall that had spirited her away. Therefore, as she was yet too young to breed he elected to sit back and watch. How was he to know that the brood selected to watch her would not be as diligent as they should have been and that eventually she would disappear in that whoresome cog called the U.S. social system. Now finally they had found what they lost and it was time to bring her home.

Therefore, he was not feeling too sympathetic right now and Edward's flippant response did not sit well with him. "Since you have such a need to speak to her then you can go and get her personally."

He gets some satisfaction when he sees what little blood Edward has in his face bleed dry, making him look even whiter than usual.

"But… but…"

"Certainly you can't have a problem with that Edward?"

"No sir… Master. I meant no offense, I just thought…"

"Silence you yapping mongrel. I don't know what I was thinking when I made you brood."

Edward slams his mouth shut and even though there is no need for his body to breathe, his chest heaves as if it now requires that he suck in as much air as possible to feed starving lungs. Of course, breathing is no more than a throw back to when he was human instead of the monster that the creature calling himself his Sire had turned him into.

"I will call Boris and clear the way for you. Now go get me some food. Make it something young, no strike that. Get me specimen 93542." He looks back to the result that he was examining before Edward interrupted him. "She is no longer producing eggs and I have a feeling that I am going to need the extra energy after I am done with Boris."

He watches the subdued Edward slump away to do his bidding. With a sigh, he turns away and makes his way to his office. He dreads the thought of having to beg a favor from Boris. He is almost tempted to send Edward in without informing Boris, but that would result in a war, a war he was not yet ready to fight.

Three hundred years ago, he and Boris fought for dominance over Europe. Even though he had the blood from his experiments, he came out the sore loser in that war. Much of that he blames on his under estimation of the size of Boris' brood, the rest to a series of bad luck over a number of years. Unbelievably enough, Boris gave him the choice between ceasing to exist or exile to this god-forsaken land when he lost. If nothing else, the war with Boris had taught him where his shortcomings were so when he had been given the choice he never even considered the alternative.

The two to them had devastated their broods in that war and contrary to what human movies show the making of more is a time consuming job.

If only it was as easy as in the movies make it out to be for then they would not have their current problem of an overpopulated food chain.

No, it is not easy at all to make a brood. It entails three bites to make a human a Thrall, and then two more to effect the change. It takes a month for the human body to process the bacteria of each of the first three bites and it takes almost three months for it to process the fourth. The last bite is the fatal one and if the human body is resilient enough a month later, it will raise as a turned. Further to that, the bite is not a simple matter of digging in the teeth to suck and tear at the victim. It is a matter of extending the piercers that usually stays safely tucked away behind the incisors, finding a good vein, and then pumping preciously horded blood back into the victim. The piercers are as fine as any needle the humans use for blood transfers and just as fragile so it is best to either have a willing or unconscious victim for a broken piercer hurts like hell until it regrows; a process that takes a couple of months to accomplish. A pint of blood needs to be put into the victim with each bite and the would be Sire runs the risk of draining his body dry, often leaving it too weak to find food afterwards and vulnerable to anything that may stumble upon it. So no, making thralls and brood is not easy and it has taken both him and Boris some time to recover from their war over Europe.

Vladimir could have elected to have his brood make turns, which in turn would speed up the process, though not nearly enough to stem the tide of the over abundant food chain. Those broods would then become Sires in their own rights. This is commonly done by some forefathers, Boris being one of them he is sure, and sometimes he allows those in his brood who please him to create their own brood. There is a problem with that for the further away a turn is from the original Sire the weaker they are and weak is not what he wants for one day he intends to achieve his goal and win Europe back, one day very, very soon. Therefore, his current brood may not be as large as Boris', however if he can be patient enough it will be much stronger.

Only if Boris had been the one to lose the war, then he would not now be facing the distasteful chore of having to call up the one he hates even more than the humans to beg a favour.

At least the humans have a use. They keep us fed. What is your contribution to us Boris? You hide your brood away from these humans and let them breed like rabbits. If you had kept things under control in Europe we wouldn't be facing the problem we are facing today.

Entering his office he looks around trying to find something, anything that may require his immediate attention. Finding nothing and admitting that he is only trying to postpone the inevitable he picks up the phone. The number that he dials is an European based number known by so few that it is a certainty that if Boris is available he will take the call, regardless of whether he still sees him as an enemy or not.

"Yes." Answers a voice that he does not recognize.

"Let me speak to Boris."

"One minute."

A couple of minutes of silence pass before Boris answers the phone making him more and more anxious as each minute pass.

"Boris, I need to send a couple of my brood into your domain." He gets right to the point when Boris finally does pick up.

"Vladimir?" A long pause follows. "Why would I allow that?"

"I lost one of my belongings some time ago and we just discovered she is in Europe, Switzerland actually."

"You lost a belonging… she…. What is she that you are concerned about the lost and retrieval?"

"That is not important. I just want to retrieve her."

"If you're asking to have some of your brood come into my domain it is more than a nothing so spill it or forget it."

He holds back the sharp reply that is on the tip of his tongue. He grinds his long pointed teeth and counts slowly to ten. The last thing he needs is for Boris to get hold of the girl.

Individually, neither the girl nor the boy is special. All of his hopes hinge on breeding the two of them. He is certain that it is their offspring that will give him what he is ultimately after and the time left for breeding them is rapidly coming to an end.

"It's just a girl. Somehow, she managed to break free from me. Ordinarily I would have her killed and be done with it. In this case I'm interested in knowing how she managed it."

A thrall breaking from a Sire is very unusual though it can happen. It is usually more likely to happen to a weaker Sire than a forefather. In fact, it is so rare for a forefather to lose a thrall that it may as well be non-existent. However, it has been known to happen. The loss of control over a brood is even more rare and has not occurred since before the last of the fairies were hunted from this world. Therefore, the pause is even longer this time. "How many of your brood do you want to send?" Boris finally asks for regardless of his hatred towards Vladimir, loose thralls or broken brood cannot be ignored.

"No more than four."

"For a mere woman. Isn't that a little excessive."

"Not so much to retrieve the woman. I need them to watch each other to make sure the woman gets back to me as she is found."

"I see." A doubtful Boris replies making him cringe for even he is having a hard time believing his lie.

"Send them and send me the details of where and when they will be landing. I will have some of my brood meet them."

"I don't need any of your brood to get her back."

"I didn't say you did, but if you think I will let your brood rampage through my domain unattended then your memory must be failing, in which case maybe it is time to select another to take your place."

It is a subtle dig, but a dig none the less so it takes all of his self-control to keep the sharp reply from spilling out of him, which he is sure is just what Boris intended all along. It has been the same since the war; even those Europeans that should know better and fear him for who he is have looked down at him since his defeat. That will change very soon. He will have his Europe back and leave these Americas to the savages. With any luck, the brood he sends back after he has Europe well in hand will depopulate the forsaken country, which in itself should be entertaining to watch. All these thoughts speed through his mind in mere seconds before he agrees to Boris' condition and then he hangs up the phone.

"Your meal Master."

Vladimir turns towards the door to see Edward holding on tightly to his shackle-bound and trembling meal. Fear radiates from her, filling the air with its heady sent. Even after thirty-seven years, she has not lost her fear of him… Ah, so splendid. The humans in Europe will learn the same fear. He can almost taste it now.

The frightful pounding of the woman's heart overwhelms his hearing and the smell of her fear fills his sense of smell. He is still savagely pissed at having to abash himself to Boris, thus needing to feel the thrill of a kill he launches at his meal. His teeth tears into her artery, the long nails of his fingers into her naked flesh. The woman can hardly be called human; in fact she looks more animal than human. The difference is that she is one of his specials, or at least was so before she became useless. This creature does have something in common with the humans though, fear, they all fear.

Her screams of terror invigorate him for they are almost as heady as the blood pouring down his throat. Specimen 93542 was a splendid choice and as he sucks down her blood its power buzzes enticingly through his body.

"Master, you will kill her if you do not stop."

His snarl causes Edward's pasty white face pale even more, making him back away fearfully. He trembles as Vladimir goes back to his meal. He watches in horror as his master tears into another artery and as his nails rips off his meal's left breast.

When a scream of terror and pain fills the room drowning out the noise of his sucking and the tearing flesh he deems it a good time to get away.

"Thomas."

"Yes Master."

"Vladimir is going to send a few of his brood to Switzerland to retrieve a girl. He is up to something. I want you to get a crew together and meet them when they come in. After you meet them and assure they are going to behave let them go on their own. Keep an eye on them until they lead you to the girl and once she is secured destroy them and bring her to me."

"You're letting Vladimir come to Europe? I can't believe it!"

"Vladimir is keeping something from me. I have no idea what he is really after so yes I am allowing him to come. I want you prepared. Use our best."

"Yes Master."

Instructions given, he turns away deep in thought. For eons they have heard of Vladimir's twisted obsession of breeding and playing with his food. There was enough concern over it that they had called a conclave. That was a waste of time for as usual it had resulted in nothing. He was not foolish enough to believe that this "girl" was anything but one of his twisted experiments. For Vladimir to even think of calling him after all these years, means something is up, something he is trying to keep hidden.

Is it possible that he finally discovered something meaningful, or is he trying to get an embarrassment back before others find out about it?

Like Vladimir, he knows that they have a problem with their food chain and like Vladimir he blames it on another. As far as he is concerned if Vladimir had not made a move to take over all of Europe they would not have the current problem they are now facing. If Vladimir would have been happy with his corner of Europe they could have kept the growth of the food chain in check as they had done for eons, but no he had to get greedy, resulting in the lost of too many broods, which in turn resulted in the explosion of the food chain.

If he could have had his way he would have destroyed him after he defeated him, however the conclave had intervened on his behalf, rightfully stating that there were too few remaining forefathers. It infuriated him, he should have ignored them for now they were all paying the price for letting that idiot live and now for him to call and say he had "lost" one of his, well nothing good can come out of that.

Just as infuriating is the fact that it had dawned on him long ago that the food chain was getting too curious about them. Not having the number in broods to make the problem go away, he as did all the other forefathers chose a different path; they pulled themselves away from the world to give the food chain time to forget about them. Feeding was now done carefully. No more of the wonton feeding of the past, no more razing townships and cities and it has worked for their food chain has all but forgotten about them. The time is soon upon them that they will be able to implement a cleansing and when that happens, the food chain will once more be under control and they, the rightful owners of this world can go back to doing as they please.

Therefore, the idea that one of Vladimir's "thrall or not" running around loose cannot be ignored for if the food chain were to discover her and in turn rediscover knowledge about the brood, well that would set them back a hundred years and the food chain has gotten so much more inventive in destroying each other, imagine what they could do if they raised once more against the brood. It would be an inconvenience, that's what it would be a dam inconvenience.

The forefathers are not the only ones having difficulty with the humans for on the Siren islands of Ospizo a long-running discussion about what to do with them is once again in progress.

The population on the islands of Ospizo consist only of women and it has nothing to do with the fact that they don't appreciate men, in fact the problem is that they appreciate them too much and intermingling with them results in too many pregnancies and this they cannot have.

Because of the limited resources and the land available to them, not to mention their long life span of a thousand years, give or take, pregnancies is something that is rigidly controlled by the Siren nation and of course, the simplest way to control it is to ban men from their island and this they have been doing successfully since claiming this island chain as their own.

Any visitor to the island would initially think that they live a simple medieval lifestyle. A closer look would reveal a much different lifestyle for their technology is just as advance in some areas and much more so in others than human technology. What gives the initial impression of a simple life is that they build to blend and work with their natural environment, instead of forcing that environment to their will. The result is a simple looking and very comfortable lifestyle.

The current siren population sits at just over two hundred thousand women who are ruled over by four queens and one high queen. The rule has been such from the day they claimed the island chain as their own and makes perfect sense for it allows each queen to concentrate and work for the betterment of their individual island in the chain, while at the same time contributing to the whole. Conflicts sometimes arise, however for the most part the queens work well together and any conflicts are quickly resolved by the quorum of queens.

Two of the islands are rural in nature and two sport larger cities, that if not on par with any city in the world population wise are much more beautifully designed than what has ever been conceived by the humans. Each island has its own speciality and they work together like a well-oiled machine to support the Siren nation.

Thus, the need for interaction with the humans is not required for they produce everything they need to survive and if not for the current problem with the warships circling their islands they would have been happy to keep things as is for the foreseeable future.

As it is, they have managed to keep knowledge of their existence from the humans for eons. Any open contact with them has been firmly controlled. The last open contact had happened hundreds of years ago when the humans knew High

Queen Sophie Lorera as The Lady of the Lake. That contact had been an attempt to control the history of the world and for the most part had been successful. These days any contact made with the humans are done on the sly so that the humans have no idea who they are dealing with, even then they are very far and few between.

The current contact or problem to be more accurate was unplanned and unwanted. For months now human warships have been circling their islands, threatening one of their petty wars and they have unwittingly placed them in the midst of it.

Normally, keeping humans from discovering their land is not an issue, for they simply sing them away. However, they have been singing to these warships for months now and instead of them going away they keep circling the islands. It is the why of this that is the main topic of the conversation that has been ongoing now for far too long.

"What are your thoughts on this Sophie? Have you discovered anything new?" The black haired beauty called Queen Accalia asks of the red haired beauty that has been their High Queen for hundreds of years.

"The only explanation I can come to is that there are too many females on one or more of those ships. We don't seem to have a problem with all of them. Just when we think they are going to turn away one and then two will come back on course, drawing the rest with them. It has to be women. It's the only plausible explanation."

"The women are getting tired of singing and frankly I am getting tired of their presence. We should attack as the other Queens and I have been suggesting."

"Oh that would be just perfect Accalia. Can you imagine what would happen if their ships suddenly disappeared. Attacking and taking their ships would be a short-term solution to what would quickly become a long-term problem. No, attacking and taking their ships is not a solution."

"Then what. You are the one that has been telling us to be patient. Well our patience is running low these days."

"I'm playing with a couple of ideas. One is to get our ladies on board and have the women killed and then we can send the men away."

"And the other?"

"The other has almost as great an implication as taking their warships Accalia. I'm considering the option of coming back out in the world."

Accalia looks to Queen Sophie aghast. "You can't be serious!"

"Very serious. The world is getting too full of humans. How much longer do you think we can keep ourselves squirreled away in our little corner of the world? Where once we would see only a ship a year we now have to deal with twenty or thirty. We even deal with the humans on the sly, something we have never had to do before. So what are our options Accalia? We can kill the women on board and make them go away until the next ship shows up, just to do it again and then again."

"What you say has some truth to it Sophie, but the implications. We are quite content here and our contacts with the humans are insignificant. What you are proposing would change much and not all of us like change and I can't say as I blame them."

"Change happens around us everyday. We need to recognize that or risk becoming an extinct race. I for one believe that we can let our presence be known in such a way as to have little impact on our society and us. In fact, I have my daughter Mariyah doing research on the Internet the humans invented looking into that right now."

"I would step carefully Sophie."

"I always do Accalia."

Chapter Three

It has been a day full of excitement. Earlier today, I had an interview with a medical research company and I think I nailed it. Best of all they have a subsidiary in the U.S. and since Mom and Dad have been talking about missing home, it is the perfect job. Then tonight and even though I can't be certain that today is my birthday we celebrated my twenty-fifth. Fact is, I asked Auntie more than once my birth date. Whenever I did she always chose a day around this one so over the years I finally decided that July 13 was as good a day as any to celebrate. Therefore, the evening had been full of good food, loud music, and crazy dancing at the bar and even more fun when we came home. Maybe just a little bit too much drinking had happened. That is okay for it is not everyday that a girl turns twenty-five. Furthermore, Mom and Dad had been outrageously accommodating when I brought my friends home. They allowed us our craziness. A perfect day followed by a perfect birthday. I loved it and I love Mom and Dad for staying up and celebrating the last of my birthday with me.

Therefore, my head is still buzzing with the day's excitement when I finally lie down and crawl under the bed sheets. This evening had been all about happiness and good times and because of that it takes me a long time to finally get settled into my bed. I can't say as I mind my settling down taking so long for at least this evening the buzzing in my head is from drinking and has nothing to do with the whispering in my ears that has been driving me to distraction for the last month, or that now familiar feeling of being watched. I think I am actually starting to get paranoid about that.

Sleep is slow to come, however come it finally does. I know it does for my dreams and nightmares come to visit me and then there is the scream. If it is not bad enough that my dreams are making me toss and turn, now this. Another scream rips through the air and only when it hits its peak do I realize that the scream is coming from me.

I watch my dream unfold around me as if I am a witness to the happenings instead of the participate. I watch as my body arches painfully on the bed. I feel the firm hands holding me, and the soothing female voice whispering in my ear. I try to wake up from the nightmare and answer that voice begging to me, but to no avail.

My back burns as if it's on fire, my legs feel as if every bone is being crushed and realigned, my hips are widening, my spine shrinking and expanding. Never in my life have I felt so much pain. Every bone in my body cracks and then melds back into place only to crack again. My head feels as if it is going to explode.

Another pain-filled scream is torn free of my now clogged throat. Strong hands continue holding me firmly to the bed; gentle ones wipe my brow. I want to wake up. I beg to leave this nightmare. I want that with every fibre of my soul and yet I can't.

My legs are breaking again… how freaky for they look like they should belong on a horse… no not horse, but a goat… my teeth hurt, my jaw breaks and still I manage to have a scream rip free from my constricting throat.

I try to bite the hands holding me. I even make a swipe at the fingers stroking my forehead and get nothing except air for my trouble. Another scream I let loose and it is not because of my frustration for my bones are breaking again, my legs are changing, and my spine is once more on the move.

Someone else invades my dream. It is that voice that has been with me for most of my life. The voice that is my insanity and that I fear, and yet at the same time the one I am drawn to. It has been so quiet for the last few months that I have almost missed it and now the voice's scream is a match for mine. It is in the midst of that pain that something reaches out for me.

Whether it is looking to give or receive comfort matters not to me at this point for I can't take any more of this nightmare alone. I cling to it and even as it takes some of my pain away, it feeds me some in return.

It seems as if I have been screaming for hours. I have no idea how my body can still have the energy to thrash around the way it is. Oh merciful mother of god it hurts. I hold onto my dream protector as it holds to me. Our screams co-mingle until they become one. Hour after hour, day after day, it goes on, or so it feels until my body finally collapses in exhaustion.

My body has finally worn itself out and thankfully the pain is receding. With the receding pain comes a cooling of my overheated body and a slowing of my heart.

Pain becomes nothing as my heart slows and slows yet again. However, even as I feel my heart stopping, I feel the other's pain. It is as excruciating as my own just was and it rips through my mind. I lend it all the support my dying body is capable of providing. Beat… beat and finally one last beat my heart gives.

My heart stops, as do my lungs. Bliss, no more pain, no more cares or worries. The other's pain now becomes nothing more than a distant memory.

Stop! What is this? Someone is beating on my chest. Someone else is crying in the distant and a voice reaches out for me. For the first time, I realize that there is more behind the voice than my insanity. The voice cannot be from just inside me for a physical something… someone has invaded my space. Too late for I no longer care. Go ahead and beat on my chest for I will not wake. No pain, such bliss it is.

NO, YOU MUST NOT LEAVE ME! Male and female voices scream in unison.

Beat- beat— beat--- beat.

God no, I don't want to come back!

Pain flares again as more bones break and realign. I reach out to what has become my support. It is male I realize even as he starts to float away from me.

"No, it cannot be happening, I will not let it happen!" I scream this; I know I do and yet the scream only echoes in my mind.

His body has finally worn itself out and he is dying. I take hold of the stranger that feels so familiar and embrace him to my breasts. My own body is still tormenting me, however I refuse to let the soul that I have just come to know as another instead as a part of me go. I will him to live. I breathe life into him with my kisses. Having little success with that I feed him the milk of life from my swollen breasts and yet his lips become cold against my nipple. He stops feeding.

Every bone in my body is breaking again. I cannot understand how a body can go through so much and not expire. I wish to join the peace that the other must now be enjoying, oh why did I have to come back. Please God take me away again. Nothing responds to my begging except for my scream of pain that once again echoes in my mind.

The body held tightly against my chest jerks once and then again. He still has my nipple trapped between his teeth and now he clamps down painfully in it. Feeling his need I allow the vital life source to flow and once again he suckles on the milk that trickles out. He drinks up that life source until his screams once again joins with mine.

He is just a shadowy figure against my breast. I watch the bones break throughout his body as mine had done just seconds, or was it days ago. It has been ongoing for so long I no longer know or even wish to know how long it has been.

Lord, either kill me, or make the pain go away for I can't take no more!

The two of us cling to each other for support, our screams continuing until blessed darkness falls once again.

"Specimen 101849 went through the change last night Master."

"What! Why is it I was not informed?"

"You were still feeling the effects the bloodlust from your last feeding."

Vladimir remembers it dimly. Edward had brought him one of his specials and he had allowed himself to become carried away. The blood had been so pure and invigorating that it had put him into the bloodlust so to keep his brood safe from him, he had gone hunting. For a week, he had hunted the countryside without a care. It felt wonderful to let himself go and to instill fear once more into the local food chain. The humans did not stand a chance as he tore them limb from limb. The best part was when he got lucky and found the den of werewolves. The two females had gotten away while he fought the male. The male had fought savagely as only one that is protecting one of his pack can. What a fight it had been and he had thoroughly enjoyed ripping him apart. It had made him feel eons younger.

"Master."

His wandering mind comes back to the present. "You videoed it I presume."

"Yes Master."

The years are flying by. It seemed as if it was only yesterday that he had pulled this specimen from its mother's body. He remembers that day well. The girl had been born and he had just laid it on the table for later examination when the female began screaming again. When he turned back, he noticed the crown of another head. Something was wrong, which was the cause of the woman screaming in pain. He had torn the mother apart and discovered that the cord had tangled around the child…. a male child. Mind filled with possibilities he freed the child from the mother. Twins! It had been eons since his last specimen had given birth to twins. It was too bad the woman had died for it would have been interesting to breed her again, maybe even to the son. At least she had given him twins, opening up new doors and possibilities.

Without really looking at them yet filled with elation at the possibilities, he had given them over into the care of the thrall that had acted as a nurse for the last ten years. She was a stupid thrall and she would never be allowed to ascend. At least she had learned enough to be competent with the small tasks he gave her. Her current task was to clean and prepare the babies for testing and he was keeping himself busy with the now dead mother while he waited for her to return from that chore.

When he had grown impatient waiting he had sent his brood to find the woman and it was then that they discovered that she had gone missing. They found the male child a few hours later screaming to high heavens in hunger. For years, he searched for that twin child in the hopes that something would come out of their breeding. However, now that her blood is no longer pumping she is of no use.

"Master."

"You have given me your news now leave me be. The specimen was of little use before the turn and now it is of less use to me so dispose of it and you may as well cancel your trip to Europe for the girl is of even less use to me now. I really don't give a dam anymore. He will find nothing if he takes her apart now so let Boris deal with whatever she becomes."

He had succeeded in bonding his genetics into this specific line of his specimens and then managed to breed and obtain an offspring from that line. The problem with this line is that he has yet to breed an offspring that lived past their thirtieth year. There is no telling when the change will come over them, but it always does and always with the same result.

A useless corpse. Why I even bother to keep that useless line around I have no idea, as it had been so disappointing from the start.

He had hoped for more and he had tried a variety of cross breeding with the male and all resulted in the same failure. What now? What is he to do with that line? He is considering his next option when what Edward is telling him sinks in.

"But Master his heart started again."

The statement shocks him. For a long time he stands there looking unbelievably. It is not possible he keeps telling himself and yet there is Edward telling him that the impossible had happened.

"Are you sure?"

"Yes Master."

"Is it pumping blood? Are his lungs still working?" The new possibilities that this little piece of information opens up is making him feel giddy.

"Yes, we checked him while he was still unconscious. A more brutal turning I have never seen and his heart did stop. One second he was well on his way into the turn, the next his heart started and the turning reversed."

"I must go see him at once and Edward I want you on that plane as soon as the sun goes down. Be in Switzerland by tomorrow and bring me that girl in one piece."

The Siren Queens are once again meeting to discuss the current problems with the humans. This meeting has already dragged on for six hours and the only two options left on the table is the slaughter of the females on the warships or informing the humans of their existence.

As expected, the queens are not ecstatic about revealing themselves to the humans and it is starting to look as if there is going to be a number of human female deaths in the coming days.

Queen Sophie looks to her daughter Mariyah, knowing full well what her choice would be if she were given an opportunity to vote in this dilemma. Mariyah's opinion, which has not changed from the start, was that they should make themselves known. This is an opinion that she shares with her, however for different reasons. She would do it because it was something that was going to have to be done sooner or later, and most likely sooner than later, while Mariyah wants to do it because she wants to explore more fully the land of the humans. Mariyah, like most children her age has an insatiable curiosity and lately she has been chaffing at the siren restrictions that are keeping her island bound.

Queen Sophie sighs at the thought of her daughter. Mariyah had recently had her one hundred and fifth birthday and yet she still has much to learn. As it is, she has always been more scholarly than warrior, which is not a bad choice for the future High Queen and even more so as there has not been any need for a siren warrior in a couple of hundred years. Often enough she is of the opinion that having her daughter experience more of the human world would be a good thing and yet the thought of sending her out into that beastly world always leaves her in dread.

As it is, she doesn't begrudge her daughter for wanting to go exploring, after all she had done her own exploring and mingling with the humans in her youth. That was back in safer days, times have changed and the humans have become unpredictable, so whether her daughter liked it or not she was going to have to get use to staying on the island, at least for some time yet.

This argument has been going on too long and the outcome is obvious. I may as well put a stop to it before I get an even bigger headache than I have now. I just hope the headache goes away before I have to deal with Mariyah's wrath tonight.

She is just about to call the Queens to order when the door at the end of the room opens up. Those who were previously trying to talk louder than their neighbor to be heard stop talking at once. In unison they turn to the door, surprised that anyone would even dare interrupt them.

The figure that is revealed with the opening door leaves them even more speechless for the person standing on the threshold is well over a thousand years old and never in the last twenty-five years has she shown any inclination towards getting involved in siren politics, never mind interrupting a council.

"This is highly unusual Saydie, what can we do for you." High Queen Sophie finally finding her voice asks.

The siren that walks into the room is one of the oldest sirens living today. Old she might be, however there is nothing feeble about her mind or the way she walks into the room. It is obvious that even though she is not a queen she expects respect and indeed the queens give this matron the respect she deserves for at over a thousand years old, Saydie is not only the oldest siren alive, she is also a seer of great power. Furthermore, she has kept the beauty of her youth so that to anyone not siren she looks to be no more than a human woman of forty or so, thus assured of her position and beauty she walks into the room with confidence.

Tossing the tail ends of her long blonde hair behind her shoulders Saydie stops in front of the queens. "I am sorry to interrupt, but this is of some concern to all the queens and I figured since you are all gathered in one place it would be a convenient time to state my case. Twenty-five years ago I informed you of the tremble in the veil. When I could not put a finger as to the why of it you replied that as long as it did not interfere with us communicating with the goddesses not to worry."

"Yes, I remember that day. Go on." Queen Sophie replies after Saydie has stopped obviously waiting to make sure everyone does indeed remember that day.

"I warned you about the implication of ignoring it and now, as of two days ago our way to the goddesses have been obscured by a shadow."

A chorus of disbelieving "what" and "impossible" follows her announcement.

"What does that mean to us?" Queen Accalia finally gets out.

"Not too much yet. I am still able to commune with the goddesses, as should every other siren, though it may be a little more difficult than before. However, as I warned you those many years ago this development is not something that you should, nay can ignore."

"But how can this be. Have you any idea what is causing the obstruction this time?" Queen Moriya asks in a trembling voice for the news that Saydie imparted is grave indeed.

"The cause, I have come to believe is that there is a siren somewhere that has not been recognized."

"Impossible, they are all accounted for and we have been even more diligent since the human blockade started." Queen Sophie snaps back, refusing to believe.

"And I think that you are correct in that. In fact, for the last couple days I have been making sure all of our sirens are accounted for. However, that does not change the fact that there is a siren out there somewhere."

"So what are you saying?"

"I am certain it will get worse, so once more I caution you not to ignore my warning." Saydie gives each Queen a stern look before continuing. "The fates of the sirens are in your hands My Queens. Good day."

That full implication of this news has already hit Queen Sophie and she feels her headache redouble. Why now she asks herself. For so long they have had a peaceful life and now everything seems to be coming apart.

"I think that will be enough for today. I suggest we all consider what Saydie has told us and we can reconvene tomorrow."

None of the queens bother to argue with the High Queen and it has nothing to do with fear of doing so. They are as tired and shocked at the news Saydie has imparted as she is, so they are all quick to make their way out of the room, leaving Sophie and Mariyah the last two occupants.

"Mother."

"Not now Mariyah."

"But Mother this is perfect." Mariyah is obviously not bothered by the news; in fact she looks smug if anything.

"I said not now Mariyah. I'm going to take a walk by the sea. We can speak tonight dear."

"Yes Mother."

Jackie and Martin are exhausted, both mentally and physically. Two nights ago Michele had waken them up from a deep sleep with a scream. Jackie thinking that Michele was having one of her nightmares went to her room to comfort her. It was only a few seconds after that first scream that Michele released another. That scream was followed by a horror stricken call from Jackie, which caused Martin to join his wife in his daughter's room. After that, the night had rapidly gone downhill.

They found Michele twisting and thrashing on her bed. Bad as that was, that was not what put the looks of horror on their face. Michele's bones were breaking. The noise of them doing so was all too audible even above her screams and as such they had little need for the following ugly twisting and reshaping of her body to tell them that something was very wrong.

In a panic Martin picked up the phone to call for an ambulance to take their daughter to the hospital. He had almost finished dialling the number when Michele went through her first major change. So shocked was he at the sight of his daughter changing into a creature he has yet to put a name to that he had dropped the phone and forgotten about it.

After that the night got worse. They watched, they tried to comfort, and they even had to hold Michele down as she went from one transformation to another. They watched her grow legs that looked like they belonged to a goat, they watched horns grow from her forehead, they watched her body shrink into a twisted, dwarfed size package and then back out to a creature of imaginable size. Even the wings and the tail were just the beginning of the living nightmare.

Her thrashing got so bad that he had to finally tie her down to keep her from hurting herself even further than what her body was already doing. Doing so caused another problem for then he had to tighten or loosen those bonds as her body shrank or grew.

When she started talking they thought she was talking to them and they were hoping that she was finally coming around. That hope was quickly dashed for it became apparent that she was talking to some inner demon instead.

When her heart stopped Martin almost sighed in relief for he was not sure how much longer he could take watching his daughter going through the horrific breaking and twisting. If left to his own devices he probably would have simply laid down and cried. Not to be, for Jackie's tearful pleas for him to do something drove him to start CPR. He knew it was no use, however he did it anyway and then the unthinkable happened. She started breathing again and her heartbeat became as strong as it ever was.

That night had been the longest, the most horrific and the most tearful night the two had ever experienced. It exhausted them mentally and numbed their minds. What they had seen was not possible their minds kept screaming and yet the truth that it was possible had been twisting and changing right there, in front of their eyes.

Somehow they made it through the night without going insane, thought if asked they would have argued otherwise and with the coming of dawn and much to their relief she finally settled down. What was left on the bed though was not their daughter, at least not the daughter they had come to know and love.

She had changed explicitly. The only saving grace was that she now looked human. That fact, as well as their numb minds was in part what helped them get through the next two days.

The next two days did not pass quietly either. Jackie was constantly at her side, bathing her with cool towels in an attempt to keep her fever in check. While Martin, having decided that what they had just seen was more than any hospital could contend with spent his time making one phone call after another; none of those calls went to hospitals.

The phone calls that Martin was making were all due to a very brief moment of clarity that finally invaded his exhausted mind. What they had just seen was not possible, their minds must have… must have been playing tricks on the two of them and if not, then what they just saw could only be the result of some twisted, out of control military experiment, either that or some mad scientist somewhere and if a scientist surely the military must know about it. Therefore, the calls to his contacts made over many years of serving in the military started. The calls were not all revealing, just enough to give them an idea of what they had witnessed. Even the little he gave made many of them think that maybe the general had finally lost his mind. Once he finished going through his list of military contacts with disappointing results he continued on to universities, which ended up in just as much disappointment.

It was during one brief break in the calls, when he and Jackie were sitting together by Michele's bedside that he approached the issue neither one of them wanted to discuss.

"Honey, you do know that the chances of Michele coming out of this without brain damage is slim don't you? After the way her skull expanded and contracted it had to be hard on her brain and then her heart stopped and she wasn't breathing for almost fifteen minutes. Nothing good can come out of this."

"I know Martin, but I will not give up on her and even if she wakes up brain dead I will not give her up."

"I know Sweetheart. I feel the same way. I just want us both prepared in case the worst happens. We must both be realistic about this."

"I am being realistic, but that will not stop me from praying."

"As for her waking up…"

"I'm keeping her clean and getting some water down her throat."

"That is not enough."

"Give me another day Martin. If she does not wake up I promise I will discuss it with you. Please give me the one day."

"One day, two even won't much matter. You can have those but…"

"I know, but I will never give up on her. Never!"

Chapter Four

"Dominic, do you know that some of Vladimir's brood have flown into Europe?" Ray asks of the Alpha in charge of the greater part of Europe.

"What are you talking about Raymond? Vladimir wouldn't dare send any of his brood into Boris' domain."

Raymond having followed Michele's progress since she was eleven was still having her watched and when he got word that some of Vladimir's brood were gathering in Switzerland he got worried. Vladimir's brood had killed Michele's aunt after all and he would not put it pass him to try after Michele.

More than once, as he watched her grow he had been tempted to take her and make her his mate. However, every time he decided to wait, to give her a chance to experience life before bringing her into his world. As it is, only a couple of times did he need to intercede on her behalf, unbeknownst to her and this it seemed was to be another.

He had brooded over calling Dominic to handle this for he really didn't want Boris involved in her life. He would rather take care of it himself and would have if him showing up in Europe had been acceptable to Dominic. Knowing that was not an acceptable alternative he finally decided to make the call.

"Vladimir wouldn't unless he has Boris' permission. I have to wonder what those two are up to. It can't be anything good I wager. I just thought that you might want to know. I've received information that the plane they took is scheduled to stop in Zurich Switzerland."

"I appreciate you calling. I have to agree that this is highly unusual. What's your interest in this?"

There it was. The question he did not want Dominic to ask yet one which he had already made up an answer for. "Nothing except that Vladimir has been giving me some problems here lately. I don't particularly want him stirring up trouble on two continents so I thought I'd give you a heads up."

"I'll take it under consideration."

"Do so. That Vladimir is a sneaky bastard so watch your pack."

"I don't need you to tell me how to take care of my pack Raymond."

"I know you don't Dominic. I didn't mean anything by it. Have to go, so take care."

Raymond hangs up the phone almost satisfied. He is pretty sure that he caught Dominic's interest and he is certain that Dominic is going to do something about it. Best of all he managed to do that without having to spill the beans about Michele. All he can do now is hope for the best.

On the other side of the world, Dominic is not so satisfied for Raymond has a point. Vladimir and Boris have been enemies for so long that he could not even conceive the two of them working together unless it spelled trouble for the pack. Neither was he foolish enough to think that Vladimir would send his brood to Europe without Boris' knowledge for that could only lead to another war.

No. Vladimir would not be stupid enough to start another one would he? The humans are starting to notice them again and another war would bring them out and leave them open for retaliation. It must be something important and if it is good for those bastards it can't be good for the pack.

"John, get in here." Boris summons his second in command.

"What is it Dom?"

"The vampires are up to something in Zurich. Get in touch with the pack and have them start sniffing around. Have them start at the airport."

"Any indication as to what Boris is up to?"

"None and it's not only Boris. Vladimir is sending some of his brood. If it was just Boris I would probably ignore it."

"Impossible! Are you sure your source is reliable."

"As reliable as can be expected and there's no harm in checking it out. It will give some of the pack something to do for a change."

It feels like floating up from the bottom of the sea. Yet, frightened of the pain that I am sure is waiting for me on the surface I try to bury myself back into its blissful depths. However, my body refuses to acknowledge my wish and keeps floating up and up. I continue to fight it for I feel at home at the bottom, so alive and so peaceful. Yet my wish for peace is ignored for even as I fight to stay in its icy depth the sea is refusing to give me its embrace and is spewing me out with her tides.

The light is blinding when I open my eyes making them water and causing me to moan in pain. Thankfully, a body imposes itself into my vision blocking out much of that harsh light.

"Can you hear me baby. Michele. Michele, stay with us!"

I blink rapidly a few times before I finally manage to orient my eyes to the figure standing above me. "Mother?" My voice croaks from a sore, dry throat.

"Yes love. How do you feel?"

"Tired. I had a horrible dream. I never felt so much pain. I'm sorry if I woke you up. I'm okay now so you can go back to bed." I start babbling and then I have to stop because the cough that had been tickling my throat forces itself out.

Mom reaches over to the end table and picks up a glass of water. As she waits for my coughing fit to end she calls out for Dad.

"Hush now Baby. Here take a drink. That's it and now another."

"She's awake!"

"Yes Martin, and she talked. She recognized me and talked to me. Tell me she is going to be alright."

Mom's worried exclamation penetrates my too groggy brain. I take a closer look at her. I see deep lines of worry that I have never seen on her beautiful face before, nor have I ever seen those dark bags under her eyes. She looks tired and worn out and when I turn to look at Dad, I see that he looks in no better shape.

If their tired demeanour is not enough to tell me that something is terribly wrong the way that Dad is staring at me is telling enough. He starts to say something and then slams his mouth shut, only to try again with no better success.

Pushing the glass from my lips I manage a question. "Okay spit it out, what is going on?"

My throat is feeling a little better thanks to the water, though it must still be raw for it sounds too deep and sultry to my ears. When neither Mom nor Dad respond I try again. "Please talk to me. You two are starting to scare the hell out of me."

Dad is the first to pull his wits together. He sits on the edge of the bed and gives me a tentative smile. "How are you feeling Sweetie?"

"Tired and a little sore. It must have been a bad dream. I'm really sorry."

"You…." Dad takes a deep breath before trying again. "Something happened a couple of nights back and you have been sleeping since. We were very worried about you."

He didn't have to tell me about his worry for I can see the worry written plainly on their faces. "It must have been one of my worst dreams…"

I stop talking when the looks that they are giving me finally penetrate my foggy mind. Suddenly I know that it has nothing to do with dreams.

The fear I heard in his voice and the worry I see on their faces causes me to slide back into my childhood. A childhood where I felt that danger lurked around every corner. "What happened that have you two so worked up papa?"

"You had an incident and before you ask, no we don't know what. You… dam it I don't know how to explain it. We were going to take you to the hospital. We would have except after what we saw… let's just say we didn't think it would be a good idea. For the last couple of days I have been making calls to every contact I have ever made trying to get answers and…"

"Papa you are really scaring me now. What happened? What did I do? Please papa, tell me I didn't do something horrible!" I ask desperately for I fear that my insanity has finally broken loose.

"You don't remember anything?" Mom asks.

"I remember a bad dream. I think I screamed. In the dream I... I don't know. It all seems impossible. Stupid actually."

"It wasn't a dream Sweetie. At least what we saw wasn't. You were thrashing on the bed for hours. I had to tie you down with sheets near the end and I'm glad I did for I would never have been able to hold you throughout the ordeal. Then when your heart stopped, we thought we lost you. I started doing CPR, your mother was crying and calling to you. It was all a mess... I'm so glad you're with us again!" Dad finishes and the tears I see are even more frightening than their worried looks for Dad never cries. He surprises me even more by lunging forward to wrap me in a tight embrace.

I squeak in surprise. I hold onto Dad with one arm and manage to snake the other around Mom. For a long time we hold onto and comfort each other, until I can no longer take the smell prevailing throughout the room.

"What's that smell?"

"Smell?"

"Yes, it smells like... old socks or something... Oh my god that's me. When was the last time I took a shower?"

"I tried to keep you clean. I gave you a couple of sponge baths. I know it's not the same."

"If you can think about a shower you really must be feeling better."

I give Dad a menacing look for his last comment before I reply. "Well I'm off to take a shower and we can talk after."

My first try at standing does not go so well as my legs refuse to hold me up. Thankfully Mom had dressed me in a long loose fitting nightgown so I don't make too much of a fool of myself in front of Dad. My second try goes much better, though only because Mom and Dad help me this time.

"Shower please." I beg to them after they have helped me stand.

Weak kneed, feeling as if my body is not my own and holding firmly onto them we make our way to the bathroom.

"Are you sure you're going to be able to shower Sweetie?"

"Get real Dad. I've been bathing myself since… well forever."

"Yes but…" He trails off lamely.

"Ah honey. There's something we should tell you before…"

Whatever Mom was going to say to me goes unfinished for we have already entered the bathroom and I have caught a glimpse of myself in the mirror.

"I think I'll leave you two to discuss this." Dad says and then lets go of me to make a quick escape.

I stare in the mirror not recognizing the person staring back at me. Unsure who that stranger looking back is, I bring my hand up to touch my face and then the world starts to spin.

"Martin!" I hear Mom shout just before everything goes black.

I hear them talking as I once more try to swim my way out of the darkness.

"Maybe this was not such a good idea Jackie."

"Well, she's just going to have to get used to it."

"Yes but…"

"No buts Martin. Have you made any headway yet?"

"Maybe… I'm not sure…"

"What happened to her Martin? What we saw. It's not possible. Someone is responsible for this and someone must know! There has to be an explanation and if anyone knows what it may be it will be…" I hear her take some deep breaths to calm herself before continuing. "You keep trying and I'll sit with her until she wakes up."

"I will honey. I promise I'll find an explanation. I wish we knew more about her birth parents or where she was born."

"Well we don't so we are just going to have to make the best of it."

"Honey maybe I shouldn't leave you alone with her."

"Don't Martin. She is still my baby. No matter what we saw she is still who she was and I refuse to think otherwise!"

"You're right Jackie. I'm just tired. I'm going to hit the phones again."

His wife is right he muses as he walks away. His daughter is still his daughter. Funny how she had crept into his life and dug her clutches into his heart. He once thought it would be impossible to replace the daughter they had lost. Somehow, somewhere along the way she had done so or more accurately not replaced, she had filled the void to overflowing. When he started teaching her self-defence, it was with a mind towards teaching her to control her temper. It didn't take long before he did it just for the joy of spending time with her. She may be twenty-five and yet as his wife had just proclaimed she was still his baby.

I come to with my head on Mom's lap and her gently stroking my hair. I am tempted to stay just where I am for I feel safe snuggled up against her. I would have done it too except Mom was right, I am going to have to face the truth sooner or later.

The first words I find coming out of my mouth are not encouraging for either Mom nor I as once more I revert back to my childhood. "Mama?"

Mom has long since learned that I only call her this when something is truly upsetting me, so I am not surprised that she uses her most reassuring voice when she answers. "Hush Dear. It will be alright."

"What happened?"

"You fainted."

"I kind of figured that one out. What happened before?"

"We are not sure Baby."

"You didn't do something to me while I was sleeping did you. I mean… oh I know that is stupid, but Mama this can't be happening."

"Well it did. Now get up and let's take a good look at you."

"I'm scared."

"Baby it's still you. Whatever may have happened you're still you… aren't you?"

I stop in the process of getting up and give her question some serious thought. Am I still me? How would I know? I look deep inside myself to see if I can find something, anything different about me. Other than not believing what the mirror showed me, I find nothing reassuring or otherwise.

"It's still me I think. Okay, I'll be brave like you are being Mom. Can you help me up?"

Once Mom helps me stand I screw up my courage and look once more in the mirror. I still can't believe that the image looking back at me is… well me.

My last clear memory is of going to bed after a night of partying and that night, when I went to bed I had scraggily short hair. It is now a brilliant sun-blasted golden brown with so much lustre that it seems to glow. I move my head to take a better look at it and the effect is dazzling. Right away I see that when the light hits it at certain angles it looks as much blonde as golden brown. Just as unbelievable is that my hair is now down to my waist and full of natural waves, whereas when I went to bed it was barely shoulder length. My hair is not the only change either, for my once ugly nose and flat face have undergone a stunning transformation.

I have never considered myself pretty. I never even dreamed of having anyone even consider me pretty. I had gotten used to being plain and now all that has changed. My face has rounded out and my nose has narrowed. My eyebrows, now a golden brown to match the colour of my hair has thinned and flow up from my eyes at a thirty-degree angle. Even my eyes have changed from a dull brown to a startling sea green. The shape of the eyes themselves is more catlike than human. I smile at the sight of my new eyes for I like the erotic effect.

That smile brings out my now high cheekbones and I release a small gasp of pleased disbelief. Next to be noticed is my now finely chiselled chin and full, unbelievable pink lips. Brushing a strand of hair behind my ear, I gasp for the top of my ear is pointed, not a real fine point, but definitely pointed.

Well dam it, but the eyebrows and ears make me look like Spock from those Star Trek movies! No, that's not quite right. Maybe a little more like those elf pictures I have seen.

Even with these strange little quirts I finally admit to myself that I am now beautiful, sensually beautiful at that and unlike before, every part of my face complements the other. My colouring is prefect. So perfect that I will hardly even have need for makeup anymore and there is not a blemish to be seen anywhere. So far so good. Nothing hideous, nothing I can't live with so gathering my courage, I turn to look at the bathroom door.

"Mom, could you close the door please."

"You sure you don't want me to leave."

"NO! I mean no. I'm not sure I can do this by myself. Please stay, please."

"Okay Baby I'll stay."

I wait until Mom has shut the door and then remove the nightgown she had dressed me in. It drops to the floor and for a few seconds I look disbelieving into the full body length mirror.

"Oh my god! Look Mom, I got tits!"

Mom smiling at my enthusiasm causes me to blush at my outburst. Calming myself I take a closer look at the changes that came over me while I slept. The breasts are obvious of course. How could they not be for they had gone from nothing to... to what?

"How big do you think they are Mom? D's maybe?"

"Maybe. Yes probably."

"Wow and look at my neck. It looks so long and slender… oh my god I have a waist and hips. I can't believe all this. It's too much."

"Don't forget to breathe Michele or you're going to pass out again."

I take her advice and inhale a couple of deep breaths, smiling brilliantly when I see what it does for my breasts. Mom had been right to tell me breathe for I immediately feel the lightness that had been creeping in retreat.

"I actually look beautiful don't I Mom. I never thought I would be you know and I was okay with that."

"Yes you are very beautiful. You always have been."

"No I haven't."

"To me you were. Now the outside matches what I always knew was on the inside"

"Not like this Mom. When I was younger, I longed to look as beautiful as you are. We have to get a tape measure!"

I come to realize that the truth in my words still held to this day. I may have convinced myself that I had accepted my plain nature, however what I had just felt when I told Mom my longing made a lie of my acceptance.

My longing to be as beautiful as Mom is not baseless for she was a supermodel in her early twenties and still holds that beauty to this day. At five foot nine, thick chocolate brown hair, full breasted and slender she had been much sought after until she met Dad. On the day she married she surprised Dad by telling him she was giving up her modelling career and that from that day forth she was going to concentrate on being his wife and a mother. That decision was her own and not something that Dad had asked of her and it was a decision she never regretted making, not even during that hard period when she was mourning the death of her daughter, or so she has told me many times.

"In here." Mom opens the medicine cabinet and pulls out the tape measurer.

"Measure me!" I realize that my voice is starting to sound panicked so I take a couple more deep breaths.

"40, 26, 36" Mom calls off the measurements as she goes along.

"And look at my pubic hair. What is that, a fish?" I exclaim as I look down at a finely detailed, multi-colour design that looks more like a tattoo rendition than pubic hair. In fact, so realistic is it that it makes me reach down, just to make sure that it isn't a tattoo. It is full of radiant blues, reds, greens, and purples. The colours seem to go on forever. So cunningly crafted is it that I can make out what looks like scales, therefore I can't be blamed for thinking it resembles a fish from the angle I am looking at it.

"It's a mermaid I think." Mom replies so quietly that I am not sure I heard her right.

"A what!"

Mom takes a deep breath before replying again. "A mermaid. Not like those Disney type mermaids. See there is the head and right there are the breasts. It looks as if she had just jumped out of the water and is making to dive back in."

"Are you and Dad Punking me? This is some kind of birthday joke right!"

Mom looks at me in worry. I'm certain she thinks I am going to lose it. So far I haven't started screaming in hysterics, yet even I know that I am not that far from doing so. As such, I can't blame her for worrying about my sanity.

"I'm sorry if I'm embarrassing you or being stupid. It's just that it is all so surreal. I hardly feel like myself." I babble, finding that talking is helping to keep my panic at bay.

"I understand. It is quite a shock. I know it was to your father and me. The good news is that your long legs look perfect on you now. I'm glad that didn't change." Mom, bless her heart tries to put a good spin on it.

"Are there any other surprises? I mean is there anything else that is strange?" I twist and turn to look at more of me in the mirror.

"Beside this whole thing you mean." Mom chuckles nervously before she carries on. "There are your shoulder blades."

"What about them."

"I don't know and neither does your father. Don't get me wrong they are still shoulder blades and all and not grotesque or anything. However they seem more define than what is natural."

"Oh my god!" A thought had just hit me making my face flame red in embarrassment. In my shame I cover my face with my hands.

"What!"

"Daddy didn't see me like this did he? I'll die of embarrassment if he did… oh god he did!"

"You were thrashing around Michele. I couldn't hold you so he had to tie you down. By then, you had already destroyed your nightie and then, well your father had to undo the knots when you finally settled down and… oh stop it. He is your father and he did what he had to do to keep you safe."

Realizing that I am being childish about the whole thing I start to giggle. The giggle is contagious and pretty soon Mom joins in. As expected, those giggles threaten to turn into an outburst of hysterics. Hysterics that we both barely manage to pull each other back from.

"Are you ladies alright in there? It's awful quiet." Dad asks when we get ourselves under control and everything has gone quiet. This causes another round of giggling to hit us, which finally escalates into outright laughter. Thankfully it is a true laughter this time instead of a plunge into insanity.

It feels good to be laughing. It lightens my worries and I see that it has the same affect on Mom. I don't doubt that an hour ago she didn't think she would ever laugh again. That was the look that I had seen on her face when I woke up. A look that suggested that all laughter had been sucked out of her life, so I am pleased as punch that she can laugh with me.

"I better go reassure your dad that we have not lost our minds." Mom finally manages.

"Oh God Mom, I can hardly breathe, but my sense of smell is more sensitive than before and right now it is telling me I stink so as much as I love to sit here and laugh the night away I really do need a shower. So go ahead and reassure Dad that we are not dying. I'll be okay."

"You're sure."

"Yes I think I am for now. At least I don't feel like I'm about to break down and scream anymore. After all, I'm a Goddess now. What could go wrong?"

Mom recognizes my flippant remark for what it is. Therefore she refuses to leave right away. She watches me carefully as I turn on the shower and continues to do so until the water has heated to a decent enough temperature for me to climb in. Even when I am inside she watches me shower for a few seconds to make sure I was telling the truth about not breaking down. I can't say as I blame her for her concern. Finally not seeing me faint, fall or scream she opens the door and exits the bathroom.

"She's all right dear so stop hovering." I hear her say to Dad, which surprises me for I should not be able to hear them with me inside the shower and the door closed.

"She's not upset about her changes?" Dad asks and I recognize the doubt in his voice.

"She thinks she looks like a goddess Martin. The truth is she is hanging on by a thread. She is doing okay for now. By the way, don't mention the changes to her until she brings it up. She is already embarrassed enough about you seeing her naked. I think that thread of sanity is razor thin right now. She always was a tough girl so we have to believe that she will handle it."

"It's not like I had any choice about seeing her naked you know." Dad grumbles.

"I know dear, now come along."

I don't blame Mom for telling Dad that my sanity is hanging on a thread for she does not know just how close I really am to tipping that balance. I look good, better than I ever have in my life. The problem is that this kind of crap just does not happen in real life. So if it doesn't happen in real life what's left?

The drug-induced specimen is laid out before Vladimir. The amount of drugs given to specimen 101849 to get him to this point was enough to have killed half a dozen humans, making him marvel at the specimen's heartiness.

Not only is the specimen drugged, he is also strapped to a metal table with metal straps that are firmly secured to the table allowing only the slightest of movement to anything strapped to it. This table is designed to keep even his most unruly experiments immobilized so there would be no escape even if the current occupant were not drugged. He knows this personally for he had seen the strength of that table tested by more than one of his specimens in its history. As for the room itself, any hospital ER or specialty laboratory would be blessed to own such equipment.

Funding his endeavours once worried him. Although, when he put his mind to it he discovered that it was all too easy. Long ago he had learned that if humans are threatened enough they are willing to pay almost anything to make those threats go away so he started selling protection to the mob. It had been his idea to sell "insurance", in the first place, which the mob quickly picked up on.

Initially, it had taken a little to convince the mob that it was in their best interest to pay. He even had to teach them to fear the shadows in the night before they did. However, after killing a dozen or so of their head bosses and leaving body parts strewed throughout their houses they got the message loud and clear.

He is proud of his laboratory and he never neglects purchasing the latest and best of equipment to allow him to advance to the next stage in his experiments. It is as much his insistence on getting the latest technology as his twisted fascination that has allowed him to get as far as he is.

He has already bled a pint of blood from the specimen for various tests and is now wondering what his next step should be. He is certain that what he has in specimen 101849 is a living brood, a living brood born, not made or turned. A brood without a Sire and not beholden to a forefather, which in turn could very well make it a forefather.

Being one such forefather, what he sees lying on his table fills him with both hope and dread.

To this day there is still a lot of debate as to how the forefathers came into being without a Sire. Many held that some catastrophic event had caused their "birth", while others support the theory that there had been one Sire to start with, a freak of nature and that the rest were born from that individual and that it was the original's destruction that had set the current forefathers free without a Sire.

Regardless of the truth, in this day and age and for ages past there has been only one way to make a brood and never since the beginning of time, as they count time, has there been a new brood made without a Sire.

Considering that there are only a half dozen forefathers left the future of the forefather's continual existence is dubious. If it were not for the continuing hatred between them and the werewolves or the increased ability of their human food to strike back at them throughout the ages the half dozen forefathers would have no worries. For the present the humans are not a problem for they have forgotten about them so the only real danger to them these days are the werewolves.

He has no doubt the time will come when the humans once again discover them, however that is a worry for another day for he has finally succeeded in birthing something capable of providing his own blood until the change and one whose body continues to live thereafter. He has managed to make something that is more than its whole, the next evolution so to speak.

He has already tested to see if he has Sire control over this specimen and is both pleased and frightened to discover that he does not. He already tested the specimen's blood and genes, already tested his regeneration ability. Everything is perfect, more than he had dreamed to achieve. To think that a few years back he had used this specimen's seed to impregnate ten of his females only to find the resulting creatures so disappointing that he had the off-springs terminated. In fact, so useless had this specimen been for his needs that more than once he had thought of terminating it.

When he had discovered how useless this specimen was he had been tempted to forget about the girl. However, the loss of the girl was a personal thing. She belonged to him and he hated losing anything that belonged to him so he had persisted. Now the unimaginable had happened with the male and he is certain that the female went through the same thing.

A completely new realm of possibilities is upon him now and when Edward gets back with the female he will have two of them to play with. Breeding the two of them to each other had always been his goal and now that goal is finally within sight.

Dam, can they still breed? Are his sperm and her eggs still viable? I have already bred something that may be a match for a forefather. Can I do better?

So many tests to be done and yet he rubs his hands gleefully together, for other than inspiring fear into the human food chain, there is nothing more that excites him than experimenting and testing.

Chapter Five

So far I have managed to keep a tight rein on my sanity. Better yet, I am sitting with Mom and Dad at the kitchen table calmly discussing the events that has transpired since my birthday. Talking is definitely helping to keep me sane, even though some of what they are telling me is both embarrassing and unbelievable.

Surprisingly enough, it is not so much the topic of our discussion that is embarrassing me the most and maybe that is a bad sign. Most embarrassing to me right now is the fact that most of my clothing no longer fits me. When I initially saw my new curves I was ecstatic, not so much now. After all, who knew that my pants would be too large and my shirts too dam tight. I finally had to settle for a too tight t-shirt or risk popping buttons and never, ever have I had to wear a belt to actually hold up my pants. Belts are "accessories not necessities" has always been my motto and I refuse to dwell any longer on the panties and bras. That is the most embarrassing part and what keeps making my face go red. How embarrassing it is to have to borrow panties and bra from your mother. Even then, I had to settle for a sports bra for Mom's breasts are now a cup size smaller than my own. I'm sure this will be the cause of many years of therapy, never mind the years of therapy I am going to need in order to live with what Mom and Dad have been telling me about the night of my birthday.

The big unanswered question for us all of course is how. How is it possible that I underwent the changes that they had seen? Such things do not happen in this day and age or in any age for that matter. This is real life not some fairy tale and yet they had witnessed my body breaking apart and reforming twenty times or more, although they readily admit they lost track in their worry. Most of what they saw they still have trouble talking about. Some they can't even describe for not only do they not have a baseline to start with, they are having trouble finding appropriate words to even begin to describe what occurred.

My parents have always been frank with me and the discussion so far has been on par with prior frank discussions. They have told me about the translucent wings that sprouted from my back, about my body compacting and expanding, about my legs changing into those of horse and goat, of me growing a beard, of it sloughing off to reveal the body I now wear. Horns, teeth, and paws, the list goes on. They tell me about the sound of my bones breaking, reforming just so they can break again, of my screams of pain as my body realigned itself, of the tears they had shed, of my pleads for help not only from them, but also from some pain induced imagined entity. It is almost too much to take and yet I need to know it all.

For the last four hours, they have been trying to explain that which cannot be explained or that, which they refuse to believe. Any one of what they saw was unbelievable, put together it is truly a walk into insanity.

That is not the worse of it. What is worse is that they tell me that some of what they saw was "ugly and evil" is what they had started with and it has not gotten much better since.

After hearing them tell me some of those horrors I come to realize that the only thing that kept them from abandoning me was their love for me. That is the only explanation I can put to it, for I am certain that if they did not love me they would have been out of there in no time flat. I know I would have been, so I wouldn't blame them if they just up and left me to my own devices when everything went to hell.

There is no doubt that they look at me differently now. I see the shivers and tremors that run through their bodies as they revisit what they witnessed. Our relationship has gone through a serious change. The love is still there and still unquestionable, however I wonder if it will ever be as it was.

I am seriously thinking over some of the more surreal details that my parents had revealed to me when a flickering catches my eye. Taking a closer look my eyes open wide. "Oh, how pretty!"

"What's pretty dear?"

"This… Oh I don't know what it is. Don't you see it?" I hold my hand just under the tiny buzzing and flickering thing to let them know what I am talking about and then… "Oh my God. Don't tell me I am starting to see things… it's a fairy!"

"A fairy! Michele, are you okay? There's nothing there Sweetie." Dad responds in his "be reasonable sweetheart" voice.

"No really it's there. I'm sure it's real. Just above my hand. It seems to be waving and blinking in and out. It's so cute, don't you see it?"

I look to them, begging them to see it for the last thing I need right now is to be seeing things that are not there. The look that I see pass between them is not encouraging, causing me to think that I have already lost my battle with sanity.

Becoming desperate for I really don't want to lose this fight I try again. "Don't tell me you don't see it. It's… it's a female and ouch what you are doing you little rascal!" I stop talking when the fairy flies from the palm of my hand in what seems to be a fit of disgust to take hold of my hair, which she begins to pull.

By the widening of Mom and Dad's eyes I can tell that they see something. It may not be the fairy they see, however they can't miss the sight of my hair moving on its own. There is no way they could miss it for a good portion of it has started floating in a way that hair is not meant to float.

Mom is about to say something about that when all contemplation of hair and fairies is forgotten. The sound of breaking glass makes us all turn towards the window and we watch mouth agape as four dark figures come hurling into our small kitchen. Mom and I scream in terror, Dad in surprise and anger.

In the dim light the men look deathly pale and if that sight is not enough to make me want to empty the contents of my stomach, well the blood covered cheeks, chins and lips is another good inducement to do so. The four are ugly to begin with, more animal than human. An evaluation I firmly believe I have a right to when their lips peel back to reveal their teeth. Then the nails catch my attention. I know women that would kill to have nails that long. That said they would certainly forego their sickly black colouring.

It only takes a few moments for me to catalogue the creatures. They repel and yet call to me. Feeling that call a part of me changes. Not all of me, just my senses. Lights, smells, vibrations, even the life force from my parents start to pound away at me. Above all, everything slows to a crawl.

In the midst of this otherworldly time drift, I watch Dad get up to challenge the intruders. I can spare only a second on him however for the sight of a projectile coming out of the barrel of a gun gets my attention. In my hyped up state, I see the object as it leaves the barrel of the gun and watch it come hurling towards me. Everything and everybody is moving so slowly that I have no difficulty moving out of the object's path. I watch it move past me, and then scream as it becomes buried in Mom's chest. My scream is drowned out by the scream that Mom releases and then I watch in horror as she clutches her chest and falls to the floor.

Screaming and sobbing fills the air. It takes a few seconds for me to realize it is coming from me and then Dad's grunt of pain makes me turn to him. He is the next one to fall to the floor as a man, no not a man but a monster tackles him. In horror I realize that everything I have ever come to love in my life is about to be destroyed before my eyes.

A memory long thought to be nothing more than the occasional nightmare comes back to me. My aunt's lifeless body is lying in a pool of her own blood. There is another body, just as lifeless in the corner. Yellow eyes glaring at me, how frightened I was and still am of them.

With that memory my mind snaps. I know it does. I have been on the brink since waking up and this becomes too much. Never in my life have I hated as much as I do right now, a hatred that is ten times worse than the hatred I felt for Mom when she first brought me home. Never in my life have I wanted to tear something apart as much as I want to tear apart these creatures that are about to destroy my life. My eyesight makes another change, I feel my lips pull back over my teeth and let out a little yelp when I feel a painful increase to my body mass.

Two of the creatures start making a move on me. These I ignore for now. I also ignore the one holding back and watching for it is the one that looks ready to tear Dad's throat open that has all of my attention.

"Nooooo. Stop! God please STOP!' I scream in fear-fuelled panic.

My yell was one of anger and frustration and I really didn't expect anything out of it. Nothing at all and yet dam if the stupid thing doesn't stop. I am so surprised by it that I literally freeze in that surprise.

I am not the only one frozen in surprise although, for the creature that was getting ready to tear Dad a new throat had turned his face to me, and now it is just as frozen in place.

I have barely a second to register our surprise for the other two creatures are reaching for me and the third is pointing that dam gun again.

"Get away!" I say in my most commanding voice, hoping beyond hope that the creatures will do just that.

It scares me somewhat that I don't even recognize my own snarling voice. My voice is of no consequence however, nor do I pay much attention to the fact that the other three have been pushed back and away from me for there is only one thing that matters to me right now.

All my attention reverts back to the creature getting ready to take away from me the only man that I love and that I have been lucky enough to have love me back.

Base animal instinct for survival takes over. There is no planning to my attack and no fancy movie star moves. No thoughts at all, other than to save something dear to me. My family's survival becomes the driving force that guides my body.

I barely register the strength that flows through my body as I push up from the floor. I brush aside the fact that I am moving much too fast, I ignore the painful lengthening of my nails, and I most especially ignore my pulled back lips for I don't even want to know if I am showing the same overbite as these unholy creatures.

The connections I feel towards them keeps building and yet at the same time the very sight of them repulses me. That feeling of comradeship is what makes me think that my teeth have grown to be as ugly as theirs, it certainly explains the nails… call me vain if you like yet the last thing I want is to look as ugly as these creatures even if there is no denying that I feel a part of them.

None of those thoughts or feelings keeps me from burying my now female perfect nails into the throat of the monster pinning Dad to the floor. So dislocated from reality am I that even as those nails dig into the creatures throat I think to myself that I have to do something about the colour… black really is not me.

Reality almost checks back in as I tear out the throat of Dad's assailant. I expected blood and lots of it. Where is the blood? There should be blood! Why is there no blood? My brain keeps screaming.

I only have a few seconds to dwell on that for the other creatures are coming after me again. I haul the monster off Dad and then almost throw up as by some mean imaginable I rip the creature's head from his body. In disgust I throw both of these out the shattered window.

I look down at Dad and whimper in relief to see him alive and mostly unharmed. "Help Mom and get her out of here. I'll meet you at the car!" I tell him, only recognizing after the fact that the voice I use on Dad is unrecognizable to me, yet one that demands immediate obedience.

The fearful look that Dad gives me when he looks up at me almost breaks my heart.

The smell of human fear coming from Dad and human blood coming from Mom is almost overpowering. It makes me want to throw myself savagely at the scents. It makes me want to tear apart the owners and bathe in their blood.

They are your parents. They are not the enemies, the still sane part of my mind screams at me and yet I want that blood. Hence, am I certain that I am losing my humanity to become the same as those creatures that have invaded our home.

Humanity. What is that but a word? It is meaningless. It is just a word to try to describe what? Ignore humanity and destroy them. The insane part inside my mind intones.

Frustrated at feeling emotions I cannot contend with I throw myself up and away from Dad. Needless to say, I am surprised to find myself clinging to the ceiling. Looking down at the faces of the creatures that invaded our home I see an equal mix of surprise on their faces. Dad I dare not look at for I can't bear to see the look of revulsion that he is sure to have now that he has seen what I have become.

Deal with Dad later, right now you have work to do.

Releasing my grip on the ceiling, I plunge down on the foremost creature. The beast in me overwhelms any human emotions I have left. Nothing now matters except to rip these creatures into shreds. How dare they ruin my life!

I am mad now. A pissed off mad not the insane type. My, oh so perfect womanly nails grow longer, thicker and sharper. They now look more like those sported by dogs or some other similar wild beast. I reach out and rake them across and into the chest of the closest of my opponent. Past the ribs I reach until I find its un-beating heart. Clutching the dead organ I tear it free from its chest cavity. Still so little blood, yet it matters not for the creature drops at my feet.

"I command you to hold!" One of the other creatures roars at me.

I laugh insanely. Some inner instinct tells me that this mongrel of a creature had just dared to take over my will. It dared to try to force me into his obedience… all that from a creature that is barely a reflection of me; a creature that I feel akin to, a kin that needs to be destroyed because of its imperfection. I spit in disgust at the thought that they have been allowed to continue their existence.

With inhuman speed, I take hold of the creature that dared test my will. A fist to his gaping mouth shatters its overabundant teeth and it does not stop there. The force that I put into the punch is such that my hand comes out the back of its head. The back of the skull explodes outward and hits the creature behind him. Drawing my hand back, I force it up into its brain. I feel around until I have a firm grip on the mush and then draw that mush down and out of its mouth. The creature looks at me wide-eyed, not yet registering what I had just done or that this does indeed mean its end.

My hunger has grown. I lust for flesh and blood. I want to devour the still pulsating brain I hold. I am about to give into that lust when the soft voice of my insanity that I now question is even a part of me knocks gentle on the backdoor of my brain.

"Do not lose yourself. I still need you!" The voice screams.

As I grew from childhood to womanhood I learned to hate that voice. That voice was responsible for getting me into more trouble than my own thoughts. That voice is what has kept me on the razor edge of insanity and yet I feel as if I have never been closer or more in-tuned with it as I am now. I remember it recently holding me to reality when I felt that all was lost. I remember the shared embrace. There was a body behind that embrace, not just a voice. We clung to each other. I fed him my milk of life when his existence threatened to end. Those were real teeth that bit into my breast in desperation as I promised to save him from his torment, just as he had saved me.

"Stay with me my love. Only with you will I keep my sanity, keep my humanity." The voice intones.

There it is again -- humanity.

Disgusted, I throw the brain I am still grasping to the floor and then snarling I take hold of the neck of the only remaining creature.

"Sister." The creature manages to croak before my grip closes off its throat.

That gives me pause. Sister. What is this creature talking about, what can this creature know about family. There is a connection; that I have to admit. However, that connection has nothing to do with family. It is an animal connection. It is the survival of the fittest. It is the connection between two animals to determine who lives and who dies.

My distraction is all the time the creature needs. With a blur of speed that astounds me even in my heighten state the creature escapes from my grasp and attacks. His attack is as brutal as it is quick. Punches and kicks pelt my body. Using what I had learned from Dad over the years and some instinct that I never knew I had I keep him from beating me senseless. Even so, it feels as if there are a hundred creatures pounding on me not just the one. I feel bones breaking and then start to heal only to be broken again. Minute after minute we fight or is it hours. As the fight continues the years of self-defence training that Dad insisted that I learn fly out the window. It all comes down to base animal instinct of wanting to survive and yet in the end my only retaliation is to bite and scratch as if I am an untutored schoolgirl. That is until stars explode and everything goes black.

When my head clears and my eyes come back into focus I am surprised to find myself on my back with the creature pinning me to the floor. I know I am in trouble and yet my fuzzy brain refuses to focus on the important things; like survival. Instead, it dwells on the creature's smell. Funny how I never noticed their foul smell before and those teeth, how could anything eat with a mouthful of teeth like that?

My fuzzy brain is still trying to make sense of what had happened when I become fascinated with the long, black and obviously sharp nails digging into and beneath my skin. The long slender fingers are much stronger than they look and the grip he has on me is beginning to crush my bones.

The creature has one hand under his overcoat, obvious trying to take hold of something, maybe another gun. That is where I would keep a gun my scrambled brain provides in a detached sort of way. That hand finally pulls out the object it had been reaching for.

"You have got to be freaking kidding me!" I yelp when I see what it has pulled out.

I finally manage to pull the rest of my scramble thoughts back to my current danger, although the sight of the wooden stake in the creature's hand almost shatters what little sanity I have managed to hold onto thus far. I am even more convinced of that loss when I release the hysterical laughter that has been building throughout the surreal evening. It is that questionable sanity causes the creature pause.

"Humanity my love. Remember yourself." The voice inside my head soothes.

Humanity! This is survival of the races and there is no room for humanity. What is humanity? Is it the ability not to kill when threatened? No that is not it. When threatened a creature must protect itself and its love ones. Is it then the ability not to kill when you don't have to kill? Is it the ability to find alternatives to dealing out death as the only means of survival? Is it the ability to keep the beast inside tucked away or the ability to recognize the right of another creature to live, no matter how distasteful you find its existence? Do these creatures even deserve to live or do they deserve total and complete annihilation?

All those thoughts and the emotions associated with them hammer at my soul.

Desperately I try to ignore the beast pushing to the fore as well as those dwelling deep inside. I finally manage to find that little nugget of humanity I still possess. Surrounding that nugget and threatening to swallow it is a darkness of bestiality. A bestiality that howls to be released, that begs to be let free.

Clamping down firmly on my inner beast I look to the creature. There is no doubt that this creature feels no humanity. The eyes, those dead red glowing eyes are revolting and I can well imagine that if I do not pull myself together quickly I will become just like it.

I pull my arm free of the creature's grasp, doing my best to ignore the skin I leave behind in the process. Taking hold of the arm coming down with that still too freakishly unreal stake I struggle to keep it away from me. The years of training finally come to the fore and I drive a knee into his privates as Dad has taught me to do when overpowered by someone bigger and stronger.

The creature doesn't even blink an eye, however I do. Dad taught me that a solid hit to a man's privates was the quickest way take the fight out of them and yet I just gave this creature a knee into his privates of such force that they should have come spilling out of his throat and he didn't even so much as freaking blink.

This can't be good! I'm going to have a long talk with Dad about this!

I feel my beast coming to the forefront again. The beast wants to survive, it insists on surviving.

The tie that the attacking creature has to another washes over me, its eyes drill into my own and shakes the very foundation of my soul. That stupid wooden stake is only a mere inch from my throat. Would it be so wrong just to let it go? It would be all over in just a second or two those eyes tell me.

Remembering that I am doing this for my parents I refuse to give in to my despair. I remember the love and support they have given me over the last eleven years, love and support I did not deserve. They believed in me even when I did not believe in myself. They had selfishly given up a part of their lives to watch over and mend my broken spirit. They would be so disappointed if I just gave up.

"I will not just lie down and die!"

Using some newfound strength I force the stake away from my throat. In doing so I lose my hold on his arm and the stake drives into and through my shoulder. The pain is excruciating, causing me to release an animal-like growl. It would be easy, much too easy to lose myself to the beast, which keeps on demanding.

"Go. Go home now before I lose what little control I have left!" I scream in frustration and pain, and then with a strength backed by all the love I have come to feel for the people that adopted and cared for me as if I was their own I throw the creature away from me.

Unbelievably enough the creature flies back with much more force than what I put behind the push. He goes through one wall before coming to a sudden halt on the next. The creature slides to the floor and lays stunned. I watch it for a few seconds to see if it is going to get back up. It does try. It is a feeble try at best and then it looks at me with such hatred that it makes me shiver.

Dizziness washes over me as the world comes back to normal. No longer feeling hypersensitive to the world around me I gasp at its lost. The sound of my beating heart roars in my ears, blood rushes to my brain, air is forced into my starving lungs. My senses dull so that the smell of fear and blood no longer overwhelm me.

Looking around I breathe a sigh of relief to see that Dad and Mom are no longer in the apartment. He must have listened to me and taken mother out when I asked. No, not asked I remember. I had commanded it of him.

Now what? The creature is not moving and I want so much to join up with Dad and yet I fear what I will see in his eyes when sees me again. It would be better if I never have to see that look for surely it will break my heart.

I rip the stake from my shoulder and then flee out the apartment and down the two flights of stairs. I barge out the front door of the building and stop, looking left and right unsure of which way I should go. I am in the midst of trying to make that decision when a car comes to a screeching halt in front of me. My adrenaline redoubles and my body threatens to go back into that hypersensitive mode before I realize that it's Dad's car and that he has gotten out and is telling me to get inside.

I want to ignore him. I want to run away and hide. However, after years of being his daughter I know that if I do not get in he will simply prolong the argument, placing himself and Mom in further risk.

Resigned and seeing that Mom is sprawled across the front seat of the car I open the rear door and get in. Dad gets back into the front and he barely has his door slammed shut before he has the car lurching forward.

"Where are you going Dad?" I wince at my use of Dad for I am no longer sure that the man cares for me.

"We are going to the embassy Sweetie. I've put them on alert and they should be ready for us by the time we get there."

Nothing rattles my dad, I have stated proudly on more than one occasion and once again, there he is proving me right. Him taking charge of the situation and his use of the endearment brings a touch of sanity and stability back into my life. Maybe there is yet a chance that he will not turn away from me.

I become suddenly thankful that he did not see me near the end of the fight with the monsters for I am not so sure he would be quite so understanding if he had done so.

Thomas observed the disaster inside the apartment from the rooftop of the building across the street. Boris, his Sire and head of the European brood told him to wait until Vladimir's minions had secured the woman before they take her away from them, and right now he is thankful for his foresight. His group is better prepared than those that just tried and failed in securing the woman so he has no doubt that he could have succeeded where they did not, although it would have been a costly endeavour.

The woman had a few surprises up her sleeves that Boris had not told him about and he wonders what other ones she may have. He has seen many things in his two thousand years and yet he had just seen something that he had never thought

109

to see. If Boris had not warned him that the woman may be more than human he would not have believed his eyes, for never would he had thought what he saw possible from the human food chain.

Therefore, he is no less surprised then Vladimir's minions to see what the woman was capable of doing. The difference is that unlike them he is still in one piece. Boris had thought he was only dealing with some twisted human breed that Vladimir had made and yes, he may have expected a little more out of her, however the woman is turning out to be so much more than any of them could have imagined. What that more may ultimately be is yet unknown and something he is sure Boris will be very interested in determining once he has the girl secured.

Her speed was astronomical and her strength unbelievable and yet it was her phenomenal mind that had him at a loss for even from where he was perched he had felt her commands trying to break through his Sire's grip. Now he knew her better and now was the time to reconsider his plan of action.

"Franklin you get ahead of that car and take out the road or bridge or whatever with that toy you love." He tells the large brood to his left.

Franklin gives him an evil smile before sprinting off. "Alive Franklin or Boris will tear you into pieces." He shouts to his retreating back.

"Bruno, Yankov, I want you two to pace the car on the left, Rizzo and Opal the right. The rest of you are with me."

Everybody scatters to do his bidding. He takes off and the four told to follow him drop from the rooftop to the street only moments behind him. Free of any obstacles they move forward at a speed that no human could hope to match and rapidly close the gap on the vehicle ahead.

"Franklin?" He yells into his microphone.

"Almost Sir. They have a bridge just ahead."

Thankfully it is late at night so there should be very little chance of having to deal with other humans he musses as he chases the speeding car.

The brood are not the only ones watching what has shattered the evening calm in this peaceful neighbourhood for a group of werewolves have been watching the brood throughout the night.

Earlier that night two groups had been sent out to spy on the going on. One group had reported back, while another is still missing. John struggled with what he should do when the second group had not returned. He finally decided to send out another group to see what was keeping the first.

Needless to say he really had not needed to be so careful for the creatures of night were not being quiet about what they were doing. However, the question that still needs to be answered is, why are they doing it?

John has never seen so many brood come down on a couple of humans and the fact that Vladimir and Boris are working together to do so is worrisome. What possible danger could these humans hold for the brood that they would mobilize such a large group to take care of them?

What the hell are Vladimir and Boris up to? That is what he needs answered. The death of the human he does not care a wit about. What he needs to find out is how this will affect the pack.

Filthy disgusting monsters. Hurry back and tell me what the hell is going on so we can get out of here and leave these things to their meals.

It is just as he is making his wish that the second group he sent out returns.

"Well?"

"We found Robert and Francis. They have been torn apart."

"Impossible."

"Not so. I saw it myself. Those fucking animals did it."

"Those bastards are going to pay!" His anger snaps to the breaking point for if it is not bad enough that they have been sneaking around following the filthy things all night now this. "Let's get us some of our own back."

The twenty with him howl in glee. The hunt is on. The time for sneaking up on the pray is long past and now it is time to retaliate for the death of two of their pack. Human forms start to undergo a change…

Mentally exhausted I slump in the back seat of the car. Now that horror and imminent death is not staring me in the eye, I have started to shake in shock. So tired do I feel that I barely remember asking Dad about Mom, or his assurance that she was only hit with a dart and that all it seems to have done is knock her out cold. Thankfully most of our worries are now behind us and my body knowing this is starting to go into full retreat.

As I try to control my shaking body I can't help wondering if what I am experiencing is what soldiers go through after battles. A couple of times I even start to ask Dad about it. The question never gets past my lips for I am still bitterly afraid of what I will hear in his voice or see in his eyes if he designs to answer me. Instead, I let myself slump into the comfortable back seat and try to wish the night away.

"Ah Sweetie."

"Yes Papa."

"I'm not sure what is going on tonight and I'm sure that we are going to have a very long talk about it very soon. Whatever it is you may want to dig deep inside again for we seem to have company behind us." His voice is strained and I can tell that he is using every bit of his military training to keep himself together.

That alone makes me sit up and look out the back window. I expected to see a car following us, not a bunch of human looking things chasing and closing in on us to boot. Human looking, but not human for nothing human could run that fast.

"What the fuck!"

"Language Sweetie."

Oh sure, trust my lovable daddy to remind me of my language when the whole freaking world seems to be coming unhinged.

"Language! Do you see those fucking things coming after us? What the hell is going on Papa?"

"Sweetie… listen to me Sweetie. I have no idea what is going on, what those things are, or what you can or cannot do about it. I do know that I dare not stop the car and that we need something right now. Think Sweetie, now is the time to dig down deep. This is the time that makes or breaks a solider. Is there anything you can do?"

Oh ya, he is in his full military mode now and yet the calm of Dad's voice has a sobering effect on me. I know it is all false bravado, but if Dad can keep it together, well so can I. So even though I fear revisiting the creature that I had been just a few minutes ago I do what he asked of me. Slowly, almost tentatively I look deep inside myself.

Kneeling on the back seat, I watch those creatures gaining on the car. Whenever they pass under a streetlamp I see the red of their eyes and the gleam of their teeth. They seem to be running easily, at times jumping to unbelievable heights to gain a few more feet of precious ground. It is surreal. This cannot be happening to my quiet life. What can I possibly do to make these inhuman creatures go away? I feel so helpless and frustrated that I want to scream.

Scream! Oh shit I really don't want to!

Without realizing it my lips part, my throat convulses, and my mouth opens. I ignore the pain as my bones shift and my neck elongates. All of the night's frustrations and fears gather into a ball at the base of my throat and then it comes spewing out.

The back window of the car explodes as a dreadful wailing pours forth. The wave of my wail hits the monsters and I watch in disbelief as they take hold of their heads and then go flying through the air.

"Opps! Sorry about the window Daddy! There are more of them out there running along the rooftops that I didn't get. A couple on the left and two more on the right of us."

"I see them. All we can do is keep going and hope for the best… What now! This really can't be happening."

I look out the front window to see what Dad is talking about and when I see it I barely manage to keep from cussing aloud again. Standing there is another one of those monsters and this one has what looks to be a rocket launcher on his shoulder. Looking around to see how Dad is going to get us out of this mess does not give me a whole lot of encouragement. We have driven onto a bridge so the option is limited to driving off the bridge, "Not!" or keep on going and hoping for the best.

I look to Mom and wish I could tell her one last time how much I love her. She is the lucky one. She is blissfully unaware of how the world has gone mad and yet I want so badly to hear her voice just one more time.

Dad floors the car. I see the tightening of his face through the rear view mirror. He is going to go for it. Bless him for never giving up.

I place my hand on his shoulder and give it a gentle squeeze. "I love you Dad. Now run that bastard over."

It is all bravado. Both of us know it is never going to happen however we know we have no other choice…

"Now what!"

I bet Dad is just as shocked as I am for an insanely huge dog or maybe a wolf has jumped onto the bridge. The creature with the rocket launcher must have heard it also and it must fear it for we are quickly forgotten as he turns the rocket launcher towards the dog. I look behind us to see if the others following us have gained and what I see is just as shocking as what just happened in front. At least a half dozen oversized dogs are attacking those creatures that have been following and gaining on us.

Both groups ignore us as they tear away at each other. I find myself routing for the dogs for no other reason than because they at least have not attacked us tonight. However, I don't care to be around here when the dust settles, apparently neither does Dad.

"Hang on Sweetie this is going to be a rough ride."

Chapter Six

For the ten minutes it take us to make it to the embassy I keep a wide-eyed look out for whatever this surreal evening may yet throw at us. Even as I do, I pray that Dad is not going to get us killed before we get there. I have never seen him drive so crazy. Heck, I would never have imagined him doing so. As such, when I finally see the gate of the embassy looming before us I heave a sigh of relief.

Whatever Dad had done has put the embassy on alert and military men in full garb wait for us at the gate. At first, I thought Dad was going to go right on through, however when he is only a few feet from the gate he lays on the breaks, bringing the car to a screeching halt.

"Sir." One man standing at the gate says to him even before Dad finishes lowering the window.

"Sergeant. Is everything in order?"

"Yes Sir. Was it your Alert?"

"Yes Sergeant. Close and lock the gate behind us. Keep the men in place and shoot anything that flies over the fence."

"Over Sir?"

"Over, under, through, whatever. Kill anything that even gets within fifty feet of this place. Shoot first and ask questions later. Do we understand each other Sergeant?'

"Sir, yes Sir."

That is what I love about the men who work under Dad. They trust him and not once have I hear about them questioning his orders. This time it is no different than any other so by the time Dad puts the car in gear to drive up to the embassy building the gate is already closing and men are ready to shoot anything that so much as moves. I pray that none of the locals are going to be foolish enough to come out and see what is happening for I have no doubt that the men will follow Dad's orders to the T and kill anyone stupid enough to show themselves.

The car stopping in front of the embassy shakes me from my wandering thoughts. I've had it. I'm done. All I want to do is go back to sleep for even my worse nightmares are not as scary as what we have been through tonight. Or maybe this is the nightmare and all I have to do is wake up, I tell myself as I crawl out the backseat of the car.

By the time I am standing outside the car Dad has gotten Mom out of the front seat. He gives her a worried look as he cradles her in his arms and then gives me the same worried look.

"Let's get inside. I'll make a few calls and see if anybody knows what is going on."

He leads me inside the embassy and into total chaos, or at least it seems like total chaos to me. The look on Dad's face as he watches his men running around, tells me otherwise. He is satisfied with what he is seeing or he would be barking orders. Amidst the chaos we make our way to the elevator. Dad pushes the button a few times and then curses. "We have to take the stairs."

"Why?"

"The elevator is the first thing that gets disabled when the embassy is put on alert. You there. What are you doing Private? Get a move on." Dad shouts to a man that has stopped to stare at me.

The man is slow to obey Dad, something I find hard to believe for nobody in their right mind is slow to obeying one of Dad's orders. Dad looks to the man and then to Mom with indecision. Seeing that he is going to have more on his plate than he is going to be able to handle carrying Mom I offer to carry her. Dad looks at me doubtfully.

"Really Dad I can do it. Trust me to take care of her while you take care of us."

"Okay, but stay close."

The private still has not moved and the look on his face is not reassuring. Dad must not like it either, for he no sooner hands Mom over to me and then turns on the private and cold cocks him.

"That will teach you to follow orders." He mumbles and then turns back to me. "Up the stairs to the fifth floor, are you sure you can handle your mother."

Amazingly, Mom feels no heavier than a feather to me so I give Dad a nod and then follow in his wake.

We make it, but not without some difficulties. Even Dad is having trouble believing how his soldiers' training and obedience is breaking down when we come around. I lose track of how many of them make a grab for my ass. Before tonight I may have been happy at getting some of that attention for I have gotten use to men ignoring my plain looks, tonight it makes me seethe with anger. Dad is getting just as angry as I am and after he lays out his fifth solider he finally starts to gather around us a few of those that don't lose their cool at our presence.

Before we even make it to the fifth floor Dad has gathered a group of ten of his men to accompany us. He orders them ahead of us to clear our path, which allows us to finally make it to his office without actually killing anybody, thank god for I hate to think how he is going to explain knocking out his own men to his superiors, never mind the explaining he would have to do if he had to add a death or two to the list.

"What are you looking at Private? To your post now before I have you court marshalled!" Dad yells to the last man standing between his office door and us and then turning to one of the men that accompanied us. "Is it secure?"

"Yes General. We started locking down the embassy the minute your alarm went off."

"I want at least two men out here and two inside." He looks to me and then shakes his head. "No, belay that order. Put four men at this door and leave us alone inside."

"Right away Sir."

Dad returns the salute and marches into his office. Right away, I note that the window barriers are down and locked. The only light, feeble as it is, comes from the small field lantern located on his desk, leaving most of the office darkness.

"Take care of your mother while I make a call Michele."

I smile at him for his very posture tells me that he has pulled himself back into his familiar military self. Such is my faith in him that I have no doubt that if anybody can put our world back to right again it is him.

I take Mom over to the sofa and lay her down on it. Sitting down at her head I lift it and lay it on my lap. She has yet to stir and even if Dad is not worried I am. I need my mother back. Dad is great at what he does however it has always been Mom's love that has made the monsters under my bed go away.

"General?" I hear Dad say to someone on the phone.

"What's going on Appleton? Why is the embassy under code one?"

I hear the voice on the other end replying and so surreal has the evening been that I don't even think it strange that I can hear the other man as clearly as if he and Dad were standing next to me and having the conversation.

"Sir, it has something to do with those calls I have been making over the last couple of days. Tonight my family and I were attacked in our home by something. I don't know what they were, but by dam..." Dad takes a deep breath to get his emotions back under control before continuing. "We managed to get away and then more of them showed up as we were making our way to the embassy. They are not human General. They walk like humans, but I tell you they are not and then there were some... dogs..."

"It just so happens that your calls, unbelievable as they were got to the right ears, or so I assume they are the right ears. You and your family have been classified as "Top Secret" even from me, so as much as I want to know what the hell is going on I can't hear anymore of this. A chopper was dispatched some time ago and you and your family were to get on it tomorrow evening. I guess this means you're going to be leaving just a little earlier. Your replacement is on board and you have a half hour to turn security over to him. You are not to tell him anything about this evening, just turn the place over to him and then get on that chopper."

"Yes Sir. Any clue of where it will be taking us?"

"Not a one. Be ready and good luck Appleton." The phone goes dead.

Vladimir Narishkin is not a pleasant Sire at the best of times, and the news he is receiving is making him even less so. He had been running another battery of tests on specimen 101849 and he had been counting on Edward showing up with the girl. What is making him even more unpleasant than usual is that instead of reporting success, Edward is reporting dismal failure, he is even praising the stupid girl's strength and speed. So where was the girl? Apparently she has disappeared again.

Even as Edward tells him his sordid tale Vladimir berates him and even as he berates him, he wonders what is going on in Europe. Was Boris asleep at the wheel and letting everything go to hell in a hand basket? Werewolves daring to interfere in a brood operation, that is something that would never happen under his watch and one of the first things he will set to rights once he has Europe back. His thoughts are wandering those pathways when something of what Edward is saying finally catches his interest.

"What?"

"I said that she managed to get through our bond. It was for only a few moments, but still. You must have felt it Master."

He had felt something a while back, however he had been so wrapped up in his tests that he had paid it little mind. Now a cold dread starts to form in the pit of his stomach.

"I felt it, but I was busy. Are you certain?

"Very certain. You have been my Sire for a thousand years and never once in those years has anyone been able to break your bond to me. Yet this little slip of a girl… what exactly did you breed Master?"

"I thought that maybe it was our salvation. Now I am not so sure."

"What are my orders Master?"

"Is there any way you can track the chopper that picked them up?"

"Maybe. It all depends on where it is going."

"Dam it we can't afford to let Boris get his hands on her. See what you can do about tracking her and then get back here."

"Thank you Master." Edward replies to an already dead phone.

For a long time afterward Vladimir looks at Specimen 101849. He knows he should destroy it right here and now and yet there is so much to learn and so many possibilities. How could he simply destroy something that may be his greatest creation without probing it once or twice?

A loud whapping noise filling my ears brings me fully awake. I come to realize that the chopper is descending and it is my lurching stomach reacting to that decent that has finally awaken me. At first, I wonder what I am doing in a chopper so it takes me a few seconds to put everything together. The chopper had come for us just as the man had said it would. Dad had turned over the embassy to his replacement and right after that we were lead to the backyard of the embassy. Four men had accompanied the chopper. Luckily Dad had kept the ten he had gathered close to him for when we showed up two of the men accompanying the chopper went crazy. By then, Mom had woken up and I saw the shock in her eyes when the men came after me. I can't blame her for her shock for this is not how men under Dad's command behave, no not at all. The ten men with us quickly put those two men out of commission and after a brief discussion two of them replaced the unconscious men. After that, we were squirreled away inside the chopper and off we went. All I really remember thinking was how I wished this night would just end.

Shaking the last of the cobwebs from my mind I look to Dad for reassurance. He is holding Mom tightly in an embrace and the two of them are busy murmuring to each other. This time it does surprise me that I can hear what they are saying to each other. I shouldn't be able to for not only are they talking quietly, the noise of the chopper should be making it impossible for me to hear anything they are whispering to each other. When Dad says something truly embarrassing to Mom it hits me like a bucket of cold water.

That's all I need. Something else that will result in a lifetime of therapy. A lifetime more than what I am already going to need that is.

Sitting across from me are the two stern-faced U.S. military men that had taken over for the two we had left behind. They have no better idea what is going on then we do yet the way they oh so casually have their guns trained on me makes me worry; surely I am not the enemy here am I?

The sight of them aiming their guns at me brings on a flash of anger. It is not the hatred anger that I had grown up with and understood. It is a type of anger I can't put my finger on. That anger almost overwhelms me and for a few seconds I fight the urge to thrown them out of the chopper.

When the reality that I actually could throw them out with ease hits me it is another bucket of cold water hitting me in the face. What have I turned into that I could think such thoughts!

Desperate not to let that animal I was in our apartment back out I sit on my hands and chew my lip until the helicopter finishes it's decent and finally lands.

We are met on the tarmac by a sergeant of some military unit I don't recognize. Thankfully he does not make a grab at me as he welcomes us to Torino Italy and then leads us and our "escort" to some waiting jeeps.

It is still evening or maybe closer to early morning, but late July in Italy means nice weather so it makes the open-air jeep ride to the hanger located at the far end of the tarmac refreshing. Waiting at the hanger there is another contingent of hard-faced men wearing military uniforms I do not recognize.

When we step out of the jeeps a man comes out to meet us and tells our escorts they are excused. Those words have barely left his mouth when all hell breaks out for a half dozen of his men turn… stupid. That's the only word I have for it. All night men have been trying to maul me for no apparent reason and I am really getting sick of it. I kick the first man in the face and break the arm of the second. I am about to take care of the third when I see that Dad and the other men that have not gone stupid are taking care of the rest of them.

"I'm really getting tired of this." I tell Dad when things settle down again.

"Me too. I don't know what is getting into them."

"General."

125

The man acknowledges Dad as his due, though I'm sure that he is doing so out of respect only and not as a military requirement, at least not his.

"So what's the story?"

"Not sure general. Our orders are to keep you people secured until the transport arrives at 0800 hours."

I look at my watch. Three hours to wait. Mom and Dad look as worn out as I feel and I'm sure we are all thinking the same thing. Three hours, that is going to feel like a lifetime.

"Who is in command here?" Dad pipes up as we are led inside the hanger.

"He was." The man replies as he points to one of the men that we laid out, and who is current being dragged away somewhere.

"That's not reassuring."

"Don't worry Sir, there has been a lot of contingent plans put into place and this was one of them. Right now the command has fallen to me and you can rest assured that I will fulfill my duty."

"After the night we just had I hope you don't take it wrong lieutenant, but your assurance means little to me right now."

My attention wanders away from the conversation for a fellow has been eyeing me up since I entered the hanger and I don't like the way he is looking at me. It is not the same stupid look that men have been giving me all night. The look he is giving me is almost insolent and positively possessive. If that is not bad enough, he then starts to swagger around me in a disgusting way, almost as if I am his prey.

That does it. All night I have been running and reacting; monsters, big freaking dogs, Mom being shot, and men groping me. I snap. My anger at the evening we had just endured comes to the fore. It is the same anger that I had felt in the chopper and this time I allow it the freedom it demands.

I'm sure the arrogant man barely registers my first hit and before I know it we are rolling around on the hanger floor. My punches to his body are brutal. I have never felt so strong and I put all my night's frustration behind those punches. His punches to my body are just as brutal as mine are to his. Heck, it does not even seem to bother him that he is fighting a girl. Then again, why should it for in truth I am trying to tear his head off.

We ignore the shouting as we snarl, bite, and hit each other. Any weakness that he shows I take advantage of and by the pounding I am taking he is taking the same advantages of my weaknesses. One minute, I am in control of the fight and I am beating the arrogant man to a pulp, the next he is on top of me and pounding on me. Back and forth it goes, neither one of us willing to give an inch.

I become thankful for the military jacket that someone had given me to wear back at the embassy for all the rolling around, punching, and scratching that we are doing on the blacktop would have torn my flesh to pieces. However, even as I am thankful for it I curse it for the jacket is much too large for me and it keeps tying up my arms, which in turn keeps me from using my newfound strength as effectively as I could.

As I tumble around with the man I briefly consider why I had the sudden need to attack him, besides being pissed at the evening that is. It was something about his attitude I finally conclude. It had almost felt like he was trying to intimidate me and after the night I just had I was no more in the mood for that kind of foolishness as I was for more groping.

That is only part of my problem for if the man's arrogance is not enough for me to contend with as we roll around the tarmac I also have to contend with his smell. The man smells musky, yet not unpleasant. It is a smell that calls to some deep instinct, which I am not ready to acknowledge, especially while trying to beat the crap out of the fool.

Private Darren Keller has been a werewolf for almost five hundred years. He has had a few Alphas throughout the ages, the latest being Dominic. Without intentionally meaning to, as he really did not like Dominic or some of the things he was into he had managed to work himself up to being Dominic's fourth in command. As it is, he would have left Dominic long ago if the wolf in him didn't insist on a pack.

Some time ago, Dominic had decided it would be a good idea to keep an eye on the military, and as he was in the position of having to make a change in his life before humans got suspicious of him he had volunteered to join this newly formed arm of the U.N. Military.

The last thing he had expected when given this assignment was to come across another werewolf, and a female one at that. When she first walked in he wondered if Dominic had placed her here to test him. That thought went out the window shortly after she engaged him. First of all, he doubted that Dominic would use a female for as far as Dominic is concerned females have only one use, and secondly, he has never heard of a female as strong as this fragile looking woman in the pack.

He had felt her the minute she came into the hanger and his wolf had automatically gone into possessive mode. This was the kind of behaviour he was ordered to keep in check by his Alpha. The very behaviour that he had spent years learning to control so that he could blend in easily with the humans. Those years of training had gone out the window when her scent swamped over him. Her scent had rolled off her and filled the hanger, it had enticed and called to his wolf. Still that was no excuse for him losing control.

He is certain that once his Alpha hears about this he is going to receive a whopping if this little strumpet doesn't give it to him first that is.

Martin is aghast at his daughter's behaviour. He has no idea what has gotten into her and at the same time afraid that the events of the evening has finally snapped her mind. She has just thrown the man off her and the two of them are now beating each other with fist and kicks. He winces as a particular nasty blow lands to her ribs and then smiles in pride as she retaliates.

Michele had never been real good at the hand-to-hand combat. He had recognized this early and had only continued her training because it helped her keep her temper under control. Later, he continued it because the time the two of them spent sparing became their time. A private moment for him and his daughter, a moment the two of them came of love more and more as the years passed.

Therefore, he cannot justify what she is doing; however he is proud at the showing she is giving.

Proud or no, he feels the need to stop this silliness or at least get these men to stop it for there is no reason for his little girl to get beaten up while she is under their "protection".

Looking to the U.S. military men that accompanied them from the chopper he sees that they look uncertain as to whether they should be stepping in or not. They fiddle with their weapons looking for direction from those who were waiting in the hanger so they are of little use.

Seeing that the U.S. men are no good to him he looks to the man that is leading the second outfit. He is not happy at the outrageous lack of concern on his part. He actually looks as if he is enjoying the show and by the looks of it seems willing to let the cards fall where they may.

"If you are not going to stop this give me your gun and I'll do it."

"Our orders are not only to protect her, but short of what happened outside, not interfere with anything and I do mean anything she does Sir. It is obvious that this is something else, so we will let it play out."

"And if she gets hurt?"

"No need to fear her safety Mrs. Appleton. She could start world war three and as ordered we would support her every step of the way. As it is, she seems to be holding her own and I will shoot the private myself if things change."

I am really pissed now. In my distraction the man's kick had gotten through and I felt my ribs break. I can feel them grating every time I breathe and they hurt like hell. With my anger my eyesight changes, not to the same weirdness as in the apartment. Something different... I literally snarl at the man and renew my attack. As I retaliate my mind brings up the image of a wolf head becoming superimposed over my own.

That superimposed image must not only be in my mind for something about it obviously knocks the man off his game. The look of surprise that he gives me would have been funny in any other situation, however in this situation I see it as my opening.

I have had enough of the arrogant male and playing with him. I release another snarl and attack him mercilessly. Putting all my anger, willpower, strength not to mention frustration of the night into the next half dozen punches, I manage to knock the wind from him and then watch in satisfaction when he drops almost lifeless to the floor, however my anger has not been soothed so I move on to kicking him.

As I land kick after kick at the man I become sorry that I am wearing running shoes instead of those military boots Dad is so fond of for with those boots I could do a whole lot more damage to the arrogant male than with runners. However, it still feels good, so dam good.

Each kick I give him sends him back another couple of feet, giving me some running room for the next kick and then another and another. I am about to give him his sixth when I take note of his posture. It dawns on me that for the last couple of kicks he has been keeping himself in the same position and willingly taking the punishment I was dealing out.

I consider his posture. It is obviously submissive, however it is something else that is catching me totally off guard for he seems to be "knocking" at my senses, asking for permission and acceptance.

He is declaring me the winner! Some inner instinct finally screams.

I stand over him, breathing hard. My ribs are still bothering me. They are getting better however, for with every breath they hurt less and less so maybe they were not broken after all. To my satisfaction the man lies on the tarmac just inside the hanger, not daring to change his posture and he is breathing even harder than me. The warning comes in the form of the widening of his eyes.

I quickly turn from the arrogant man and take note of the man running towards me sporting one of those huge freaking military knives; the kind I am sure that they use to kill bears with. I wait for him until I judge the time to be just right and with a speed that takes my breath away I move to the side. The man's momentum forces him to continue pass me and it is just as he is passing me that I take hold of his military outfit and using his own momentum against him I help him into the wall of the hanger. The man hits the wall with a solid thump and then slides fifteen feet to the tarmac.

"Stand down and that is an order!"

At first, I think the man is talking to me and being strung so tight I am more than willing to take him and all of his on. A quick look at him although shows me the truth. He is not yelling at me. He and his men have their weapons trained on the one man that I had just thrown to the wall as well as on a couple of their own. One look at him and it is obvious that he is more than prepared to shoot anyone that does not listen to him.

Still, it takes everything I have left in me to keep from reacting to the danger that hangs in the air and the smell of human fear makes it doubly hard.

"Miss. It's okay Miss. Nobody going to hurt you. I'm told that this may help. Drink up." The lieutenant tells me calmly once he has a semblance of order restored.

Hurt me. I feel invincible right now. None of these puny things could hurt me. How dare he even think such an outrageous thought!

"Dear. Michele… listen to me Dear. It's okay. They are here to protect us. Everything is okay. Look at me baby. That's it."

I look to Mom dreading what I will see in her eyes. What I see rocks me to the very marrow of my bones for instead of fear of what I have become I see acceptance, complete acceptance and infinite love.

Everyone else holds their breath as I take one deep breath and then another. Seeing that I am not going to lose it they start to relax causing the fear in the hanger to subside. Half dozen deep breaths I take before I get myself under control and then I take a drink of what the man handed me. He was right it helps. The drink taste strongly of blood and something else I can't place.

"What is this?"

"Blood mixed in some broth."

I spit out the mouthful I had been in the process of swallowing and stare daggers at him.

"You fed my daughter blood!" Mom beats me to the punch.

"I was told it might help. Am I right?"

Ya okay so he was right, but still…

"I won't have you feeding my child something so disgusting so don't do it again." Mom tells him and then taking the container from my hand she throws it away.

I feel the same way as Mom. I mean how disgusting and yet as I watch the blood spill over the tarmac I can't help feel some remorse at not finishing it.

"Are you okay now Baby?" Mom asks, taking my mind off the slowly spreading pool of blood and broth.

"Yes." I say distractingly and then pulling myself together I look directly at her. "Yes, I'm okay now Mom. Thanks for being here for me. Just give me a sec."

I turn back to the arrogant male still lying submissively on the ground. "You saved me. Thank you."

"No I didn't. You would have thrashed his ass."

"Regardless, thank you. Let me help you up. What is your name?"

"Private Darren Keller, Miss." He replies and then offers me his neck.

What a strange thing to do I think, however instincts take over once more and I find myself sniffing and then nipping his neck. When I feel that I have asserted myself I thank him again.

"What are you?" I whisper to him when the realization of what I had just done hits me.

"You know what I am. I see it in your eyes."

"No I don't know."

"Are you going to deny the wolf we all saw come out of you?"

Wolf! God this is the last thing I need to hear tonight. "Whatever!" I tell him still not ready to admit to something so stupid and then turn away.

"What was that all about Michele?" Mom asks when I return to her.

"Just a friendly little tumble."

"Friendly. Oh dear you're never going to attract a man that way, although if you don't cover yourself back up that may do it." She states jokingly, trying to lighten the tension I'm sure.

I look to my clothing. Sure enough, I lost the borrowed military jacket in the scuffle and my poor worn out t-shirt is showing much more skin, in many more places than I am comfortable showing. Red with embarrassment I turn to look for my borrowed jacket. Much to my relief I discover the lieutenant standing behind me offering me that very jacket.

"Thank you Sir." I tell him with as much dignity as I can muster under the circumstance.

"Lieutenant Knoll, Miss. Is there anything else I can do for you?"

"Not right now thank you."

"Then let me clean up this mess."

Lieutenant Knoll nods to me, and then turns around to get some semblance of order back. "You two get that man to a hospital. Private Keller, you are excused."

"No."

He turns to me with a questioning look.

"I like and trust him." I reply firmly.

"Like him. Hell miss I hate to see what you would do to someone that you don't like. Okay then, Keller looks like you're stuck with the lady.... "she likes you", as for the rest of you, we are here to secure these folks and keep them safe, not to act like a bunch of asses. If any of you don't think you can handle it leave now because one more incident like this and I will personally shoot you." He glares from one man to another.

There is a couple of seconds of uneasy silence and then one man's eyes glaze over. He makes a move towards me and true to his word Knoll shoots him, although admittedly the wound is a minor one all things considering.

As it turns out, I am hell on men tonight for in the end, only ten of our previous twenty or so "protectors" are left standing in the hanger.

Private Darren Keller is still in shock. The strength of a werewolf is based in part on the amount of anger they can generate. The other part is the amount of willpower they can enforce onto another wolf. This in turn decides their positioning in a pack. Therefore, if a four-foot werewolf could generate enough anger and willpower he could conceivable beat the daylights out of a wolf twice his size.

All wolves generate the two to some degree and Alphas are by far the best at it. It is the amount of these two things combined that determines whether a wolf is an Alpha or not and that which determines the strength of said Alpha.

Therefore, he is at a loss. Not only did this little slip of a girl just kick his ass, she had done so with enough anger and willpower that she had just changed his pack alliance, which is something he was totally not expecting.

Even as he considers the implication of this, he touches the threads of the alliance he just formed and finds it new and raw, therefore he is not surprised to discover himself the lone member in this Alpha's pack, however he has no doubt that he will not be the last.

He shivers at the thought of what will happen when the quiver of his broken alliance to his prior Alpha hits home, for his prior Alpha is not a very forgiving man.

As for whether he is sorry or not for the change in alliance, he has yet to decide. Dominic is a good enough Alpha for the most part. A little crude and resistant to change, making him a little too old fashion for his taste and Dominic gets into things that he does agree with. Overall, he is not the worst Alpha he has been under. As for this she wolf, what will she have to offer?

What the hell are you thinking Darren? A woman. There hasn't been a bitch Alpha in... has there ever! I get a feeling that things are going to get interesting around here.

Dismissing Dominic, he probes the threads tying him to Michele only to discover that she has not yet learned to acknowledge the probe.

Don't worry about it old man, your Alpha, whether she knows it or not will make certain that you don't end up a stray.

As order is re-established I find Private Keller giving me the eye. Not the arrogant look that he had been giving me earlier this evening. This one is more curious than anything else. As if he can't believe what had just happened. As if he is wondering what kind of creature I am and what I am going to do next. It is in the midst of this that I feel the knocking on my hindbrain, much like the knocking of the voice had done in our apartment last night. When I open that door it is with a shock that I recognize the person doing the knocking to be Keller and not the voice.

Shit, I can't deal with this right now!

Slamming that door shut and firmly ignoring Keller I turn to the man that really means something to me in my life. "Sorry Daddy."

I really am sorry for the scene I made, although the "Daddy" part is all calculated, calculated to keep Dad from going into one of his long "you have to learn to be more responsible" speeches and Mom knows it for I see her grinning at me.

Jackie grins when she hears Michele call her husband "Daddy". *You're such a pushover. Now please, please show her you still love her... you do still love her don't you?*

She breathes a sigh of relief when her husband smothers Michele in a tight embrace. Even with all this strangeness going on, she again thanks god for giving them Michele to care for after the death of their own daughter. For a certainty it has been a trying time and more to come by the looks of things. That is okay for just as certain is the fact that the bonds the two of them have forged over the years is still strong and unbreakable.

"So did someone mention coffee and food?" Mom finally pipes up.

"And a shower. God how I could use a shower."

"Sorry Miss a shower will have to wait, however coffee and some of our best military "breakfast in a can" is available in the back." The grinning lieutenant informs us.

I scowl, Mom sighs and men chuckle.

"Lieutenant, I thank you for your intervention. Can you please inform me as to what military outfit you belong with?"

"Sorry for my lapse General and welcome under the protection of the U.N. Security.

"U.N. Security!" I hear Dad's breath catch, but he keeps his worries to himself as he joins us for food.

Michele let me in.

Leave me alone I'm tired.

I just want to make sure you are okay and ask why I can't slip into your mind as easily as I use to. Are you blocking me on purpose?

I don't know what you are talking about. What do you mean slip into my mind as easily as before. How long…

I've been with you for a long time, forever it seems. It is with you that I learned how to talk and how not to be an animal like the rest of what it has caged here.

You're the one who has been haunting me all my life. You're the one that has made me think I am mad.

Not haunting Michele.

Are you real then?

If I were not real would I hurt so much?

Probably not. Why are you hurting?

He is doing things to me. Experiments, like you use to do in university. It hurts Michele. It was

139

bad enough before that night, but now... I heard him talking about how he sent some of his people to get you. I was out of my cage and he was working on me when one of his men came and told him that one of his thralls recognized you. He was even talking about breeding us together. That I wouldn't mind. I have never felt so comforted as when you let me suckle at your breast the other night. I could easily stand to feel that way again.... He's mad as hell right now so I assume you got away.

My face flames red in embarrassment before I can reply.

Yes we got away. Where are you? Who has you?

I don't know on either count.

What can you tell me about them?

Not much, they have me in a dark room most of the time. I did hear him talking and apparently what we just went through should have killed us.

It sure felt like it had and I wished for it more than once. What did we just go through? What has happened to us?

Sorry Michele for I really don't know. As it is, if I didn't spend all those years inside your head, going to school with you and learning as you learned I would not even understand half of what I do. I just know that it was expected. What was not is what we have become.

Who are you?

A very long pause before I finally hear the whisper of a reply.

I don't know.

Boris is no happier than Vladimir at hearing the news about the girl. At least he is able to moderate his anger with the knowledge that he is right about Vladimir withholding information from him.

Thomas had just briefed him on all the facts and angry or not he takes some time to maul over what he has learned. For a good half hour he considers one action and then another. He looks for weaknesses, flaws and repercussions. Ever since he got Vladimir out of Europe, he has been able to keep his brood from attracting the human's attention and he is not so eager to get the girl as to blow the lid off that secret. That said, the danger of not acting might very well "blow" the very lid he is trying hard to keep firmly in place, and the werewolves, what the hell was up with them.

"So only two of you came back." Boris finally mumbles.

"Yes Master. It wasn't the girl or at least not directly. It was those dam wolves."

"What the hell were they doing there and in such numbers at that? We haven't heard anything about them massing. Get in touch with those who are assigned to keep watch and find out why they never reported in and then poke around and try to find out what the wolves may be up to while I do the same."

"And the girl, Master."

"Yes the girl. What are we to do with Vladimir's sick experiment?"

"I have word that they have left Torino and headed towards Naples. I wouldn't be surprise if they plan an extended stay there."

"Dam it. If that group get their claws into her there could be problems. Send word to the brood and our thralls in Naples and have them keep an eye out for her. I want this creature dead Thomas. Dead and buried, and the sooner the better."

"I'll see to it Master."

"I know you will my friend. Once we have more information on the dam wolves we will deal with them also." He grins evilly at his long-time friend. A grin that is readily returned for there is nothing that they love better than tearing up a wolf den or two. Even if he finds the wolves' interference to be nothing but a fluke, he may let his brood loose on them for it's been years since they have had the opportunity to teach the wolves a good lesson.

Dominic has also just been briefed on what the creatures of the night were up to in Switzerland and the ensuing fight. He is not concerned about his pack taking out the brood although he is worried about what those creatures were up to. Therefore, having no idea of where else to turn he calls the very one that warned him in the first place.

"Why would they be after a human family Ray?" Dominic asks the U.S. Alpha.

"Human family? That doesn't make any sense. I mean Vladimir would have no qualms about taking out a family, but to send his brood so far to do so does seem to be a little excessive." Ray lies smoothly for he knows exactly what Vladimir was after.

"Does he have something going on in the U.S. that I should know about?"

"Nothing that impacts Europe. Is there anything special about the family he went after? Who does the father work for, the mother, what about the children?

"Nothing on the mother and only one girl child. The father was head of the Swiss embassy. Do you think that may have something to do with it?"

Ray pretends to consider the question. Steering Dominic's attention to the father is just what he needs and yet not able to think of a credible lie he finally decides on keeping it simple. "Maybe, but I can't imagine what. It might be best if we keep a closer eye on these two for the next while. I'll let you know if something leaks on my end."

"Thanks Ray. I don't like this. I don't like it one bit."

Chapter Seven

I was a little disappointed at the jet. When they told me "jet" I pictured a real jet with nice comfy seats, wine and stewardesses. The kind of jets you see in the movies that all those special units use when they fly, those that house all the good things in life. On the other end of the spectrum of my expectation was a fighter jet. How I would love to fly in one of those, not to be. Oh no, neither one for us, the stupid thing turned out to be a transport with the most uncomfortable seats I have ever had the displeasure to sit on and I can't believe how cold the cargo section of one of those things are; cold and noisy. It was so bad that I was sorely tempted to jump out the back just to get away.

At least once we arrived there was a little surprise waiting for instead of jeeps, there were black, window tinted Mercedes idling on the tarmac. When I questioned the number of cars, I was told it was all part of the deception to get us safely tucked away. I didn't bother asking about how that deception worked out although it must have worked for we had arrived yesterday and nothing of excitement has yet to happen, other than a shower, god how I loved that shower and I had soaked under that showerhead for an hour before I finally fell to my bed in exhaustion. For the rest of that day and night I laid on my bed tossing and turning.

That sleep had been restful enough before the first of the nightmares had begun. Every nightmare ended up with me screaming myself awake and then huddling in a ball until sleep finally overtook me again, only to wake up screaming when the next nightmare visited me. I was not foolish enough to think that I was the only one having nightmares for I am sure that Mom and Dad were having the same trouble sleeping as I was. The difference being that they had each other for comfort while I had nobody. The voice had gone silent again and as it is my thoughts kept going back to Keller. More than once I thought of asking if they could bring him to me so that I too could have some company.

I am not sure why my mind kept going back to Darren. It had nothing to do with sex, that I am sure of, however there is something about him that is tickling the back of my mind. I can almost grasp what it is however every time the answer seems within reach it slips away again. Regardless of that, my instinct tells me that if I could crawl in his arms I would feel comforted.

The sleep was not restful, but at least it was long so this morning when I wake up I feel only a little gritty-eyed and almost fully rested. I make my way into the bathroom to relieve my bladder and then prepare for another shower in the hopes that it will clear away the last of the cobwebs. It is just as I am getting ready to step into the shower that I catch my reflection in the mirror.

It's funny. A person looks at themselves so often that they don't even think twice about what they see in the mirror and I'm certain I use to be the same. Now, everything is new and strange to me. I don't recognize my nose, my eyes are a different shape and colour and my chin so much finer than it used to be. The naturally wavy golden brown hair is still a little of a shock, but other than the length no worse than if I had gone in for a dye. Then there are the breasts. How often I wish I had bigger breasts, make that any breasts for before I changed I was as flat as a board. Well the joke is on me, for now all I can think of is how they keep getting in my way and how heavy they feel. The waist and hips however, now there is something I can live with. I have always wanted a waist; almost as bad as I wanted boobs and both I definitely have now.

I look at myself for some time, trying to memorize each feature so that the next mirror I pass will be just a little less shocking to me. When I get tired of trying to memorize the new me, I turn on the shower and jump in. I am showering for a good fifteen minutes give or take and more than willing to go another hour when I hear Mom calling from the bedroom. I automatically yell back that I am in the shower.

Duh, as if she can't hear the noise.

"Are you about ready for breakfast Dear?"

"Soon, but I have nothing to wear."

"There's a nice lady here with clothing for you and she will be showing us the way to the mess."

"Great, I'm starved and then I hope someone is going to tell us what the hell is going on!" I turn off the water, open the curtain and give Mom a pout.

"You are so beautiful Michele. You now reflect on the outside what I have always seen you possessed on the inside. That pout just makes you much more enticing. No wonder we had so much trouble with the men at the hanger. I wonder if that is what it is going to be like for you for the rest of your life. Men fighting and killing each other over you."

"I certainly hope not. Call me wishy if you like. Before I changed I would have killed to have men look at me like that, now I just want them to go away. So have they told you anything?"

"Not yet. Don't worry I'm sure they will tell us what's going on soon. I'll let you dry and meet you back in the bedroom."

A short time later I walk out of the bathroom patting the last of the water from my waist-length hair. I find Mom and a good-looking female officer who is standing all too erect waiting for me.

Our eyes meet and almost immediately I see the hate. It is the same hatred that I saw in the eyes of many of the women in the foster homes I stayed at before moving in with my parents.

Seeing that hatred brings back my past. For just a second I feel as if I am eleven again. My aunt has just died and adults are deciding my fate as if I am not even in the room or too stupid to understand what they are saying.

"If you will excuse me I have to go." The young lady blurts out.

"But…" Mom starts obviously startled at the young lady's sudden change in attitude.

"I will send someone else. She will be here by the time she is dressed." The young lady puts enough emphasis on the second "she" to let me know to whom she is referring to and exactly what her feelings are about me. In her haste to escape she bumps into Dad as she runs out of the room. Mom and I look at each other in surprise and then turn to Dad as he steps into the room.

"What happened?"

"I'm not sure. She was certainly nice enough to me when she brought me here. That changed the minute she saw Michele, she turned…"

"Ugly." I finish Mom's sentence for her.

"Well I guess that isn't working out the way they wanted. They told me that they had cleared the area of men so we wouldn't have to put up with what we have been, now I see they are going to have to do the same with the women."

"The lady said another would be coming for us."

"I guess we wait for her and see how that works out.'

The wait is only a couple of minutes or so. When she finally arrives we stare at each other for a long time, waiting to see who is going to break first I suppose.

"Hi, I am First Lieutenant Andrea Kinsley. I will be your escort for now. They are just clearing out the women and then we can make our way to the mess."

"What happed with Jenny? She seemed so nice and then…" Mom asks still feeling perplexed over the young lady's sudden change in attitude.

"Not sure. That is something we are going to have to work on. While you have breakfast we will be introducing people to you. I hope you don't mind Michele. We have to start somewhere and determine whom in this compound you are safe being around. Before Jenny's outburst we thought it was only men, now we are going to have to test them all."

I groan at the thought.

"Don't worry, until we find a good ring to put around you we will only bring in one at a time. Your father and I should be able to handle any outbreaks."

"Gee thanks. I'm starting to feel unwanted."

The laugh that Andrea gives makes me like her a whole lot more. Therefore, the few minutes we have to wait until they clear the women from our path turns out to be more enjoyable than it would have. When she finally gets a call on her radio telling her the path is clear she leads us to the mess.

Queen Sophie is yet again in another meeting thrashing out the same problem that has been plaguing them for months now.

Humans, why is it always the humans. I can trace all of our problems since the dawning of time to humans and here is another one. How I wish I would never have been elected High Queen. If only Queen Amora had not gotten herself killed when she went out to find someone to father her child. How differently things would be and best of all this would have been her problem not mine.

They have been going in circles for too long and it is time to call a stop to it. She can't really blame the queens for there are pros and cons to either action they have been contemplating. All these have been discussed and debated to death although and now it is time to call for a vote and let the chips fall where they may.

The Siren islands consist of four islands with a queen overseeing each Island. Queen Accalia is queen of the southernmost island. The farmlands throughout her island supplies much of the Siren nation their plant based food. Queen Moriya is queen of the middle southern island, which is one of the two islands with a major city and its contribution to the Siren race is the processing of the food sent to them from the various islands as well as their own contribution of seafood that the women on the island cultivate. The middle northern island contributes animal base food and is the other island with a major city. That city's major industry being the processing of minerals and ore shipped to them from the northernmost island, which Queen Kimi oversees.

As for the High Queen, she does not rule over any one island. As High Queen she is expected to move from one island to the next every couple of months. This constant moving being their way of making certain that the High Queen does not come to favour any one queen or island over another.

When it comes to contentious issues or issues that affect the Siren nation as a whole, each queen gets a vote. The necessity of having the High Queen make the swing vote is rare for the four queens rarely disagree. When they do come to an impasse such as they now face the High Queen's position become very important.

Currently the queens are split down the middle in what action they should take against the humans. In times like these, it is the High Queen that breaks the tie and Queen Sophie does not relish doing so for she sees herself losing whichever way she decides.

"Enough. Time to decide. Those in favour of letting our presence being known to the humans." Queen Sophie asks those gathered.

Queen Accalia and Queen Moriya stand, showing their support for that idea.

"Are you two certain you won't change your minds?" Queen Sophie asks the two remaining queens.

"And make it easy for you Sophie. I think not. We know there is going to be no winners, whichever way the vote goes." Queen Moriya tells her.

"Be assured we will support you regardless of what action you decide to take." Queen Kimi pipes up right after, giving her High Queen a charming smile.

Queen Sophie knows that the four queens have just played her. None of them want to be responsible for the decision and yet none will object to whatever she decides. She fumes at the thought that all the by-play over the last few days could have been avoided if only they would have admitted the truth in the first place.

"It is time we let our presence be known then. I will make the arrangement."

Queen Sophie's daughter Mariyah lets out a squeal of joy at that announcement, only managing to stifle it at the last second.

Queen Sophie does not miss the little peep that comes out before it is stifled. She gives her daughter the look that Mariyah has long learned to associate with her displeasure. When she is certain that Mariyah has herself under control she turns back to the gathered queens.

"As you all know the humans have been Mariyah's pet project for a long time now. When we started debating our latest action she turned her curiosity into a different direction and much to my chagrin has come up with a creditable plan."

"Mariyah, if you please." Sophie tells her daughter after the laughter ceases.

A red-faced Mariyah takes her place at the table. "I have come up with an idea that may kill two birds with one stone so to speak. Doing this we will let the humans know of our existence and our rights and laws, more importantly it should attract the attention of our missing cousin. Here is what I propose…"

Now that he has lost the girl, Vladimir is giving a lot of thought about what his next step should be with specimen 101849. If he had a thousand pints of his blood he could take back Europe. However, he is a long way from a thousand pints. In fact, there is no way to harvest a thousand pints, not even a hundred from 101849. What he needs is more of him.

He looks at the results of the sperm tests. That too came back positive, a little low on the count, most likely due to the death and rebirth, but it is still more than enough for his purpose. Without the girl it comes down to whom to breed specimen 101849 to.

The girl had already showed him some risk associated with 101849 and those risks would increase if he started a breeding program with 101849 as its seed. Those risks he considers manageable. Breed him with the wrong cross however and it could result in disaster or a waste of time… who…. who?

He slams his fist into the metal table, leaving an indentation in its middle. Not for the first time in over 500 years he wishes that some of the fairy folks were still alive, but no, they had been hunted into extinction.

As it was, he was lucky that he had already captured and almost finished the fairy folk portion of his breeding program before they disappeared from the world, a problem that he blames on Boris.

Back then the fairy folk had the best blood, so sweet and succulent. One drink of their blood was enough to make even them feel alive again. To drain the body of a midsize fairy folk in one feeding would bring on a bloodlust of unimaginable pleasure and power. In fact, it was the discovery of this bloodlust that had started the mass annihilation of the fairy folks in the first place.

Ruefully, he has to admit that he was the one that discovered the true benefit of draining the fairy folk bodies of blood in one feeding. The power of fairy blood was so overpowering that to drink up the larger of the fairy folk of all its blood was enough to send most broods into a never ending bloodlust and a bloodlusted brood becomes a killing machine. The problem is that they do not bother to distinguish between killing for food, for sport, or even the destruction of their own kind. Furthermore, the longer a brood is under the influence the worst the problem becomes. Because of the instability associated with the bloodlust, brood that dared to succumb to a fairy bloodlust were destroyed and because of this and for a long time after the fairy folks were avoided.

However, they were losing the war with the werewolves and he had become desperate. He used himself and his own brood as test subjects. He discovered that most brood would come back from the bloodlust if they had no more than a half pint of fairy blood, while forefathers could handle four or five pints. He passed this knowledge on to the others and with the use of this discovery, the war turned. Neither side really won, but at least the brood were not wiped out, not by the werewolves at any rate.

He should have been recognized for his discovery. He should have been the one to gain and the one to rise in power. Instead Boris managed to steal his thunder. In his anger, he turned on his brethren and for over a span of a hundred years brood killed brood with the use of fairy blood until at last, the fairy folks disappeared. By the end of the brood war he had almost accomplished what the werewolves had not been able to do and it was a much-weakened nation that came out of that war.

Now he is on the brink of bringing that blood and even better back into the world and once he does Europe will once again be his. Only if he dares to continue that is. Only if he dares to breed something that if not managed better than their human food may be dangerous even to him.

For the last two days, now going on to three, our lives have been put on hold. Dad has been meeting with the general of this underground base, on what I have no idea and whether these meetings have resulted in any revelations he has not told me, so I admit I am starting to get impatient.

When I had awakened after my birthday my change had been a novelty and then everything started happening. I had not been given any breathing room to spare the time to think about my change. That has changed for now that I have rested and hung around with nothing to do for two days, other than being tested around hundreds of men and women who still want to rape or thrash me, things are starting to come to a head.

The shock, the same shock I am sure Mom and Dad have been going through since my birthday is starting to sink in and in the quiet solitude of my room I am starting to get seriously concerned, voice aside, about my sanity. To make matters worst the buzzing that I have been hearing for the last few months has gotten worst, making it even harder for me to think rationally.

Thankfully, I have my parents to run to when things are at their worse. Hours and hours we had spent talking. They have no better idea than I do about what is going on, but that is okay for at least they are someone for me to babble with. Someone who listens to my fears and someone that hugs me when I need to be hugged and how I so need those hugs.

The first day had been at least partly interesting. Andrea had shown us around the base. I was equally impressed and disgruntled about what we discovered. There is only one way in and god himself couldn't get in without the proper passwords, fingerprints, eyes, and card. Getting out, she made sure to inform us is just as difficult as getting in.

After the chaos of the first day and them having to clear the base so we could get to the mess I was banned from the mess hall. They had tested a number of people with me. Way too few seemed indifferent to me. Most men tried to maul me and a good number of women downright hated me so breakfast is now brought to my room.

The following day they were better prepared. There were still incidents for with the number of personal inside the base, there was no possible way to keep me from being seen. The up side is that I now have a dozen people around me able to keep me safe… or are they there to keep others safe from me?

The second day I was shown where I could get some clothing; oh joy army grays and blues plus bras and panties that are sure to turn off any man and thus protect the virtue of any woman in "this man's army".

Once the tours were over and with nothing else to do, I spent the rest of the time swimming laps in the pool and exercising in the gym to use up my pent up energy. When I had asked to do this it had not gone over well for once again the call had to be made to clear the areas. I'm sure they hate me for more than one reason now. I would have felt badly about this if not for the fact that I was starting to feel like a prisoner.

This is now the third day we have been trapped inside here and I am ready to test their so-called security system. It's not that I am not thankful for the quiet and "protection" they have provided the last couple of days. It's just that I am starting to feel like a prisoner and the fact that neither Mom nor Dad can tell me about what to expect is not helping my mood.

Therefore, as I finish off my breakfast this morning I am planning how to get out of here when I hear a knock on my door. Answering the door I find Dad on the threshold.

We spend a few minutes talking of nothing of consequence until I finish my breakfast. Once I am finished, Dad tells me that a resolution has been reached and that we have been requested to a meeting to be told "something".

Oh gee Dad thanks a lot for that insight.

I know I am being unfair and that it is not Dad's fault. An army, regardless of who is at the head, is still an army and will work as all armies' work. Still, it is Dad who is in front of me right now so he is the one to feel my displeasure. Not that he seems to be paying it much mind; something he has been too dam good at for eleven years.

Breakfast finished, I let Dad lead me to the common area where Mom joins us. As we wait for whoever is suppose to join us we can't help noticing that the place is as eerily empty as it was the first day we were here.

A few minutes later Andrea meets us and guides us down a hallway to a steel door. This door we had seen on our tour the first day. When we asked about it we had been informed that our current security would not allow us to get inside or allow her to tell us what is behind it. This time it opens for us as we advance. Waiting behind the opening door are half a dozen heavily armed, hard-faced men in full military garb. Almost instantly, two men make a move on me, one grabbing my ass the other trying to grope my breast. These men had already been tested with me and earlier they had showed me indifference. Their reaction now makes me realize that I will always have to be on guard.

Dad and one of the other men quickly put the man that took hold of my ass out of commission. The one that tried to grope my breast however is all mine and he ends up on the floor with a broken jaw and wrist. So okay, maybe I got carried away, but come on enough is enough.

When the others see that man laid out on the floor I see a couple of them open their mouths to ask what I had done, and I can't blame them for it, as I had moved fast, dam fast and I am not surprised that nobody saw how I handled the man. The look I give them however, makes them snap their mouths shut and keep from asking.

A couple of men pick up and drag the comatose bodies away from the door and then the door closes behind us. With everything seemingly back in order we continue down a long brightly lit hallway that reminds me too much of a hospital.

One benefit to being behind this door I notice right away is that the buzzing that has been making me question my sanity has stopped. I am just relishing that quiet when the hallway spills out into a room that is staggering. The room is mostly natural rock and it is unbelievable large. It is filled with computer screens, communication devices, observation platforms, firearms, and a whole lot of other things I cannot even guess at.

Feeling a tickle on the side of my neck, I absently brush my hair back.

Dam it! There goes that freaking buzzing again!

Dad touching my arm brings my attention back to my surroundings. We are led to a room with a stainless steel door, which slides open almost noiselessly as we approach it. When we enter we discover a half-dozen people in the room. For a couple of minutes we stare at each other. I am ready to start breaking bones again. I wait for something, anything… These people were also tested with me earlier. That said, after what happened at the door nobody seems inclined to take anything for granted. The time drags on slowly and when nobody feels the need to kill or grope me the door closes behind us and the room starts to turn.

"Oh cool!" I exclaim causing the first smiles I have seen on any face since coming through that last steel door.

Once the room has stopped spinning introductions are made. The three-star general introduces himself as Lieutenant General Lawrence Macklin in charge of this U.N Security base. The general is a little taller than my father's six feet by a couple of inches and heavier around the stomach by maybe twenty pounds with a little more grey in his short cropped hair, however his eyes have a sparkle to them and his smile seems genuine. Right away I like him for I recognizes a lot of Dad in the man.

The next man introduced is a Major Anthony Gazinno. This man is only five foot eight, however even his military uniform cannot hide the fact that he is built like those so-called tanks these army boys like to play with. He has dark hair and I imagine that if he were to let it grow it would have a beautiful curl to it.

The third person introduced, or re-introduced is First Lieutenant Andrea Kinsley. Andrea is only five foot seven and as I have discovered she is a bundle of energy. Her dark brown hair, cut military style of course, frames a beautiful and seemingly delicate face. She has the kind of body that I had long since dreamed of having, at least what I dreamed of having before my change and maybe what I would still have preferred, for I am certain that Andrea has one of those so-called perfect bodies at 36-28-36 making her look outstanding in her military garb.

The next woman introduced is a Captain Laura McNeal. She is an older woman of about five foot six with greying hair and a kind face. When her position as a psychiatrist is stated, I can right away picture myself spending hours and hours talking to this woman. I jokingly tell the assembled group just that. They laugh at the joke as I intended, however deep down inside I know that I really do need to spend a lot of time with the woman.

The next three men introduced are a Second Lieutenant Neely in charge of day-to-day operations at the base, a Sergeant Major Riley in charge of logistics and Master Sergeant Wright in charge of Special Unit 502. These three men are so alike, so army through and through. They are typical of the type of men that Dad had brought home when he was getting me use to men and then later to spar with. They are no nonsense, stern looking and rough and tumble types. So well had Dad done in chasing away my fear of men that I have learned that these are the type of men that makes my stomach go into jitters and my brain turn stupid. They never seemed to fear anything and I can only imagine the kind of trouble I could get into with any one of them. Not that Dad was likely to leave me alone with any one of them, regardless of the fact that at twenty-five I should be able to make my own choices.

The one exception of the three is the Master Sergeant Wright. I can't put her finger on what it is with him that troubles me. There is something about the way he is looking at me that makes me uncomfortable. It is as if he is gauging me up as an enemy. Even as I come to that conclusion I can't help thinking that there is something more wrong with the man and if pressed, I would have attached the word evil to him.

Once introductions are complete we take our seats around the table. When we are settled General Macklin starts off.

"I know you must have a lot of questions." He starts and Dad gives me the look when I release a un-lady like snort.

"Sorry, carry on." I tell the general by way of apology.

General Macklin gives me a reassuring smile before continuing. "As I said you must have a lot of questions and we are going to try to answer them for you. I'll start by giving you a little insight as to how you came to be here in the first place. A few days ago we started hearing a lot of chatter from a group we have been monitoring about a girl. Of course, we didn't put two and two together until you started making those phone calls of yours General Appleton."

"Why is this group so interested in my daughter and do you know what happened to her?" Dad asks wanting to get right to the point.

"As for what happened to her, nobody has a clue. Maybe those who seem so interested in getting her back could answer that question. After what happened I doubt you want to go asking them however. The one group we had been monitoring was talking about finding the girl they lost when she was a baby. There was a lot of excitement over her discovery and plans were put in the works to retrieve their "lost item" as they put it. It is our understanding that is what the night you were attacked was all about. Even more interestingly, if you will forgive the term is the second group we accidentally stumbled upon. It was just fluke that we caught their transmission in the first place. This second group confirms some of what we have learned. They have a deep-seated hatred for the first group and apparently they were not happy about what they were about to do. It didn't have anything to do directly with you Michele, but they were obviously not happy about the first group getting together to hunt you. A couple of days later, after you were safely tucked away in here, we intercepted another call between them where they were questioning why you were so important to the first group. They did not seem to have any better explanation. However, their interest has been peeked and now they are combing everything that they can find about all of you. As their intention seems to be one of interest and not to harm any of you in any way we have allowed them to carry on their investigation, even supplying them some false information when we can. At any rate, it was when your phone calls came to our attention General Appleton that we started putting two and two together. It is now obvious that Michele is the girl they were after. We had already obtained authority from the highest sources to bring you in before you were attacked. They were on their way to pick you up when all hell broke out."

"So that explains why the chopper was already in route when I called from the embassy."

"Yes and we learned something during this. We knew that these groups were spread throughout the world, what we didn't know is that there seems to be fractions of them and that they do not like each other, even among there own kind."

"Their own kind." I ask and I'm sure Mom and Dad caught that also.

"I think this will be a good place for First Lieutenant Kinsley to take over."

First Lieutenant Andrea Kinsley is given the floor and as such, she will forever be remembered by me as the first one to shatter what I once thought of as a perfect little world.

"What I am about to tell you is top secret and has been so for the last couple of years. Contrary to popular belief we are not alone on this world and I am not talking about cute little space aliens here." She touches a button on a remote, the lights dim and an image lights up the screen.

"This is what we have come to call a vampire. As you see, they are pretty much as they are portrayed in the movies, although with much more teeth and not nearly as cute."

The picture shows a human looking creature with an abundance of long, sharp teeth and very pale skin. I shiver, Mom releases a yelp and Dad goes pale for these creatures are definitely the creatures that had attacked us the other evening.

"Just like the ones portrayed in the movies they feed on human blood and more often than not they do not leave their victim alive afterwards. We are still gathering intelligence about them so some of what we know is guesswork for as you can imagine there is some difficulty in getting any information from them directly. We have reasoned that there are two different purpose for them coming after us. The first is for nourishment. The second is to infect us. We believe that a certain bite of theirs carry a toxin that is capable of making a human very sick, a disease if you like. Up to three bites does not seem to be fatal to a human, as long as the victim lives through the infection that is. It is the fourth that seems to bring on a change. We have come to believe that the fourth bite changes the human into something like a slave."

What the voice had said to me the other night pops into my head. "Thrall." I say before I can stop myself.

"Thrall?" Andrea asks me questioningly.

"Something I heard somewhere." I reply with a shrug wishing I had kept my mouth shut.

"Well that is as good as what we have been calling them, so thrall it is. We expect that any subsequent bites to one of these thralls will put them closer to becoming a vampire. That is guesswork and we have yet to determine how many that may require. From everything we have been able to gather, which your recent experience confirms, vampires are ruthless. They see us as food and as such not worth having a conversation with, much less a truce of any kind. We know for certain that they are exceptionally fast, incredibly strong, and by all accounts almost impossible to kill. Well let's not say kill for they are already dead, let's say destroy. We have had a few encounters with these over the last two years and needless to say we rarely come out on top."

"I think I am going to be sick!" Mom manages between gasps of air.

Dad and I both reach over to comfort her. As I comfort her, the itch that has been bothering my neck for the last little while becomes even more bothersome, so I scratch it, which in turn causes the buzzing in my ears to increase ten-fold.

"Michele, this is mostly for your benefit so if at any time you need a break for any reason please speak up." General Macklin states in the ensuing silence.

Dad squeezes the hand I have on Mom encouragingly so I give him the bravest look I can to reassure him that for now I am okay. It is when I am giving him that look that a thought suddenly hits me.

"Is that why you had that man feed me blood in the hanger. Do you think I am one of these vampires?"

"No, at least we hope not. We were not even sure that you would like the blood. We have also been putting blood in all of your drinks since you came here. Has it been helping?"

I give her a sour look, as does Mom. We had no idea that they had been feeding me blood. Sure, the drinks they have been giving me mostly tasted… well I wouldn't say awful for as much as I would love to admit it I mostly liked it.

"Maybe" I finally tell her.

"Well that's a start. But no, we do not think you are entirely vampire. From your father's phone calls and from what we have discovered and seen since then we do feel that may be a part of you that we would be unwise to ignore."

"Please enough." Mom whispers so softly that I am sure I am the only one that hears her.

"Let's leave that for now." I tell Andrea, feeling Mom's pain.

Andrea gives me a nod before continuing. "Next we have what we are calling the werewolves, once again after the movies. Actually, we are beginning to wonder if one of these two species didn't make the original vampire and werewolf movies. The werewolf being the most likely candidate for the movies comes close to some of the realities that we have discovered. We speculate it may have been their first attempt at "coming out" so to speak. To test how we would react to the knowledge that they exist or maybe even to cover their tracks. Make us think that anyone who would report seeing them "is off his or her rocker" so that we won't go looking."

The image shows an ordinary looking man. There is nothing spectacular about the man that would make a person think that he was anything but human.

"We are not even certain that this man is even a werewolf. Contact with them has been very limited and if this fellow is truly a werewolf, well as you can see they are hard to identify so we do not know a lot about them. We have no idea if, when or how they change to wolf or even if they do. We have only had a couple of tentative contacts with them, or at least this man who claims to be one. As it is, the contacts were more probing than anything else. As if they were trying to discover what we knew about them. Much of the information we do have on them is more eyewitness and historic reports than anything else. We believe they are meat eaters so they are in direct competition with our food chain. That said, as long as that does not include humans we are willing to talk to them if they so desire. We are going on the assumption that they are not quite as fast as a vampire, although we think that they may be stronger. We thought we were going to get somewhere with them after they had made their initial contact, but then after the second meeting, nothing."

Dad and I look to each other and I am sure that just like me, he is thinking of the big dogs that had attacked those creatures the night they had attacked us. Unable to keep silent I speak up. "Are there any werewolves in the military?"

"Of course not. Until we learn more about them we can't trust them." Neely replies.

"But."

"What is it Michele. Is there something you want to share with us?" McNeal asks.

I take a deep breath and then another. I started this and now I have to either spit it out or put a stop to it. Deep down I know I should tell them what I suspect. However, by the end of the fight with Darren I had begun to feel a bond with him and as such I loathe the thought of turning him in. Just as loathsome is that I know I have a connection to these so-called werewolves. I can't deny the connection I had felt with what they are calling vampires, but that connection had been sickly, dark and tormenting, not at all the same kind of connection I had felt with Darren.

"Maybe later. I don't know enough right now and I'm sure I'll just mess things up. Shit, I actually think I am going mad and what you people are telling me is not helping any." I tell my first lie.

"You are holding up better than we thought you would."

"Thanks to Mom and Dad, but that is only going to take me so far."

"You need a break Michele?"

"I'm okay for now Dad. How about you Mom?"

"Oh, we may as well see what other bad news these people have for us." Mom has been a military wife for a long time and has gotten use to the life and its uncertainties.

Andrea takes a deep breath before continuing. "There is not a whole lot more to say, but only because we really don't know. Up until a couple of years ago, we didn't believe in vampires or werewolves. This unit has been in the discovery stage since its inception and we have done our own investigations of some of the crimes being reported throughout the world, mostly those that involve murder or missing persons that local enforcement agencies have not been able to solve. Our data suggests that we are encountering these two races frequently even though we are only now starting to put things together. Up until a couple of days ago we had hoped that would be the extent of the surprises we had to deal with, until she showed up."

This time the screen shows a picture of a woman of astounding beauty. Her dark, thick, wavy hair falls down to her waist, her face is the very image of a goddess, her breasts very generous, and her curves outstandingly lush.

"My god, that's you Michele!" Mom exclaims.

"No it's not. She's stunning and she does not have my eyes or eyebrows."

"Take another look in the mirror Dear. She may not have your eyes or eyebrows, but you and she are one of the same. Who is she?" Mom turns to Andrea to ask.

"She is the reason we took so long to talk to you folks, for her sudden appearance has kept us busy for the last couple of days. She looks human and yet she claims she is not. If we wanted to, we could easily conclude that her race, if the rest of her race is the vision of womanhood that she is are the inspiration of the Aphrodite legend. When she made contact with us she told us that we could call them Sirens. Whether they are the Sirens of legends…" Andreas shrugs before continuing. "The one thing we can say is that some men and women react very emotionally to her picture, not as much as they do when they see you in the flesh Michele, but still. Contact with her so far has been by email and telephone so they obviously have some technology. We are told that she sent a package to every country in the world and that she has asked to speak to the U.N. in six weeks. At that time, she promises to give us more information about their race and from where they hail. We had asked that she come to The Hague to speak. She refused that, telling us that she has feelings of unease towards Europe so we are thinking of taking advantage of the G9 meeting happening in Washington D.C. She has requested half a day to speak. We do not know much about them for they have just made contact. In fact, if it were not for discovering the other races first I doubt we would even be taking her claim seriously. The little that we have learned was in a package delivered to the U.N. so that we can prepare for her visit. On the top of the list is that she is not to be in the company of any women having relationship problems. From that and from what we have seen with you over the last couple of days we have made some educated guesses, with varying degree of success. As you can well imagine we hope to learn much more of them when she visits."

The buzzing in my ear is almost a roar. It is obvious that the men in the room are in love with the lady. Even the women are not unaffected. I can only imagine what kind of chaos the woman could or will cause in person. As I contemplate the beautiful woman, the itch on my neck increases making me brush at it in annoyance.

"We now begin to wonder what else may be living on our little planet that we don't know about. The vampires are certainly a direct threat. The verdict is still out on the werewolves, the sirens we are yet unsure of, but only because of lack of information thus far."

Andrea sits down and the silence in the room stretches on. It is obvious that the others are giving us all the time we need to absorb what we have just been told. Minutes tick by before Mom finally finds her voice. "I think this would be a good time for a break."

"Of course. There is coffee and food available. Let's take an hour."

"Wait…." I dread the answer to the question I want to ask and yet, "Are you telling me I may be one of these Sirens? Could one of these women actually be my birth mother?"

"You do have to admit you resemble her in many ways, and we have seen the reaction of both men and women around you so there is a possibility."

"But that is just fucking crazy!"

"Michele!" Mom and Dad both reprimand me at the same time.

"But it is! This is all sorts of craziness. First you tell me I am a vampire and then this!" I don't mention the wolf on purpose for I am already feeling enough of a freak.

"Let's take that break Michele. I think we all need it." Dad consoles me.

I breathe deeply while the room spins back to its original position. In a daze I wander out with the rest of them. I have no idea how such things can be possible in the twenty-first century or how I fit into it all. I had always wondered about my birth parents and the suggestion that I may come from some up to now unknown race is almost too much for me to take.

Pouring myself a coffee, I tell everyone that I need to be alone to think and not having any particular direction in mind I wander away across the huge room. I don't miss the fact that as I move out, a few heavily armed men follow in my wake. The "escort" is very casual about following me. However, there is no mistaking their purpose. It makes me wonder what I have walked into and if it was not a mistake for Dad to bring me to the attention of the military.

Ignoring them the best that I can I start thinking some deep dark thoughts. What did these people want with me and why were they going through the trouble of showing me all this. If all that is not bad enough, the buzzing in my ears has now changed from a constant buzz to an annoyance and that dam tickle on my neck refuses to go away.

Once more, I reach up to scratch it. The buzzing becomes a roar again and then another surprise pops into being.

"Oh!... were did you come from! Hey haven't I seen you before?"

All I hear is the buzzing of its wings. The fairy, as I think of it, is tiny, less than six inches tall. The breasts marked her as a female if they follow the same biology as any earthly mammal. Her hair is long and blonde. The wings sprouting from her back move blindingly fast and are almost transparent with bright red veins. Her skin is a creamy white and her clothing dazzlingly bright blues and yellows.

"You're a pretty little thing you are." The fairy seems to bounce up and down at my complement.

"You understand me don't you? Do they know you are here?" I point back at the others.

"Oh I guess not and by the looks of it you don't want me to tell them either, do you?" I reassure the fairy after seeing her look of panic at the very suggestion of informing the others.

"Well then you better go back into hiding or they will see you."

The fairy shakes her head from side to side.

"No. Are you saying they won't or can't see you?"

A double question so all I get is a lot of buzzing to my question.

"Let me try this again. They can't see you."

An agreeable bob, so I continue. "Then why can I?"

That gets me a shrug.

I suddenly notice the lack of buzzing. A strong suspicion settles deep within my bones.

"You're the one that has been driving me crazy!"

She gives me an uncertain look, as if the little fairy does not understand the statement.

"The buzzing in my ear and lately the tickling on my neck." I touch each spot to demonstrate what I mean.

The shrug this time is more of a maybe shrug than one of unknowing.

"But now I can see that it is not your wings making noise so why the buzzing?"

This time the fairy opens her mouth and it looks like she is talking. Not hearing anything I put my ear closer to the fairy.

"Oh my gosh. You have been trying to talk to me haven't you?"

I get an enthusiastic nod of the head at that.

"Oh that is so sweet, but I really can't hear you, you sweet thing. It's all... well as I said a buzzing. As if you are talking much too fast. Do you understand me?"

The pout and following nod makes me laugh.

Master Sergeant Wright is on this base for one reason only and that reason seems to be losing her mind right now. He is sure that he is going to have to kill her. She, like any animal will show her true colours and when she does it is his job to put her down like a rabid dog. He is looking forward to that day for as far as he is concerned Michele is nothing more than an abomination that needs to be disposed of.

When they first offered him the posting he thought they were pulling his leg. However, after seeing her he is convinced that for once his superiors know what they are doing.

As it is, he has had a long history of doing the tough jobs. Jobs that the military needs done. Jobs that most people are too squeamish to do. He is good at what he does, the best if you were to ask those he knows, and there is no job too ugly that he is unwilling to do.

For this operation he is in charge of a five-man team and he is not the only one on the team that thinks like he does, nor is he the only one who will not think twice about fulfilling their orders. They have been keeping an eye on her since she entered the compound and keeping an even closer eye on her since she has entered this secured area. All he has to do is wait, he is sure of that.

He has no say in what the general decides to do with her, or have her do and he really doesn't care. On the other hand, the general has no power over him or his unit either, as long as they can prove the kill is justified that is. Hence, Special Unit 502 waits for that justification.

"Michele."

I startle and turn to face Laura with a look of guilt plainly written across my face.

"Oh… hi!"

"Are you okay?"

"Ummmmm ya… I mean ya, everything is cool." The buzzing has started in my ear again so it seems that the fairy is back in hiding.

"Let's take a short walk and talk for a while okay."

"That would be nice. I so need to talk to someone. Mom and Dad are great but…"

"I understand. So what would you like to talk about?"

I take a look around at the men still following us. "How about if we start with those men and Wright."

Laura is obviously surprised at my choice of topic. "What about them."

"Why are they here… wait let me guess. They're here to take out the freak when I finally snap."

"What gives you such an idea?" She replies with an offended look.

"Laura I'm not stupid. If we have any chance of getting along you need to learn that and if you want my trust, then you have to stop lying to me."

She looks at me for a long time. She probably knows more about me than I care to guess so she obviously knows I am not lying when I tell her I am not stupid. "Okay, I won't lie to you. Yes they are here to make sure you do not become a danger to us."

I give a satisfied nod. "And you? How much of what we talk about will get back to the general or his superiors?" Now there is a much more serious question and one I am much more interested in.

"They want it all. I am arguing for none."

"And?"

"There has to be a compromise, however we have not reached it yet."

"I'll make a deal with you."

She eyes me up warily for I'm sure that this is not how things are supposed to be going. "And what would this deal be?"

"I really do need to be able to talk to someone, but I can't trust you unless we come to an understanding. I know why they would want what they want. So here it is. If it has to do with my mental health, you know what I feel and why, that sort of thing is personal and ours. Everything else you can give them."

She thinks about my proposal for a minute before answering. "I think they may settle for that."

"I'm glad. See I'm not some irrational monster, but sometimes, god Laura for the last few days I really do feel like one."

The two of us walk away together. I notice that the group that has been set to watch me relax as we begin to talk. As we make our way around the compound I try to ignore the rest of the people there and that is harder than it sounds for another half dozen have to be pulled out as we make our way past them.

"I feel sorry for them." I finally tell Laura.

"Why's that."

"It's not their fault."

"It's good that you feel that way. At least it shows that you still have what we would call human feelings."

"I am human dam it!"

"In part maybe. Let's be truthful like you promised Michele. Do you really think you are human like, say me?"

I growl at her for the last thing I want to admit to is not being as human as her.

It is more than an hour before Laura and I rejoin them. It is obvious that General Macklin is getting restless to get started again, however the positive look that he and Laura share when we get back soothes him.

Therefore, just over an hour after our impromptu break we find ourselves locked and seated back inside the room. This time however, Second Lieutenant Neely takes the floor.

"So you now know things you never knew before. You have learned things that have maybe altered your view of our world, and now you are wondering what our part in this may be. It's not all that complicated. For the last couple of years we have been tasked with gathering as much information on these races as we could and now, mostly due to you Michele and what happened in Switzerland, our superiors think it is time we take it to the next level. We have been tasked with finding the vampires and when we do to destroy them. We are to confirm without a doubt the existence of werewolves and once we do to decide the best course of action to handling them. We are to be judge, jury and executioner if need be. The final say regarding these nonhuman races. As for these so-called Sirens, we have yet to learn what part we are to play with them. We are also charged with continuing to learn everything we can about any of these species or any others that we may discover. Michele, this is in part where you come in."

"Me!"

"Yes. What are you Michele? From the phone calls your father made it is easy for us to guess that you certainly are not the same young woman you were just a few days ago. Who were your birth parents? Were you ever bitten or mauled. Have you ever bedded one of these non-human species? What knowledge can you provide us?"

I look uncertainly from face to face before replying. "There is very little I can give you. I have no idea about what I am as you say and surely, if you asked me that question a couple of hours ago I would have easily answered I am human, just like the rest of you. I have no idea who my birth parents were. I have never been bitten or mauled that I know of and I am still a vir… never mind that is none of your business." My face goes red only realizing after the fact that I may as well have screamed it to the world.

"Then we would like to study you." States Neely in a matter of fact manner.

I get the impression that it is not really a request that Neely is making. I look to my parents and see that they have come to the same conclusion. I wonder what would happen if I refused. Would it put in danger the only two people I truly love in this world? Is that why they were there, to pressure me into making the "right" choice?

"Okay, but no cutting me open and no knives. I swear if you try I can and will kill the whole lot of you."

"Come now Michele, we are not that barbaric. We only want to run some blood tests, take a few x-rays, run some scans, and monitor you under various stress levels. We will put you through some military training to see how you handle it and last but not least, we want you to spend time with Captain McNeal so she can get to know what makes you tick."

"I think I can live with most of that." I reply, no longer sure I like the good Second Lieutenant Neely.

"Very well."

"I think we have a lot to talk about. So now that you have made your wishes known can we go?" Dad speaks up for my benefit I am sure.

Major Anthony Gazinno speaks up for the first time. "Not quite yet. There is one more thing that we want to ask of your daughter."

"And what may that be Major?" Dad, now wearing his military face asks.

"We would ask her to join our little "group" and use whatever abilities she has to assist us in meeting our mandates. The team we want to build to handle these nonhuman species we want to build around your daughter."

Total silence is the reaction to Major Gazinno's statement. I feel like the trap has been sprung. Dad's face is as white as... well one of those freaking vampire faces and Mom looks about ready to faint.

"I'm not joining the military." I finally manage to say in the ensuing silence.

"We are not asking you to."

"How do I even know you guys are on the up and up? I've seen movies showing what horrors groups like this are responsible for. How do I even know that..." My accusations peter off when the image of a man brightens up the screen. The military personal quickly stand to attention.

"Hello Michele. It seems you have some doubts. Do you know who I am?"

A few months ago that question would have elicited a "no" response, however the Secretary-General of the U.N. has been very much in the news lately. So much so, that only those living in dank dark corners of the world would not recognize the man. "Yes, Mr. Secretary-General."

"Good and to assure you that this is not a recording and that it is happening in real time look at the date on the calendar and the time on the clock behind me. There is no way they could have set this up so perfectly."

Sure enough, the date is correct and all three of us check our watches to verify the time.

"Also, to assure you that we are not a rouge part of the U.N. working without the knowledge of other world powers."

Another half dozen screens light up sporting the images of various world leaders.

"What may I do for you Mr. Secretary-General?"

"Do. Well I would appreciate it if you did what these gentlemen are asking you to do Miss Appleton. We have been listening in, and we have discussed you at length for the last couple of days. There is something special about you and we ask you to use whatever special abilities we find in you to help the human race, your race, your people. That can't be too much to ask can it?"

I am having trouble breathing. My eyes feel gritty, however I refuse to let myself spill tears in front of these men. "And have you decided what to do with me if I refuse." I manage without choking on my words.

The quick look he directs to Wright confirms my suspicions. "I, we do not wish to go there Miss Appleton. We ask that you take some time to consider the offer we are giving you. Not everyone has the opportunity to do something that may touch the lives of so many other people on earth. We have faith that your star will shine, now we ask that you have faith in yourself and let us help you make that star shine."

It's all I can do to keep from weeping aloud, although I am certain I will be doing a lot of that later. "Thank you Secretary-General. I will consider the offer seriously."

"Do that Michele. An offer like this does require serious consideration, however, please don't take too long."

"Yes Mr. Secretary-General."

The screens fade to black. "Let me out of here." My voice is no louder than a whisper.

"Michele, are you going to be okay?" Mom's voice is just as quiet.

"Yes Mom, but I need to beat something up and if I don't get out of here these nice people may not look so nice when I am done."

A gentle knocking inside my head gets my attention.

What's wrong Michele? Your emotions are swapping my senses.

These assholes have put me in a bind.

Get away from them then.

I can't. Mom and Dad.

I can't say as I understand your attachment to your mother and father.

Attachment? They are my parents. The ones that took care and watched out for me. The ones that had faith in me when nobody else did, not even myself.

You would have grown up without them.

Yes, but what would I have been then? Would I have liked what I grew up to be?

Do you like what you are now?

I give this question some serious thought before answering.

Yes. How about you?

Unlike you I have no idea who or what I am and nothing to measure what I am against.

Yesterday I may have agreed to run away, but like you I don't know who or what I am anymore.

You are my reason for continuing, the only brightness in my dark world.

Ah, now you understand what my parents are to me.

A long quiet ensues before the next reply comes.

We need to learn.

Yes!

Chapter Eight

"So where are we at Thomas?"

"She has gone to ground Boris. We have all of Italy and France on alert especially those in Naples where we lost her. If and when she comes back out of the hole she crawled into we will know about it."

"We need to do this quietly. I have a feeling that the humans know more about us then we have been led to believe."

Boris could almost be a twin to Vladimir, with the same dark hair, pointed ears, and pinched face. The resemblance is even more pronounced when he frowns in thought the way he is currently doing.

"I think we are going to have to lay low for a while. We won't give up on the girl of course. We need to retreat until we discover how much these humans really know about us. There have been some things lately that we blamed on the werewolves, now I am not so sure it was them. Send out the word Thomas, until further notice we feed only on the homeless and there will be no more turnings or thralls."

"Yes Master. Speaking of werewolves, I have not been able to make any headway. Have you been able to determine why they attacked that night?"

"I have to assume it was for revenge. Vladimir's brood found a couple of wolves and spent some time playing and torturing them before finally doing away with them. Bad enough that they killed them without my permission, but to kill them so brutally was uncalled for. I assume it pissed

Sabatino off, and I presume he decided it was time to teach us a lesson. I can't say as I really blame him after I saw the mess myself. You just happened to get caught in the middle. It's really my fault for agreeing to let any of Vladimir's brood into Europe in the first place. That reminds me, I am putting out a destroy order on Edward so let the brood know not to hesitate if he is spotted."

"I understand Master and I will put the order out right away. As for Sabatino?"

Dominic Sabatino has been the leader of the European werewolves for at least the last half thousand years, so long so that Boris has some difficulty remembering whom Sabatino had defeated in order to win his place. It has also been many years since Boris has seen Sabatino. He has no doubt that the creature has not changed since their last encounter. Sabatino, he remembers is Italian in every way. Dark hair, dusky Italian face, five-ten to six feet tall, muscular and not an ounce of fat on him and of course he has the typical Italian temper.

Boris finally answers after some thought. "Sabatino will need to be taught a lesson. A quick strike will do. Not enough to stir up any noise with the humans."

Back in North America Vladimir Narishkin is no happier than Boris is with his human food. Just like Boris, he is beginning to believe that the humans may know more about them than they let on. The bothersome part is how.

It is not that he or any of his brood ever takes any great pains to segregate their food. A senator was just as likely to be chosen as a penniless beggar is. However, there has always been one rule that he has insisted on… no proof of what has killed the food.

Statisticians wonder why the missing and murder rate is so high in North America. He does not wonder, he knows. Except for food found in the wilderness, where they can leave the body to be chewed upon by wild animals, all traces of feeding on any of the food chain in populated areas is destroyed. He does not give a dam about the authorities identifying the name of the body, however they must never suspect the true nature of the death.

Therefore, for years he and his brood have been doing whatever they wanted to do. For years, the humans have been screaming about the deaths. For years, the humans have been trying to put things together to no avail. Any human that he even suspected of getting close to the truth, and there were not many, found themselves targeted for food. Therefore, what has changed?

He would be tempted to blame it on idiotic werewolves, however he didn't think so, for if the truth came out in regards to the brood how much longer before the truth came out about the werewolves.

What he needed to do was strengthen his position. "Edward, get your incompetent ass in here."

Unknown to Boris, after losing all hope of finding the girl, Edward had managed to get crawl into the belly of a jet flying to the U.S. Losing her has put him even more out of favour with Vladimir, so he answers quickly in the hope of getting back into his master's good graces. "Yes Master."

"I need you to put out the word. I want the brood to double the number of turnings and triple the number of thralls."

Edward is stunned for Vladimir has restricted the brood from making their own turns for hundred of years and now he is giving them free rein. Furthermore, he knows the current problem they are facing with their food chain and to follow his Master's suggestion is risky, very risky. The humans breed so quickly and they have become so inventive in killing that if they were to rally things could become very difficult.

"Well!" Vladimir snaps, bringing Edward thoughts back to his master.

"As you say Master. I will let them know immediately. Are we to gather?"

"No, not right now. Just make sure they know to hide their houses well. I will let them know when the time to gather has come."

"As you wish Master."

It is with dread that Edward backs out of the room for he has a feeling that Vladimir has just made a very grave mistake. However, to argue would result... no better not to think about that. If only he could get that girl back. She had almost shattered Vladimir's hold over him. If she could have, she may have become his Sire. This he knows and yet it does not bother him as much as the thought of his continuing service to Vladimir. He has already been Vladimir's servant for over a thousand years and he has no desire to serve him for another thousand. She could never be as bad as Vladimir, he tells himself as he moves on to carry out his master's wishes.

He stops in shock at his next thought. The woman is not the only one. It would be risky, especially since he is not sure the extent of its abilities, but he could do it. He would have to be careful. Gain its trust somehow, do a couple of experiments, maybe even teach it. It could be done, he is sure it could.

He has never had such a treasonous thought. Before meeting the woman he never would have been capable of even thinking such a thought, never mind acting on it. Is it possible that even though she did not sever the link she weakened it? A shiver of mixed fear and delight runs through his body at the possibilities.

The only problem that he sees standing in his way is that Vladimir currently has specimen 101849 breeding. From past experience he knows that these specimens can get very unpredictable when they are breeding so he will have to be careful and take the time needed to gain its trust. He only hopes that he will be given that time.

For the next couple of days I take out my anger at the situation in the gym. My newfound strength is amazing, and frustrated as well as angry over the situation I let it all out. I manage to destroy every punching bag in the compound and tear a half dozen weight-lifting machines from the wall. Needless to say nobody minds for this was exactly what they were looking for. They wanted to see what I could and could not do so as I break them they are replaced. That is until they started running out of spares.

The fact that someone seems to be feeding me anger doesn't help the situation any either. By the second day I can almost place that anger. It comes in burst and as much as I try to put my finger on it, it keeps eluding me. There are times when that extra anger fills me to bursting, making my nails grow and my eyesight go weird. Instead of letting it frighten me the way it should I use those nails to rip and tear at more of the gym equipment, causing those watching me even more glee I bet.

The one thing I become grateful for is my enhanced hearing; something I am determined to keep from them for it allows me to overhear a lot of conversations I am sure they do not want me to hear. It is some of what I hear that keeps me from trying to get out of there I suppose. I hear them talking about the increased "chatter" in both Europe and the U.S. If what they are saying can be believed the hunt for me has intensified, there are even groups staking out our old apartment and the last thing I want to do is put Mom and Dad into any more danger.

Therefore, for two days I try to beat that anger out of me. I am not even fit company for my parents, therefore I banish myself to my room with my only company the little fairy that seems determined to stay by my side. Having never been away from Mom for so long does not help my attitude either. I miss her and yet the last thing I want to do is have her bare the brunt of my anger so stay away from her I do.

The third morning I know I have to face the truth so when Andrea drops off breakfast I tell her I will not need her to guide me for the rest of the day as I would be spending it with my parents.

The sight of Wright and his cronies pacing me as I make my way to my parents' room does little for the anger that is now always simmering just beneath the surface. As tempted as I am to tear him and his group to shreds I fight the instinct and ignore them the best that I can.

It is with dread squeezing my heart that I raise my hand to knock on the door. I have not been a good daughter for the last couple of days. Not since I moved in with them have I been away from Mom for two days and truthfully, that as much as anything else has been wearing me down.

As I wait for the door to open I dwell on the fact that I am unworthy of their love and totally unworthy of the years that they put their lives on hold for me. Unworthy of being called their daughter and I would not blame them one bit if they pushed me out of their lives forever.

When the door opens I become even more ashamed at my thoughts for the door has barely opened when Mom launches herself in my arms. Her eyes and face are puffy from crying and I become even more ashamed at my actions of the last couple of days. Somehow Dad manages to get the two of us inside and close the door to Wright's prying eyes. In my need to feel my mother against me I squeeze her so tightly that I make her yelp, yet when I go to loosen up my hold on her she clings to me even harder and begs for me to do the same. Dad lets us cling to each other for a long time before he joins in. God, how could I ever think that my parents would hate me for what I have become. For a long time, we say nothing to each other for the way we hold each other is more telling than words and all that we need right now; well hugs and tears that is.

"I'm sorry for being such a piss poor daughter and I can't even begin to tell you how sorry I am for getting you two in this mess." I tell them when we finally part and Mom and I get our tears under control. Mom tries hushing me before I even finish, but this is something I have to say so I push myself on until it is all out.

"You are not a piss poor daughter and I won't hear that from you Michele."

"Your mother's right Sweetie. Things have changed, but we will never give you up. Remember we are army and I am not talking about just your mother and I. We are use to change and this is just another that we have to deal with."

I look around the room and see that Dad has been doing some "renovations". "What's with all the wall sockets and lights?"

"Looking for bugs." Dad replies and when I raise my eyebrow in question he continues. "Listening devices. I wanted to make sure it was safe for us to talk in here."

"And is it?"

"Either they are very good at hiding them or it is safe."

"So now what do we do. I could probably get us out of here if we really want to leave, but I have overheard some of their conversations and apparently those monsters are still looking for me."

"Then it is probably best we stay here for the time being. What else have you learned?"

"Nothing of much importance. I'm sorry Dad, but the last couple of days I have not been myself."

"That's understandable Dear. Tell me Michele are you still drinking that blood that they have been feeding you?"

I chew my lip for a few seconds before I answer. "I don't know for sure Mom, but the drinks they are giving me have that taste in them."

"Well I want you to stop."

"But Mom what if I need it. What if I turn into something ugly if I stop taking it!"

"And what if it's that blood that turns you into the monster you fear."

"You're mother is right Michele. Take as much control of your life as you can. You decide what you need and don't."

"And what if I change into something ugly and do something even uglier before I can stop myself."

"Do you really think I won't be able to tell if you are changing into something you shouldn't baby?" Mom replies, giving me a stern look.

I don't know what to say. A lump is caught in my throat and I can't reply. Mom's next words don't help.

"Trust me to keep you safe Baby."

That does it. The tears come rushing out once again. How could I ever have been so lucky to find loving parents like these two?

For the next two days I refuse to leave their room. We spend that time going over our options forward and backwards and over again. I am not ashamed to say that my mental state reverts back to childhood. I spend at lot of time being hugged by them. I even refuse to sleep anywhere except in their bed with them on either side of me. This causes Dad some issues the first night for I have never slept in their bed, especially with him being a man and his grumble that, "we don't do this kind of thing in the military" does not help his demeanour. Mom and I both ignored him and finally get him to settle down beside me and as bad as these two days are emotionally those nights will be nights I will never forget.

After two days Dad tells us that it is not doing us any good to stay hiding in our room so he drags me back to the gym. We have not sparred since my change and apparently he thinks it is time we do so again. We spend three hours sparring that day and by the time we finish I feel like shit for I am still not use to my increase in strength and by the time Dad calls it a day he has so many bumps and bruises that it makes me wince just to look at him.

That night I let Mom and him have their room back so that Mom can work on his aching muscles. I thought I would have to sleep alone that night. Not to be and I have to say that I am more than happy when Mom comes to my room late that night to crawl into my bed.

I am not surprised to discover that only with Mom lying beside me does the anger I am continually feeling fade. Dad has told the two of us more than once that we have an unhealthy need to be with each other. He even admitted to me once that was why he took Mom out that first night they left me alone. He told me how Mom had almost broken down until he had agreed to stay parked just down the street and watch the house. He had forced us to be separated for those two hours, which up until now had been the worse two hours of my life. I almost hated him when he told me that for that was one of the hardest nights in my life and if Mom had been feeling what I had, I can only imagine the panic she was in. In the end, I have to admit he is right. Mom and I do have an unhealthy need for each other. That had been part of the problem with the two days I spent away from them. I needed Mom. It was only my fear of what I would see in her eyes that had kept me away. I should have known better for only with them is my world right and that night as I snuggle with Mom in my arms I am able to think clearly and come to a resolution.

"I'm going to agree to their terms Mom." I tell her the next morning.

"Are you sure about this?"

"It is not like we have a choice. Besides they know more about me than I do. I need to learn what they know and learn what they can teach me."

"Don't forget your father's advice."

"What advice"

"You still have some power here. They want you so use that."

That very morning I do just that. "I'm here to see General Macklin." I tell the lady sitting outside his office.

"He's expecting you. Go right in."

Of course he is expecting me. I can't do or think anything in this place without it being broadcasted all over the freaking place!

"Michele."

"General. I have come to say that I agree to join your unit, but with conditions."

"Conditions." General Macklin replies with a twinkle in his eyes.

I had thought over what Mom had said to me this morning and decided that if I was going to join I was going to make them pay. Furthermore, some day I was going to run and when I did we would need money so I had to get a nest egg put away. Therefore, I had every intention of making them pay through the nose for me.

"Let me start by saying that I agree to join your group, however not as part of your army. Let's call me a subcontractor."

"I can live with that."

His agreement to that so readily should have made me suspicious. Instead emboldened by my easy victory I move on to my next demand. "I want fifty thousand Euros a month."

The general's eyebrows shoot up. "I was thinking more along the line of starting you at a private's pay."

"Ridiculous. I will settle for forty five thousand however."

"Come now. I don't have that kind of budget. I will agree to pay you a sergeant pay and tie you into military pay raises."

"That won't do. Forty thousand tax free."

"Five thousand, after all we will be paying for all your living expenses."

"Thirty five thousand for surely it can't cost you more than that to keep me fed."

"Seven thousand for there is a lot of overhead costs and you have to admit your hell on my men."

"You're not going to make this easy are you?"

"I'm just starting to get warmed up."

I blow out a frustrated breath of air. "Thirty thousand for having to be locked up in here."

"Ten thousand as we are providing you twenty-four hour protection."

"Thirty-five thousand as I have no doubt what you have planned for me will be dangerous and I will have to buy life insurance."

"Eleven thousand and we will provide the life insurance."

It goes on for some time and in the end we finally settle for fifteen thousand Euros tax-free per month. It is not until I am walking out of his office that I realize how much he had worn me down. That thought causes me to start cursing and dam if I don't hear him chuckling. The dam man enjoys his haggling much too much.

Later that day Dad is called to General Macklin's office and offered a posting. When I hear about it I am outraged. Dad, funny enough takes it with his usual military stride. When my voice starts to raise too high he promptly shuts me up by saying, "I'm still working for the good guys, besides it will allow your mother and I to stay by your side."

What could I say? This is so obviously not my day so instead of turning into an even bigger bitch I choose to shut up and spend a night of love with my parents; once more taking over their bed.

As we settle down in bed Dad says something that really hits home. "Things have changed and there is no guarantee that we will be able to stay together."

That statement keeps me awake long into the night. Not being able to get to sleep I keep myself occupied by caressing my parents' faces, trying to memorize every line in case the unthinkable happens.

The next five days are so full of test that I can't even remember them all. They start with an I.Q. test. When they tell me that I am in the top twenty in the world for genius I am not surprised nor am I proud. For a long time we have known that I am a genius. When Mom started teaching me we discovered that I had a photographic memory. Today, I can read a lengthy novel in just under an hour and spew back any page and line number word for word. However, it has always been Dad's words that I have strived for, "Sweetie, it is all fine and good to be smart, but wisdom on how and when to use or not use what you know is what is important." He would tell me whenever I got too cocky about it.

My dad may not be a genius like me, but he is so much smarter and wiser than me that I can only hope to achieve some of his wisdom. He tells me that wisdom comes with age and that pisses me off for I need it now as I get the feeling that I am in so over my head.

Following are so many x-rays, blood test, and cat scans that it makes my head spin. I become convinced that they have taken at least a gallon of my blood. They have me go through enough cat scans and x-rays that I am positive that I will set off any radiation detectors I pass, and more mental and physical examinations than I care to count. Funny enough, I await the results of some of those test as eagerly as they, however what comes back is a disappointment to me, however I am sure not for them.

Blood tests. "We have never seen that and there is no such blood type. Are you sure the tests were not contaminated. I guess we should take more blood… inconclusive."

Cat scans. "You have a busy brain. Lots of reds and blues and see those neurons firing…. inconclusive."

X-rays. "Well you look normal…" Whew! "but wait what's this… inconclusive."

Mental health. "Currently stable and yet… inconclusive."

Physical health. "Ouch and dam, but you are fast and you need to learn to control your strength."

Knife! "I warned you… do you really want to die?"

They still don't have a clue of how to categorize me or how to tell me what I can and cannot do. The only thing they tell me with certainty, which causes me to crawl back into my parents' bed, is that there is nothing about me that is human. I cry about that long into the night as Mom soothes my hurt emotions away. Poor Dad, he has not seen us cry so much before and I know he is having difficulty dealing with it.

Throughout those trying days, that little fairy stays by my side every step of the way. We can't talk to each other vocally, or at least I can to her, however I get nothing more than buzzing from her. Yet, with each passing day I get better at having those one sided conversations.

She is a silly little thing that gives me a lot of comfort when I am feeling down. We have started a game where I am trying to guess her name. I think she is cheating, after all how difficult should it be to guess a name when you know the first three letters to be "Sor".

Much to my mixed feelings the fairy's favourite position becomes sitting on my shoulder where she snuggles up against my neck and drapes herself with my lush hair. This often results in that part of my hair moving every time the little fairy moves. Some days it is as if a breeze is continuously blowing around me. Why nobody has asked about it I have no idea. I'm sure that they must think that it is just another one of my strange quirks.

The little fairy takes to sleeping with me at nights and more than once I am awakened from a deep sleep to the sound of some very angry buzzing. I finally figure out that this happens every time I roll over and lay my head on top of her. I can't help it for she insists on sleeping on my pillow. I try to get her to sleep elsewhere, however no amount of nagging or bribing has managed to budge the little creature's stubbornness.

I know she is trying to talk to me and sometimes it almost seems that I can understand her. As if something deep inside me recognizes her buzzing and tries to process it. So far it has managed to elude me in the most frustrating of ways. However, even without the ability to communicate I feel a deep-seated friendship forming between us.

Five days of tests I go through. I expect a sixth, however on the sixth day when I show up in the inner compound instead of leading me to the infirmary they lead me to the gym to put me up physically against men. Some of them flatly refused to engage me, even when I beat the crap out of them. They do find some that don't have any problems engaging, however most of those I immediately get pissed off at and they go away with a variety of broken bones, most especially the first few as I am still learning to control my newfound strength.

For two days it is the same thing. They try to work out the reasons for the men's refusal to fight me, and the only common ground they have found so far is that those men are either single or in rocky relationships.

On the eighth day they make me spar with some women. This results in almost the opposite reaction. The women either hate me outright or feel indifferent to me. When they hate me, the hatred is so intense that once engaged their only thought is to annihilate me; often resulting in them taking hold of the nearest weapon they can lay their hands on to accomplish that end. The ones that tolerated me do okay, however like the men, they often go away with a broken bone or two.

The breaking of bones is not really my fault. Well it is I suppose, although it's not as if I do it on purpose. Still unsure of my strength I do try to hold back when I spar with them. The problem is that most of the men and women they have me spar with are much better trained than I am. Dad and I have sparred for many years and even he admits that I just don't get it, so when we spar these people manhandle me easily. As such, after being on the receiving end of a few of their blows the anger that is now always lurking just below the surface explodes and bones start breaking.

After I break a few of the women's bones they stop putting me up against anybody and for the next two days they do not allow me to spar with anyone except Dad or my shadow.

It is on the tenth day that George Matten shows up.

George is a big man. Big, powerful and extremely skilled I soon learn. He is one of those "bull in a china shop" type of man that looks like he can break a man's body as easily as "normal people" break crystal plates. He is six feet six of brawn and muscle and as I was about to learn a master in the art of hand-to-hand combat. I am certain that our initial meeting does not proceed, as anyone would have hoped. I am just as certain that his arrogant act is his attempt to put "the little girl in her place".

"Go ahead and hit me sissy." He tells me the second we square off.

"You're not really going to pull that macho shit on me are you?"

George is standing there with his hands on his hips daring me to punch him in the gut. It is obvious that nobody has told him what I am capable of, or that he is suffering from an over bloated ego. I am leaning towards the latter.

"You're such a sissy. I can't believe that they have you here."

I look to my parents who have been spending the days watching over me. They shrugged at my unasked question. So I sigh and hit him.

George goes flying back fifteen feet, lands hard and lies there gasping for breath. Those who witnessed his foolishness laugh at his expense and I can't blame them. He is still gasping for breath when I give him an insolent shrug and walk away.

I thought that would be the last time I would see George so when I get to the sparring compound the next day and see him waiting there for me I am more than a little surprise.

"Ready to try again Missy."

"You must be a sucker for punishment."

This time he is the one that gives me an insolent shrug and this time I am the one that goes after him too cocky.

I have never been real good at hand-to-hand combat, even with all of Dad's drilling. Still, Dad has been the best I have ever been put up against so when George starts to move he catches me by surprise.

My first flight through the air has me thinking "nobody is suppose to be better than my daddy, this just isn't right!" and then I find myself flat on the floor trying to catch my breath.

Getting back up, I face him again and this is when I learn about George being a genius in hand-to-hand combat. Before I know it he is manhandling me like a child. I become certain that he is holding nothing back as he literally thrashes me.

The sparing match reminds me of my first year of sparring with Dad. The man is never where he is supposed to be and he just keeps on hitting me. I have no defence against him. Time and again, I find myself trying to catch my breath as I lay on the floor wondering where the hit had come from. That is until a particularly brutal hit to my nose pisses me off.

The next thing I know my eyesight is changing and time slows to a crawl. It feels as if my teeth want to grow. I really hope they are not, however there is no mistaking that my nails do when they come out long and black. Every sense becomes hypersensitive. I smell George's sweat, but no fear. This man does not fear me, not even a little.

It becomes as if I am watching a movie in slow motion. As I watch his fist coming towards my face, my uppermost thought is that the man really should have some fear, especially from me.

I wait until his fist almost lands and then I make my move. Ending up behind him I give him my best punch to the back of his kidney. Dam does it feel good! This is the first good blow I have yet to land on him. Any other hit that I managed to get in thus far was feeble at best, well the punch I give him this time is not feeble at all.

Now that I have gone weird he does not stand a chance against me. He moves as if he is moving through mud and it makes it so easy for me to finally turn the thrashing around. The punch to the kidney I follow up with another half dozen. It is so satisfying to finally be able to hit him back that my weirdness rejoices in it.

Seeing him go down like a sack of potatoes is satisfying enough that my world rights itself again. I look down at him laid out on the mat trying to catch his breath and give him a grin. I have obviously hurt him badly, but all I can think of is that it serves him right.

Of course that brings to a halt of our sparring for the day and he ends up being hauled away in a stretcher. As I watch them haul him away I truly believe that I will never see the man again.

The monster of the man turns out to be even better than I thought, or maybe stubborn for the next day when I show up he is standing there waiting for me.

"You're kidding right?" I tell him when I see him waiting for me.

"Not likely little missy. I learned something yesterday."

"Ya, like how to take a beating."

The dam man actually smiles at me before replying. "That and more, so are you ready."

Dam it, but I learn to hate the man. He has no right to be so freaking good. He trashes me and then thrashes me even more. I am just building up a good head of steam and about to give him some of that back when he holds up his hand and calls a halt.

"What!" I am seething with anger and the last thing I want to do is stop.

"I need a second."

"You're kidding right. Come on you bastard let's do this."

"No, just give me a second." He replies with his arms crossed against his chest.

What can I do? There is nothing more that I want right now than to beat on him and yet he has asked for a time out. I could ignore it and go after him, but how would that be fair. So fuming I sit myself down and wait for him.

"Okay, ready to go again." He asks me after five or ten minutes.

"Sure."

Dam it all, I should never have agreed. Once more he thrashes me. I try to grapple him. I try to hit his smirking face. I try every dirty trick Dad has taught me… he just pisses me off.

"Hold."

"What! What the fuck are you up to George, you can't just stop a fight like that!"

"Watch your language little missy. As for stopping, I think I can."

I think it is the fact that he tells me to watch my language just like Dad would do that allows the anger that has been boiling inside me to settle down enough for me to sit and wait.

The third time he pushes me too far. This time when he calls for a stop I ignore him. He has me so frustrated and mad that all I can think of is killing the man. I beat on him to do just that. How I hate his smirking face, how I hate how much better he is than my dad, how I hate how easily he manhandles me. It all explodes like a firecracker making time come to a crawl.

The day turns out to be a lucky day for George. Today, Mom had not been feeling well and she had almost decided against coming to watch me spar. If she had not shown up I am sure things would have gone very badly for George. I was so ready to kill him by this time that if she had not thrown herself on me when she saw me lose it I would have. So not only does she throw herself between George and I, not fearing me one bit she takes me in an embrace and then refuses to let go.

Even in my heighten state I recognized her. For a long time, even before my change Mom has had that effect on me. Her smell, her touch, even her soothing voice is all a part of me so when she takes hold of me I don't even fight her. God I am glad of that for the last thing I want is for Mom to fear me. I'm sure it takes her some time to bring me back to my senses and in the end we sit there embracing and crying like a couple of school children.

That surly should have been the end of George. He does not show up for the next two days and I actually find myself missing his presence. On the third day he is back.

"No George I don't want to hurt you again." I tell him and dam if he isn't still sporting that silly grin.

"Not today you won't."

"Oh, and how do you think you are going to keep me from doing so?"

The blow he gives me to the side of my head makes my ears ring and then we are at it again. This time he calls the halts more frequently, not letting me get as mad as before. I argue with him each time he calls for a break, but nothing I can say makes him start up again until he is good and ready. It is the end of the day, with me feeling all battered and bruised that he calls a halt and then sits down beside me.

"You have no idea what I am doing do you?" He asks me as I seethe there in anger.

"Other than keeping me from beating the crap out of you no. I think you broke my nose you know!"

"And I see that is has already healed… Remember I said I learned something that first day."

"Yes."

"Are you interested in knowing what I learned?"

I give him my best glare. "You're just bursting to tell me so go ahead."

"When you get mad enough your eyes change. Sometimes they are yellow, at other times red. I've notice that it is when they change that you lose it. When you do something happens. You just seem to disappear and pop up somewhere else and the next thing I know you're hitting me much faster and harder than before."

"Time…" I start, but George holds up his hand to stop me.

"They are listening so be careful what you tell me."

This is the first time that anyone other than my parents has warned me that it may be in my best interest to keep my mouth shut. The fact that he is not trying to pry information out of me raises my respect for him. I actually start to think that maybe somehow we can become friends. So for a long time I just look at him, working through my mixed emotions. He sits there patiently waiting for me, brushing my hair out of my face on occasion, even touching me gently once in a while. I find it strangely peculiar that he can do that for other than Dad no man has been able to touch me like that.

Finally, I give him a tentative smile and shrug. "When I get the better of you it is as if time slows. I see every move you make in slow motion so it is easy for me to get out of the way and sneak up behind you."

That admission actually causes him to laugh so it takes him a while before he can reply. "What you need to learn is to get to that state without losing you temper. When you are in a fight you can't afford to lose your head, it will get you or someone else killed."

"Dad always tells me the same thing."

"Then if you will not listen to me, listen to him."

"I am not use to being manhandled like you are doing to me and especially not by a man. Dad is the only one that I let do that to me. When I was younger he would bring his army buddies over to spar with me. For the most part, that did a good job at teaching me not to fear men outright. You on the other hand… well, will you help?"

"That's what I have been doing."

"Ya well I've still been losing it."

"Time little missy. It takes time and if I can I will get you there."

"Thanks George."

"No problem, however I have had it for the day. Monica will have a fine night working out all my sore muscles tonight."

"Monica?"

"My wife. I think you would like her."

"Women are not always good around me. Tell her I'm sorry."

"Will do, see you tomorrow."

Sure enough that becomes the building block for our friendship. Over the next few weeks he brings me time and again to the brink of madness. Time and again he makes me stop. Time and again he beats the crap out of me. He actually becomes a test of my healing ability. We discover that the more internal and lethal my injuries the faster they heal. Bruises take almost a day to heal, whereas broken bones a couple of hours, broken or ruptured organs almost immediately.

Even as George is breaking me to pieces my respect grows for the man and I come to believe that his respect for me grows also. The fear at being so easily manhandled by a monster of a man grows dimmer each day. It comes to where I no longer panic at the feel of his hands on my ass when he grabs it to give me a throw across the room, or when he crushes my chest to squeeze the life out of me.

It is when I start to relax at his "groping" and manhandling me that it comes to me. With the fear gone I am able to concentrate on George telling me when my eyes are changing and with that knowledge I learn to identify that little seed that makes time slow to a crawl as well as the one that gives me more strength than ever imaginable. A couple times he even tells me when the head of what looks like a very angry she-wolf super imposes itself on top of mine. Not being a stupid man, on those times he calls my mother to him, knowing full well that I will not go through her to get to him.

Surprisingly, it does not take long for me to learn how to pull on those small seeds of internal energy to give me those boosts. The first few times I succeed those watching tell me that I am teleporting from place to place. I try telling them they are wrong, however it takes them reviewing and slowing down the video of George and I sparing to convince them that I am telling the truth and that I am in deed only moving very fast.

As the weeks go by and my control becomes better they start to introduce others to me. It is a trial and error thing with each one of them. This time at least I don't break bones. It is for George however that my respect grows and I like to think that his respect for me grows just as much.

Another benefit of sparring with George is that it has the same effect as sparring with Dad had over the years. I find I am better able to handle my anger while sparing with him, until he frustrates me pass reasoning that is. The end result is that I get better at keeping my anger around others.

My strange night vision, I discover accidentally one evening on my way to visit my parents. The lights have been turned off for the evening making the hallway dark. I discover that I can make out a red shadowy figure at the end of the hall. Angry at the thought of being spied upon, my eyes do that strange "twist" that it does whenever I get ready to do a hyper move on George. The figure became more defined. A vibrating red outline and yet I still cannot identify the individual. Another twist of my eyes and the strange red vibrating figure disappears and in place the pitch-black darkness turns into a dusky darkness, allowing me to see that the man standing at the end of the hall is Wright.

I am bitter to discover that Wright is keeping tabs on me even late at night, so it is a couple of days before I tell General Macklin about my strange discovery, and of course thereafter I have to undergo more tests. We discover that it is when my eyes glow red in the dark, that I see the red shadows, and when they glow yellow in colour, the lessening of darkness into dusk.

When I try to explain the red shadowy figures in more detail, they tell me that it might be the same as using one of their night-vision goggles that uses heat signatures to help their men see at night. They give me one to test their theory, however, the second I put them on I end up disoriented and throwing up. They finally settle on showing me a film of a solider using the contraption. I admit to them that it does look similar to what I see and what they plan to do with that information I don't have the slightest idea.

Over the weeks I spent a fair amount of time talking to my assigned physiatrist Captain Laura McNeal. At first, even though I knew I really needed it I was not completely happy with it because regardless of what the captain said, she is military and I was never sure how much got back to General Macklin. However, I know I am skating on thin ice when it comes to my sanity and that I am still struggling with what has happened to me so talk to her I do.

I make a lot of progress with Laura over the weeks. I even begin to accept what I now am, whatever that might be. Unexpected anger still creeps up on me, especially when facing George. The up side is that I have not broken someone's bones in the last week, or pulled a weight machine off the wall in three, and it has been a week since George has had to call my mother to him.

As promised Mom starts taking care of my diet. The need for me to have blood is undeniable so we start testing how to cook my meat. When I suggested just eating it raw Mom gives me such a look that I promise myself never to suggest such a thing again.

I discover that the more I pull on those special abilities of mine the more need I have for blood. If I don't have blood the headaches start and then my gut starts clenching. The more that George teaches me to pull on my abilities the worse it gets.

After some experimenting on Mom's part she finally agrees that allowing me to eat my meat rare is no more inhuman than how many people eat their meat. I can't say as I love the thought mentally, although there is no denying that I feel a whole lot better after eating one of her rare steaks.

My hand-to-hand combat never really improves further than what Dad has taught me. It is only my strength and speed that even allows me to be a match for George and the others they put me up against.

That said, that is a much better experience than what I have with the firearms. I find that I have a deep loathing for the things. Even after six weeks of daily drills I feel sick every time I pick one up. Just as bad is the fact that I can't shoot worth a dam. On my best day I can be no more than a few feet from the target to hit it, on my worse, when the sickly crawly feeling of handling a gun gets to me, my hands shake so much that I have to be practically touching the targets to hit the stupid thing.

All and all, I cannot complain about my treatment. Yes, I have to work out every day, yes I have to learn how to use various weapons, most of which still make me sick or scare me to death, yes I have tests after tests, examination after examination, however they are teaching me and this is something I take very seriously. At present I am not sure if I want to get away from this hellhole, but I know that if or when I do, I will need every skill they are teaching me to survive.

The only real problem we encountered is trying to build a team around me. How many people we have to go through before they find enough to make a team I lose track of. I actually get frustrated with the process as some that I think will do, they dismiss. In my frustration at the process I talk to Dad about it. It is not until he explains how members of a unit have to learn to fully trust one another to be truly proficient at what we do and keep each other alive that I manage to keep my temper in check over the process.

It takes time to find them and in the end the unit consists of nine men and two other women. The members they finally find to be not only compatible with me, but who also feel comfortable enough around me are Anthony Gazinno, Andrea Kinsley, George Matten of course, Mitch Knoll, Lori Trenton, Tom Jeffers, Brent Lambert, Evan Williams, Antonio Gambino, Mark Brighton and Marcus Peters.

Building the unit around me is not the only problem they have with personal however, for after being in "The Hole" as we have come to call the base, for a couple of weeks, Mom, Dad and I have to be moved into the inner compound because of the disturbances that I cause whenever I enter or walk around the outer compound. None of us are completely happy about it for the outer compound houses a more comfortable living environment, if even by just a little. However, in the end even we have to admit that it is the right choice to make. They have been changing personal around to try to accommodate me and I feel sorry for those that are "shipped out" and replaced, but this is their army so they will do what they will do I suppose.

My new room turns out to be pretty similar to my old one. It still only consists of one room that houses a bed, a desk, a comfortable chair, closet space and dresser with a bathroom off to one side. The upside is that it is a little larger than the other.

The little bigger room does little for me missing the outer compound for at least there a person could find some entertainment. Even do some shopping, while the inner compound is military through and through, except the one place I find by accident.

Before they moved us to the inner compound I had been kept so busy that I had not had much time to explore. Whenever I was released for the day I was more than happy to get back to my room for some peace and quiet or just to crawl into my bed. That changes when we are moved to the inner compound for now when I am released for the day; well I am stuck in the inner compound so I take to exploring.

The room I discover is incredible. It is like an underwater grotto with a glass dome over the front. The walls are natural rock and the sea pushes against a glass dome built over its front. In this room I feel truly at home. It does as much to keep my temper under control as the sessions with George and Doctor McNeal. The sea serenades me like a lover and keeps coaxing me to come out and play.

The first couple of days upon the discovery I spend with my nose pressed against the glass. I stand there for hours losing myself to the sea life and listening to the sea's song.

However, it only takes those couple of days for the sea life to discover me and when they do, every time I go in there they start beating themselves against the glass to get at me. After watching a few do just that a few times I start sitting in the dark back corner of the grotto to keep them from seeing me. It is not the same as being pressed up against that glass, but at least it still allows me to watch and listen.

One day, after a particular gruelling day of them trying to get me use to guns I go there for some peace. I am so exhausted from trying not to throw up all day that it does not take long for me to fall asleep. The dream that comes to visit me is so real that I am not so sure if it is a dream at all. I am being embraced naked in the sea's icy depths. The sea life swims around me, caressing and playing with me while others clean my pearly skin of its above water impurities. I should be freezing, however I am not. For the first time since my change I feel totally at peace. There is no anger or uncertainties. My world becomes perfect once more, and I loath the thought of ever leaving its perfection. However, loathe it or not I do wake up. I wake up flushed and full of excitement and absolutely convince that it was no dream at all.

It is a couple days after that dream that General Macklin finds me sitting in the grotto's darkness. My entire being is begging me to submerse myself into the sea and I am having difficulty fighting off that urge.

"Why are you sitting way back here Michele?" He asks when he discovers me there.

"Because those stupid fish keep trying to kill themselves getting to me whenever I get too close to the glass."

"That's interesting. I spend a lot of time here myself and I have never noticed them do that."

"Maybe they are not in love with you." I answer glaring at him. It is not the general I am mad at, but the sea life, for it really does feel like they have fallen in love with me, however, much like that day with Dad when I went off on him for no reason, the general is the one that is available to me just then, so I take out my displeasure at him.

Much to my surprise General Macklin laughs at my comment. Bolstered by that I ask the impossible. "What would be real nice is if you could design this so that they could come in to visit me or better yet, so that I could go to them."

"That would take a real feat of engineering, besides you would drown or freeze to death."

"I'm not so sure about that."

"What are you saying Michele?"

"I don't know. They want me to come out and play with them. It's stupid I know, but..." Not having any way to explain it I just shrug my shoulder and leave the General to his own thoughts.

Of course the grotto has not changed. In fact, my one and only success in regards to the unit, which is not really a success at all was to get Private First Class Darren Keller assigned to the compound. I had thought long and hard on the implication of taking on this fight for I know he is more than what he seems.

Something had happened during our little scuffle in the hanger causing Darren to be forever on my mind, as if there is some kind of physical umbilical cord tying us together. I feel a need to have him close by as well as a need to see him and be assured that he is safe. There is something about him that calls to me night and day. As before, it has nothing to do about sex, but something that goes so much deeper. As such, I struggle with the possibility of putting someone in place that could endanger the military, according to them that is. My instincts tell me otherwise, that I can trust Darren with my life; something I may very well need someday.

When I insist that Darren be allowed to join the unit, I am told quite firmly that he does not have the clearance and no amount of posing on my part changes that old military machine. I argue long and hard about why I want him here. In the end, the best I come up with and that works, much to my surprise was that his presence comforts me. We reach a comprised, which has him assigned to the outer compound, where he can be near, but not near enough to learn the inner secrets.

Darren showed up after we were in The Hole for four weeks. I have managed to spend only a little time with him, which considering my "banishment" from the outer compound was not the easiest thing to do in the first place.

Initially, I thought I could sneak off somewhere private with Darren and have a long discussion. That delusion was quickly snuffed out, for when I start making noise about being too cooped up and needing some escape General Macklin finally relents, however only agreeing to allow me into the outer compound if members of the unit accompanied me to "keep me protected from their own" as well as to teach us to form a cohesive bond.

Even then I was certain I could divest myself of the "unwanted guests" whenever I wanted, but to what end? My parents would still be stuck where they are and I will do anything to keep them safe. Therefore, I settle with only casual conversations with Darren and the occasional bouts. Even this is paying off, for every time I visit him I can feel that unusual bond between us building.

Every visit with Darren I discover something new about him. I learn that he is a charming man. He is entertaining to be with and full of life. Much to my surprise, I discover that he has a beautiful singing voice, although it is always easier to get him to sing after a few beers. He does have one bad habit and that is when he drinks too much beer he starts singing songs in a language none of us understand.

Those songs are old songs I am sure and they affect me in an almost physical way. I have begged him time and again to tell me more about the songs and yet no amount of begging has gotten him to tell me anything worth a spit.

I keep my secrets of course. I never tell them what I suspect about Darren and then there is the fairy. It still amazes me that nobody has been able to spot her for if that little fairy isn't whirling around my head like a bumblebee she is sitting on my shoulder and what a troublesome little thing she has become. I have come to love her to death and yet some days she can be so frustrating, not the least is her insistence on showering with me.

Still hating the military blues and grays my greatest victory comes when I talk General Macklin into allowing Mom and I to go on a shopping trip outside of the compound. When I first ask, he offers to have a female officer do whatever shopping I need done. Of course that is not the point in the whole exercise. It takes some pressure from Dad in the end to get him to agree to the excursion and even then he insists that every member of the unit accompany me or it is a "no go".

Freaking Military. How many times have I heard Dad say that to me? Do this or that or it's a no go Sweetie…. I'll no go the military's ass someday, just wait and see.

Therefore, after almost six weeks of being locked underground and seeing nothing but harsh lighting and the sea beckoning outside my glass cage I get to leave the compound for the first time.

Chapter Nine

I had succeeded in talking General Macklin to let Mom and I out shopping for the day. What I didn't expect was the condition he put on it. Initially, I was furious at the General's insistence on the unit accompanying us, for I had planned to make shopping just a by-line of the day. What I wanted was to be alone with Mom, to feel the sun on my face, to just sit somewhere peacefully with my head on Mom's shoulder and let the sea serenade the two of us. Even something as small as feeling a sea breeze blowing across my face hour upon hour would have done. Not to be, for he pulled some more of that military crap on me. When he tried to insist that Wright and his team follow us, well that was a line that I would not allow him to cross and we argued over that for some time.

Therefore, when the day comes my anger at the intrusion of the unit into what I had wanted to be quiet time with Mom is palpable as we make our way out of The Hole.

Most of the outer compound is clear of personal when we get there. Darren, having proved himself totally immune to me is exempt from evacuation. If only they knew for he is not an exception. He wants me, as badly if not more so than most males, it's just that with him the tie that we have allows me to push him into behaving. This is a little quirk I have learned with him over the last couple of weeks and one that I wish I could do to the other males I have to contend with and believe me I have tried.

When I see him in the outer compound my anger at the general is roiling just beneath the surface so that when he catches sight of me he bends his head submissively and refuses to look me in the eye.

I really wish I could spend more time with him to learn what it is between us. Whatever it is will have to wait, however I know that I have just done something uncouth so I growl something unintelligible to the rest and then ask them to give me a minute.

"Sorry for what I just did."

"You are Alpha, there is no need to apologize."

This is the first time Darren has ever called me Alpha and it catches me off guard. I look at him speechless for a good half minute before I find my voice. "What do you mean by that Darren?"

"You know what I mean. You feel our bond. It gets stronger every day. You may want to deny it Alpha, but denying it will not make the truth go away."

Why today of all days he has to get into this I don't know. All I want is to get away from all this and he goes and throws that in my face. Crap and double crap.

"What am I suppose to do with that Darren. Why can't anything be fucking simple anymore?"

"Do with that as you wish. You are Alpha and I am pack."

"I can't deal with this right now. You want to come shopping with us and maybe when I get my head on straight we will find more time to talk about this."

"As you wish Alpha."

I growl in displeasure before answering. "No, as you wish. Do "you" want to accompany us?"

Darren gives me a grin, making me want to smack it off his face.

"Certainly."

"Then come along." I manage almost without any anger.

It is a beautiful autumn day and the wind is blowing from the sea filling the air with its briny smell. When they look questioningly at me for our first destination I point towards the sea and then drag them along with me. We end up on top of a bluff overlooking a sandy beach and the urge to throw myself into its icy depths becomes overwhelming.

"Let's go for a swim!" I say breathless with desire.

Much to my surprise it is George that voices the first refusal. "Missy, even if we had a hundred men my size we could not keep you safe on a beach with you in a bathing suit. Hell, I can't think of any world power that could. I tell you if my daughter grows up to be even half as beautiful as you I will lock her up until she is old and grey. Now why don't we just make this a test trip and see how things go. If we do well maybe we can do the sea thing another day."

The rest agree with him, even Mom is against it, so in the end I relent and agree to a compromise suggested by Lori. "I grew up around here. I happen to know of a stretch of rocky outcrop that gives a magnificent view of the sea. It's beautiful there so why don't we give that a try?"

I do some grumbling and then relenting I ask her to lead the way. It is still early in the morning so there is not too much foot traffic. The few people that we do encounter react to me, causing the unit to tighten the ring around me until Mom and I become all but invisible to those we pass.

Arriving at the outcrop I smile appreciatively to Lori for the spot is a perfect alternative. The rocky outcrop sits right up against the sea and looks out over the great watery expanse.

Asking Mom to sit beside me I move forward as far as I dare and settle in. For an hour I sit there with my head on Mom's shoulder memorized by the sights and sounds. The sea calls to me and I want to answer that call. One look at those with me is all I need to know that it is not going to happen without me breaking some bones… something I have been trying very hard not to do lately.

Therefore, instead of following the call I sit, letting the peace and calm wash over me. I mummer softly to Mom about what I feel. How the sea is calling to me. I tell her how it wants me to come and play and how the sea is lulling the anger that always seemed to be skirting the surface of my emotions.

After an hour I decide I have tortured everyone enough. Thanking them for their patience I inform them I am ready for the next part of the day. When they ask to where I give them a rueful smile.

"I have no idea. This is the first time they have let us out and neither Mom nor I know the city. Why don't you take the lead Lori?"

"I do know of some nice little shops that shouldn't be so busy as to cause us trouble."

"Then you have the lead." Mom and I both say at the same time causing us to smile at each other.

Once again, they place Mom and I in the middle of the group and once again, for the most part, those we pass ignore us. When we initially discussed the excursion there was talk about taking a car. General Macklin had even offered one. I had declined for part of the whole idea of the excursion was to get out and feel free, not to be ushered from one spot to another under tight security so even though I feel like I am being smothered by them it still turns out to be much better than what taking a car would have been.

This is the first time that Mom or I have been out since being squirreled away in The Hole, as such we gape like country bumpkins at some of the various sights we pass. Thankfully, the rest of the unit understand for most of them are new to the area and have spent enough of their leave doing just what we are now doing. Therefore, they are patient with the two of us as we pass one sight or another. Lori turns out to be a wealth of information and becomes our unofficial guide.

We have only gotten about halfway to the lane where the first of our shopping experience is to start when I start to get that familiar feeling of being watched. Having felt that feeling most of my life I try to shrug it off. That is until I notice that I am not the only one feeling "twitchy".

I had thought that whoever had attacked us that night in the apartment would have forgotten us after all this time. However, watching the overall nervousness of the group I become unsure.

With that uneasy feeling crawling over me I beckon Darren to me and as quietly as I can I ask him to watch over Mom. Darren, obviously feeling what I am feeling looks at me grimly and nods. Fear of what could happen to Mom if things went to hell is so overwhelming that I almost call off the trip. However, Mom eyes are alight and I can't blame her for her obvious excitement at being out. She has been locked up as long as I and with not nearly as much to keep her busy as me so the thought of cancelling dies in my throat before I even voice my concern.

We make it to the lane without mishap where much to the delight of us women the shopping commences. The men in the unit, being typical of men, especially typical military men are not interested in shopping if it has nothing to do with "boy toys", preferable boy toys that go boom so they allow us to lead them from shop to shop. Amazingly, the little shopping excursion becomes our first true bonding experience.

The four of us, that being myself, Mom, Andrea, and Lori use the opportunity to shop to the fullest. We drag the men from one clothing store to another. I soon discover that there is nothing quite as funny as the look and posturing of stern military men having to stand around a women's lingerie store as the women get excited over panties, bras, and nighties.

Noticing their reaction, we become merciless and start showing and asking them what they think of each piece of clothing. By some unspoken signal that men will never understand a contest starts to see who can find the tiniest and sexiest set of panty and bra. Much to my surprise and with everybody in agreement, even the men, Andrea wins that contest.

I purchase, socks, nylons, dresses, shirts, high-heeled shoes, bras, and panties. When I will ever get a chance to wear them I have no clue, however once again, that is not the point. My greatest treasure of the day is finding a pair of jeans that fits me like a second skin. Everyone agrees they are nice, too dam nice George growls and as such they flatly refuse to allow me to wear them out of the shop.

The fairy of course has a heyday. She has been no happier than me at being cooped up and even though I'm certain she is able to get out whenever she wants she has never bothered, so she makes the most of the day. I have never seen her interact with anybody other than me so I had no idea that she could. When my mind had refused to see her she felt like a tickle whenever she touched me. Now we are able to interact as any other two individuals. In fact, she often caresses me to sleep at night with her wings. Therefore, after I finally get tired of her making herself a pest with me and shoo her away she goes on to make herself a pest with other shoppers. Just watching her flicker around them and seeing their reaction to her pulling on their hair and flying around their bodies soon has me balled up in gut-wrenching laughter. When I see the looks of concern on the faces of Mom and the unit I try to keep that laughter under control. It is hard, dam hard for she looks so cute flying around and being a pest the way she is.

For the most part the unit keep me protected from the local populace. Whenever we move from shop to shop they have me tightly surrounded. Even after we enter a shop they keep me in place until they have scoped it out and then brought the shopkeepers to me to see how they would react. If they react badly, they turn us around and out we go. It makes for a lot of shop hopping, but hey that was the whole idea anyways.

The only outbreak we have comes when we are making a move from one shop to the next. Mom says something to me, which makes me smile. Nobody should have been able to see me for as usual Mom and I are well surrounded, however with that smile comes a stampede of men. I am not even sure if they know what they were stampeding towards, however it is obvious that they want what the group was hiding… me.

Seeing the men descend on us the unit circle Mom and I even more tightly than they had been. After ten minutes of defending me from admirers, things are getting pretty ugly. Lori finally pushes me into a shop and tells me to lock myself into the back room, much to the dismay of the shop owner. Not wanting to make things more difficult for them I drag Mom behind me and lock us behind the door. With me tucked away the men are not so madden and the unit slowly get matters back under control.

That is the only major incident for the day. After that I make sure not to smile where men can see me and the unit do a good job at keeping the crazed women away from me so all in all we have a good time. We even find a dark corner in a little restaurant where I manage to stay hidden from view, thus allowing us to enjoy a little down time in a public setting. That was so cool for I had come to expect that I would never again be able to enjoy such a thing.

As fun as the day is, that feeling of being watched and followed prevails. Even in the midst of our gaiety that crawly feeling persists. So bad does it get on our return to The Hole later that evening that it begins to feel like I have insects crawling all over my skin. By the way the others are looking I am not the only one that is feeling that way so I finally point out an almost deserted restaurant and tell them to get us inside.

I am not totally surprised that when I tell the rest my suspicion that none of them question me. What does surprise me is that after we have discussed alternate plans it is Darren that volunteers to create a diversion to allow the rest of us the opportunity to slip away. I counter back that I can cause just as much of a diversion by simply going outside and smiling at people. Well that does not go over too well and I suppose I should have known better than to even offer.

Therefore, Darren ends up taking the lead, however I suspect I am not the only one that has second thoughts as to whether that was a good idea after cars start crashing and what seems like a hundred Italian men start yelling at each other.

During the confusion, we manage to slip into the watching crowd and then away. The night sky was already darkening when we started on our way back to The Hole and as it gets darker the more nervous I become. The first six blocks go without a hitch. It is when we make a turn and start working our way down a laneway that is even darker than the lanes we have been following that a feeling of dread overcomes me. Halting the group, I kick myself mentally for allowing us to be drawn into such a narrow and dark lane. True I was not leading, but dam it I should have known better.

Angelo watches the group make its way into the narrow lane. The thralls had been following these humans all day and had reported the group to him just as twilight was falling. Once the sun had set and using the rooftops it had not taken much for the six of them to get ahead of their quarry.

"What do you think Mitch is that her?" Angelo whispers to the brood lying in wait next to him.

"Two possibilities down there. I don't think it is either of the older ones or the blonde. Either one of the other two I think. Too bad we couldn't stir the rest of the brood quickly enough. It's going to take a while to take them all out and that is going to cause some commotion."

"I know and yet we can't risk missing this opportunity. Boris did say dead or alive. What do you think about putting two of us against the others to create a distraction and two each against those two women until we know for sure? Once she reveals herself we can all converge on her. If it turns out that it is not possible to take her alive we will just kill her."

"We still have a couple of thralls following so they should be able to help with the distraction."

"There's a wolf with them Angelo."

"I see that. What is a wolf doing with them?

"No idea, however we can't let that stop us. I say we put Larn against the wolf. He should be able to keep him busy until we have resolved this."

"Good thinking. So are we ready?" Angelo looks around to see if there are any dissenting voices. Seeing none, he starts appointing assignments.

I turn to Darren, who has long since rejoined us. "No matter what happens I want you to watch Mom and Mom…"

"Yes Dear. I have been a military wife for a long time. Watch yourself."

"Love you Mom." I tell her and then off I go down the laneway with the rest of the unit following.

We have gone no more than fifty feet when a group of them drop down around us. Even though we expected something their sudden appearance is a surprise, causing us to come to a quick halt.

Half frightened out of my wits by their appearance I freeze in my tracks. The memories of that fateful night comes back to swamp me. The knowledge of what we are facing paralyses me.

Thankfully, the others are faster than me in recovering. They are military through and through and unlike me, the rest of them are armed in one manner or another. It is the flurry of weapons coming to bare that finally frees me from my paralysis.

The only saving grace for us is that there are twice as many of us as there are vampires and that for some unbeknownst reason two of the vampires chose to move from one of us to another only to harass and distract us instead of trying to score a kill. Two vampires come after me and two go directly for Andrea.

Making a quick decision and praying it is not the wrong thing to do, I tap into those abilities that I dread and yet have learned to use.

Even with two to one odds we experience trouble right away for the vampires are much too fast to allow us to make any kind of defence, never mind offence and when a couple of thralls come barging into the mix it gets worse.

I go into action and like those vampires creating chaos and distraction I unwittingly follow their lead, hoping to slow them down enough to give the rest of the unit time to defend or attack.

It becomes immediately obvious to me that these vampires, unlike those that attacked us in our apartment recover much quicker at their initial shock of my speed and strength and soon, as I had hoped, their attention starts to gravitate towards me.

The rest of the unit are much more experienced at this kind of thing then I am and even though they are outmatched, they give it their all. The sound of grunting and swearing, our own, quickly fills the air. If we had been properly armed for this kind of encounter we may have made a much better showing even considering the vampires unnatural speed. However, the attack had been unexpected for who would have thought that a simple shopping trip would end in a fight for our lives.

My decision to put the vampires off-balanced instead of engaging directly seems to have been the right one. I think it is what makes the difference between life and death for us, that and the fact that the rest of them quickly pick up on what I am trying to do. Every vampire I hit I manage to slow, giving the others time to retaliate in some manner and what started out as a death trap for us starts to turn into a much more equal fight.

After what seems an eternity of breaking bones and smashing in faces, I find myself facing off with one particular fast and astonishingly strong vampire. Thrice now, I have tried to hit him and thrice I have missed. It, on the other hand has yet to miss, or so my swollen face and sore abs are telling me.

"Hold still dam you!" I finally yell in frustration, tapping even further into my reserves and putting all the force of a command learned from many years of living with my military father behind my voice; much to my surprise he does.

By the look on the vampire's face I am not the only one that is surprised. One minute he was throttling a wimpy little girl and then I tell it to stop and what does it do, but listen to me. I'm sure that is it's last thought as my fist goes through its brain to exit out the back of its head.

When I turn around from destroying my nasty I see that the four remaining vampires are also in trouble. They had been trying to cut me off from the rest of the group and as such they were no more immune to my command than the one I had faced. The initial force of my command had caused them to halt and the rest of the unit, although surprised at the turn of events quickly took advantage of the situation. Now it is the vampires' turn to consider the likelihood of continued existence instead of us.

Even as the rest of the unit beat and blast away at them I see their calculating look. Bullets riddle their bodies and they ignore them. It is me that they want and it is obvious that they are not at all pleased with what I had just done. They hit me in mass, smothering me with their bodies and causing me to fall to the ground.

"You are even more dangerous than we thought. You must die!" I hear one of them hiss.

The combined weight of them threatens to suffocate me. Worse, the mind numbing pain in my shoulder as their nails dig in incapacitates me. Even as I scream in pain, I feel one trying to latch onto my neck. It does not have much luck for my hair is on the move causing it to get nothing more than a mouthful of it. Frustrated from its goal it finally settles on incapacitating me further by thrusting its nails into the flesh of my other shoulder. Another scream rips out of my throat and echoes down the laneway as the third vampire, having no better luck with latching onto the back of my neck because of my twisting and maddening hair starts to shred my back to ribbons.

The sound of my scream is quickly drowned out by the sound of more gunfire. Bullets spattered with brain ricochet next to my face, throwing up chips of paving stone. The fairy, still holding desperately onto my hair buzzes to and fro, confounding the vampires every time they try to bite me. However, it is obvious that the poor thing is tiring.

In desperation I push my chest up in a last ditch effort to free myself of the leaches clinging to my back and shoulders. I get a few inches off the ground and I am about to give another push that I hope will launch me into the air when a bullet goes clean through a vampire clinging to my back and into my shoulder. The bullet, already bent out of shape with its travel through the vampire sears a ragged burning path through my shoulder, causing my arm a moment of weakness and making me fall back onto the paving stones. Multiple gunshots follow and then blessed silence as the guns finally click on empty breaches.

Shortly thereafter, nails are pried from my shoulders and then the weight of the three vampires weighing me down disappears. Relieved of my burden I am able to turn over to I look up at those standing directly above me. George and Lori stand only a couple of feet from me with their guns still out and smoking while the rest drag the bodies of the destroyed vampires aside.

The last six weeks had taught me something about how to gauge my temper. George has even told me that the madder I get the more yellow my eyes shine. What I have noticed is that the angrier I get the stranger my eyesight becomes and I have learned to use the degree of strangeness to gauge the depth of my anger. That current strangeness is telling me that I am very angry indeed. Very, very freaking angry. To make matters worse something or someone seems to be fuelling even more anger into me.

I fight my first instinct to reach out and kill. Mentally, I know that neither George nor Lori purposely shot me, or at least I hope they had not. Emotionally, I do not care.

Laura and I have spent a lot of time talking about my anger and trying to find ways to defuse it during our sessions. I have been given some suggestions as to how to control it, like the deep breathing I am now doing. However, even this is not enough to keep me from wanting to tear these two limb from limb so I start imagining the sea as I experienced it that very morning. It helps and yet it is the fairy's gentle caresses along my cheek and neck that is as much a credit for me not exploding, as is that deep breathing and lulling sea.

It only takes me thirty seconds or so to get my anger under control, however it feels like an eternity. Luckily, my comrades know me well enough not to intrude. I do not doubt that my eyes are yellow; a clear indication that anyone who so much as makes a quick move is bound to lose a body part or two.

Remember what Laura suggested. Make light of it. Control your anger instead of letting it control you…

When I think I have some semblance of control on my temper I attempt what Laura had suggested. I try for, and almost succeed in expressing joviality. "You shot me! I can't believe you shot me! Which one of you mother's shot me and where the hell did you get the gun from Lori?"

Lori is wearing a short, tight fitting dress and as far as I am concerned she should not have been able to hide a Tic-Tac without it showing, never mind a freaking forty calibre Glock.

Lori grins down at me before replying. "I'll show you later and he shot you."

"Like hell I did. I went for the one on the left and it's the right shoulder that got shot."

"You can't aim worth a shit George. You should keep to your fist. You shot her so admit it and take your lumps like a man."

"Did not, beside you'll be right as rain in a few hours Michele so quit whining like a girl."

"Hey George I have a surprise for you. I am a freaking girl. See I have tits!"

Another thing that I have learned about George over the last few weeks, and something that was very unexpected in a six foot six giant, is that he is easily embarrassed. Thus seeing his face go red as a beet does a lot towards getting rid of the anger still boiling inside me. Furthermore, George is right in a way. It had taken me a while to get myself under control and although both of my shoulders are burning in pain, my healing is well underway. Therefore, by this time I can't even remember which shoulder had actually been shot so I really don't know whom to blame. That, on top of their six-year-old playground antics helps to relieve me of the remaining anger.

"Enough with you two miscreants!" I try a glare, which only makes them grin. "Help me up."

George hauls me to my feet and then being the gentleman he always is he tells me straight out. "You look like hell."

"Gee thanks, I'd look a lot better if I hadn't been mauled on and then shot by my own team. Are we all okay here?"

The three of us look around. The rest of the team is piling up the bodies against the buildings and then I scream for reasons other than physical pain.

"She's okay Miss Appleton. She just got knocked back a little when this here one came after me."

Sure enough, a destroyed vampire lies not ten feet from Darren and Mom. Mom is just sitting back up and she is giving Darren a look; a look that I had long ago learned to interrupt.

Please mother no!

"We'll have to send a team back for the bodies as there isn't a hope in hell we can get them to The Hole ourselves without answering a lot of questions. Besides, its more important to get you two back than taking care of the bodies." Gazinno states the obvious.

With everyone in agreement we leave the remains in the laneway and make our way back as quickly as we can. We arrive a little ragged for wear, but alive and most importantly as far as us women are concerned, none of the purchases we had spent the day shopping for had been ruined.

We are a grateful group that lean back against the thick steel door when it closes behind us. For the few minutes we simply stand there in disbelief that what had just happened had actually occurred.

Once we get our breath back and our wits together we look at each grimly for we know what we need to do next. I apologize for the inconvenience. They shrug at me and wave it aside.

"We'll call you when we have the area secured. Just stay here until then." Andrea tells Mom and I.

Darren, only able to go as far as the first secured area volunteers to help, which the rest accept gratefully. He starts to follow, however before he can get away I stop him and no doubt surprise him by taking him in a bone-crushing embrace and thanking him repeatedly for watching after Mom.

During the embrace I decide it is time to acknowledge the man. "I feel something. I'm not sure what it is. Actually I'm too scared to delve in it, but thank you again and I ask that you give me time." I whisper in his ear.

Darren's reply is a sniff of my neck and then an offering of his own. I smell his musk. It is much more intense than what I have ever smelt on any other man and so unlike other males, for his scent has much more to it than the smell of his maleness. The smell is individual to him and identifies him more deeply than his name. It overwhelms my senses and it becomes buried deep inside my brain. That scent and his exposed neck scream to me that he is mine to with as I please.

"Dominic is not going to be happy with you taking one of his, nor happy with me for that matter so watch yourself." He whispers back in warning and then he is gone.

Dominic? Who the hell is Dominic and why should I care? What does he mean take one of his? Why can't anyone just give me a straight answer?

I growl under my breath as I watch Darren make good his escape and then wait for the signal from the unit that the coast is clear.

"I need a very rare steak Mom. A big one at that." I finally confess when Mom and I are alone.

"I'll make sure you get one the minute you are free to eat."

"I hope I can hold on that long."

"If not tell them you need some food. Don't be shy of asserting yourself."

I take Mom in a hug. I can't believe how she is taking such good care of me, when by rights I am of age where I should be taking care of myself. I keep her crushed to me, willing her to know how much I love her until the rest of the group return.

When we finally manage to make it to the second security door we all breathe a second sigh of relief as it closes behind us. As expected it was too much to hope that I could escape to my room unnoticed for sure enough, once Mom has been safely tucked away, we find ourselves in front of Lieutenant Neely receiving a proper dressing down, as Dad would say.

In the operation center General Macklin looks on grimly as Neely addresses the unit, however his thoughts are far remove from what he is looking at. They have been given a job and he has only one day left to start getting his people into position. It is that job that occupies his mind.

"Send Michele's unit." He hears Captain Laura McNeal say as if she is reading his mind.

"What! Why?" The general turns to Laura.

"I have a feeling." Laura replies with a grimace for she knows what is coming next.

"A feeling. Great, we are going to start basing our operations on feelings now. That woman is addressing the U.N. in three days. She will be here in two and we have been made responsible for her. We know almost nothing about her except that her picture generates strong emotions… and you have a feeling!"

"Think about it General. Where else are we seeing those emotions being exhibited?" Laura does not wait for the general's reply, but barges on. "When it comes to Michele, feelings are all we can go on until we learn more. We can't deny the truth that is right in front of us; Michele is of this Queen's race."

General Macklin glares at her for some time before finally replying. "Half the time she still keeps her eyes closed when she shoots a gun and her hand to hand combat is still appalling, Well maybe not appalling, but certainly not up to par. If it wasn't for her strength and agility she would be useless. On top of that I'm not so sure she is ready and I don't mean physically, but mentally. Can we count on her not to snap or not coming back in when the operation is over?"

"She is surprisingly stable and as long as you have her parents here she will come back."

"They are not her parents!" General Macklin growls back obviously displeased.

"We all know that, even Michele acknowledges that. She loves them more than she would a parent. Don't tell me you have not seen it.

Her and Jackie have an unhealthy dependency on each other. She will never abandon them."

"Dam it. It feels so barbaric to be keeping that kind of hold on her."

"Yes it is, but we have our orders." Neely, who managed to return for the last couple of comments, throws in his two-cent's worth.

"Whatever. So what happened?"

"Seems like some vampires decided to attack them on the way back. This is the first true encounter we have had with them and by all indications they made a decent showing for themselves. None have come back with anything more than a few cuts and bruises. Except for Michele that is, but you know her, she'll be back to full health before the day is out. Amazingly enough one of them shot her and she didn't kill whoever it was. They are being debriefed now and we should have the full story by this evening."

"One of the vampires shot her? We've never heard of them using guns before."

"No, either George or Lori." Neely replies with a wide grin.

"She knows this and they are still walking? Was it on purpose?"

"Accidentally by the sounds of it."

"I'm still surprised she didn't kill whoever it was. McNeal thinks we should use them to protect Queen Sophie. What's your opinion?"

"I think she may be right and they did account for themselves out there today."

"Well then get them briefed and have them on their way tomorrow morning and god help us if we are wrong."

An hour later I am back in my room. I had overheard the tail end of the conversation in the operations room and the thought of being sent out is not making me happy. Worse yet, is that I am finding even less solitude in my room than I did while Lieutenant Neely was dressing us down for now it is Dad giving me the dressing down. The difference is that here at least, Mom is on my side.

If Dad is not enough to deal with the little fairy that has insisted on becoming a part of my life has been buzzing in my ears non-stop since we arrived back in the room and I am just about ready to crack from the double attack.

"Honey, you can't expect us to stay locked up in here the rest of our lives." Mom speaks up in my defence and not for the first time.

"No I can't, but dam it!"

"We did okay. It was scary and I probably have grey hairs now, however Michele and her unit did well."

"That's the point. They should not have had to!" Dad states, obviously frustrated by the whole situation and his inability to make it go away.

I can't blame him for his frustration. From the very day I woke up changed I ruined their life. They are now as good as prisoners inside this compound as I am, and to make matters worse we have just received proof that outside is no safer.

I finally crack because I have had enough of the fairy taking Dad's side. "Will you stop nagging at me and stop taking his side?" I say between a mouthful of the rare steak that Mom brought me.

The fairy stops to hover a mere inch from my nose. Her surprise is plain to see, though I suspect my own face shows just as much surprise. The two of us stare at each other.

"Michele. Don't talk to your father like that! He may be acting like an ass, but he is still your father."

"What!" Mom's condemning voice shakes me from my shock. "No, I wasn't talking to Dad. I mean I was, but I wasn't…. I am so messed up right now. It's been a tiring day. I'm sorry I screwed up your lives. I really am." I tell them truthfully for what must be the thousandth time in the last six weeks.

"You didn't mess it up Honey. I am a military wife and have been since I married your father. He's the one that messed it up."

"Well your father was happy enough to get your temper out from under his roof. He practically pushed you at me."

I give my parents a wan smile. For as long as I have known them they have joked with each other thus and hearing them now makes it seem like everything is okay, as if they we are back in our little flat in Switzerland and nothing has changed.

"Still I'm sorry, but Dad you can't expect us to stay in this…. this prison forever. We need to get out occasionally. We need to see real sunshine, to feel it on our faces, to breathe polluted air. I need to see the sea. And not only Mom and I, you have to get out occasionally too. You need to start taking Mom out and start living again, like when we were in Switzerland. I know things have changed, but we can make the best of it, can't we Daddy?"

"Oh, you're getting better Michele. You saved that for just the right time." I hear Mom whisper so softly that I am sure I am the only one that could ever have heard and then I see Mom try to hide a chuckle behind a cough.

"Of course we can Sweetie. I'm just acting like a worried parent and husband." Dad states as he gathers Mom and then beckons me to him so he can have the both of us in his arms.

I have always felt safe in his arms and this time it is no different from any other time. I snuggle against his chest and breath in his scent. Funny, I have never noticed before how manly he smelled.

Oh geez Michele stop that already!

"Thank you Daddy… you want to hear a secret. Mom brought some real sexy underwear today. I'm sure you're going to love taking them off her." I have long since learned that the easiest way to get away from my parents is to bring up the subject of sex, most especially theirs.

"Michele!" Mom's face flames red.

"Well you did and he will."

"Urmp….um, I think this is where I make a tactical retreat. Are you coming Jackie?"

"Yes, just give me a sec."

"You going to be okay Dear."

"Yes Mom and thanks. By the way, I overheard them say that they are sending us to the U.S. tomorrow."

Mom freezes. I see the panic on her face. The same panic I felt when the truth of what being sent meant to me. "We knew this day was coming." She finally says haltingly.

"I know, but I hate it just the same."

"Mind if I sneak back in your room tonight."

"I was hoping you would. I don't know if I can do it Mom."

"You can… we can. We have to grow up."

I smile at her knowing she is putting up a brave front. I only wish I could feel so brave. "I'll keep the door unlocked for you." I tell her as I crush her with a hug.

"You do that. I'll be back after I have mollified your father."

"Oh ya, get a room and have fun." I shout at her retreating back.

Once the door shuts I lean back against it with a sigh and close my eyes in a feeble attempt to get some sanity back in my life.

"It's about time ye learned to listen to me." A primp little voice exclaims.

I wasn't imagining it then!

"I was always listening to you. You just weren't talking right." I snap back.

"Well I never..." The fairy starts, however doesn't get a chance to finish for I gathered her up in my hands and hug her to my breast.

"I can't breathe."

"Sorry. I can't believe that I can actually understand you!"

"And it be about time too."

"Oh I'm sorry. We have never really introduced ourselves. I'm Michele, Michele Appleton." I state with as much grace as my still shocked brain allows me.

"Sorcha Mac Giolla Riabhaigh. It is a pleasure to formally meet ye at last." Sorcha gives me a flowering bow, which looks cute as hell with her floating no more than a couple of inches from my nose.

"My god what a name. No wonder I couldn't guess it. Well, nice to meet you my dear. So why is it that I finally understand you? This is just too cool!"

"I knew ye would in time."

"You did how?"

"Ye be kindred."

"Kindred. That must have a different meaning for you than me." I answer, confused at Sorcha's use of the word.

"Kindred is kindred and ye be kindred. I feel it and ye would never be able to see me, never mind hear me if ye weren't."

"But how. Was your race once human?"

Sorcha bursts out laughing until tears of laughter stream from her eyes and down her face. It is a long time before she gets herself back under control. Her laughter becomes so infectious and so out of place in this dungeon that I can't help smiling and then finally joining in.

"We be never human. How ye managed to get so large be the question that needs to be asked, but kindred we be. Don't ye feel it? Sorcha finally manages once she gets her breath back.

I look at Sorcha with no more insight than I had just a few minutes ago so she flies down to my breasts and places a dainty hand between them. "Feel it Michele. Touch that part of ye that makes ye, ye. Feel my touch, feel my essence and find that which is I inside ye. That's it. See. I know ye feel it! Go on and tell me I am lying!"

Sorcha is right I do feel it. There it is, hiding deep down inside me. That little bit of me that acknowledges Sorcha for what she is. The little bit that surged to be noticed when she had touched me.

"Yes, I feel it, yet I don't understand. How is this possible? There is so much about me that I don't understand and it scares me. It was not so long ago that I thought fairies were nothing more than something created by Walt Disney."

"That be the way we wanted it, or at least thought we did. A long time ago the fey were a hunted race. The vampires sought us for our blood, the werewolves for food and the humans for sport. We be long lived, but we have few children. The killing was so abundant that we became a dying race so the fey decided on using the great magic to make us disappear from the eyes of anything not fey. The elves…"

"Elves. Don't tell me there are elves also!"

"Yes elves and ye be looking a little like them to. I no longer know if they exist although. They led us in the great magic and made us disappear in the eyes of our enemies. Little did we realize that it would also take away all of our abilities to reproduce, but at least we be no longer hunted. It has been eons since I have seen another fey so when I came across ye I was ecstatic. I have been with ye for a long time Michele. At first, ye didn't even hear me, even when I screamed to ye, but I felt the kindred in ye so I persisted. I be so happy ye finally found the fey in yeself!" She dives down around my neck giving me the best hug that her tiny figure can.

"How long do you fey live?" I ask dazed at what she has been telling me.

"Almost forever."

"Almost forever, then how can there be so few."

Sorcha flies up to my eye level. "We can still die by accident and some just fade away when they get tired of living. It has been so many years since I have met another of my kind and even I was getting to the point where hopelessness was starting to overwhelm me." Another dive down she takes, however this time she ends up inside my t-shirt where the playful Sorcha commences to tickle me.

Peeling in laughter I try to free myself of my mischievous friend.

"I will never leave ye again Michele. Wherever ye go, I go." Sorcha pipes up once we finally settle down from our play.

"It is nice to have a friend Sorcha. Thank you for being here for me and now that we can talk..." I turn to kiss my new friend, engulfing her head, which starts another round of play housing.

Chapter Ten

"The bitch. That's how the humans are learning about us." Vladimir exclaims in fury.

He had just finished watching a newscast where Queen Sophie was the headline news. The news did not report her as a Siren, and he has no doubt that this is a little bit of information that she is not going to give up. The newscast had gone on about her visit to the upcoming G9 Summit being held in Washington in three days. The newscaster proclaimed her as the monarch of some country that was of such insignificant that it had never before been worth even marking it on maps, never mind newsworthy.

He knows better. The "woman" is of a species he had not seen for hundreds of years. So long in fact, that it was his hope that they had finally passed from the face of the earth.

Sirens and brood have been at war for hundreds of years. Who started it or why no longer mattered for now only hatred existed between them. Therefore, it takes only a very small leap for him to associate the siren with the human's obvious growing knowledge of the brood. Never once did he consider that the human's knowledge might be due to his own mismanagement of his brood.

The fact that Sirens have long since been their natural enemy is not the only cause of his hatred. The intensity of his natural hatred increased tenfold when he had gone after one for his breeding program. He had mistakenly cornered the High Queen and her party of ten elites. It had cost him almost eighty of his brood to finally subdue the queen. She had been a grand prize. However, the cost had been more than he had wanted to pay. In fact, he still blamed her for weakening of his brood, which in turn was in part responsible for his loss of Europe.

"I want her dead Edward, her and any other Sirens with her. Use whatever resources you have to, just bring me her head."

"As you wish Master. I will get on it right away."

"Don't fail me in this as you did the girl Edward."

"I won't Master."

Edward bows his way out of Vladimir's office and then hurries off quickly to get things in order. She is to be here in three days so that means he only has a couple to get everything ready… two days, not hardly enough time. He would be lucky if he could get twenty or thirty of the brood gathered in two days. Vladimir still tends to forget how big America is and how thinly spread out the brood are.

He was there the day when Vladimir had captured the High Queen for his breeding program. He saw the brood fall beneath them like wheat to a scythe. As such, he knows that taking the High Queen with bare hands with only twenty or thirty is not nearly enough to guarantee success. He will have to do as the humans do, he finally decides; use guns. Guns are such a great equalizer and twenty or thirty of them should make short work of this job.

Sometimes the human's propensity towards annihilation can be so useful. Edward grins as he thinks about the eons that humans have been designing new and better ways of killing each other.

Thinking of humans reminds Edward about his last visit with specimen 101849. He has finally gotten pass the point where the creature tries to tear his head off whenever he goes to his cell. It had surprised him to discover that the creature had some intelligence. Once he discovered this he even started having discussions with it.

Shortly thereafter he had started the training. It has turned out to be a slow process. However it has been progressing nicely.

Quickly deciding on his priorities Edward makes a detour to the holding pens.

Boris has just seen the newscast of Queen Sophie. Like Vladimir he has no love for Sirens, although his hatred does not run so deep. He does know about Vladimir's deep-seated hatred for them however and as such he is worried about Vladimir's potential reaction to the queen.

A few hundred years ago, he, as did most of the other forefathers came to the realization that humans bred too fast. They bred faster than they could feed on them. By the time the brood came to that realization it was too late to reverse the trend and not even the couple of world wars they helped along was enough to keep their food chain from becoming over abundant. With the over population of their food chain came the discovery of the brood and that was followed by the human's rage.

It was then that it was decided that it was time to pull back from the world to give the humans a chance to forget about them again. It was his suggestion of pulling back long before the last couple of world wars that was the basis of his and Vladimir's disagreement that caused the battle for Europe, which he eventually won. He should have destroyed Vladimir completely when given the chance. Instead the council had intervened, so he had set him afloat, forever banishing him from Europe. He never thought Vladimir would make it through the journey, however even if he did, he had not been worried for nothing lived on the land that Vladimir had been banished to except a few savages. Another mistake he has had to deal with for he never expected that land to become such a beehive of activity.

He has been careful in Europe. He has ruled his brood fairly and with an iron fist. He had insisted in spreading his brood thinly over Europe to keep the humans unconcerned or at least no more concerned than normal over the occasional dead they found. Whereas Vladimir is still under the misguided assumption that the brood are still lord of the realm, and as such, he gives his brood free rein over their feeding grounds.

There is no denying that Vladimir and his brood have been very lucky and for the most part has been able to stem the flow of their knowledge, but he can't help feeling that has come to an end. Human knowledge of brood has now become a very real possibility and they are starting to retaliate.

So far, the retaliation has been limited to a few encounters here and there and mostly without success. However, knowing humans the way he does he knows that won't last.

One or two of the brood have been caught from time to time. Yet so far, there has been no world resounding scream to eliminate them. In fact, most of the humans still don't believe in their existence, making it so much easier for them to continue preying on them for food. All that can and most likely will change if Vladimir went after the sirens, as he is sure he will.

"I don't like it Thomas. Do you think that she even knows that Vladimir has control of that land?"

"I doubt it Master. Of all the brood that the sirens hate, Vladimir is on the top of the list so if she knew he was there she would be coming with many more Sirens than they reported as coming."

"Unless she is keeping the true numbers from them."

"That's possible, yet I don't believe it is likely Master."

"Then why is she doing this Thomas?"

"Maybe she thinks it is time her Sirens came back into the world."

"Can she really think the humans have become cultivated enough to accept them?"

Thomas shrugs in response.

"We can't have him doing this. Even if the humans are willing enough to accept that Sirens live in their world, they will never accept wholesale knowledge of the brood. I am sure he is going to make a play for her and when he does, he is going to crack wide open everything I have been working towards for the last couple of hundred years."

"What can we do Master. North America is his and he can do with it as he pleases."

"Don't you think I know that dam it? I can't have him just fling us out there. We either have to do something to stop him or make it seem like humans are responsible... That's it Thomas. I want you to gather a force of mercenaries, no better yet get a force of those stupid Taliban together. Fly them to America with whatever promises you can. Vladimir has no imagination for this sort of thing and I'm certain he will go after her at the airport. Here's what we will do…"

"Please mother. You know I will be of help. I know more about the humans than anybody else and you know it." Mariyah tells her mother for the hundredth time.

Queen Sophie sighs. How did she ever spawn such a wilful child? "They are only allowing me four escorts Mariyah. The queens are insisting that they be…"

"I know what the queens want, but what if everything does not go as plan. You are going to need someone who knows about the human world and what if our cousin doesn't make herself known. Then what. Have you any idea how to proceed?"

Queen Sophie hates it when her daughter is right. Still, she loathes the idea of letting her daughter leave the island even more so she tries again. "You haven't even taken your warrior chaste yet. All you do is study. Don't get me wrong as the future High Queen your education will be valuable, but you need to acquaint yourself of all the chaste."

"We have not had a need for our warriors for hundreds of years Mother."

"And yet, here we find ourselves in the middle of one, surrounded by warships and about to step foot in the human land. We are lucky that not all our women feel the same way you do for I have a feeling this is not going to end well. Your plan is good, but I fear that the humans are greedy."

"All the more reason you will need me with you."

"The Queens will not like the two of us going. What if something were to happen."

"Mother!"

"And if you go that will be one less warrior."

"Mother!"

"And the humans can't be trusted."

"Mother...!

"You're not going to give up on this are you?"

"Please mother. You know it's the right thing to do."

"I will allow it on one condition." Queen Sophie states after releasing a resigned sigh.

"Anything."

"When we get back you must go through the warrior chaste and I am speaking to you as your High Queen now, not your mother."

Mariyah does her best to keep from jumping in joy at finally wearing her mother down. "Thus I swear My Queen."

The call comes first thing in the morning for us to gather in the operation center. Once gathered, Neely gives us our assignment and any information they have gathered to date.

"We have picked up a lot of chatter over the last couple of days. We are not certain it has anything to do with the Siren Queen, however after yesterday we are not taking any chances. They keep calling her "she" and other unflattering names. At first we thought they were talking about you Michele, but the chatter continued all night long so we now suspect it is the Queen they are talking about. Apparently they are not happy about her revealing herself after such a long time. They are even blaming her on us knowing about them and they are less than happy about her talking to us at the summit. So far we have what sounds like four groups involved. The first seems to be led by someone called Vladimir and from what we are hearing it is obvious that his hatred for this queen runs deep. There is every indication that he is going to try something at the summit so security has been tightened and we need you guys to be in top form." He stops to make sure we are paying attention before continuing.

Sorcha picks that opportunity to tell me that Vladimir is the Sire, the boss so to speak of the U.S. vampire group and that yes he has a deep hatred for the sirens. His hatred for them goes even deeper than what is natural between the two races. If anybody, she goes on to say, is going to make a move on the queen it would be him. Before I know what I am doing I am relaying this information to the group causing them to stare at me as if I have grown a second head.

I ignore them as Sorcha continues to relay information, which I continue to share. "It is rumoured that Vladimir once captured a Siren Queen. He lost quite a few of his brood capturing her, however it was after, when the rest of the sirens discovered what he did that he really felt their wrath. For a hundred years they hunted his brood and destroyed them whenever they could."

They are staring at me even more wide-eyed now. The silence stretches on for a couple of minutes before General Macklin speaks up. "Where is this coming from Michele?"

I stare daggers at Sorcha. It's all her fault, for if she would not have said something I would have kept my mouth shut. I have to think of something however. Sigh, another lie…

"Something happened to me after the attack yesterday, and no don't ask. Trust me you would not believe me, even Mom would have trouble believing me and if you have learned anything from our time here you know the true depth of that statement. I don't want to start a debate, nor do I think this is a time for argument. Trust me that if any information comes my way I will reveal it, for it's going to be my ass as well as theirs on the line out there."

"Okay we can deal with that so what else can you tell us?"

"Not much, until you talk about it I know nothing. It just pops to me." I finish lamely.

"How good is this information you seem to be getting?"

I think about that for a few seconds before replying. "I don't know. I can tell you what comes to me and you can decide what, if any value it has."

"Well don't be shy about sharing." General Macklin tells me and then nods to Neely to continue.

"The second group is led by someone called Boris. We picked up on his name a couple nights before you were attacked Michele. He does not like the queen either, but apparently he is more worried about what actions this Vladimir is going to take against her than in the queen herself. There was mention of using the Talibian to stop Vladimir from… what did he say, yes here it is, from doing something stupid. We picked up one real nugget from him. It seems that these vampires have been keeping themselves hidden from us on purpose for a couple of hundred years so we will forget about them. What is interesting and worrisome at the same time is that they are talking about a cleansing and getting their overpopulated food chain back under control. That is a worry for another day however." Neely looks to me to see if I have anything to input, which I do for Sorcha has been relying it to me even as he was speaking.

I cock my head toward Sorcha as she continues to fill me in. Now that I can understand her she is being a font of information. "He's the Sire of the European vampires. He does not like the sirens any more than Vladimir. Sirens and vampires are natural enemies. Interestingly enough Boris and Vladimir hate each other. Apparently they warred over Europe a few hundred or so years ago. Boris won, mostly because the sirens had depleted Vladimir's vampires, which may be the cause for Vladimir's deep hatred of the sirens. Vladimir was banished to the North American continent after he lost. There are three other Sires. One rules over England, a Lydia Hall another in Africa, Zubair Okeke. Morrell Diaz is Sire of South America and Chin Chan is Sire of the Asian brood. " I finish dry mouthed at what they may be thinking of this information magically popping out of my mouth.

"That is more information that what we have been able to gather in two years Michele. We are really going to have to talk about where this information is coming from when you get back from the U.S." General Macklin states in the ensuing silence.

"The third group we picked up on came from some chatter in the U.S. Somebody called Raymond has some interest in the queen, but even more interest in you Michele. We have no idea why, but it sounds as if he has been watching you since you were a child. We have no reason to think he is going to interfere in this operation as he has yet to make a move on you or any of us, however I want you to keep your eyes open out there and if it looks like his actions are going to risk the queen's life we need you to separate yourself from the unit, understand?"

"Yes Sir." I reply all primp and proper. "And his name is Raymond Clarkson. He is the Alpha of the U.S. werewolf pack. He has no particular liking for Sirens, however he hates the vampires even more. Like the sirens, they are natural enemies of the vampires. They too warred in Europe with the vampires, but that war was one meant to eradicate the vampires not to take over a country. I have no idea why he is interested in me except for some rumours that have been floating around for the last few years; rumours that I can't quite put my finger on."

This earns me a real eyeing from the group. This is all interesting information that Sorcha is giving me, but what really catches my attention is the term Alpha. Darren had called me that yesterday... I stuff that piece of information aside for later consideration.

"The last group is another group that we have not heard of before. They are located somewhere in Europe and led by a man called Dominic, or so we have come to believe. Their interest seems to be nothing more than to see what it is the queen wants to say to us. This queen coming out must be a big thing for it is all any of these groups are talking about so we have to assume that what she told us when she first made contact with us is true."

"Dominic Sabatino, Alpha of the European werewolves. He and Raymond tolerate each other as much as two Alpha's can do so. Apparently two Alpha's can't stand to be close to each other for extended periods of time so they tend to avoid each other. Dominic is said to rule his pack with an iron fist, while Raymond tends to be more democratic about it."

I hear General Macklin groan as I rely this information and I can't blame him. I also know that he is not groaning because of the information itself, but where I am getting all this from. I look to him and give him a wan smile before I turn my attention back to Neely.

"I know I don't have to say this, but I am going to do so anyway. Nothing must happen to this queen while she is in the U.S…"

Neely continues on for a while. I lose much of it as the mention of Dominic's name occupies my thoughts. Darren had mention it yesterday and had said that Dominic would not be happy with either him or I so I'm hoping that Neely is right and we are not going to have to worry about him also.

I have come to the decision that I am not so fond of flying, especially in an Air Force transport. They are uncomfortable and noisy, not to mention a real ear popping pain in the ass. Sorcha does not find it any better and has already told me in no uncertain terms that there is no way that I am ever going to talk her into taking another one. The next time, she tells me she will follow, or better yet fly ahead instead of ride.

Our role in this assignment is simple. At least it sounds simple for all we have to do is protect the Queen and her escorts while they are in Washington.

We still don't know what Queen Sophie has to say to the U.N. In fact, it is doubtful that anybody knows what it is this queen wants to relay to the U.N. countries. All that is known for sure is that she requested to have her speech telecasted to countries not in attendance. A request they are currently working on to fulfill. Communication is the "bosses" problem however. Ours is to make sure that the queen doesn't get even so much as a scratch between now and then, even if she threatens world war.

Arriving into the U.S. we are immediately taken to the hotel where the queen will be staying. The whole of the top floor has been reserved for her and we are not there for more than a few seconds when we are put to work.

Any of us that had hoped to do some sightseeing that evening are sorely disappointed for Riley, the man in The Pit back home is in charge of the operation and he denies all of our requests. He has us test the personal assigned to guard excess rooms and doors, not once but a couple of times and then scour every room from one end to another.

It turns out to be a pain in the ass. A thousand men and women are brought forward to have a quick chat with me. We have learned some of what it is that sets off men and women against me during my time in The Hole so most of the personal picked for this has already passed a basic criteria, happily married and none involved in rocky relationships that is, so it is not as bad as it could have been. Still, it makes for a long and gruelling night for we have yet to perfect the selection process.

When I finally get to retreat to my assigned room that night I feel worn to a frazzle and yet restlessly awaiting Queen Sophie's arrival I take to talking to Sorcha as we lay on the bed. "Do you know anything about Queen Sophie Loreral and Sirens."

"Some." Sorcha replies with a tired sigh.

"So tell me what you know Sorcha?"

"Sleep Michele."

"I can't sleep. Please."

Sorcha flies onto my chest and gives me a tired look. "A short history then. What I know is that much of what ye humans know about Sirens holds a degree of truth and mostly because the sirens have indeed been luring humans to them with their beauty and songs for centuries."

"Where did they come from?"

"That is something that is much debated. There is no real proof for they just seemed to appear. Rumours have it that the sirens were the original Amazon warriors."

"Amazons?"

"Ai. In the height of their power the amazons were warriors through and through. They were never known for their hand-to-hand combat, however give them a broad leaf spear or sword of almost any design and they were lethal. They lived and breathed war until they were forcefully retired, which usually only happened when they were severely injured. Once retired their sole purpose became the breeding of more warriors, and to that end they would search far and wide for not only

men of courage and strength, but also beauty. Male
children were given away, usually to be raised by
peasants, females were kept to repopulate their
army and finally to breed their own children. If it
had not been for the arrogance of the one called
Queen Ernesta Lombardi they may well have
conquered a goodly portion of Europe. As it was,
Queen Lombardi's arrogance and pride was the start
of their downfall for she had unwittingly crossed
swords and had words with Julius Caesar. Mind ye,
Julius was just as prideful and arrogant as Queen
Lombardi so maybe it be wrong to blame the
Amazon's downfall all on the queen alone, but such
is history."

"They fought. I have never heard of this."

"Ai, they fought long and hard. Caesar's
army was just coming into the height of its power
and Caesar cared little about the men he wasted, and
waste them on this war he did. Thousands upon
thousands died pushing back the queen and her
army. The last battle they fought the queen and her
army had the sea to their back and the might of the
Roman Empire to their fore."

"Why have I never heard about this before
Sorcha. I studied history and there has never been a
mention of the Roman Empire getting into a battle
with an army of women."

"The history of the Fey as recorded has it
that it was a historic battle whereas Roman history
all but wiped the battle from their records. They did
not want to be shamed in the eyes of the rest of the
world. The truth of the matter is that the Roman
Empire spent the lives of four thousand men against
the last five hundred Amazons before they finally
managed to push the amazons into the sea. That

battle alone lasted three days and when it was over everybody thought that was end of the amazons."

"Thought?"

"Ai. Years later rumours started that something intervened in that defining moment. Some claim it to be Eldin magic, others the magic of the Goddess they worshiped. Ye see, when the Amazon women were pushed into the sea they did not drown. The rumours claim that they were changed and swam away."

My eyebrows lift in doubt.

"Be truth." Sorcha replies when she sees my look. "For years there was no sign of them, in fact as far as history was concerned the Amazon race died that day. We of the long-lived know better and we knew we be right when years later, sea faring men started telling tales of being enticed into the sea by mermaids."

"What does that have to do with the disappearance of the Amazons?"

"Before the Amazons disappeared there had not been such a creature as a mermaid. The few men that survived the mermaid song claim that they were taken to underwater grottos where they spent their time in leisure and loving. It be hundreds of years after the tales of the mermaids commenced and then dwindled, that those of the sirens began."

Long tale completed, Sorcha settles onto my breast. "Mind ye, what I tell ye may not be accurate as both the mermaids and sirens were a secretive race that kept itself hidden away from the going on of the world."

"If they are so secretive and have managed to keep themselves hidden for so long, why now?"

"That be a real puzzle. I can't say as to why Queen Sophie has suddenly decided that it be time to bring the knowledge of the sirens back into the world. Mind ye, it is not like she doesn't do that from time to time. The last was in the time of King Author's rein when she was known as The Lady of the Lake and yet I have heard naught of much importance happening in the world right now to warrant her actions."

"Yikes! You're pulling my leg."

"I be nowhere near ye leg."

"I mean you're stretching the truth."

"Why would I do that?"

The tale and impact of what she has so casually told me stuns me into a long silence. I find it hard to believe that the history of the world, as I know it, could be so wrong. If it were not for the fact that this fiery little fairy is quickly becoming the best friend I have ever had, I simply would refuse to believe what she is telling me.

Then there is me. What am I? I have already admitted to myself and had it proven by the military that I am more than human, if human at all. Sorcha calls me kindred, however what she means by that is still hazy. Long discussions between us have resulted in very little insight to this except... well except that is exactly what we feel like, kindred. If push came to shove, I would be as hard pressed as Sorcha to explain it, so I have already accepted it as just another one of my oddities since my change.

"You and I are going to have longer talks someday for I feel that there is much you can teach me Sorcha." I manage when I get my thoughts back in order.

"I will spend the next couple of hundred years teaching ye if ye like my friend."

"Couple of hundred years!"

"Of course… there is so much to learn Michele. Get away from these humans and ye and I can spend all the time we want in learning from the past and watching what unfolds in the future."

"You know I can't just disappear Sorcha. I cannot abandon my family, no matter how much I wish to."

"I understand and I be sorry. It was careless of me to even mention it."

"What did you mean by a couple of hundred years?" This is the part of Sorcha's statement that really bothers me for I have never given any thought to my life expectancy.

"Ye be Fey Michele. We live a very long life, almost immortal in the natural sense. We went over this remember."

"But…"

"But what?" Sorcha asks kindly, no doubt seeing my look of panic.

"That will mean that I will watch my parents grow old and die, while I will not age a day."

"Ai Michele, but that be the way of the world, regardless if ye are human or not. It is the natural order of life for children to watch their parents age and then pass. That will be ye natural order also, if ye don't let these humans get ye killed that is."

"I guess I never thought of it before. I don't know what I will do without Mom and Dad."

"Ah, but ye are young yet. When ye grow out of ye childhood ye thoughts will be more ordered." She replies much too smugly.

"And how long will that take?"

"A couple of hundred years."

I stare daggers at her and then pounce. I need to stop thinking for I know that if I dwell on what she has just told me I will become paralysed with hopelessness. Let it sink in slowly instead of letting the unknown drive me crazy has become my recent motto.

Noon the next day finds us sweating it out on the Tarmac. We have searched the entire area over twice and feel pretty secured in the fact that nobody is there that is not suppose to be. All personal have been evacuated except for us, which did not go over particularly well with a couple of senators or the multitude of reporters. As a first line of defence, a hundred U.S. soldiers have all the access points to the tarmac blocked and anybody foolish enough to get past them is fair game to whatever we want to deal out. Two black limos await the queen's arrival, and the drivers of these limos are no happier than the senators at being replaced. They did not argue long however for you only argue so far when faced with the borehole of a M16. We have just been informed that the Queen's plane has landed making all of us thankful that the long hot wait is coming to an end.

A Learjet 85 comes to a stop only a short way from our position. We wait as the pilot shuts down the engine and then disappears into the back of the jet. A few minutes later, the door opens and stairs come down.

We had been told what to expect, we had even been shown what to expect, however nothing could have prepared us for the reality. The first four women out of the plane are obviously bodyguards or at least acting the role.

I can't help but think that this is a perfect role for these women for nobody, man or woman would ever dream of hurting someone so beautiful looking as these; well except the crazed women I amend my thinking.

The women are dressed in loose fitting outfits, which do little to hide their shapely bodies. They are all approximately five foot ten to eleven inches tall. Their legs look long, their hips wide, their waist trim, and their breasts outstanding. Their bodies are perfection, magnificent to behold.

However, it is when you get past those bodies that the blood starts to boil. Their hair range in colour from a dark, lush brown to black, all are of waist length and flowing around their faces as if it has a life of its own. Their eyes are a deep sea green colour like my own, that are capable of trapping and sucking in a person's soul. Their cheekbones are high and perfect. Their noses and chins a plastic surgeon's dream outcome and their lips so full that I ache to see them smile.

I am convinced that these women are the most beautiful ladies I have ever had the pleasure to lay eyes on, and I am not the only one for the rest of the unit stand as speechless as me. That is until Queen Sophie makes her appearance.

Once again we are caught flat-footed. The pictures of Queen Sophie did not even come close to preparing us for the truth of her beauty. Rich red hair flows around her, her eyes a deeper green than the others, her cheekbones higher, her lips fuller and the tighter clothing shows much more of the shapely body and legs. Like the others, it is the eyes that draw and capture a person. They are ancient and yet they have a twinkle of mischievousness in them that makes the whole of her beautiful face come to life.

An ear-piercing squelch in our earpieces manages to free us from our paralysis.

During our briefing it had been decided that it would be best if a woman took the lead with the sirens so Andrea walks forward and graciously apologizes to the queen for the lack of a proper welcoming and escort, however considering the circumstances it was deemed to keep their contact with us to a minimum.

"Of course my dear, but if you will excuse me for a minute." Queen Sophie interrupts Andrea's pre-arranged speech.

I start to fidget for Queen Sophie was looking directly at me when she put a hasty stop to Andrea's speech and now she walks towards me. God help me, I feel a connection to her. However, I have the overwhelming feeling that something is amiss. The woman is regal in every way. Her posture demands obedience and yet something deep inside me screams that I should never bow to this queen. Sorcha is not being of much help either, for she has become a statue upon my shoulder.

"Cousin. Only in my prayers did I imagine it would be this easy. How is it that you come to be here?"

I try my best to ignore the traitorous thoughts rattling around my brain and bring my concentration back to Queen Sophie. As it is, it takes a few seconds to register what it was that she actually said to me.

"Cousin? I'm sorry I don't understand Queen Sophie?"

"Of course cousin. Don't tell me… no I see that you don't. Well we can't have that. You will ride with me. What is your name child?"

I look to Andrea. This is not how things are supposed to be going. Andrea gives me the nod. "Michele Appleton and I would be honoured to accompany you."

"Excellent. You will be one of my personal guards then."

Needing to escape those piercing eyes of hers I move over to the black limo and open the door for her. "In that case, if you will get in we will make sure your bags are stowed away and then we can get you somewhere more comfortable."

Queen Sophie and two of her bodyguards get into the limo. The other two bodyguards get in the other. Once they are secured inside and the bags are loaded into the trunks, we go into action. Two of the unit take the driver's seat, another two settle into the front passenger seats, three into the armoured vehicle idling at the front of the line, two in the middle and two more in the rearmost armoured vehicle.

I have never been in a vehicle as lush as this limo. The carpets are so thick that my feet feel like they are sinking into the floor and the leather seat more comfortable than any sofa or chair I have ever sat on. I am just thinking how I could live in such luxury when my thoughts are interrupted.

"What are your orders Michele?" Queen Sophie's stern voice catches my attention.

"To protect you at all costs." I reply promptly and truthfully.

"All costs Michele. What if I decided that I wanted to harm some of your citizens? Would you still protect me at all costs?"

"Of course. Although I would hope that you would have no cause to harm them and that my method of protecting you from bodily harm if you did may surprise you into… oh let's just say not harming them." I reply with what I hope is a winning smile.

Queen Sophie's laughter causes me to heat up in places I don't want to think about or dwell upon.

"You are truly a cousin. Now I understand why they were so assured that they could provide me safe conduct. Where did you come from cousin? How is it that you are in the world of humans without our knowledge?"

"I really don't understand what it is you mean by calling me cousin or what it is you are asking." I finally manage, though the lump in my throat threatens to cut off my breathing.

Queen Sophie looks at me long and hard before replying. "Never mind that for now. We will have time to look into it later I think. For now, let me make you acquainted to your other cousins. The black haired vixen in the other car is my daughter Princess Mariyah, the women with her is Vani, and that is Capri." Queen Sophie points to the golden blonde haired beauty sitting beside her, "and that is Lia." Lia being the lush sable haired woman sitting next to me.

"Honoured…. cousins.' I try out the term causing smiles all around.

"Now that we know each other we can get down to business. I have a busy day tomorrow and as I have been allowed only today and tomorrow in this land we will not have much time to look around before I have to fly back home. Mariyah has an urge to see the White House that these people are so proud of as well as the Smithsonian that she has read much of. I have decided to indulge her. Can you arrange that for me Michele?"

"I will try Your Highness."

I pass on Queen Sophie's request to The Hole and it only takes a few minutes to obtain permission for her to visit the White House. In fact, the U.S. President turns out to be ecstatic that she has decided to visit. I'm only hoping he will feel the same way by the time we leave again.

We no sooner arrive at the White House when chaos breaks out. It certainly becomes a lesson learned. The sirens have barely left the car when men come running in adoration and women in hatred.

I am embarrassed at their behaviour, while the sirens find it delightful that much of this adoration is directed in my direction. Their ensuing smiles as they watched the men charging towards us causes pandemonium and it takes us a half-hour to get things back under control. Deciding not to take any more chances I am put on display again. I am not happy about it, but we have a mandate to fulfill so I bear it. We finally manage to evacuate the premises of everyone except those mostly immune.

As expected the President has to use the opportunity to meet privately with Queen Sophie. That causes us some worry for we really do not want to have to take the U.S. President out of commission. It causes me even more worry for I am presented to him in advance of Queen Sophie. Therefore, if anyone is to take him out it will be George and I. That I am sure would not make us popular and yet I am more than ready to do so after what I had just gone through.

As it is, I do not have to restrain the president and we only have to put down a dozen of his Secret Service men. Something we are sure will do nothing for our popularity with the Secret Service or this country.

The queen and the president spent an hour together. Half of the unit spend this time cooling their heels outside his office, while the other half of us follow the rest of the sirens on their tour.

"It is nice to finally meet you Michele." The one called Princess Mariyah says to me as I follow them on the tour.

"Finally. I don't understand."

"Yes finally. Even though we did not know of you personally you have been the cause of much debate back home."

I look at her blankly, which causes her to give me that stunning smile of hers. "Twenty-five years ago the goddesses warned us of the existence of a Siren born that we lacked in acknowledging. That caused the veil between us and our goddesses to become obscure. Just over six weeks ago something changed that caused that veil to close even further. Finding you and acknowledging you is just as important to us as what mother has to say to the U.N. We never imagined it would be this easy to find you. I'm happy we have however for we have much to talk about and little time to do so."

There is not much I can say to that. I still don't understand a half of it and my brain has gone stupid at her stunning beauty so the best I manage is. "Well I'm glad I have made it easy for you."

Hard to believe that I am suppose to be a freaking genius after that reply. Thankfully, Princess Mariyah just gives me another of her winning smiles and then her attention is pulled away by something said by the fellow giving us the tour.

Her hour with the U.S. President must turn out to be satisfactory, or so Queen Sophie's smile when she leaves his office indicates. So meeting finished we gather them all up and get them in the limos to make our way to the Smithsonian.

Having learned from the White House and having the time it was decided to clear the Smithsonian of people before getting there ourselves. A request was made to the U.S. President during our tour of the White House to do just that. The request was initially frowned upon, however when the First Lady, who is getting along famously with the sirens, asks to tag along, well it is not easy to ignore the wishes of your country's First Lady or that of a queen who is surround by twelve people immune to your country's prosecution.

Therefore, by the time we get to the Smithsonian we only need to restrain a half dozen civilians who managed to be missed in the quick sweep, two military personal, one more Secret Service man, and two screaming, hate filled women, who I am sure will wake up with abysmal headaches.

Just as she did in the White House Princess Mariyah acts like a child in a playground on this tour. Her eyes are wide and bright. She is so full of questions that I start to wonder if she ever pauses to take a breath. Some of the questions seem so obvious to us that we have difficulty even understanding why she is asking, never mind trying to explain something so second nature that we hardly ever think as to the why of it.

Finally, it comes time to go to the hotel. I dread what we may have to go through to get them safely to their rooms, but having learned all day from the school of hard knocks this time we plan better.

Getting to the hotel we park by the external elevators. We make sure nobody is in the elevator or in the vicinity before allowing Queen Sophie and her escorts out of the limos and then they are quickly ushered inside. Once inside, two lines of bodies block the front of the elevator as it ascends. Nobody gets in and nobody sees what the line of bodies spread across the front hides. Up to the top floor we go without incident. Arriving at the top floor we stall the elevator while six of us move forward to do one more sweep of the queen's suite of rooms. Once that is declared cleared, Queen Sophie is allowed to enter and then we go through every crook and cranny on that floor one more time.

Concerned over what we may be facing tomorrow I radio in. "Are we sure that everybody that is physically going to be at the U.N tomorrow has been tested against the Queen's picture?"

"Yes Michele and now that we have even more pictures of her and her entourage we can do further testing. As you know it is not perfect, however it is the best we can do for now." Dad replies, surprising me for I had no idea he was in The Pit.

"Good, because I am really getting tired of this."

Dad chuckles for a long time before answering. "Not feeling so much of a Goddess now are we."

It takes me a second to remember why he would say such a thing. I flash back to our first night in the apartment after my change, which in turn makes me chuckle. "Love you Dad and give Mom a hug for me."

It has made for a long tiring day and the last hour of going over every aspect of this floor has made it even more tiring. I have just finished the last sweep of the Queen's chambers and I'm done in. Queen Sophie is safely in her room. The entire floor has been checked and cleared. Men and women previously tested to see how they react to me block the elevator, the stairs, and guard every doorway down the hall. Two members of the unit block the queen's door and will do so throughout the night. All that is left is for me to get some sleep before my turn to guard the door comes.

As we have to be ready to move on a moment's notice we have been assigned the rooms next to the Queen's for the evening, and in that room resting is where I want to be right now.

"Unless you need anything else this will be a goodnight Your Highness." And even though I still have the feeling that I should not be bowing to this queen, I give her a tired half bow anyway.

"But you must not. There is much you must learn. I insist that they release you of your duties for the night as you must join us for our meal so that we can get to know our cousin as our cousin can get to know us." Queen Sophie states with a prolong pout.

"I would be honoured my Queen, but it has been a tiring day." And honoured I really would be for I want to learn what, if anything these ladies can reveal of me. However, I am exhausted and it would be poor taste if I fell asleep during the meal.

"Nonsense. You are of size of Lia no?"

I give the siren called Lia the eye, wondering what Queen Sophie is thinking. "I suppose."

"Good. Lia why don't you get her a gown and while you do…"

Lia leaves to do her queen's bidding and while I wait the queen commences a low soft song. At first, it is only a whisper on the breeze, however as the revitalizing energy of the beautiful song soaks into me I come to hear it much more clearly. The song is in a language I do not recognize, however the voice behind that song is easily the sweetest yet most powerful voice I have ever had the pleasure of hearing. That voice can do no wrong, it calls for me to come, it fills me with energy, and it makes me one with her.

I am not sure how long the song flows through my body or how long I lose myself in its melody with my eyes closed and body trembling, however it is long enough that when I manage to pry open my eyes, Lia is back with a colourful silk gown. More of a surprise is that a short time ago I was ready to crash and burn, but now I feel as if I have the energy to party all evening long.

"You are so much a cousin!" Princess Mariyah exclaims and then enfolds me in an embrace.

"Go wash and come back to us Michele. We have much to talk about." She whispers to me during that embrace.

"It will be my pleasure." And this time I mean it for fully revitalized I am ready to learn all I can about these women that insist on calling me cousin.

Promising to return soon, I make my way back to the room assigned to me, which I am sharing with Lori, who at twenty-three is not only one of the youngest members of the team, but also the most junior. I inform her that I am having supper with the queen and then tell her of Queen

Sophie's request to have me released of my duties for the evening.

"What do you think, will they give it to me?" I ask her worried.

"I think so. This is a perfect opportunity for us to learn about them."

"Can you make the call?"

"No problem. I'll put a good spin on it so go ahead and shower while I make the call."

"Thanks Lori."

She waves me away so I head for the bathroom for a quick shower.

"Ye be drowning me again!" Sorcha's high pitch voice complains.

"If you're going to keep insisting on having a shower with me we really need to figure something out." I reply indignant.

Sorcha is taking this never leave you again thing too far. It is a pain in the ass, yet I actually feel sorry for her loneliness. When she started showering with me I put up a little bit of a stink, however I have an idea of what it is like to be the only one of something so I really did not put up much of a fight, in fact, I gave up trying to shoo her away after the second shower and have become resigned to never having a shower alone again. The problem we have not been able to resolve is that the shower, while perfect for me is like a rushing waterfall for Sorcha, making it impossible for her to keep to wing. Therefore, she has to stand on my shoulder and hang onto my hair during our showers, which of course results in me having to be careful of how I let the water splash on me or how I wash my hair and shoulder.

I am getting use to it however, so the two of us manage to finish showering without any major mishaps. I dry off and then dress, or at least try to. It is not until I unfold the gown that I realize I have a couple of problems. The first is the army issue underwear, which is all I packed, looks ugly as hell compared to the gown. I would have worn them anyway, however right away I see that is not an option for when I put the gown against my skin I discover that I am able to see through the gown to the underwear below. Furthermore, the design of the gown is such that it is meant to be worn without a bra, so off comes bra and panty.

The next problem I encounter is that I am not even sure if I am putting the dam thing on correctly. Luckily, Sorcha is somewhat familiar with the style of gown, which to me looks a lot like the type worn by Hawaiian women I have seen on television. A few minutes of fiddling and we finally manage to get the gown wrapped and tied.

Hair blow-dried and a touch of makeup later I admire myself in the mirror. I still find it hard to believe the change in me, from dud to goddess, or so I still think of myself, and this time my change along with the incredible beauty of the gown with its vibrant colours of blue and greens takes my breath away.

When I exit the bathroom I discover that Lori has the same opinion of the gown for she spends some time admiring me, although her comment about the "silky thing hugging my body so tightly as to make it appear non-existence" gives me some pause.

Oh well it's not as if I have far to go.

"The Pit gave you the night off or should we say the night to learn what you can." Lori tells me still grinning after she has admired and teased me for a time.

"Great! Ah Lori, is this gown really okay?"

"It's magnificent and you look good in it. Too good in fact so watch yourself out there."

"Thanks Lori. See you later."

I manage to get back into Queen Sophie's quarters without having to kill anybody or getting too much of a teasing from Gazinno and Knoll who pulled the first shift at the queen's door this evening.

Once inside I see that the rest of them have also changed and that they wear the same type of gown as me, yet I can't help thinking that theirs look so much better on them. Capri gives me a critical look and then smiling friendly she comes over to readjust my gown; I glare at Sorcha who gives me an insolent shrug.

"You do not need any of that." Princess Mariyah tells me as she wipes away the little makeup I had put on.

Deeming me suitably prepared, we sit down to a lavish meal. The meal consists of lobsters, crabs, prawns, shrimps, and a variety of other seafood. The food is succulent and easily the best that I have ever had the pleasure of eating; Mariyah, go figure, pronounces it edible.

The drink chosen to accompany supper comes from their travel bags. Capri tells me that it is made on their island and is called Louval. The liquid is a dark green in colour and when I see it I almost turn green myself remembering my first few weeks in university where I drank myself silly on just such a green colour drink. The day after I swore that I would never drink it again.

Yet, not wanting to offend them I take the offered glass anyway. The drink turns out to be thick, sweet tasting, and heady. The first swallow burns down my throat and almost turns my stomach. Seeing my reaction to the drink they giggle friendly at me and then show me how to combine the drink with various morsels of seafood to soften the blow. It makes such a difference that before the meal is complete I fall in love with its sweetness.

The food and drink is excellent, however the conversation is better. The first topic of choice is trying to figure out who my birth mother could have been.

Queen Sophie explains to me that they keep a tight control on Siren births. When I ask why they would do such a thing she tells me about the limited size of their island and their long life span of a thousand plus years. The current population she goes on to say sits at just over two hundred thousand women and that is about as much as they can comfortably house and feed. I can understand the limited size island and I take that piece of information in easily. It is her claim that they live a thousand or more years that has me reeling. However, that does explain the look of ancient wisdom I had noticed in her eyes when we first met.

We spend more than a few frustrating minutes trying to figure out who my birth mother could have been and how, as they put it, I can even exist without them knowing about me. Queen Sophie claims that I resemble someone she once knew, however every effort to put her finger on who that may be is for naught.

Having no clue myself I am of no help so after a while, the question about who my mother can be is put aside. I am a little disappointed for I would have loved to learn that I had relatives somewhere. However, the following topic is just as interesting for they start telling me about their home.

I become engross in their home. The things they tell me seem unbelievable. Their island chain is approximately twice the size of the Hawaiian chain and located in the South Pacific. Why it has been undiscovered to this point, they tell me is due to their ability to turn men's minds away from what they think they see. Queen Sophie goes on to explain that if it were not for the current situation, it would have been the increase in female military personal that would have caused them to "come out" eventually.

The island chain itself is made of four islands, all tropical in nature, mores so on the southern islands than the northern. The island chain they call Ospizo. When I ask what the name means, Queen Sophie tells me that once they were a lost nation and that it had taken them many years to finally find a place that they could call their own again…. Hence the name, "Home".

The way they talk about living as one with the land, initially gives me the impression of some backwater place surviving a couple of hundred years in the past. This impression is dispelled when they begin to tell me about their cities, their advanced energy system, agriculture, scientific, and medical faculties. Two of the islands are rural in nature and two sport larger cities that if not as large as ours are on par with any city in the world, yet much more beautifully designed than what has ever been conceived by the humans or so Capri claims. Each island has its own speciality and they work together like a well-oiled machine to support the siren nation.

They go on to explain to me that unlike humans they build to blend and work with their natural environment, instead of forcing that environment to their will. The result is a simple looking and very comfortable lifestyle.

The next topic they go on to teach me about is the politic structure. Ospizo is ruled over by four Queens and one High Queen. The rule has been such from the day they claimed the island chain as their own and makes perfect sense for each island is ruled by a queen who concentrates and work for the betterment of their individual island in the chain, while at the same time contributing to the whole. The High Queen is there to make sure they play nice with each other. As Queen Sophie explains it, the rule of the individual islands belongs to the queens whereas the rule of the people themselves is her duty.

Therefore, Queen Sophie explains the need for interaction with the humans is not required for they produce everything they need to survive and if not for the current problem with the warships circling their islands they would have been happy to keep things as is for the foreseeable future.

"Not to be disrespectful or anything, but why are you telling me all this?" I finally ask.

Queen Sophie finally decides to drop a bombshell. "The real reason we contacted the humans was because of you Michele. We will tell them something else tomorrow, which in part is the truth. However, we have been leading their warships in circles for months now and could have done so indefinitely or chosen to do away with the women on those ships that keep leading them back to us."

"Why would you even bother with me?" I ask, trying not to think about what "doing away with the women" meant.

Queen Sophie looks at me so long in silence that I start to squirm. "Whether you believe it or not, you are a Siren Michele and as we have already explained we Sirens control the birth of children very rigorously, so the first problem is how is it possible that you can exist without us knowing about you. The second problem, which I believe my daughter has already told you a little about, is that our seer told us that something is disturbing our bond to the goddesses. That can only happen if there is a Siren alive that we have not acknowledged. We searched to make sure all of our women were accounted for. Not finding anyone not accounted for we then started to question births, however we found no problems there either. You see Michele you simply cannot exist."

"I am sorry to be the cause of so many problems Your Highness."

"Not problems my dear just confusion and it goes deeper than your birth. Our seer tells us that it is more than your unexplained existence that is causing the tremble in the veil. She warned us of the first tremor just over twenty-five years ago, and then felt it again and yet more strongly just over six weeks ago. Since then our link to the goddesses has been obscured. No more can she give us for the goddesses have not been forthcoming. You are Siren however and as I said earlier, it seems that I can almost recognize your mother in you."

"I don't understand how the birth of one person can cause so much trouble." I answer perplexed yet worried, for the time frames mentioned are too close for comfort.

"That is because you do not know the siren part in you Michele. The life of every Siren forms an intricate link to the goddesses and any disturbance in that link is felt, first by the seers and then by the population as a whole if it becomes too great. In order to fix the veil we have to at least acknowledge your birth and that is why we made contact with the humans. We knew that if we made our existence known that you would find us. The Siren in you would demand it. We just didn't expect it to be so easy." Queen Sophie's statement causes a ripple of laughter from everyone in the room.

"Then I am glad that I was able to make some things easy for you and now all should be as it should."

"You must come home with us." Queen Sophie states suddenly.

The comment stuns me. I am so tempted to take up that offer until I remember that my parents are being held on my good behaviour. Even knowing it is impossible for me to accept her offer, it still takes me a couple tries to get out a simple. "I can't."

"Can't or won't?"

"Can't. I'm really sorry. Your home sounds wonderful and I would love to see it, but I can't."

"What is it that is keeping you here?" An excited Princess Mariyah asks.

My mouth opens and closes a few times. I feel like they are family already, however, how can I tell them the real reason why I cannot go with them and if I do what would or could they do. Finally, I settle for a half-truth.

"I have to take care of my parents. They taught me how to love. Without them…." I finish with a shiver.

"You can bring them. I would even allow your father to accompany you."

I release a long frustrated sigh. "If only things were that simple. I would love nothing more than to just disappear right now, however things are not as they seem."

"Are you in need of help cousin?" The beautiful Vani asks and I so want to scream yes to the world.

"No, the time has not yet come for that, but thank you. However, if you could leave that offer and the offer to come to your islands open it would be much appreciated."

"I can and will, yet… and look at me Michele." Queen Sophie puts her finger under my chin to make sure she has all of my attention. "This offer is for you and your parents only, if they so desire. It is not for any other human or for you to come to our home to work for the humans. You will understand more tomorrow after I speak to them I think."

"Of course Your Highness."

"Good and enough serious talk for now. We have acknowledged you Michele and taught you a little about our land, maybe that will be enough to please the goddesses. There is much more I would teach you about us… about you. However, our visit is short so there is no time to teach you everything it means to be a Siren on this visit. There is some we can and will teach you if you are willing and swear not to pass that knowledge on to the humans."

"I swear!"

"Not so fast. This oath is binding. It will be sealed with magic and to break the oath will result in grave consequences. This is a secret that only those who are Sirens are permitted to know. So do you still want to swear?"

"Oh God yes Your Highness. I need to learn about myself. So much has happened to me lately and most of the time I feel lost in my own skin."

"Then swear on the Goddess Aphrodite that you will never share with anyone that is not Siren what you learn this evening."

"Does she actually exist?"

"Don't be pert child or you may discover the truth the hard way." The smile that Queen Sophie gives me does not match the sternness of her voice, however it still sobers me up.

"I do swear Your Highness."

"Excellent. Now come to me and seal the oath."

Even though I feel it should be the other way around I kneel in front of Queen Sophie. She bends forward and placing her hand gently behind my head she draws my lips to her own. I almost swoon. It is not so much the feel of Queen Sophie's full lips against my own that makes my head dizzy. It is the feeling of the electrifying tingle that passes between us.

Is this what magic feels like? I really didn't credit her talk about magic, but I can feel…

The force of the sealing causes such a backlash that I find myself sitting on my butt. "Wow, that was awesome!" I manage after a few shakes to clear my head.

"Awesome." Queen Sophie raises an eyebrow and breaks out in laughter. "I can't say that I have ever heard it called that before."

I see this as my opening. All night I have been embarrassed to find my eyes going to the tops of the breasts of these well-endowed women. I have been trying not to look with little success so now that she has promised to teach me I become bold. What keeps drawing my attention is that all of them except Mariyah have fanciful tattoos of naked women imprinted on the swells of their breasts.

"May I ask a question then?"

"Of course."

"What are those? You all have them except Mariyah. Is there a special meaning behind them?" I ask, pointing to their breasts.

Once more Queen Sophie's laugh is friendly. "The meaning of these I am afraid I cannot tell you. However, if and when you decide to come to Ospizo that will change. Either that or when you discover the truth for yourself."

"But I thought…"

"Sorry Michele, but not this. You are not ready for it yet and there are much more important things we must teach you. Lia, if you would be so kind as to do us the honours we can start teaching our cousin her music." Queen Sophie stands and offers me her hand.

"Music, but I thought… oh!" I clue in before I make too much of a fool of myself.

Lia returns from the bedroom with an instrument that resembles a guitar. The instrument has sixteen strings, wooden pegs, and a pregnant looking body. It looks very old and at the same time very well cared for.

"Once you learn you will not require an instrument. Tonight it will help you with the learning process by keeping you in sync with the songs."

"I warn you I sing like a frog." I say truthfully, for having been told a hundred times or more that I suck I have been careful not to sing in years.

"Nonsense, no Siren sings like a frog. Close your eyes and listen. Feel the music thrumming across your skin and flowing through your body. We are music Michele. Our very essence is made up of music. Music comes from the land, the stars, even the very air that we breathe. This is one of the gifts that the Goddesses give us for they appreciate music even as they appreciate beauty."

By now, Queen Sophie has me pulled back against her chest and wrapped in her arms. The breath that accompanies her whispered words tickles my ear. Slowly that even fades until there is nothing left, but the music and the dance.

I close my eyes and allow Queen Sophie to lead me, to take me away from the troubles of the world. The smell of a sea is a sharp sweetness to the senses. The distant cries of gulls, the playfulness of the sea life, and the echo of waves pounding unerringly against the shoreline becomes my being. Eons upon eons of wave after wave chip away at rock and sweep away sand. Erosion of ages past, present and the possible future fly before my eyes. The mysteries of the past no longer become mysteries, the present a whirlwind of possibilities, the future unknown, but bright if allowed to stay under the guidance of the Goddesses.

The dance is seductive in both body and power. I feel every line and curve of the body pressed tightly against me. The rhythm, hypnotically and purposely slow demands that awareness, demands that I give my body and spirit totally over to the song.

The music of the strange instrument, once being the centre of my world slowly fades to the background. In its place comes my music. Compared to the sweet melody of the instrument my music sounds flat, almost jarring the nerves. Hands tighten around me, pulling my hot naked body against another hot naked body.

The thought of the loss of my gown almost jars my music to a halt. However, hands caress it back into existence. A pandemonium of colours explodes and settles, bringing back the rhythm of my song.

My music is beautiful I finally admit. It is the core of my new beauty. I come to realize that this is what Queen Sophie had tried to tell me. This music is the core of the Sirens and to be cut off from that core is death. To be in the center is life and yes I can just barely feel the tantalizing link to something much greater than myself. That music is to be in the embrace of the Goddesses where they shower me with love even as they demand the impossible.

"Listen carefully. The sharing of energy both mental and physical." A voice whispers.

The music takes a subtle change. Sweet and clear it becomes. So beautiful is it that I cannot stop my voice from joining the perfection. My voice is a match for the music and the power is exhilarating. I share myself with the hot bodies pressed to mine, one to the front the other the back. I give and then I take. I feel my flesh meld into theirs… so erotic.

I gasp aloud when those perfect bodies pull away from me leaving me feeling more naked than I have ever felt in my life.

"The music of the world." States the voice of the body that next presses against me.

I throw my head back and groan in delight as the most perfect of melodies overwhelms me.

The world is not a simple thing and its music, though perfect in every way threatens to shatter me to pieces and throw those pieces to the heavens. It is the music of all living things, be it human, animals, sirens or gods. The music is the originating piece from which comes the root of all other music and the song serenades the soul.

I give another gasp as the hot flesh pressed against me abandons me, and then a sigh as another's flesh melds into me. The song makes another change.

"The song of war" is the soft whisper in my ear, a whisper that is a direct opposite of the song's demands and intensity. The other's body presses firmly against me, the tempo increases and the speed becomes dizzying. Someone gropes at me harshly and demanding, making my body response to those demands. However, even as I submit to their demands I make my own. Smooth thighs press firmly together, stomachs breathe in rhythm, and breasts heave in unison. I sing of war, death and destruction and my enemies fall in hopelessness around me.

This time when the hot body leaves me I am so immersed in the song that I barely notice, although not for long for another soon presses against me, and the song changes once more.

Tranquil as the ocean waters in the deepest of deeps. It slows and lulls. It is never ending and never still. The smell of salt, fish, sea mammals, and crustaceans overwhelm me. These waters are the very lifeblood of the living when clean and death if otherwise. "The song of the Mermaid", says a distant voice before it flows away from me as does the body belonging to the voice.

"The song of the Goddesses. The song of the Siren. The song of love." The voice, which I barely hear states for a new melody is filling me. My voice rises in joining, although how I could ever hope to give justice to music so pure I have no idea. A body moves sensually against me making my own respond. Hands explore places they should not be exploring. Hair tickles my sensitive flesh, but all that is peripheral to the music.

I lose myself in the song. I sing the glory of the Goddesses. Goddesses that only a moment before I did not believe existed. More hands and bodies press against me demanding my love and affection and I give it to them shamelessly.

I wake up with a groan. My head feels like it is splitting wide open and my mouth taste like cotton. At first, I can't reconcile the daylight glaring through the window with my belief that it should still be evening until a faint memory of the last evening invades.

Shocked, I sit up to discover the presence of four beautiful and perfect bodies scattered around my bed… no not my bed, the queen's bed. A quick look reveals that Queen Sophie is not among them and I silently thank the Goddess for that. As I acknowledge whom the naked bodies spread out on the bed belong to, I am shocked into full wakefulness when I realize that I am as naked as those bodies lying beside me.

Still, I can't help but admire their beautiful perfection. Never have I thought a woman's body could be so perfect. Never would I admit that my own is now as perfect as those sprawled out around me.

Taking another look at the tattoos on their breasts I feel them calling to me, making me tempted to investigate them more fully. There is nothing more that I would love to do then trace those designs to see if that will provide any insight, however already embarrassed at being caught naked in the same bed as them I decide it best to forego my investigation. Therefore, confused and as carefully as I can I get off the bed. I find a robe on the floor and wrap it around my naked flesh.

Last evening is a distant memory to me. I remember the music, and the beauty of my songs for they still resound deeply inside me. I remember the joy I felt as I sang and danced. What I don't remember is how I came to be naked in bed with these beautiful Sirens. An even better question is why am I naked.

Still drawn inward on my thoughts I do not realize that Queen Sophie is sitting in the room I just walked into until I hear her chuckle. Startled I look up.

"It can be very overwhelming the first time." Queen Sophie tells me good-naturedly.

"That's one way to put it." I answer uncertainly.

"Come here and give me a proper good morning."

I surprise myself by giving Queen Sophie a very un-queenly kiss, knowing deep inside that even if she did not put it into words that was what she was asking from me. In the midst of that kiss I realize that my perception of the world I live in has changed. How much it has changed is something better left undiscovered for now.

"That's better, but you stink of sweat, magic and sex so why don't you go wash up."

"Magic!.... SEX! By the Goddess what happened last night?"

As I yelp my disbelief, I think it strange that twice already this morning I have called to the Goddess.

"You sang Michele. You came to know your Siren and by the Goddess it was most beautiful. I have not felt a power as I felt in you for eons and I can almost place your mother now. When I get back home, I will search our archives and find her for you. That I promise you, however if you want to wash up before we have to leave you better hop to it and do not worry overmuch about last night it will come to you when you are in need."

Deciding I am more in need of untangling my confused mind than cramming even more information in I hurry to the bathroom to take that shower.

"Ye be drowning me again!"

"Oh! Sorry Sorcha. I don't feel like myself this morning." I move so my right shoulder is turned away from the showerhead's spray.

"Last night was wonderful Michele. I have never seen the rituals of the sirens. It be so beautiful." She finishes with a sigh.

"Shhhh Sorcha. You can't tell anyone!"

"Like whom am I going to tell?" Sorcha replies scornfully.

"You're right. Sorry love I panicked."

"That's okay. It was exciting however!"

"Hummm…. ahhhh, Sorcha were you there all night?"

"Of course. I told ye I would never leave ye again. I almost lost ye once, never again."

"Oh…. ummm. Sorcha did I have sex last night?"

"What a silly question. Of course ye did and by the looks of it not only did ye enjoy yeself, but you were very good at it."

Dam it all to hell! For five years, I have been more than ready for sex. I had dreams of wild parties when I started university, but being so plain my parties consisted of only me until I met a couple of girlfriends and even then no freaking parties. I was willing to jump the bones of any man that even looked at me crossways and finally I get what I want and I can't even remember it…. Fuck, how freaking frustrating.

Amazingly enough it is not the fact that Sorcha is telling me I had sex with women that is bothering me, something I would not have thought of ever doing, but the fact that I do not remember having that sex that is pissing me off.

"Are you okay?" Princess Mariyah asks as she joins me in the shower.

I am both embarrassed and shocked. Embarrassed that what may have happened last night happened, and shocked at Mariyah's casual invasion into my shower. Then there is Mariyah's body. I know without knowing how, that I am acquainted with every aspect of her body. That thought makes my face heat up causing me to look down demurely in further embarrassment.

"You should have told us last night that you were a virgin Michele. We would have gladly sung you the song of purity if we had known."

"Dam it Mariyah. I had no idea that what happened last night was going to happen, worst yet I don't remember!"

"Ah, so it is not shame with whom you laid with that is making you hang your head, but shame at not remembering."

"Yes." I manage to mumble.

"I think we have time for one more lesson. As it is with the Goddesses, there is the good and bad that comes with every gift. The good that Aphrodite gave us is our beauty, our long life, and most of all our song. The blessed-curse is that we are very fertile, which she reminds us with our pubic hair. It is not that we do not love men, but to lie with a man once is a guarantee of becoming with child, thus the reason we don't unless we mean to give birth. Every birth results in a girl and that may not be bad considering who we are. The bad that comes with our gift is not remembering. We cannot remember our sexual encounters. We remember lust, wants and even great loves, but never the sex. Even I do not remember all that happened last night. It is our custom that for evenings such as last eve, to have one not participating so that they can pass on any important happenings to the participating parties the next morning and that is what mother did for us. The only reason I know that you were a virgin is because mother told me just now when I talked to her. I must say she was not pleased to discover you were a virgin and very unhappy that it was I who had the honour of taking that virginity, until I reminded her that we would not be here long enough for it to matter so… well never mind about that. When we have sex we suspect that it has happened because it tickles the back of the mind like an itch, but never the particulars unless…."

Mariyah's voice is soft and inviting. When her voice rises, it makes my heart flutter and when it lowers my loins scream with desire.

"The song of remembering Michele, with that song you can remember anything. The more you know about what you are looking for the faster you will find it in your memory, but even if you don't know what it is you seek you will eventually find it. With that song, even the bad can be changed to good." She finishes with a sly grin.

"Meaning?"

"Sing it Michele and I will show you. Think of our evening of dancing and making love. Open yourself to the experience, remember me taking your virginity and I will show you the good with the bad."

I eye her warily. *What the hell. They didn't harm me last night, at least I don't think so.*

I open myself up to my music. I hear Mariyah's voice far in the distance leading me to where I need to go. I find my rhythm and put what is mine and mine alone into the song. Before my change my voice sucked, however my music and song is now the sound of angels singing to the Goddesses.

What I am searching for slams back with clarity. So clear that I can feel the bodies pressing against my own, the hands caressing my body, the tongues whispering their way across my breasts, my nipples and then down my body and between my thighs. Again I feel the sharp piercing pain that came with the loss of my virginity, and then the sweet bliss that followed. I throw back my head in delight and part my thighs. I barely make note of the scream of ecstasy that breaks the silence that had descended in the bathroom.

When I come to it's to find myself lying on the bottom of the tub. "What happened?" I ask the floating face of Mariyah hovering above me.

"You just experienced the good with the bad. By singing the song of remembering you remembered last night while I made love to you just now. It increased the sensation of everything you felt. I believe what you would say is "I just had one hell of an orgasm." Mariyah smiles down wickedly.

"And ye be a screamer Michele!" Sorcha supplies teasingly.

I give Sorcha the look and then turn back to Mariyah. "You are so naughty Mariyah. Does your mother know how bad you are?"

"Oh yes. Mother knows me very well, however as long as it is not with a man she is happy to allow me my naughtiness. Now let me help you up and then you can give me a proper thank you kiss."

There are so many questions I want to ask, so much more knowledge I want to absorb. That has to wait for being embarrassed once again I decide it best to just settle for the kiss.

"No Samuel you must put your will into it. You need to find that spark deep inside you. You'll know that you found it when you feel the change in your eyes… yes that's it. No don't do it now Samuel! Vladimir will feel it and we are not ready yet."

Edward's tense body relaxes once he sees the power drain from Specimen 101849's eyes.

He has an uneasy feeling that things are going to come to a head very soon. He managed to get thirty of Vladimir's brood in place in Washington and another half dozen thralls, but even those numbers have not reduced his unease.

Therefore, for the last couple of days he has been spending much more time with Specimen 101849 or as he now calls him, Samuel than he use to.

He had decided on the name in the hopes that giving the creature a name would make him more amendable, which so far seems to have worked. His first real breakthrough with Samuel occurred only a couple of weeks ago, for much to Edward's surprise he had discovered that Samuel was intelligence. For so long he had thought of Vladimir's specimens as nothing more than animals hardly worth the notice. That has change for he is now under the opinion that he may have underestimated some of these specimens. Furthermore, he does not think he is only one that has underestimated them, for he knows for a fact that Vladimir thinks of them as mindless stock.

When he had made the discovery that Samuel had intelligence the depth of that intelligence came to light for he soon realized that Samuel's mind was a steel trap and that he absorbed every nibble that he threw at him.

Front and foremost of his concerns is getting free of Vladimir's control and to that end he has been teaching Samuel how to force his will onto another. He is certain that Samuel currently has enough control and more than enough power to command any human. Still, that is not enough for what he is after is so much more.

He is after his freedom, freedom from Vladimir that is. He's not certain if it is possible, however the force that the girl used on him in Europe makes him think that the possibility exists. When she had hit him with her mind she had just gone through the change and no doubt untrained, however the raw power she had used had stunned him and shaken his tie to Vladimir. If she had that much power untrained then what could Samuel accomplish trained. His future, if he is to have one hangs on that very thin thread.

"How will I know if it works if I can't use it?"

Samuel's voice breaks into his straying thoughts. "The next time you are brought a woman use it on her. Don't use it on any of the brood until we are ready or he will know and if he discovers what we are up to we can expect a very short life to follow."

"Since I killed that one monster he wanted me to breed he has them strap me to the table first."

"But they leave you alone after, so once you are alone with her drive your will into her. Once you capture her you can get her to do anything. Just make sure you have her put you back the way you were afterwards and don't forget to release her when you are done with her. You still remember how don't you?"

"Of course I do."

"Good. Now I want to show you one more thing. Only if and when you master this, will we be ready."

"What is it?"

This is dangerous. This is knowledge he is not sure Samuel should have. However, without it there is less hope of success. "There is another power that we have, or at least the stronger ones have. You must understand there is a hierarchy among us. It is not as easy as the oldest being the strongest, although that is often the case. Who turned who also has to be considered in our hierarchy. Those that are the forefathers are the strongest and it goes to follow that they are the oldest, but even more important is that they were not turned and Vladimir is one of these. We are not sure how they came about, or at least they are not forthcoming with that information, but be assured that they are by far the strongest of us. Next to consider is who turned a brood and how old they may be. If a forefather makes a brood and that brood in turn makes another, the brood maker will almost always be stronger than the one he turns, even if they are the same age. Do you understand?"

"I think what you're saying is that the closer one is…. let's call it "related" to a forefather the stronger they will be."

"Yes exactly and then there is how long they have been turned."

"Okay, I can follow that. It's like generations. The forefathers would be the first generation and any they turned could be considered second and any the second turned would be the third and so forth. The closer to the first generation you are related the stronger you can ultimately be."

"Yes, yes exactly so."

"So Vladimir being a first generation is very powerful."

"Yes and that is why we must be careful. However it is not hopeless, for whatever he did to you has made you of the same strength as a forefather, however you lack the training and years."

"Okay, I can follow that. So what is this other power you speak of?"

This is the point of no return so he pauses to consider the wisdom of what he is about to do before plunging in. "I was turned by Vladimir making me what you called a second generation, however I am a mere thousand or so years old, as such I have developed the skill, but it is not nearly as strong as Vladimir's."

"And I'm what… twenty-five, if what you tell me is correct. If you are a thousand years turned and don't have the strength, then what makes you think I will be able to even do it, never mind be strong enough to make it effective?"

"Just like I believe you have the power to break my link to my sire I believe you can do this. I have never heard of anyone breaking a link and I have never heard our forefathers talking about it. I recently came across someone that gave me such a "whack" that it strained the link. That is how I have come to believe it is possible to break it entirely. This other thing I more than believe you have the potential to master and the strength to make effective. You see the older brood, Vladimir included of course, have the power to use their minds to push."

"Push? I don't understand."

"Yes push, however the first step is that you have to believe in the possibility."

"Okay, but I still don't know what you are talking about."

"I am talking about the ability to use the power that runs through you to push things away from you or for you to be able to push your own body through the air. We cannot fly per say. However, those with the power can use it to help them glide over land, making it look as if they are flying. That is one way to identify a very powerful brood. If he can glide over the ground you need to be very certain of your own power or get the hell out of there as fast as you can."

"And you say you and Vladimir can do this?"

"Yes, but there is more. He could for instance use his power to push against you. If he did it with enough force it would feel like you have been hit with a battering ram. I have seen him throw humans forty, fifty feet through the air with only the use of this power."

"And you think I can learn this. Don't be silly."

"Yes I think you can. You must if we are to succeed!"

"Give me a thousand years then."

"You're not listening to me. You have a very sharp mind. Vladimir has kept you in the dark for all of your twenty-five years. You have had nothing else for company except that mind of yours. I have never come across such a structured mind and that is what will allow you to learn this quickly."

Samuel is still uncertain as to Edward's beliefs. What he says is true in almost every respect except for one fine point which Samuel has no intention of letting Edward or anyone else know. Long did he spend alone in the darkness, however almost fifteen years ago he learned to latch onto Michele's mind. It was his ability to learn and experience life through her mind that has kept him sane. If Edward or Vladimir gave it any thought they should wonder how he learned to talk, to associate with others, to even be able to reason for all they have ever taught him is how to breed and that is such a base animal instinct that even the lowest of animals can accomplish it. Until Edward starting showing up in his cell, he had almost no social contact and definitely no learning. However, he had learned. He learned with Michele, he graduated high school with her and then university.

He saw what she saw and experienced what she experienced. His drive for new experiences was half the reason she got into so much trouble in her youth. The last few years he had kept himself silent and simply rode along with her. She was and is literally his whole world and if Edward thinks he has a fine mind, he should spend some time in hers.

As it is he fell in love with Michele immediately and for fifteen years he has had the joy of living in her mind. However, since the night of the change things have… well changed. The night the two of them went through the change they became one. To this day, he swears he had touched her physically, just as he swears she had touched him. He still has a vivid memory of the feel of her firm breast beneath his fingers, the feel of her hard nipple between his lips as he suckled her and most of all the feel of her hot skin against his. She was his comfort as the pain ripped through his body and he hoped that she had drawn as much comfort from him.

Prior to the change, he was able to come and go into her mind at will without her knowing. Now he has to ask permission and "knock" gently for her to acknowledge him. This is his secret and something he will share with nobody but her.

All this he acknowledges in a few seconds and then he asks the question that Edward obviously wants him to ask. "So what is it I have to do?"

"You need to learn to focus your mind. You must have done that wonderfully all those years in the dark. Now use what you learned in the darkness to focus the natural energy of your body and mind into a pinpoint of power and then imagine pushing with that pinpoint. Many of the brood find it easier to learn if they use a gesture with it, like a hand motion. That is all show. It is the gathering of that energy and then the push of the mind that does all the work. Watch."

Samuel keeps a close watch on Edward. He sees the strain build behind his eyes, the trembling of his limbs, and then a push against him makes him stumble back.

"Well?" Edward is obviously tired from the effort and his voice is strained.

"I was pushed back a few feet."

"Yes and I did that by simply thinking about it and using my energy against you. Do you think you can match it?"

"That I do not know. I will think about this and let you know the next time you visit."

"Belief Samuel. Belief is half the battle. I have shown you that it can be done. Now you have to believe that you too can do it."

"I will work on it."

Chapter Eleven

The last twenty-four hours has been full of adventure, surprises, learning and self-gratification for me and right now I am praying to the goddess that the rest of the day will be just a little more boring. No sooner am I wishing that, when my wish for peace and quiet is shattered. Feeling the mental knocking I open my mind to the knock.

"I'm learning Michele!" The voice tells me.

"So am I. The sirens taught me last night. You would not believe the knowledge they gave me."

"Nor you the knowledge that I am getting. Look…"

Images flash back and forth between the two of us at a rate too fast for words.

"You are being held by vampires!" I exclaim when I learn whom it is he is talking about teaching him.

"Is that what you are calling them?"

"Yes. Are they hurting you? Have they bitten you? How are you faring?"

"They do not bite me, however they hurt me all the time. Lately, they even have me breeding with some of the other monsters they have down here."

"Can't you get away?"

"Not yet, but with any luck what the vampire called Edward is teaching me will help me get out of here. The one called Vladimir is up to something and Edward is not happy about it so he is teaching me in the hope that I will be able to break his bond to his sire. He said that you almost did it to him in Switzerland."

"By the Goddess so that is what I have been doing! Wait, he was one of them?"

"Apparently on both counts. You have been commanding them the same way that they command humans and that hard push you gave him almost broke his link. He tells me that it should not be possible, however something in us allows us to do what they themselves cannot do. Believe me, that is something else that Vladimir was not happy to discover. He almost did away with me on the spot when he found out. You will need to practice to get better at it. You also need to practice that pushing thing that Edward has been teaching me. A push with your mind can accomplish wonders or so he tells me. Edward is so happy with my progress that he has even given me a name."

"A name"

"Yes, for the first time he sees me as something other than an animal for them to play with so he named me Samuel."

"That is a good name. A strong one."

"Thank you. I am happy with it. Make sure you keep practicing Michele."

"I will just as you need to."

"I will, however I doubt that I will be able to access the siren part of me. I know it exist because you just told me so and yet the goddess, if that is what you want to call her, did not allow me to see far into what you have learned."

"Of course, you can. If I can do it, so can you! We are one are we not?"

"No, I don't think so. I can feel something of it inside me, however the goddess or whatever is not allowing me to work with it. Even as you were giving me the songs I felt them slipping away from me. In fact, I can't even remember any of them now."

"Keep trying anyway."

"I will… I have to go someone is coming. Be careful today."

"Why?"

"I just don't like what I am hearing. It has something to do with the sirens so be ready."

"Have you made any headway as to where you are?"

"No and I really have to go."

The presence disappears, slamming me back to the limo.

"Daydreaming?" The erotic blonde-haired Capri asks.

"A lot has happened in the last couple of days." I give her a wan smile and then look around to see where we are. "We should be at the conference in a few minutes."

I spend the next few minutes checking my weapons, which I admit I will most likely not use for I still have not gotten use to firing guns. In fact, I still have a deep aversion for the things. Aversion or not I have to at least look as if I am willing to use it for part of the deal with allowing Queen Sophie to speak in front of the G9 members was that none of the sirens are allowed arms. Therefore, it is up to us to make sure that none of them come to harm, although I now realize how naive the no weapon thing is considering what they have taught me.

"Okay people let's get ready. Michele and George you will be the first to go. When you're sure everything is clear give the go ahead. Err on the side of caution people for I have no intension of failing our first real assignment." Riley declares over the radio.

George is in the other limo with Mariyah and Vani, while I have Sophie, Capri and Lia with me. The rest of the team is spread out the same as when we left the airport, with an armoured vehicle in the front, middle and rear of the limos.

Let this day be boring Goddess.

The cars barely come to a stop when I open the door and hop out. Even then, I see that George was faster than me, and that he is already out and scowling at the crowd.

"I can't see anything, but can you take a quick look Sorcha love."

"Oh, this be so fun! Be right back."

I giggle silently at Sorcha's enthusiasm. As she checks the high ground, I search the low, taking special notice of the gathering crowd and coming to understand George's scowl.

"This could be ugly Sergeant Major." George relays to Riley.

"What is it?"

"The people. No radicals by the looks of things, but people galore. It will make yesterday look like a boy scout exercise if things break out here."

"Shit, we don't need this crap. Okay let's surround the sirens so the population don't get a good look at them and then lead them inside. Can you get Queen Sophie's cooperation Michele?"

"I think so. By the way, I just got almost confirmation that the vampires are going to take a stab at the sirens."

"And we have been picking up a lot of movement from some of the Taliban groups. I've traced them back a couple of days and they seem to be converging on your location so we need you guys to be extra alert." Dad says over the radio.

"Great, just great." I growl and then open the limo door. "Your Highness, there is a lot of people out here. Will you permit us to surround you and your women so they can't see you?"

"Of course my dear. I am not here to wave and be friendly with the humans so do whatever you think is required."

"Thank you and please whatever you do don't smile. Okay George, gather up around the princess and then come to us and we will tie them all in a neat little package and deliver them inside."

For the most part our plan works like a charm. The population is already being held back by the military and as such only a few people actually notice the sirens. Quick action by Gazinno with only slightly firm knocks on a couple of heads puts an end to the couple of threats that do occur. Admittedly, by the time we get them inside there are others that are starting reacting to the sirens' "auroras" is the best I can describe it, however we hustle them inside so quickly that by the time the crowds' forward surging threaten to become a danger we are long since out of sight. Once inside, we hurry the group into the elevator.

"I hope you don't mind me asking Queen Sophie, but how do you intend to keep those in the meeting from being affected by you. Not that I mean them any offence and they have been tested against your picture, however I'm sure at least half of them will be trying to get to you before you even make your way to the podium." Andrea asks once the elevator is on the way up.

Queen Sophie gives Andrea a shocked look. She obviously had not thought of this. "Michele will think of something." She finally replies.

I groan and then look long and hard at Queen Sophie. How can someone with a face so pure and beautiful be so....

"I got it. At least I think it will work! Send the elevator back down."

They all look at me askew. "So what if she is a minute or two late." I reply defensively.

The elevator comes to a stop, the doors open and the mob waiting outside to take pictures are kept back until the elevator doors close again and back down we go.

"When we get down you guys wait here for me. I will be just a few minutes."

"You have the ball Michele. I hope you know what you are doing with it?" Andrea tells me.

Goddess so do I!

The elevator door opens and I go outside to find the vendor that I had barely paid any attention to on the way into the building. Finding her, I beckon her inside and thankfully find her to be one of those that do not take an immediate dislike to me. I spend the next few minutes selecting and then haggling over the cost. Once we come to an agreed upon price I take my purchases and hustle back to the waiting group.

"Here. These are for you ladies and this one is yours Your Highness." I hand out the ceramic masks holding back the most gorgeous of them for Queen Sophie.

The masks are made of delicately thin porcelain with fantastic artwork. Once in place they will cover the forehead, eyes, nose and cheekbones of the face, resulting in cunning artwork covering well over half of the sirens' faces. As the sirens look at the artwork appreciatively I don the one I purchased for myself, which in my opinion has quite a devilish design and suits my current attitude to a tea.

"At first, I thought this one most suited you Mariyah, and I was going to give it to you, but…" I can't finish my thought for the look that Mariyah gives me makes me burst out in laughter.

"There is more to being a Siren than the face Michele." Capri finally speaks what I am sure they are all thinking.

I get myself back under control. "I know that. I'm hoping that these may at least confuse them a little. Throw them off balance so to speak. They have been tested with your pictures so with any luck this will allow them to have just a little more immunity towards you. Just don't smile, whatever you do please don't smile." I finish, remembering the one time I had smile on our ill-fated shopping trip.

"Well, why not. They are quite pretty and if they will help all the better. I must agree with you Michele that yours looks absolutely evil. Maybe you should give…"

"Mother!"

Sophie smiles at her daughter. "If we find out they work, maybe next time we visit we can use these so we can be "tourist" without causing the chaos we did yesterday."

"I'm sure it would break your heart not to cause at least one riot Mother."

"I see the time you spent with Michele this morning has made you a little frisky daughter."

"I was teaching her." Mariyah replies too quickly and I notice that her cheeks are as red as my own feel. I may not remember the act itself, however I dam well know there was an act.

"Then you need to re-evaluate your teaching methods dear for there was much too much screaming for a proper teaching."

The sirens laugh, I go even redder, the rest of the unit have looks ranging from uncertainty as to what the sirens may be talking about to knowing. Sorcha falls off her usual perch on my shoulder and tumbles to the floor.

"It will served you right if you get stepped on and I wasn't screaming." I growl softly to Sorcha when she finally regains her seat.

"Oh yes ye were and such a lovely scream too." She replies still grinning. "Admit it Michele ye be a screamer."

I glare at her and then the door to the elevator slides open saving me from further embarrassment. As one, we turn to face our first test.

There is a lot of yelling and picture taking, however the masks work amazingly well for the chaos is no worse than what could be expected when what looks to be a hundred reporters come swooping down on our charges to get a story.

We manage to make our way pass the crowd of reporters and finally through the door into a room filled with the G9 leaders and their aids. The bluster of noise falls into silence and every eye locks onto the women being escorted towards the podium. As we pass the electronic room, Queen Sophie nods to her daughter, who splits from the group, dragging four of the unit responsible for her safety along with her.

"And you would be?" The man currently standing behind the podium asks when the party arrives to the front of the room.

"This would be Queen Sophie Loreral. High Queen of the Sirens." Vani replies with the same snarky tone the man had used.

"What's with the masks?"

This time Queen Sophie answers herself. "They are Miss Appleton's idea. She believes it may help you men keep your hormones in check."

"And I suppose you think you can just come up here and take over."

"Not at all. If we have any gentlemen in this room they may find me a seat and I will patiently wait for my turn." Queen Sophie replies much too sweetly.

The man is obviously shocked back into civility by her too sweet remark. "No need Your Highness. Ladies and Gentlemen it seems we have a guest among us so allow me to turn over the floor to High Queen of the Sirens, Queen Sophie Loreral."

"Stick to her like glue Michele." Riley blares in my earpiece.

I know the job I have been assigned so there was no need for Riley to remind me. As such, I am only a step or two behind Queen Sophie as she makes her way onto the podium. Once there I glance around nervously. This is a decisive moment. Either the testing and the masks work or all hell breaks loose.

Queen Sophie looks to her daughter who nods. "Thank you sir. Ladies and Gentlemen, I want to thank you for allowing me to speak here in front of you today. I understand that I should be doing this at what you call the U.N., however at present I have an aversion to Europe." Queen Sophie gives a slight grimace at what seems to be a distant memory before continuing. "I also see that you have kindly started the monitors so that anybody who is interested can listen in so let me begin." Queen Sophie gives her daughter a nod. Princess Mariyah signals the technician she stopped to talk to.

"As you already know I am High Queen of our people and we call ourselves Sirens. For over two hundred years, we have called the islands of Ospizo our home. Nobody lived on these islands when we inhabited it and nobody outside our women have stepped foot on it since, or know of its existence. That changed recently when we became entangled in the middle of your war. If you will please look at the monitors." Queen Sophie directs them to monitors that now show a half dozen war ships surrounding an island chain.

"Prior to this we were able to direct the minds of men to ignore our islands and this we have been doing since the beginning of days in order to keep our islands peaceful. As you can see by the way that your warships are positioned things have changed and you have placed us directly in the middle of your war. The fact is, we have been leading those ships in circles for a few months now. This morning the leaders claiming ownership of these ships most likely received calls from the soldiers on board telling them that an island has suddenly appeared in the midst of your precious battle. That is because after a long debate and after months of you people circling our islands and refusing to take your war elsewhere we have decided to once again allow humans to know of our existence."

"What else could you have done?" A sleazy looking political calls out.

"What we could have done was utterly destroy your precious warships or your poor excuse of soldiers and taken your ships away from you.

Instead, we come to you to make our claim. Mr. Secretary-General of the U.N., are you with us and of clear mind?"

"I am on both counts Queen Sophie."

"Then please hear this as our claim. I Sophie Loreral, High Queen of the Sirens claim the island chain known to us as Ospizo as our own. We claim territorial sea up to twelve nautical miles from our baseline. We claim a contiguous zone of twenty-four nautical miles from our baseline, and exclusive zone of two hundred nautical miles from our baseline. We expect everyone to respect our waters under the same rules as every other country respects another country's waters. We will permit nobody to enter our territorial waters or permit any activity in our contiguous waters except what is required as a waterway. Furthermore, our laws do not permit visitors or immigrants without prior written approval, which believe me, will be very rare if at all given. Any intrusion into our land will be seen as breaking our laws or an act of war and the trespassers will be dealt with severely. I tell you now, we believe in the death penalty and we will have no qualms dealing out that penalty. The sentence for stepping foot on our island chain without written permission is death. There are no prison terms and there is no day in court for the very presence of the trespasser is proof of breaking that law. Every country should by now be in possession of the details of our land and people."

The room is silent. Most of the leaders are slacked jawed. I can't blame them for not only is this beautiful woman claiming a nice chunk of land, but she just told them in no uncertain terms what will happen to anyone who so much as steps a baby toe on the lands she is claiming; something I bet that some of them wished they had the guts or military power themselves to proclaim.

"Mr. Secretary-General let this be our notice for those who would claim ownership of the warships around our sovereign land. We give them a half hour to have their warships outside our territorial zone. They have ten hours to get them outside our exclusive zone, whereas they can go back to their petty war."

Conversations break out throughout the room as leaders talk to their aids.

"I am lead to believe that your island is only populated by women. Do your seriously expect that you can do anything against a half dozen warships. I have a mind to go in and teach you "women" a thing or two and put you back in your proper place" A dark skinned looking man on one of the monitors speaks up.

"Don't even try it. Gentlemen I ask you not to make us do this. We do not look forward to making our first contact with you humans in over two hundred years a bloody one. We ask you to stand down, and we ask you to leave peacefully. Mr. Secretary-General please use whatever influence you may have over these leaders to make them understand. One half hour gentlemen. Thank you."

I feel the movement behind me even as Sorcha calls out the warning. Without thought I find myself in action. I turn and move towards the man that is rushing forward. Getting to him quickly I take hold of the barrel of his gun and tear it out of his hands. His momentum continues to carry him forward until his chest comes up hard against the flat of my palm, whereas his body suddenly stops. As the bones break, my hand caves in his chest. I give him a push and then watch his body fall and slide fifteen feet along the floor.

Dam it all! I curse when I feel a bullet pass through my shoulder. *Go figure, shit!*

I turn to the person that shot me. The first thing I notice is the blank look in his eyes, as if he cares little if he succeeded or not. It is the same look that the first man had, and right now he is repositioning to take a shot at Queen Sophie.

Not!

Pulling on that little seed inside me gets me next of the man in a blink of an eye, whereas I take a firm hold on his neck. My eyesight changes and I feel the anger explode allowing me to pick the man up by the neck and shake him like a rag doll. The man's face turns purple and he starts to gurgle so I give him a couple more shakes. Hearing his neck snap I throw him away like an unwanted toy.

I then notice that I am not the only one busy. When the first man attacked, so did others and the rest of the unit as well as other security personal in the room find themselves pressed from every side. The sirens having doubt in our ability to control the outbreak surround their queen, fully prepared to dispatch anybody foolish enough to come too close. Mitch, realizing that the doors are the key to keeping the chaos contained runs to the door nearest to him and I see him jam a wedge under it to keep it closed. Other members of the unit take care of the attacking humans scattered throughout the room little realizing or caring what kind of enemy they may be. Shots are fired and some of those who were previously posing as security guards go down. The hardest part is trying to determine foe from friend.

An explosion coming from up above makes me look up. The ceiling comes falling down upon those below the exploding upper floor.

You have got to be kidding me!

The ceiling in this grand room is easily twenty feet high and repelling down from the blown ceiling are a half dozen men. Or so I think of them until their smell hits me.

"Vampires!" I yell to anybody willing to hear me.

I try the trick that Samuel had shown me. I gather my inner force.

Just a push he said... Not to be... *Oh hell!*

Even so, the jump I make is impressive. As I fly through the air, I pull my knife. The first rope I pass I slice in half and the gracefully descending vampire no longer gracefully descends. He thumps to the floor where three of the unit pounce on him. I miss the rope of the second vampire, but manage a deep gash across its neck. The deep cut would have dropped any human, although I suspect that it will hardly slow the vampire down. The third one I end up body slamming and we engage.

The vampire I slammed into is massive. He looks like he was a body builder in a former life, and then he goes and proves to me that he may just as well have been as he wraps his arms around me and starts to squeeze. The rope snaps and locked together the two of us fall to the floor. I scream when my injured shoulder hits the floor and then all my attention turns towards staying alive.

The vampire facing me is big, strong, and exceedingly ugly with plenty of scars across his face and one eye, the other eye being nothing but an empty socket. His knife is more of a short sword than a knife and he knows how to use it not only to keep me at bay, but also how to be a real threat with it. We circle each other warily, each waiting for an opening; he faints towards me. I block and push his blade aside and then he moves with such speed that all I see is a blur until he stops once more in front of me.

I give a yelp of pain as what feels like a hot poker burns its way through the same shoulder that had taken the bullet earlier. Grasping my shoulder I look down in confusion as the point of a blade comes sliding out the front instead of the other way around.

It takes me a few seconds to understand what I am seeing. The vampire I was fighting is still in front of me, still holding his blade, and yet… my brain finally registers and I turn to see the grinning vampire behind me.

All reason leaves me and a deeper anger then before fills the void. Since my change I have been having anger management issues, but prior outbursts have been nothing compared to what I now feel.

This time, I don't even try to hold that anger back. A growl starts low in my throat, which changes to a snarl by the time it escapes from between lips pulled back firmly against my teeth. My eyes complete the change. I'm sure they are now a bright yellow instead of the sea green I have gotten use to seeing in the mirror. Everything comes to me in surreal clarity. I look into the vampire's eyes and for a brief couple of seconds I see the image of a wolf head superimposed over mine.

My hand shoots out and I bury it to the wrist inside the chest of the stupidly grinning vampire that owned the knife still buried in my shoulder. My fingers clench around the heart. By the time I pull the creature's heart from its chest cavity my nails have changed to six-inch black claws. The claws dig into the heart and blood that it has been storing spills out. I wonder who the poor soul may have been that contributed its blood to the monstrous creature, but only briefly for I then force my hand through the vampire's forehead, into and out the backside of its skull, leaving the heart inside to replace the brain that I have just forced out the back of his ruined skull. The vampire drops and I turn to my original opponent.

It had taken only a few seconds to take out that stupidly grinning vampire, however those few seconds were enough to give the other vampire time to zero in on it's real prey; the Queen of the Sirens.

In one way, I am thankful that the vampire has turned away from me for I have no illusion that if it would have continued against me I would be dead right now.

Everything is not as it would have wished however for his target is being well protected. The vampire seeing the Queen surrounded by two other Sirens hesitates and that is when I hit him in the back, whereas we both go rolling onto the floor.

My anger has not been soothed and the knife still sticking out of my shoulder causes a fiery pain that burns through me with every movement I make, causing that anger to flare ever more intensely.

I use my claws to shred the vampire as we roll onto the floor, but he is not defenceless and I feel teeth and nails tearing at my skin. We roll apart, stand and crash together again. Fists fly at a speed that is too quick for the eye to follow. I feel my ribs crack and then the knife being torn from my flesh. I howl in pain and redouble my attack forcing the vampire back with brutal efficiency.

Before I know it, I am flying through the air and my back slams into the wall. My fuzzy brain tries to put together what just happened for I was certain that I had the fight under control. I am just as certain that the vampire had not laid a hand on me for the last couple of minutes.

The older a vampire is the stronger they become. They learn to use an inner force, which they can use against a victim or enemy. I recall Samuel saying. *Oh goddess he has to be real old!* My still jumbled brain provides.

I scream when I see Princess Mariyah throw herself on the creature's back.

Others are rushing towards the vampire and Mariyah. However, it is obvious they will not be on time. Groaning, I pull myself off the floor. A thrumming music begins to fill me. The song entices me to do better, to rip the savage creature to shreds. It fills me with so much energy that it makes my skin itch.

The creature reaches back and takes hold of Mariyah's long hair, and pulls her over his shoulder. It holds her six inches off the floor with just her hair and then it opens its jaws. My head explodes.

"It's has been a long time since I have tasted Siren blood."

"I command you to Stop!" I scream in desperation, putting all the force I can behind that command.

My command does not stop him. It does slow him however. Slows him enough to give me the time I need to reach them. As it is, I just barely make it on time for when I slam into him he is starting to get his wits back. He flings Mariyah away from him like a rag doll, ripping out a fistful of her hair as he does so.

I was on the edge before, but seeing what this monster has done to Mariyah puts me beyond reason. I attack him savagely with claws and teeth. The foul leathery taste of his skin makes me gag, but I do not relent. I go to punch out his chest and he brings up an arm to stop my downward strike. The arm breaks, however it manages to slow my momentum enough so that I only break a few of his ribs instead of getting to its heart. In turn, his teeth take hold of my lower arm and tear at the skin. As my blood flows into his mouth his eyes light up and he starts to emanate an eerie glow.

Oh shit that can't be good.

Frustration, anger, and despair overwhelm me. The song of the siren propels me. The savagery inside me compels me to destroy my enemy. I rip my arm free from his teeth, leaving a fair chunk of skin and muscle behind and then I wrap my hands around its throat. I relish the feel of its neck constricting as I squeeze with all my might.

I squeeze the vampire's neck not to choke him for I know that the creature has no need to breathe and by its bulging fear filled eyes the vampire knows what it is I am up to. In its panic to continue existing it paws at me ripping even more skin and tearing even more muscle from me and yet I refuse to give up and continue to squeeze. My eyesight tunnels, nothing matters but destroying this creature.

A gun going off near my ear deafens me and the next three shots going off in rapid succession don't help bring back that hearing. The vampire's head explodes and the body goes lax. The suddenly lax muscles allow me to accomplish my goal and I rip the vampire's head free from its shoulders. The destruction of the vampire is not enough to sooth my beast however for the beast is demanding. I give in to that beast and taking hold of one of the vampire's arm I tear it from the body. Next, I go for his chest. I rip apart the skin and clamping down on its ribs I pull them apart. The ribs spread and then break leaving the heart exposed to my attack.

I hear someone calling to me, but I ignore the voice. I feel hands on my shoulder, squeezing gently; these too I ignore. All that matters to me is tearing the creature that dared to touch one of my cousins into as many pieces as I can. The heart comes out and this I shred with my long nails. Still not satisfied I reach for his other arm.

The song is beautiful. The sound of the ocean fills me. Waves crash softly against the shore and then the water retreats. In the far distance there is the sound of porpoises singing. The smell of salt fills my senses. The music and gentle caress of those waves sooth my spirit. The music comes to fill me completely.

When I slam back to my senses, it is to find the burly George standing over me. He has his hands lying reassuringly on my shoulder and I see a mixture of fear and companionship in his eyes. I take a deep breath and immediately regret it for the smell of fear that lays thick in the air awakens a hunting instinct in me. Clamping down on that instinct, I look around.

The room is a mess. Tables and chairs are overturned and half the roof now lies on the floor, leaving a wide gap to the floor above.

George offers me a hand, which I accept. I allow him to pull me from the floor as I take a closer look around. I sigh in relief when I see no more moving vampires. I give an even bigger one when I see Mariyah sit up, although I almost cry at the sight of her missing half her hair.

The desire to run to Mariyah is overwhelming and yet I still have a job to do so instead I hobble over to Queen Sophie to assure myself that she has not been harmed. I find one dead vampire not five feet from her and when I look questioningly at it, Capri grins and then pipes up. "You really didn't expect us to stay out of the fun did you?"

I laugh along with them until I notice a man lying next to where Vani stands. "What happened to him?"

"The bastard groped me. Can you believe it? In the midst of all this mayhem he takes a grab of my ass!" Vani replies with fire in her eyes.

I grimace for yes I can believe it.

"Make sure you have them cut off the heads and crush them to dust. Then take their hearts and burn them to ashes Michele or they will come back." Queen Sophie tells me.

"What?"

"That is the only way to make sure they stay destroyed."

"Oh great. That means all those others that I thought I destroyed I only pissed off. Great, just terrific, just freaking peachy. Let's piss off the creepy crawlies so that the only thought they have afterwards is to rip your heart out. You hear that Lori?"

"On it."

"As much as I like to change my agenda as to why I am here I can't. So if you will excuse me."

I watch Queen Sophie walk back to the microphone with pose and confidence. When

Mariyah walks up to me I turn to her and give her a hard hug. "You scared me to death. Don't ever do that again!"

"Just having fun."

"Fun. Look at your hair. It's half gone. Whatever were you thinking?"

"My hair is already growing back."

I give her a very un-lady like snort and hug her. Even as I hug her I notice that she was not lying to me for I can actually see her hair growing back at an unbelievable rate.

"Wow that's a useful trick." I say in wonder.

"You're a mess Michele." Mariyah manages after I have finished squeezing most of the breath from her.

"What she said. Ye look like hell!" Sorcha pipes in deciding she needs to put her own two bits in I suppose.

Their comments make me take note of my condition. I am not surprised to see that they are telling the truth. The bleeding from the tear in my shoulder is only now starting to slow, as is the one on my lower forearm, although it still looks like a mauled piece of raw meat more than an arm. While checking out the cuts and scratches on my face I sadly note that my mask is missing. It had been broken during the scuffle and I feel a piece or two of it still embedded in my skin. More of my body screams for attention, however I refuse to look any further.

I really suck at this. I know I do and if it were not for my freakish nature I would be among the dead right now. The upside is that maybe those back in The Hole will finally admit to it and let us go back to living our lives as we see fit. Maybe I'll even take up Queen Sophie's invitation and we can all go live on Ospizo.

"I would have thought that you humans would have eliminated these animals by now." Queen Sophie states, bringing silence back into the room. "Well, nothing to be done about it right now I suppose. I swear to you that I will give your Secretary-General all the knowledge I have about these creatures. I believe we have a book or two about them in our library that may also be of some use. However, now that the excitement is over we have to get back to the business at hand. You heard my demands before all this started, however due to the interruption I will allow an hour to have your warships out of our territorial zone and twelve to get them out of our contiguous zone. I will leave you gentlemen to your work and pray that you make the right choices for I think enough blood has been spilled for one day."

Statement made, Queen Sophie walks off the stage. Still nervous about what may be awaiting them we surround her and lead her through a door into an abutting room.

The smell of coffee floats in the air as well as the scent of food from two heavily laden tables. The room is meant to hold dignitaries in comfort and the sirens looking for that very thing head straight for the food; embarrassingly I hear my stomach growl.

"Get yourself something to eat Michele before you fall over. In fact, all of you eat or you will be of no use to me before the day is out." Queen Sophie raises her voice so everyone hears her.

The one thing that any military personal learns, and learns quickly and well is to eat when given the chance. I am not technically military, but I have learned this lesson over the last couple of months so I am just as prepared to dig into the food like the rest of the unit. Before I get my own however, I fill a plate and bring it to George, who has planted himself directly in front of the only door into the room.

"Thank you for your help in there George." I tell him as I hand him his plate of food.

"Think nothing of it. It's no more than what you would do for me."

"You're right, but we both know that I was on the edge. Not all of them would have done it or stuck with me afterwards, so thank you."

"It's the least I can do for your mother for her saving my hide from you." George replies with a wide grin.

I know he is saying more than he is. This is the military and in the military we don't do this kind of thing. How many times I have heard father tell me that I can't even begin to imagine, however I know that George knows exactly what I am thanking him for and he in turn has just given me more of a your welcome than he had.

I give him one last smile and then move off to get my own plate of food. Plate of food in one hand, superb coffee in the other I make my way to Queen Sophie.

"Thank you for the song earlier. I thought I was going to lose myself. I really don't know what got into me. Something just snapped when I saw that creature hurting Mariyah."

"Of course you did." Mariyah, who has sidled up beside us says before her mother can reply. "I'm the one that took your virginity. That causes a special bond that will persist throughout our life. I knew that if I attacked it, it would rile you up and it looked like you needed riling right about then. Maybe mother was right to be upset when I took your virginity, but it all worked out in the end."

"Shhhhhh!" I reply aghast in equal measure that Mariyah can speak so freely about, well things that should not be spoken of so freely, especially around a mother, not to mention within earshot of the unit. Then the rest of what she said hits home. "You did that on purpose. Are you out of your freaking mind?"

I growl at Mariyah's responding smile.

"Settle down. See my hair has already grown back."

I see that she is telling the truth yet it does little to make me feel better about what she did and than it dawns on me. "Does that mean I will never be able to wear my hair short?"

"Never and believe me many of us have tried." She replies with the same off-handed grin.

"Come and sit down Michele and let me look at you." Vani interrupts us.

"I'm okay."

"Sure you are. Now come and sit like a good girl."

"You're as bad as my mother."

"And mother I been to a number of children, not all my own of course, but that is the way of the siren. I've already taken care of the rest of your crew so now come and sit."

Vani gives me a sweet smile that makes me tremble to the very core, for I have often seen that same smile on Mom's face and it always leads to a sense of guilt on my part, whether warranted or not.

Vani waits patiently until I sit on the seat in front of her and then she goes to work on my cuts. She works quickly to clean my wounds, however before she can finish the two of us become engrossed in watching my muscles knit together and finally the skin grow over. So engrossed are we in watching me heal at a pace that is at least a hundred times faster than a human that the other forgotten wounds close before Vani gets around to them.

"You are more than what you seem Michele." Queen Sophie whispers in the silence.

Her voice next to me startles me for I did not realize that she had snuck up on us. "I'm a freak. You call me a Siren, but I am not. I have no idea why you felt compelled to acknowledge me for I am an abomination of some sort, a nothing and a no one!" I reply bitterly.

"No Michele you are not a nothing. I'll give you that you are a confused young lady. Give it time and you will come to realize how special you are and never doubt that you are not Siren."

I am unable to meet her kind eyes so instead I look away and brood.

"My dear you need to start using a weapon. The Kardia-daru should be your weapon of choice, but if nothing else you should be using a sword." Queen Sophie states in the ensuing silence.

"Kardia-daru? What's that and why?" I look at her in confusion.

"A Kardia-daru is something like a spear. It has a broadleaf head and the edges are sharp making it equally good for cutting as stabbing. There is a chain attached to it that we wound around our wrist and arm. That chain allows us to throw and retrieve it easily. That is our weapon of choice Michele. Sirens do all right in hand-to-hand combat and you are stronger than most from what I have just seen, but you will never really be real good at it. It's just not in our.... DNA so to speak. Give us a Kardia-daru or even a sword and it becomes a different story. That is what makes us the warriors that much of the world once learned to fear and will fear again before this day is out I am afraid to say. With a Kardia-daru we are almost invincible and only slightly less so with a sword. Part of the agreement I made in coming here was that we would not wear any weapons, and leave it to the humans to provide for our well-being. I kept to that agreement, however if I had known that those beast still roamed freely I never would have."

"They use guns. I should have gone for mine."

"And do you like guns?"

"No, but they are effective enough if you pump enough lead into the right areas."

"You will never like guns Michele and you will find that you can do better with the Kardia-daru than any human with a gun."

"And where would I get such a thing and learn how to use it?"

"I will think on it. Maybe some kind of arrangements can be made. As for learning how to use it, its use is ingrained into every fibre of your body. Every Siren is born with the knowledge of how to use one. That is part of the gift from Athena. Use the song of remembrance and it will come to you." Queen Sophie points to the top of her formidable breasts, leaving me even more confused than before.

Queen Sophie leaves me to contemplate her words and then turns to Andrea. "What are your orders regarding us young lady?"

Andrea blinks at her a couple of times in surprise before she replies. "I'm sure Michele has told you. We are assigned to protect you and your companions until you are safely back on your plane."

"And what if I have to do something very distasteful when I go back in the room. Then what are you to do?"

"Distasteful is not for me or us to say one way or another. We received our orders before we flew out and I intend to keep to the letter of those orders. If you plan world destruction or something stupidly hideous we will personally stop you, but otherwise." Andrea takes the earpiece out, throws it to the floor and crushes it underfoot. "Oh, what a shame. I bet that thing cost quite a bit."

The rest of us look at her in shock for Andrea is the most "by the book" person on the unit. Our looks of shock turn to grins a few seconds later and then a few moments after that more of those earpieces end up in the same state of disuse.

"I am so going to hell for that." Andrea states when the sound of grinding electronics fades.

"Maybe I'll let you visit our home so you can mediate on your wrong doings." Queen Sophie tells Andrea and then turns to Lia. "Would you like that dear. I've been watching how you have been eyeing up the young lady."

"She does have a nice rear." Lia replies so innocently that choir boys would have looked like the antichrist next to her.

Andrea sucks in a shocked breath, causing the sirens to break out in laughter. When she realizes that she had been made the butt of a joke, or at least by the look on her face she hopes it is a joke, she joins in.

Finally, Queen Sophie wipes the tears of laughter from her eyes. "Their hour is up. Time for us to get back to business."

During our absence the room had been cleaned of both debris and bodies. Queen Sophie goes back onto the podium and then nods to her daughter. Mariyah goes over to the technician and a couple of minutes later the scene of the siren's islands fills the screens. The image shows us that the warships that were previously surrounding the islands are gone except for one.

"Whose warship is that?" Queen Sophie asks with obvious displeasure.

"That would be ours."

"And you are?"

"I would be the President of Iran foolish woman."

"You have a warship? Strange, this is the first I have heard of this. At any rate you refuse my orders."

"I refuse you like I refuse those of my enemies, but before I command my ship to take control of your small empire I give you the opportunity to bow before me like a proper woman."

"I am sorry. May the Gods or Goddesses your people pray to be with them in their hour of need." Queen Sophie replies and then nods to her daughter.

Mariyah takes a device out from her bodice and speaks quietly into it. Those of us gathered in the room hold our breath in a mixture of fascination of what may be about to happen, and morbid wonder of how these beautiful morsels are to make good their threat. Our questions are quickly answered, but in a way we would never have imagined.

We watch enthralled as over a hundred women line the shore of the Island closest to the warship. Each are dressed in alluring tight fitting silk gowns much like the one that I had worn the evening before and each woman is more beautiful than the next, or so it seems to me. It is a breathtaking display of beauty that I am certain none of us will soon forget. Sadly, sound does not accompany the image being displayed, however when the women open their mouths there is no doubt that they are singing.

Nothing seems to happen for a minute and then two. Those of us holding our breath in anticipated fear remember to breathe again. Maybe the ship is too far away, or maybe these women are not a threat they claim to be.

An evil smile spreads across the face of the Iranian President. "Prepare to be conquered bitches."

The President looks around to speak to someone, but the wide-eyed look that man gives his president makes him look back to his monitor. His smile turns very sickly at the scene that he beholds. Soldiers on the Iranian warship are throwing themselves into the waters. Some swim to inflatable boats that had been thrown in. Others, and even though the distance from ship to shore is much too far to swim, commence doing just that. Sharks fins break the surface of the ocean water and shortly thereafter bodies start thrashing and disappearing.

Then the great beasts of the oceans come into focus; Killer, Blue, and Humpbacks whales to name a few and in their midst are the porpoises.

They do not come alone for beautiful, embarrassingly clad women are riding each one.

Each woman carries a weapon, which I recognize for Queen Sophie had described those weapons to me just moments ago. The metal of their broadleaf heads glitter in the sunlight. The chains attached to them and winding its way around the wrists and arms of the beauties look more decorative than purposeful. The women open their mouth, whether in song or otherwise we cannot tell.

The sirens on their ocean manuals speed towards the boats and men throw themselves down to embrace such a beautiful death. Inflatable boats and bodies are crushed beneath the whales' massive weight, and those who think themselves unlucky in not finding death in the face of such beauty soon have their wish fulfilled by porpoise riding females and their sharp edged Kardia-daru.

The Kardia-daru wielding women are beautiful to behold. They move with such grace and pose that it is difficult to believe that their every movement results in the death of a human. Down under the water they go and back out the manual riding beauties come. Kardia-darus fly through the air finding their mark and come back dripping with the blood of their victims.

Neither is the ship itself spared for large flocks of birds are attacking those still on board. However, they are not the only creatures or the most dangerous that have come to the siren's call for giant squids crawl over it snapping up those too slow to disembark.

It is a slaughter and only handfuls make it to shore whereas they immediately prostrate themselves in front of the still singing women. I am certain that the sirens and their allies could have stopped the men at any time before hitting landfall. I am also certain that they have been allowed to get to shore for a purpose; the purpose of which now becomes clear.

None of the kneeling men take notice of the sword that comes down to behead them. Once the bodies cease their jerking, bodies and heads are thrown back into the surf to feed the still hungry sharks.

The entire battle, if it could even be called such, is gruesome to watch and in the end not one Siren was harmed and yet not one Iranian lives.

"I am sorry you had to witness that ladies and gentlemen." Queen Sophie states in the ensuing stunned silence. "Believe me when I say that what you just saw was the least bloody of what we can bring to bear upon any invasion, and I assure you that we do have the means to repel any invasion force, even as far away as a couple of hundred miles."

Lai checks some device on her wrist and whispers something to Queen Sophie.

"We also keep a close watch on any underwater activity and our airspace so please do not try to get close with your submarines and airplanes." Queen Sophie looks to the U.S. President, who smiles back at her and then signals to one of his aids.

"Furthermore, the Iranian government has kindly donated another warship to our arsenal and I thank them for their generosity." Now she has to wait until the nervous laughter calms down before she can continue. "We insist that you recognize our sovereign rights to our land and our laws. We have no wish to war with any of you. We are self-sufficient so we are not in need of trade, although I will personally review any request that come our way. I tell you now, do not expect too much for we love our quiet little islands and our life as it is. We have no wish to get involved in your... rat race. I will now make myself and the others in my entourage available in the room next door to answer questions or inquiries that you may have for the next four hours, and then as agreed we must be gone."

With the last of her message given Queen Sophie and the rest of the sirens make their way back into the room we had just recently exited. We follow in her wake and position ourselves around the room and at the door. Thus we wait.

They start filtering in slowly, as if they are lambs being lead to the slaughter, although once started there is no pushing back the flood. For the next four hours we are kept busy trying to keep chaos from reigning and protecting the virtues of the ladies that we have been sworn to protect.

Countries propose alliances and these are gently rebuffed. Request for embassies are duly noted to be taken under consideration. Most requests for trade rights are immediately turned down although there is a couple that seem to intrigue Queen Sophie enough for further consideration and these she tells the delegate will be taken back for contemplation. Such does the onrush become that before I know it the four hours have expired.

Chapter Twelve

We are a weary group that finally makes its way down the elevator and then into the sleek black limos four hours later. This time, Mariyah insists on riding in the same limo as her mother so I find myself in the midst of their recap of the last few hours. When asked about some particular or another I provide honest answers and opinions, otherwise I stay silent.

"You have healed up nicely Michele." Mariyah takes hold of my once mangled arm after silence descends between her and her mother.

"It is surreal isn't it?"

"Very. Mother and I have talked and she agreed that I may give you this." She holds out a pendant to me.

The five-inch pendant is a beautiful representation of mermaids at play in the ocean waters. So intricately carved is it that I can almost make out each of the mermaid's individual characteristics. In the middle of the mermaids are porpoises and sharks at play and what looks like the tentacles of a squid wrapping around their naked bodies. The metal of the pendant as well as the chain is silver in colour, though it glitters with a sheen I have never seen before.

"It's lovely, thank you." I finally reply in shock at the extravagance of the gift.

"It's our pleasure. Lift up your hair and I will put it on you."

I lift the back of my hair and she leans forward to snap the link of the pendant's chain around my neck. She then brings the clasp around front and pricking my finger she places the bleeding tip onto the clasp causing it to fuse close. "Siren blood fuses it and only Siren blood can release it. If nothing else this should convince you of your true blood."

I give her a grin as she arranges the pendant between my breasts.

"Oh, I thought it would be heavier!" I exclaim after she has the pendant arranged to her satisfaction.

"It is made of a combination of ores that we find on Ospizo. The combination makes for a very light and almost indestructible metal. The pendant is more than a pendant however." She pushes herself against me so she can whisper into my ear. "The pendant is a communication device that works almost like your telephones. If you know the frequency of another such device you can call it directly. This one was mine. We just tuned it to you and I've pre-programmed it with my own and mother's signals. You open it like this."

She shows me how the pendant opens and then closes it again. "The rest I will allow you the pleasure to discover on your own." She tells me and then tucks the pendant down between my breasts again.

"Thank you again. You leave me speechless. I'm sorry I have no gift for you in return."

"Don't be silly. You have given us much, not the least is the idea about the masks and the masks themselves. It's not a perfect solution however you were right in guessing that it would throw confusion in the mix. One of the reasons mother has refused to let any of us wander far from Ospizo is the stir we cause. Now you have given me a weapon to use against her."

"As if." Queen Sophie pipes up.

Mariyah pokes her tongue out teasingly at her mother and then turns to me. "Promise you will call me when you figure it out Michele."

I feel my insides turn to butter for the look that she turns on me is unbearable in its beauty. "I will." I finally manage after swallowing the lump of desire that has built up in my throat.

"You are so wicked Mariyah. I can't wait to see her turn the tables once she comes into her own." Thankfully Queen Sophie's following chuckles releases the sexual tension that had been building inside me since Mariyah's first touch between my breasts.

"Look alive people, we're almost there." Lori states from the front seat of the limo.

Sure enough, we are turning onto the road leading up to the airport. It had gotten dark during the drive and a large almost full moon is just making its presence known. Everything looks so beautiful and peaceful and yet…

"I don't like it Lori." I reply upon seeing the quiet.

"What don't you like?"

"I don't know. It feels like an itch in the back of my mind."

"Well scratch it and be done with it." She replies with a grin, although I don't miss the fact that she starts rechecking her weapons.

Having replaced our "accidentally" broken earpieces upon our return to the limos, they now come to life as Lori cautions everyone to prepare.

I stare out into the darkness. The limo turns, putting us in full view of the Queen's Learjet sitting in the middle of the tarmac. Everything is as it should be. The place looks deserted, as it should be.

The door to the jet is open in invitation for the High Queen.

It is the sight of the open door that finally hits me. "Stop. Something is not right."

The three armoured vehicles and two limos come to a stop a few hundred feet from the LearJet. Nothing looks out of place except for that door. The LearJet glitters under the harsh glare of the floodlights. Dark hangers sit empty to the left and right.

"What are we waiting for Michele? If you have something say so, otherwise it's a go." Andrea states over the radio.

"Give me a sec dam it!"

"Sorcha can you take a look around for me." I whisper to my perky friend posed on my shoulder.

Sorcha gives me a wink and is gone.

"Michele?" Queen Sophie finally speaks up.

"Just give me a couple of minutes."

"A couple of minutes to do what?"

"If I told you, you would not believe me so I ask that you trust me on this."

Queen Sophie looks intently at me for a few seconds before nodding. No more than a minute later I feel the insubstantial weight of Sorcha on my shoulder.

"Well?"

"Ye be right. There's a group of those disgusting vampires in the left hanger and a group of humans in the right."

"Human. Photographers maybe."

"Not unless they be taking pictures with bombs."

"Shit. How about the jet? Is it clean?"

Sorcha gives me a put upon look.

"Please."

I watch Sorcha fly away again, while those in the limo look at me clearly thinking I have lost it.

"We have company guys. A group of creepy crawlies in the left hanger and a group of bomb carrying humans or thralls in the right."

"Ideas anyone? Andrea calls back over the radio.

"Working on it. Give me a minute of two. Can you get a hold of the tower to make sure Her Majesty has takeoff rights from now until…"

"On it." Riley back in The Pit informs us.

Those in the limo continue to look at me uncertainly for I am sitting placidly on the lush limo seat and frankly I don't seem to be working on anything at all.

"It's clear."

"Thanks and watch yourself out there Sorcha for bullets don't need eyes."

"The jet is clean." I tell the rest of the unit over the radio.

"Okay here it is. We assume that the jet is clean, as Michele has informed us so we pull the limos right next to it. The Queen's limo on the jet's door side and the other limo on the far side. That should give us some cover from both hangers. Once we have stopped, the sirens and Lori are to go directly into the jet. Lori makes one last sweep and then they take off. Meanwhile, I'm pretty sure we will be very busy keeping the vamps off them. Any better ideas?" Gazinno puts in.

"We can fight also Michele." Mariyah proclaims earning her glares not only from us of the unit riding inside the limo with her, but also her mother.

The radio stays silent. "I guess there are no other takers then, any better suggestions from The Pit?"

"You people have the ball, do what you think is best. Just make sure you get the sirens out of there." Neely responds from The Pit.

"By the looks of things we are not going to have time later for a proper good-bye so this is it and safe journey." I say to Queen Sophie and Mariyah.

"Not good-bye Michele, we will see each other again and soon."

I give Queen Sophie a wan smile. "Sorry about your luggage too."

"Nothing important in them that can't be replaced. Why don't you take care of them until the next time we come to visit or we send for it?"

"Deal. Can I…"

"Yes you can wear the gowns if you want or anything else that turns your fancy. You may be surprised what you find in there for mother did not completely keep to the agreement with the humans. Remember Michele it takes the blood of a Siren."

"Mariyah!"

"I will not let the humans get our cousin killed Mother."

"Of course and you are right dear. Michele if you find what Mariyah is eluding to you may use them in good health. We will pray to the Goddesses that you will come to visit us soon."

Quick kisses and brief parting words are exchanged. The limos surge forward. My heart starts pounding and my mouth goes dry. I give my cousins a smile that is much more encouraging that what I am feeling inside.

The limos barely come to a stop when the serene evening is shattered with the sound of gunfire.

"Just fly away. Don't worry about us." I yell to them and then jump out of the door closest to the jet.

Why the vampires decided to use guns instead of just coming after us I have no clue for it is obvious that they are an even worst shot than I am. That said, there is no mistaking that the gunfire coming out of the darkness is impressive and enough to make anyone cringe as the flashing of thirty machine guns spew bullets all over the tarmac. Furthermore, even though they are poorly aimed those spewing bullets turn out to be a problem for after they hit the tarmac they are just as likely to ricochet, as they are to dig in.

I hide behind the front tire well of the limo and swallowing my distaste for my firearm I return fire. Lori followed by Queen Sophie and then Mariyah head directly to the jet. From the other limo Lia, Vani and Capri spill forth. They are halfway to the jet when a bullet whines off the tarmac and hits Capri in the chest.

I suppress a scream of anger when I see Capri go sprawling down upon the tarmac and then growl at the sight and smell of the blood spreading across her chest and stomach.

"Go. I'll get her." I tell the other two and then effortlessly pick up Capri.

The jet fires up as I am making my way to the door with Capri. When I reach it, Lori comes bouncing out and takes cover behind the limo. The roar of the engines starts to build up speed threatening to burst my eardrums. I pass a weakly breathing Capri into waiting arms. Jet engines are still whining up as I help close the outer door. We get the door shut and I am just diving for cover behind the limo when a sharp pain rips threw my shoulder.

Dam it not again!!

I have barely made that mental curse when another one rips through my upper thigh.

Ah shit… well at least that's somewhere new!

I grit my teeth against the pain and duck down below the limo. The jet engines continue to roar and the plane starts to roll away. The firing of the engines heats the surrounding air until it feels hot enough to scorch clothing, hair and skin. The force of the backwash causes the limos to vibrate making it just as risky for us hiding behind them as the open bullet ridded tarmac.

The plane rolls away and we breathe a sigh of relief, which is short-lived for we must now turn our attention back to the firefight. The vampires are getting better with their guns for a least half of the bullets now seem to be hitting the limo.

"Thank the Goddess it's not my credit card these things are on!" I yell to Lori eliciting a chuckle.

For the next couple of minutes we exchange gunshots with the vampires, but even in the midst of this I am thinking; thinking that something is not right.

The Queen is now gone, so if she was their target it is no longer available to the creatures in the hanger. Therefore, they should be dispersing. If not dispersing they should at least be pressing their advantage. We are caught between the two limos with nowhere to run, speaking of which, why hasn't the group in the right hanger done anything yet.

Could Sorcha have been wrong about someone being inside?

"Shit, this is just a ploy. It has to be the plane, a bomb probably." Gazinno, who obviously was on the same track as me, but faster at coming to a conclusion, yells into the headset.

"A bomb!" I am stunned that I had not thought of that.

Oh dam... ... oh dam it.... oh dam it all... dam, dam, and dam again.

Sorcha, Sorcha where are you.... dam it.

"Sorcha!" I yell, deciding that the safety of my cousins is more important than whether anyone thinks I am crazy.

"What!"

"There you are! Sorcha you have to catch up to the Queen's plane. Can you do it love?"

"Maybe, but why would I want to?"

"These vampires don't really care if they hit us or not. This is all a diversion. It kept us from checking the plane as we should have and it's now keeping us pinned and occupied. Sorcha, I think there may be a bomb on, or attached to that plane!"

Sorcha looks at me in horror and then looks to the darken sky. She puckers her lips in thought and then gives me a wicked smile. "This could be fun."

"Love you and be careful."

I watch Sorcha fly away for a couple of seconds and then turn back to the hanger housing those firing at us.

"Riley has been trying to contract Queen Sophie's plane, however they are not answering." Lori tells me when I settle back down beside her.

"And at this rate we could be trading bullets all night. Any ideas on how to get them out Michele?" George yells.

"Maybe I'll just sing them out!"

My reply causes both Andrea and Lori to snort in diversion and George to chuckle.

"The sirens are gone so no more playing nice. Jeffers, Lambert, light up that dam hanger!" Andrea orders.

Only a few minutes have passed so far, however in those few minutes no less than an thousand rounds of ammunition has been fired. The noise of that gunfire has long since dulled our hearing, but even dulled senses cannot block the sound of guns firing grenades or the aftermath. Six explode in rapid succession with no apparent effect until finally a vampire stumbles out of the hanger.

"Oh dam. He's got a rocket launcher!" Jeffers shouts.

The rest of the unit turn to the figure stumbling out of the hanger and open fire. Bullets riddle its body with little effect. The figure raises the rocket launcher to his shoulder.

Blessed Goddess no!

I stand up and start running towards the vampire. I open my mouth and dig deep down into my being. If my freakish nature is ever meant to be of value, now is the time for it to prove itself.

Give me this Goddess and I will love you forever.

A screeching wail starting from the very depths of my soul vibrates every bone in my body. My throat convulses and changes. Thus changed, it allows the wail to pass and disgorge from my mouth, which to my horror does not even come close to resembling that of a human.

The call of a banshee. Some inner sense provides.

I know that if the vampire had been human the wail would have incapacitated it in the most painful of ways. It is more than human however, so instead the force of the wail hits the body knocking it sprawling, although not before it manages to fire the rocket. Where that rocket goes is not even close to where it was intended to go.

Yikes!

I react with speed and strength that is more than human. I jump into the air. My foot hits the rocket, driving it down into the tarmac. The resulting explosion flings me much farther into the air than I ever intended on going. I spin out of control certain that I have met my end.

Even as I am thinking of my impending death I catch sight of the men that Sorcha had reported as being in the second hanger. They have been sneaking across the Tarmac and have gone un-noticed while our attention had been focused on the vampires, and this is about to become a deadly mistake.

I am about to scream a warning when I hit the arc of my unplanned flight so instead of a warning comes a squeak of surprise as my stomach lurches into my throat as I fall back towards the ground.

Funny what a person will think about when they come face to face with death. For me it becomes the fact that I now think in the terms of Gods and Goddesses. I have never been overly religious, and any discussion on God I would have had up to yesterday would have revolved around the one God and Jesus Christ, so as I plunge to the earth

I find myself surprised to be praying to the Goddess Aphrodite instead.

A bedlam of screaming comes from below, sounding much like those fanatics you see on television running headlong to their deaths. Goddess protect them is my last prayer as a searing pain of unimaginable intensity rips through my shoulders.

Fuck, not again!

There is more to flying than the flapping of wings and she has been flying long enough to learn every trick. There is the wind to consider, the angle of accent and decent, the form of the body and most importantly of all, the magic. Just a little touch of magic is all that is needed to assist flight, although a great deal is needed to have her go as fast or faster than modern day jets, and the one flying the queen's Learjet is not being chintzy on fuel. Fuel can be replenished cheaply and easily, magic can't for a body can only store so much before it has to rest and replenish its store. Therefore, even though she has managed to build up more speed than the Jet and is fast approaching it, she is having doubts as to whether she has enough of that stored up magic to catch it.

It is just as she is starting to give up hope of catching the Learjet, when the flare of the jets subsides and she slams into the belly of the plane.

Ofphhh...ye are so going to owe me for this Michele.

She has watched humans make weapons of mass destruction for years so she has some idea of what she should be looking for, therefore once she gets her breath back she starts the search. She examines the wings to no avail. Next she checks the underbelly and yet nothing. She checks the topside, the tail, the nose and still nothing.

Oh please not inside!

Sorcha makes one more desperate search of the exterior and still nothing. Reluctantly she admits to herself that if Michele is right about there being a bomb, it has to be inside.

The great spell the elves had cast so long ago and which still persist to this day did nothing more that make the fairy folk invisible to those without the fairy blood. It made the minds and eyes of those not fairy refuse to acknowledge the presence of the fairy folk. Hence they live in the same realty as all other living things and have to live with the same rules.

The aircraft, having neither brains nor eyes causes a problem for her for to get inside she has use some of her precious store of magic to slip into another reality. Usually it would not be much of a problem however her store of magic is already getting dangerously low. Finally deciding that there is nothing to be done about it she shifts her body into the other reality to slip inside the jet.

She comes back with an audible pop that makes the sirens inside look up, but their attention quickly goes back to the body laid out on the floor. Capri is bleeding profusely from the ugly tear in her chest. It is obvious that what had hit her was an already mangled bullet for a clean hit would not have left such a gaping wound. Lia is stuffing Capri's wounds with gauze, Sophie is giving her chest compressions, and Vani is breathing into her mouth. Mariyah would be there too, she is certain, if she was not the one flying the jet. Siren music fills the air so thickly that it is smothering.

No time for gawking Sorcha or they will all be dead!

Taking a gulping breath of air she turns away from the grisly scene and resumes her search. She starts in the cockpit and finds nothing, then into the fuselage, over, under and around the seats and still nothing, from front to back and front again.

Maybe Michele was wrong. There is nothing here.

Thinking hard about her knowledge of the makeup of an airplane, which she admits to be sadly lacking, she tries to figure out where else a bomb may be placed. She had found nothing on the outside and now the inside seems clean. There is no space inside the walls to place such a thing, so where?

Think Sorcha. Ignore the sirens and think. Michele could be wrong, but she felt so sure. There must be one and if not ye have to make certain that ye have checked everyplace possible…THE WHEEL WELLS!

She groans at the thought for it means another shift and her magic is dangerously low.

Three wheels, with not that much room once retracted so probably a smaller bomb. Ye don't have much magic left so ye better make the right choice. Which wheel be it Sorcha. Think! If I wanted to blow one spot to cause the most damage, which wheel would I go after? The front of course. There is nothing like taking the nose off a creature to interrupt its flight and if ye take the brain out with it, well the result of that is obvious.

She shivers almost uncontrollable and releases a long groan of agony as she passes through the floor and phases through into the undercarriage of the plane. A few seconds only does she allow herself self-pity and then she is looking again.

Sitting almost right in front of her is a huge bomb; huge looking to a mere six-inch fairy that is. There are two digital clocks attached to it -- no not clocks she corrects herself. They are measuring something, at least one of them is. One is sitting level at ten thousand and the numbers on the other digital readout are currently moving upwards.

If there is one thing that a fairy knows well, that is flight so it does not take her long to realize that the digital readout with the moving numbers is tracking the airplane's altitude, the other she guesses is the altitude that the bomb is set to go off. She doesn't know much about bombs and bomb making, however it takes no imagination to figure out that once the two numbers match, things will get nasty.

She thinks hard upon the decision she has to make. She does not owe the sirens anything and she has used almost all of her magic catching the jet, and then finding the bomb. The only way for her to be able to take the bomb away from the plane is to use what is left of the little magic energy she has, which will leave her weak and vulnerable.

She is certain that Michele would understand if she went back and told her that there was nothing she could do. She knows that Michele would believe her. The problem is that Michele has fallen in love with her cousins and she is certain that Michele would always wonder. Could she live with that doubt between them, could she live with the look that would be sure to come into Michele's eyes whenever she thought about her cousins, and then the look she would turn towards her? The two of them had become good friends in such a short time, but could doubt and guilt on her part allow their friendship and joy to continue growing, never mind survive?

She has had a long life. A much longer life than many and until a few months ago, before she found Michele she was ready to fade away. Without Michele she would end up back in solitude, so if she did not do this… could she go back to that loneliness? No, she could never go back is the truthful answer.

Say good-bye to her for me Goddess and look after her always.

The sound of explosions greets me when I come back from unconsciousness. Pain flares throughout my body and all I want to do is lie down and forget this day has ever happened.

I quickly forget about my aching body when the surface below me starts shuttering. Looking down to see what I have landed on. I only just register that I am on the roof of the hanger when the roof starts buckling and I start sliding down its rounded slope.

In desperation I grasp for a handhold. The hanger roof is made of smooth steel making handholds non-existent so my groping does me no good. Another explosion rocks the hanger, setting my teeth on edge and propels me even faster towards the ground. I clench my teeth to keep the panic at bay and continue to claw at the steel roofing, wishing beyond hope that my nails would change into those sharp ugly claws.

Oh, it worked!

The scrape of steel against my bare skin reminds me that I am still not out of trouble. I bury my now six-inch nails into the steel. However, my momentum is such that I continue to fall as the steel parts and tears in my wake. Over the edge I go. I slam into the side of the building and then down the steel sided wall.

Another explosion. This one farther away and high in the night sky makes me look up in dread. I scream in grief and despair at the significance of that explosion. The thought of having failed my cousins and sending Sorcha to her death overwhelms me. The emotional grief associated with losing Sorcha and what I hoped we would have become to each other threatens to paralyse me. Up to a couple of months ago I had only once raised a hand in anger. I wonder how anybody could have thought that I was capable of handling this crap.

Have faith dear one. States a voice deep in my soul that resounds with power and love.

The subsequent explosion rocks me free of my mind numbing paralysis, although when I refocus on what is happening around me, my first instinct is to crawl back into myself.

My favourite movies are action movies where the hero bravely fights his way past all obstacles put in his path to save the girl. I had always fantasized of being that girl, waiting for my true love to come and rescue me. That perception changes now that I am in the midst of that reality. My first thought is that the movies do not do it justice. Men are screaming like idiots and running out of one hanger towards the other. These men literally exploded into gory chucks of flesh as they make their way across the tarmac. Those that do make it causes the very walls of the hanger to tremble as the explosions they are carrying detonate.

Meanwhile, the unit is pinned down behind the limo trading gunfire with those left inside the one hanger or shooting any of those scary, crazy madmen blowing themselves to pieces. I have never seen such chaos or imagined such senseless loss of life.

Gathering my determination, I am about to make a sprint towards the rest of the unit when there is a sudden lull in gunfire and explosions.

Silence descends over the field. The lights had long since been extinguished by the firefight so the area sits in darkness. I peer into the ensuing darkness, which causes my eyesight to change into that strange hypersensitive mode.

The silence is so deep that it is as if the world has stopped to hold its breath. One minute passes and then two. The silence stretches to a third minute and still nothing. Just when I come to believe that the firefight has come to an end the night explodes with a flurry of bodies hurling themselves bodily at those behind the limos. The speed of the onrush is such that they only manage to get a couple of shots off before they are over run.

It quickly becomes apparent that the team is overmatched. The vampires swarming them move much too fast for human senses and they manhandle the members as if they are toys being discarded by wilful children.

Since the night of my change, and except for my recent success with my nails my changes have all been due to circumstances forced upon me, and a need to react to those circumstances. My body has been reacting to its own need for survival to the dangers presented to it instead of doing what I want or wish. Seeing that my unit is about to be eradicated I scream with the urgency to have my body act instead of react. My mind filters through everything I have learned about myself, all the improbabilities that have become probabilities. I have no doubt that I can take on any one of the creatures attacking them, any two or three even, but that would be small consolation for the rest of the unit, for surely by the time I took care of that two or three they would be dead.

I need to do more; I need to give something of myself to them. That thought makes me realize that the members of the unit have come to mean something more to me than them just being my keepers.

My mind flickers back to the night with my Siren cousins. They had not only showed me the joy of sharing they had also taught me how. They had taught me not to fear sharing that part of myself that humans never share. That part of my soul that makes me shine much brighter than a human could ever hope to shine. This is the magic, the real magic of the sirens, not their beauty, although that is unquestionable. However, sharing that night was accomplished with the song of the siren and for Sirens only.

But even humans must have a song!

Without really understanding what I am doing, but knowing that if I don't all is lost, I reach out to the members of the unit. I latch onto George, that big burly man that is as strong as an ox, but as gentle as a lamb with those he cares about. I look into his soul and feel the love he has for his wife, how gentle yet stern he is with his son and daughter.

These love ones are his reason for living and fighting for the better good. The song associated with that love resounds gently yet strongly within him. I laugh aloud for Dad is a sports fan and I can't count how often I have heard that song throughout my life. "We will, we will rock you…" and on it goes. I reach into that song and pour my strength into him.

Lori, the ultimate show tune girl resounds with Christina Aguilera's Burlesque and after allowing myself a small chuckle I pour another part of myself into her song. Jeffers calls to The Beatles, Lambert to Mariah Carey, Andrea to Meatloaf, Williams to Aqua and on it goes. Antonio though, his song is gone and his body lies lifeless on the tarmac. Grieving for his death I do not allow it to paralyse me again. Instead I take hold of another song, a song of the sea, a song of strength, endurance and speed. The song of the warrior.

I sing the song of sharing. My body feels as if the eleven songs are tearing the very fabric of my soul apart and yet I give unselfishly and then give even more. I give them my strength and speed. I pour into them encouragement from the Goddesses. I give them my finesse when I go into hyper speed, and valour I had not known I possessed until now. The joining is heady, so joyful and pure.

By the Goddess, if this is what the Amazon's felt it's no wonder they loved war!

Songs intertwined I explode into action. What had seemed certain defeat a few seconds ago is now not so certain. The vampires are still blazingly fast and strong, but now they are being matched hit for hit, strength for strength. I jump and smash one vampire in the back of its head with my foot, the vampire next to that gets a fist through his skull, and the next, six inches of claws tear it from neck to sternum. I lose myself in destroying the creatures that crawl the night.

I turn to the sound of gunfire. There are still some inside the hanger and they have opened fire again. With the unit out in the open fighting hand-to-hand for their lives the gunfire is more dangerous than before, so I turn to the new threat.

In three steps, I match the speed of those inhuman creatures attacking us, in four even they seem slow, in five there is no stopping my forward momentum. Into the absolute darkness of the hanger I plunge. My eyes adjust quickly. I know they must be glowing a bright red and then I am upon them. Another half dozen creatures are inside and when they see me coming, they drop their weapons and come at me with the weapons they truly know how to use.

A fist to the head extinguishes the first vampire before its weapon fully settles on the floor. I am upon the second and burying my claws inside its chest even as the head of the first vampire is exploding. My momentum carries me past it, causing that vampire's body to twist to follow and then my hand comes free, still grasping the creature's undead heart. The third creature is reaching for me as my body slams into his, throwing us both back against the steel hanger wall. Forward momentum comes to a screeching halt. I scream as a jagged piece of metal slices through the vampire's body and into my shoulder and then scream again as I rebound from the wall, causing that metal to rip out of my already torn skin and muscles.

As I slide across the floor I feel Mark's song die, but there is yet hope, for nine still make demands of me.

The sound of the ocean and all its manuals is deafening and yet I rejoice. I reach out for the ocean so far away from me. It responds and gives to me a portion of its life. My soul absorbs what the ocean is giving me and then I pour more of my music into my unit, giving as much as they can take, causing my own song to respond in its high, sweet melody.

The floor is covered with multiple body parts of both vampires and humans so I slide easily across it. However, my slide comes to an abrupt halt when I bump against one of the creatures. It gives me a kick that causes all the air to leave my lungs making me gasp for breath.

Without air filling my lungs I am unable to continue singing my song vocally, however it thrives with a life of its own inside me. Pulling on that song and all the strength now available to me I burst up from the floor and high into the air. The two remaining vampires follow me up. At the apex of the jump my shoulders tear again, the pain only slightly less painful than that pain I had felt after the explosion that had sent me to the hanger's rooftop.

The vampires' leap turns out to be a match for mine so I can't spare any time to wonder about the way the air buffets behind me or the way my thick hair moves around me in waves of glory. Only fleeting attention am I able to give these peculiars for my whole world becomes fist, kicks, claws and teeth. We reach the apex of our jump and the vampires' eyes open in surprise as they start to fall to the ground. There is another searing pain in my shoulders and then I find myself tumbling to the ground entangled in their midst.

The fall ends with one body under me, cushioning my fall and the other on top of me. The air whooshes from my lungs once more. I gasp for breath, my eyesight starts to turn to dark pinpoints and my world begins to go dark for lack of oxygen. The songs begin to die and pain flares across my back as nails flay my skin to bloody ribbons.

Gunfire threatens to burst my eardrums. Pain that I have come to associate with bullets ripping into flesh makes me scream and then the weight of the vampire vanishes from my back. Still gasping for breath, I roll over and look up at what new danger I may be facing.

By the Goddess George, I think I have fallen in love with you!

For the second time this day, George has come to my rescue. The gun he holds still bellows smoke and then flares again and again as he pumps another four shots into the vampire that I was so recently lying upon.

Managing to take a large shuddering breath, I pull myself to my knees and look upon my savoir. George still holds the gun in both his hands, his legs are spread for support and his eyes are glued onto his recent victim. I look to the vampire and wince at the sight of its head, or at least what is left of it rolling across the floor.

All around me silence has once again descended. Not trusting that silence, I listen carefully for even the slightest noise. So focus do I become on listening for further danger that I jump in surprise when George's body thumps to the floor.

I release a scream of concern and rush to my saviour's side. He still grips his now empty revolver so I gently pry his hands loose of it and manage to get him to lower his arms. His clothing has been torn to shreds and I look in disbelief at the spreading pool of blood spreading across his chest and abdomen.

Horror at the sight of his lifeblood pumping freely from his ragged wounds causes me to yell in fury. I place my hands onto of his wounds to stem the flow of blood and yet his blood still spills out between my fingers. There seems to be no end to the red flow.

In desperation, I reach into him for his song. I search for the rhythm of his soul. What I find is feeble and weak and yet it still has a will to live. Images of his wife, son and daughter flood my mind. It is his love for them drowns out all my doubts. This I can do. This I must do!

I barely take notice of the others reaching us. I barely take notice of them calling for medical assistance. All of my attention is turned inward. I take hold of that feeble soul that is struggling to hold on and feed it my will to survive.

The song that flows from me is sweet and clear and it takes command of the body's responses. The heart slows so that it pumps only enough to keep the body alive. Next to respond to my song is his breathing. All of my attention and song is on keeping the body alive, on keeping the heart from pumping out the last of the body's blood, on keeping what little blood remains oxygenated.

When hands take hold of me to pull me away I snarl and tell them to leave me be; the music continues. Just barely do I realize that the medics have arrived, just barely do I register the ride in the ambulance, just barely the run down the halls of the hospital. That sweet song pours forth from my throat. The sound so pure as to make even the most harden of hearts melt. Only when I feel his lifeblood

being replenished and his heart strengthen do I
release the man physically; even then the song
continues.

Chapter Thirteen

The light causes my eyes to water when I wake up so it takes me a minute or so to recognize that the figure to my right belongs to Lori and the one to my left Andrea. Needless to say, they look like crap. They are not standing or sitting beside me as a loved one visiting a patient, but as one guarding a precious cargo. I am still trying to put two and two together when some telltale sound or movement I make gives them the warning that I am awake. Both of them turn to me in a mixture of surprise and concern.

"Michele…. Michele do you hear me?" Andrea asks as she gently pats my cheek.

I try to respond, however my throat is raw so only a croak comes out. I try once more with no better luck and end up coughing on my words. Andrea reaches behind my back and holds me upright as Lori dribbles water into my mouth. I can't remember the last time I drank something so sweet. A couple more swallows and I finally manage to find the strength to wrap my fingers around the cup. When I have drank down all its contents I lean back with a sigh.

"Michele?" The voice sounds commanding.

"What?"

"I asked if you can hear me."

"You know that really should be one of the top ten dumbest questions you can ask a person."

My comment causes the two of them to glare at me so I decide I better give them a straight answer. "Yes I can hear you. Happy."

I receive another glare from Andrea and then memory of recent events comes crashing back. "How is George?"

"We are not sure. Nobody has come to give us any news. You stopped singing about fifteen minutes ago so I sent Lambert to check."

"Thank the Goddess he's okay."

"We don't know that yet. I swear it was only your singing that kept him alive. Even as the doctor was cutting and prying bullets from you, you sang. You've been singing since we found the two of you, and you wouldn't give him up until the doctors were pumping blood back into him. It's no wonder that your throat feels raw. Speaking of which, drink more water."

I take the cup gratefully and down its contents in a couple of swallows. "Did we get them all?" I ask after I finish the cup of water.

"Either that or they ran off."

"During the fight it felt like we lost…"

"Shhhh. Don't worry your head about it Michele." Lori tries to sooth me.

"Antonio and Mark wasn't it." I finish my thought anyway. "Dam it!"

"It happens Michele. It sucks but it happens." Andrea tells me grimly.

"I just wished I could have done more."

"We all do. The good news is that the sirens got off okay. There was an explosion reported to occur near their jet. We were tracking the plane and it continued on its flight afterwards, so either no damage was done to the jet or it was minimal. By all accounts it got to where it was going."

"That is good news, for a while I thought we lost them also." Then remembering Sorcha, I look around in desperation. I feel a part of my soul die when I find her absent.

"We really blew this didn't we?" I look from one to the other.

"We weren't prepared. Considering that we are lucky any of us are alive, but yes, the operation was less than stellar."

"Why are you two here like this anyway? Have the doctors checked you out, you look like shit."

Lori and Andrea manage a chuckle. I glare unhappily at them until Lori gets herself under control enough to answer. "You were in…. let's say a daze when you got to the hospital and even more so when you finally released George. An orderly managed to get you into another room and then all hell broke loose. The poor man got a broken nose and two black eyes protecting your virtue. Luckily, we were not far behind. We heard the commotion when we got here and it did not take much to put two and two together. Lori and I managed to rescue the poor fellow and restore order, not once, but three times for the next two doctors that came to see you were just as bad as the first. We finally managed to hook onto one that actually did an examination, cut out the bullets and clean your wounds, which by the way are almost all healed now. At any rate, we have been watching over you ever since. Jeffers and Lambert have been blocking the door and before you ask, we all look like hell, but we have all been checked by the doctors. So far they agree that we will live to die another day."

Understanding dawns as to what they thought was so funny, however I still have some worry. "Nobody managed to… well you know."

"No… oh god no Michele. We got here in plenty of time thanks to that orderly.

"I'm going to have to thank him personally. How long have I been here?"

"Thirteen hours."

"Thirteen hours!" I squeak in surprise.

"Yep, so did you enjoy your rest because it will be time to get back to work soon?"

Just then, the door opens and Lambert pokes his head inside. As Lori stated he looks like death turned over. "He's okay Andrea, oh hey Appleton, you look like shit."

"Gee thanks. I bet your wife just loves you, by the way have you looked in a mirror." I shoot back pretending anger. Nobody takes me serious, not even myself for I do feel like hell. I might be mostly healed as they said, however every part of my body aches, making me feel fifty years older.

"Of course my wife loves me. Don't you know that I am the love of her life? You ready to go?"

"Can I get dressed in something that won't show my ass off first?" I reply tartly.

"No need on my account and I'm sure Jeffers won't mind either. In fact, he was just commenting on how cute…. Hey!" Lambert ducks the boot flying towards him and backs out the door.

I had been looking for something to throw at Lambert myself. Lori, being of like mind had beaten me to it so satisfied I lie back onto the bed and sigh.

"He doesn't mean it. You know that is only his way of blowing off steam, don't you Michele?" Andrea asks with some concern for if there is a problem she will have to be the one to report it. Something I'm sure she really wouldn't relish doing.

"I know. We just can't let them get away with it or pretty soon we are going to be nothing more than eye candy to them." I give Andrea a reassuring smile to make sure she knows that everything is okay with me.

"I hear you there. By the way, we really are going to have to find an alternative to you coming to hospitals. I never knew doctors and orderlies to be so dam horny! The doctor also had a hell of a time getting the bullets out. He had to keep cutting you open because the wounds kept closing before he could extract them and for a while I thought he was going to give up on you. I'm sure he is going to be doing a lot of talking to his peers over the next few days and that you are going to be his topic of choice." Lori tells me as she helps me out of bed.

Getting dressed takes some time, for even though I am mostly healed my body still protests at having to move. As I dress the air hangs heavy with the ones that we have lost. The thought of lost ones eventually leads me to thinking about my loss of Sorcha. That alone becomes enough to double me over with grief and more than once I have to swallow bile.

"You must be ready soon Samuel." Edward tells him in his ranting.

"What happened that has you so upset?" Samuel has a good idea what it is for he got some flashes of what was happening at the airport. However, he has no intention of letting Edward or anyone else know what he knows.

"That bitch did it to us again and Vladimir's steaming. He went into a rage and ordered a blood hunt. He then took one of his specials and drained it of blood. It will take him a week or so to get full control of his senses and when he does...." Edward shivers and is unable to finish his thoughts.

Samuel isn't happy about having Michele called a bitch, however that is another thing he has no intention of telling anyone around here so he grimaces along with Edward. "I have made some headway. Watch."

He would have preferred not to show Edward, but unless he can prove that he is ready he doubts that Edward will ever let him out of this cage. Therefore, he reaches deep within himself to that place that Edward taught him to seek the true power of a vampire. Taking hold of that rolling ball of energy he compresses and forces it to obey his will. The result when he releases it is Edward flying through the air.

Edward thumps against the wall and then slides down to the floor. He glares up angrily at Samuel who is looking smug behind the bars of his cage. That glare suddenly changes to laughter or at least Samuel is almost certain it is laughter although the dry raspy huffing coming from Edward sounds more evil than friendly.

"Very good. I'll make sure you keep getting decent food for the next week and you keep practicing. You just proved you have the power. Now you have to learn to reach for it faster until it becomes second nature to you, and don't forget to keep practicing the force of will!"

That is all the encouragement that he gives Samuel. Getting to his feet he lets himself out of the room and locks the door. He is very pleased indeed, for Samuel's power is very promising. He is not sure that Samuel will be able to best Vladimir and he really doesn't care one way or another, as long as he gets his freedom that is. After that he does not give a dam what happens to Samuel for what he is really after is having Samuel break his link to his Sire.

He has not told Samuel the whole truth. Has not told him that he had recently come to suspect that once the link is broken he will no longer have a Sire. Once free Samuel and Vladimir can kill each other as far as he is concerned. All of his training thus far has been to attain his goal of freedom. Without a Sire he would become a forefather. The thought is enough to make him giddy.

We are flying back to Italy when I feel the knock at the back of my mind.

"Soon Michele. Very soon now, we will be together."

"Have you figured out where you are?"

"No not yet, but I have learned and Vladimir is not happy right now, neither with you nor his minions and I think that is going to push Edward into letting me free."

"I still do not understand why he is teaching you."

"I'm not sure I understand it all myself. Edward does not like Vladimir. That I know for sure. Vladimir has control over him however and because of that he has to do what Vladimir tells him to do. I'm sure if Vladimir knew what he was up to he would tear him to pieces."

"Vladimir sounds insane."

"Oh he is. Believe me he truly is. Even as he cuts me open and runs his experiments on me he rants and raves about losing you. He rants and raves about wanting you here so he can breed us and in the same breath about how he wants you dead. He even rants and raves about other Sires and how weak they are to let their food chain breed so that they are now out of control."

I shiver at the thought. "You will need to be extra careful around him. Have you learned enough?"

"I hope so."

"I wish I could help you more."

"As do I my love, but I am afraid I am in this on my own."

"Be careful."

It was another uncomfortable flight back to Italy and thankfully it is over. Still, I can't help but make my displeasure known. "You really have to find us a better way to fly if we are going to keep doing this Andrea."

"Yes Andrea, use your pull." Lori puts in right upon the heels of my comment, which does not surprise me for she had been spewing out her displeasure for the last couple of hours.

"Michele probably has more pull than I do right now." Andrea replies ruefully. "Besides, after the showing we just made we will be lucky if they don't make us walk to the next assignment."

"Well, all I want right now is to walk into my room and lock myself away for a couple of days."

"And sleep."

"Oh yes sleep and more sleep."

"Which you will not get until we finish the debriefing so we may as well get it over and done with." Andrea says ruefully as the vehicle comes to a stop.

The minute I get out of the car I am assaulted with a musky male smell. The smell is familiar to Darren's, although much more powerful. It brings me up short and makes me turn my face to the wind and sniff.

It's coming from down there. A stranger and Darren.

"Are you okay Appleton?" Lambert asks at my right elbow as he looks warily around.

"What?"

"You look like…. I don't know like you are sensing something."

"Sensing? No, I'm just tired and happy to be back. I'm going to stretch my legs for a couple of minutes and then I will join you inside." I reply as charmingly as I can.

"I'll come with you." Andrea pipes up beside me.

"I'd rather be alone. I just need some time to relax and think."

"But…"

"Oh come on Andrea. I've come back and Mom and Dad are in there. You don't really think I'm just going to disappear do you?"

"It's not that Michele."

"Then what is it?"

Andrea glares at me in displeasure. "I'll wait by the car." She finally replies and then leans back for the wait.

I give Andrea a long look. I am tempted to say something cutting back. Deciding otherwise, I slam my mouth shut and give her a wan smile instead.

I walk down the road tracking the scent. It gets stronger with every step I take and every corner I turn until it threatens to overwhelm all of my other senses. Turning one last corner I see the source.

I take note of the good-looking man that is towering over Darren. The man is a typical dark skinned Italian, tall probably six feet give or take. The clothing he is wearing is tight enough to reveal that he has a well-formed muscular body and my fingers itch to caress those muscles. He is one of those "kiss me once and I'll swear off ice cream" type of man and my knees go weak just looking at him. His face is beautiful, or at least would be if he were not currently scowling down at Darren.

Darren looks as if he has taken a beating. It is obvious that these two have had a confrontation and that very thought is enough to bring me back to my senses for nobody, but nobody harms something that belongs to me.

"Get away from him you animal!" I hiss in anger.

The way the stranger looks at me with his smoky brown eyes almost undoes me. I bite my lip to firm up both my resolve and my trembling knees.

"So you're the one that stole him away from me. I should kill you for that."

"Try it."

The stranger continues to look me over, unconcerned at my threat, and then with a switch so quick that it leaves my already weak knees trembling he smiles. Never have I seen such a good-looking man and never has a man affected me this way. It takes all of my will power to keep from throwing myself at him and his scent. I want so much to snuggle my nose into his neck and breathe him in deeply.

So paralysed am I by his overpowering presence that before it registers he is beside me. His scent leaves me breathless, even the heat of his body close to mine sends shivers of delight through my entire being. I am ready to submit to him, ready to give him whatever he asks, ready to give him all of me.

The touch of his nose along my neck makes my body ache with passion. The feel of his teeth trapping my earlobe makes me whimper in need and the tongue he runs across it makes me melt into him.

"Come with me." He whispers in my ear.

Go with him, as if I can refuse. I am incapable of refusing this man anything he wants. My entire body trembles with desire to please him. I am his.

No! You are mine! Nobody can have you but me!

The anger of my lifeline flays my mind. He has never before forced himself into my mind like that. It is what I needed however and luckily it brings me back to my senses. "Stop." I croak out and then even more firmly. "I said stop it."

The man steps back from me smiling, although not without a look of surprise in his eyes.

"Who are you and what do you want?" I manage between gulping breaths.

The stranger looks to me as if I have lost my wits. All along I wish that my knees would stop trembling. The look he gives me sets off every nerve in my body.

"Excuse me for forgetting my manners. Dominic Sabatino at your service Perdere and you."

The force of the man's will is so overpowering that I have to swallow twice before I can answer. "Michele Appleton. Why did you do that to Darren?"

Dominic looks back at the battered Darren still sitting in the middle of the lane. "I was teaching him a lesson. I don't look kindly on losing one of the pack. However, seeing you I can now understand why he did it."

Oh for the love of the goddess please stop looking at me like that!

"He is mine now, so leave him alone." I state with much more confidence then I feel.

"Yours. Do you even know what you are talking about?"

I bite my lower lip in uncertainty. "Maybe not, but…"

"Come with me Michele. Leave these humans and run free as you are meant to do."

"No." I answer back even though even fibre of my body is screaming yes.

"Why! Do you think that these humans can teach you what you need to know or teach you about what you are?"

"No I don't think they can, but you never know."

"They can't teach you to be wolf!" His anger flares such that I can actually feel it pushing against me.

My breath catches. Until that moment, I had been and probably would have gone on blissfully denying the truth. I can still yell and scream that it is a lie, but now that it has been said aloud I will never again be able to believe my denials.

Sigh, ignorance was so bliss.

"No they cannot teach me to be wolf and all what that means, but I am more than wolf. I am a freak and they can help me a little with that."

Dominic leans forward to sniff my neck again. I tense in fear that my body will response uncontrollably to him. "You are more than enough wolf. I can feel the anger rolling off you and that anger will demand a change in you soon. It can be very frightening to go through it alone the first time."

"I have Darren."

Dominic gives Darren a long look before turning back to me. "Yes you do, but it is best for a new wolf to be with an Alpha the first time they change. It keeps them from getting lost in their wolf. I'll let you keep Darren…"

"He's not yours to give away. He's mine." I growl as that very anger he was talking about flares.

Dominic grins at my defensiveness. "You are going to make a dam fine wolf. I look forward to the day. I'll leave yours alone, but don't try to take anymore of mine or I may have to take you over my knee and spank you as a child."

"Try it and you may find yourself short of your testicles." I hiss back sweetly.

"You are going to be such a pleasure to take. If you need anything, be it help getting free of the humans or the desire to come to my bed give me a call." Dominic hands me a card with his phone number boldly printed on one side.

"Your bed. You wish."

"You are wolf! Wolves need the pack and your time of need is going to come upon you. When it does you will come looking for me. I have decided that you belong to me and I will own you."

"Never! Never will I let anyone own me!"

"We shall see. Until the next time we meet." Still smiling Dominic takes my hand and kisses my wrist. Luckily, he drops it and is gone before he sees me start to swoon. It is with longing that I watch him walk away.

"The first time meeting him can be quite earth shattering." Darren tells me after a couple of seconds of silence.

"To say the least."

"Lets go home."

"Good idea. You and I are going to have a long talk pretty soon and if you ever need help again call me."

"I can take care of myself." Darren replies with a very wolf like growl. "Well except against him and you I suppose. What were you thinking coming at him unprepared?"

"Unprepared. Well the next time he roughs you up let me know. That way I will be prepared and I'll kick his ass, or better yet shoot him from a distance, a very long distance at that."

Darren laughs long and hard. When he finally pulls himself together, he asks. "So how did you find me? Did you finally allow yourself to touch the bond?"

"No I smelled the two of you."

"As Dominic said, you are more than wolf enough. When are you going to admit it and allow us to be a pack?"

"We are not much of a pack Darren."

"Not yet, but like any new Alpha you have to start somewhere."

"Does pack mean that much to you?"

"Yes. The pack is everything."

"And Dominic just warned me against stealing anymore of his."

"We can worry about that later if need be besides there are packless wolves. The younger ones don't always see things the way the old wolves do."

"I need to think on this Darren. For now, tell me why is it I felt as if I belonged to him. If I am Alpha and he is Alpha doesn't that make us equals?"

"Part of that was his charm and Dominic can be very charming when he is after something he wants. Mind you, if you cross him or he thinks you are going to be a threat to him or his pack, he can be very ugly. On top of all that he used his Alpha on you, and as I said you came to him unprepared. You allowed him to have dominance over you." He waits to make sure that has sunk in before continuing. "Not all Alpha's are created equal Michele and Alphas do kill Alphas. It's the quickest way to gain a pack after all."

The all-consuming thought running through Samuel's mind is that he has to get out and help Michele. The last encounter with the wolf showed him just how vulnerable she is, and how unprepared she is to deal with her new world on her own.

His anger at not being by her side as she struggles sends him into a rage of such magnitude that the bars of his cage threaten to break as he bashes himself against them. Getting a better grip on the bars and feeling them give way he pulls, hoping that this time he will finally make his bid for freedom.

Gas commences to pour into his cell. He growls, for he had hoped his rage would have gone unnoticed. The continuing hiss of gas fuels his rage onward causing a change in him. That change gives him more mass and strength and he uses it all against the bars keeping him from going to his love one…He feels them give a little more.

About the Authors

My spouse and I have always had a love for fantasy books. We read enough of them throughout a year to keep most bookstores in business. In fact, it was late one evening when we were enjoying a warm summer evening with a glass of wine and discussing one of the latest fantasy books that we had read that Michele was born, so to speak.

Michele was just a thought that first night, however as we continued to enjoy the warm summer evenings, and wine, she became more than that; she became a part of us; almost like a child.

The bonded in blood sage became a collaboration and has since become a book written by the two of us. We may not always agree as to how Michele may evolve as the series progresses although there is one point we agree on whole-heartedly. Michele is no super hero, at least not yet. She is like a teenager learning to get use to her latest growing spurt. She tries and in that trying gets herself into all sorts predicaments. Only time will allow her to get that new body and tangled feelings she now possesses under control.

We hope that you enjoy reading our endeavours, as much as we enjoy debating over her next adventure as well as the next hurdle our little girl may have to overcome.

We love you hear from you so don't be shy and visit our blog page at:
http://www.wsicebooks.com/authors/?cat=1
or email our publisher at
publisher@wsicebooks.com

www.ingramcontent.com/pod-product-compliance
Lightning Source LLC
Chambersburg PA
CBHW062003170626
46813CB00001B/24